'One of the hallmarks of Lerner's fiction is the way that it brings a single consciousness into collision with broad sociopolitical movements . . . In *The Topeka School*, Lerner writes from the vantage of 2019, and from the premise that the collective is broken and common discourse has been derailed. The implicit bid of the book is that exploring myopic white male monologuists, simmering with rage in the Midwest in the late 1990s, might shed light on today's America' ***Atlantic***

'[An] impressive investigation of gender and language . . . One of the great joys of *The Topeka School* is Lerner's description of various linguistic modes – rap, poetry, debating – as they pass through different realms . . . Some of the novel's most breathtaking moments come in its rapid movements through time and place . . . Brilliantly flexible, it's a work whose form expresses Lerner's remarkable intelligence and attention to the entwined workings of language and masculinity' ***Literary Review***

'A funny, penetrating book about language, politics and masculinity . . . there's so much going on: connections everywhere, layers of irony, several narrative procedures running concurrently. Above all, it is fascinated with the possibilities and plasticity of language: talking therapy, policy debate and rapping all ferociously scrutinised. What stops it from being dry is Lerner's wit, his eye for period detail (whether it's Bob Dole or Eminem) and his poet's ear for sounds (the distant whistle of a Union Pacific train or the beeps and hisses of a dial-up modem). Lerner never shies away from emotional or intellectual complications. If anything, he feeds on them' ***Evening Standard***

'How do you write your way out of autofiction's cul-de-sac? Masterfully. Lerner stays close here to his own life and occasionally lets the mask of fiction slip, but his account of an overeducated family in a regional capital of toxic masculinity has all the pleasures of a traditional novel – a more self-aware Franzen' ***Vulture***

'Lerner is [an] author who has spent his career dwelling in the gaps between what language can and can't communicate. The multi-faceted roles he inhabits as poet, essayist, and critic (as well as a former champion debater himself) are on full display ... There is emotional excavation; political exposition and critique; historical exploration; burgeoning poem fragments; even a long Molly Bloom-esque post-cunnilingus monologue' *Vanity Fair*

'Ambitious and original ... like no other American family saga I've ever read' **Editor's Choice, *Bookseller***

'A kind of writing that is self-consciously literary and intellectual ... but that also has a thrilling imaginative vigor. By fusing therapeutic monologue, allusive poetry, critical theory, and social commentary, Lerner has turned a familiar genre – the adult writer revisiting his painful high school days – into something genuinely new' *Tablet*

'The novel lurches towards the final launching of the cue ball like a tornado swerving over open country' *Arts Desk*

'Ambitious ... In this frequently virtuosic novel, we glimpse the seam between the human-constructed world and the abyss beyond' *Irish Times*

'Polyphonic ... Brilliantly realised ... [Lerner] remains uniquely good at conveying the energy of emerging intimacy, the moment things quietly yet fundamentally change' *Spectator*

'The structuring throughout is brilliantly done: the main chapters are standalone episodes, or mini-memoirs, which reverberate against each other thematically rather than chronologically, opening up yet more fertile spaces for the reader ... If one of *The Topeka School*'s many miracles is the way in which its proliferation of ideas are held in place, entwined, made to reinforce one another ... then this exhilarating feeling of composed artistic plenty stands in contrast to the preoccupation with uncontrolled babble coursing through the novel ... [Lerner] has written a perfectly weighted, hugely intelligent, entirely entertaining novel that does more than simply

'*The Topeka School* is what happens when one of the most discerning, ambitious, innovative, and timely writers of our day writes his most discerning, ambitious, innovative and timely novel to date. It's a complete pleasure to read Lerner experimenting with other minds and times, to watch his already profound talent blooming into new subjects, landscapes, and capacities. This book is a prehistory of a deeply disturbing national moment, but it's written with the kind of intelligence, insight, and searching that makes one feel well-accompanied and, in the final hour, deeply inspired' **Maggie Nelson**

'Ben Lerner is a masterful writer who destabilizes the very notion of what a novel can achieve by making it new at every turn. *The Topeka School* is not only a fiction for our times, but for the ages: insightful, humane, politically astute, and true' **Hilton Als, author of *White Girls***

'In Ben Lerner's riveting third novel, Midwestern America in the late nineties becomes a powerful allegory of our troubled present. *The Topeka School* deftly explores how language not only reflects but is at the very centre of our country's most insidious crises. In prose both richly textured and many-voiced, we track the inner lives of one white family's interconnected strengths and silences. What's revealed is part tableau of our collective lust for belonging, part diagnosis of our ongoing national violence. This is Lerner's most essential and provocative creation yet' **Claudia Rankine, author of *Citizen: An American Lyric***

'Ben Lerner has redefined what it means for a writer to inhabit an American present by showing how a family reckons with its past. Here the personal and political are masterfully interwoven. *The Topeka School* is brave, furious, and finally a work of love' **Ocean Vuong**

'*The Topeka School* is a novel of exhilarating intellectual inquiry, penetrating social insight and deep psychological sensitivity. At every turn, its beautifully realised characters are shaped, even in the privacy of their inner lives, by the pressures of history and culture – this is a book not only about how things really feel, but what things really mean. To the extent that we can speak of a future at present, I think the future of the novel is here'
Sally Rooney

'Ben Lerner's third novel, *The Topeka School*, is an education in the sympathetic imagination, a deep and bracing intellectual challenge, a powerful political statement. As usual, Lerner plays winningly in the fertile ground between fiction and memoir, as usual he is often hilarious and occasionally infuriating. Wider-reaching, subtler and kinder than his earlier works, this is a novel to cherish' ***Observer***

'*The Topeka School* is . . . a novel of intellectual integrity and deep concern for words and meaning(s). Lerner's novel is cleverly set pre-9/11 and pre-Trump, but shows the seeds of hatreds were already stirring . . . structurally, the novel is pleasingly intricate . . . this is a serious book for serious times' ***Scotland on Sunday***

'*The Topeka School* – as dazzling as anything Lerner has written – is also his most successful effort at navigating between communal experience (the shared tropes, ideologies and clichés of a culture) and individual feeling (the specificities and textures of poetic expression) without denaturing either' ***Guardian***

'Extraordinarily brilliant . . . Through the wizardry of Lerner's prose, this battle of adolescent elocution becomes an emblem for the fiery state of American culture . . . Among the myriad miracles of *The Topeka School* is that it accomplishes so much, captures so much and questions so much about America in fewer than 300 pages. Here is that all-too-rare masterpiece: a svelte big novel. I'm as awed by Lerner's artistry as I am by his insight, which seems downright forensic in its ability to trace the pathologies consuming us'
Washington Post

mine his childhood or explore what it is to be an author; he has taken on American masculinity, group identity and marginalization, political messaging and generational exchange, and has done so not didactically but generously and with admirable sensitivity' ***TLS***

'A masterful exercise in language' ***Dazed***

'Exceptional' ***Art Review***

'When early copies of *The Topeka School* arrived in London and New York, I heard stories of people cancelling dinner dates in order to read them . . . Lerner doesn't just tear down the curtain between the reader and writer, as in his previous books, but allows the reader to flicker between the first and third person, to see a boy's sentimental education as dynamic, resolving one inherited trauma, repeating another, and making new ones of his own to visit on his daughters . . . The nice thing about Ben Lerner is that he identifies the space [between what has gone before and what a writer can do now], shows us how it works, what can be said there, how it can be said, and then he humbly sends in a man-child to make it all look less like the aesthetic and philosophical feat it actually is' ***LRB***

'Brilliant . . . Gripping . . . Lerner succeeds, where Roth and Updike succeeded before him, in painting ordinary scenes of suburban life with vibrant colours on a lavish canvas, the details emerging with a mixture of humour and horror . . . To our parents especially, we seem like we are all our ages at the same time, a phenomenon Lerner represents with elegant ease . . . Lerner knows what he is doing in one of the best and most satisfyingly provocative large-scale social novels I have read for some time' ***Prospect***

'I admired so much about Ben Lerner's *The Topeka School*, an object lesson in less-is-more . . . Lerner inhabits [his characters] voices so subtly it makes most other first person narratives look like ham acting . . . [he] knows exactly when to hold back, using silence to complicate the texture and expand the scope of a big novel that fits perfectly into just 304 pages. Judicious metafictional touches not only comment on the act of writing, they also heighten the novel's verisimilitude. That's a hard trick to pull off, but in Lerner's hands, a magical simultaneity occurs: we get the apples, the fermentation process, and the sparkling cider all at once' ***TLS*****, 'Best Books of 2019', chosen by Claire Lowdon**

'Rising star Ben Lerner came into his own with the stunningly multi-layered *The Topeka School*, exploring voice, power and masculinity in the 90s and now' ***Guardian*****, 'Best Books of 2019'**

'It's official. Ben Lerner is America's trendiest writer . . . Lerner is a dazzlingly intelligent writer, and for anyone looking to understand contemporary America this tale of toxic masculinity, resentful outcasts, rigged high-school debates and political disaster is a good place to start' ***The Times*****, 'Best Books of 2019'**

'Lerner's dexterous prose is the ideal tool for excavating the gulf between those who have power over language and those who haven't' ***Financial Times*****, 'Best Books of 2019'**

'Taking aim at toxic masculinity, Ben Lerner's latest novel explores, in part, how American culture has twisted young men and created our contemporary political moment' **GQ magazine, 'Best Books of 2019'**

THE TOPEKA SCHOOL

BEN LERNER

GRANTA

Granta Publications, 12 Addison Avenue, London W11 4QR

First published in Great Britain by Granta Books, 2019
This paperback edition published by Granta Books, 2020
Originally published in the United States in 2019 by Farrar, Straus and Giroux, New York

A CIP catalogue record for this book is available from the British Library.

1 3 5 7 9 10 8 6 4 2

ISBN 978 1 78378 537 7 (paperback)
ISBN 978 1 78378 538 4 (ebook)

Designed by Jonathan D. Lippincott
Offset by M Rules
Printed and bound by CPI Group (UK) Ltd, Croydon, CR0 4YY

www.granta.com

For my brother, Matt

CONTENTS

[Darren pictured shattering . . .] 3

The Spread (Adam) 5

[May break my bones . . .] 37

Speech Shadowing (Jonathan) 39

[Things Darren dreamt . . .] 69

The Men (Jane) 75

[Darren would help his neighbor . . .] 111

The Cipher (Adam) 115

[Frost had hardened . . .] 149

The New York School (Jonathan) 157

[From the ceiling . . .] 185

Paradoxical Effects (Jane) 191

[Darren thinks of it . . .] 229

Olde English (Adam) 231

Thematic Apperception (Adam) 261

Acknowledgments 285

THE TOPEKA SCHOOL

Darren pictured shattering the mirror with his metal chair. From TV he knew there might be people behind it in the dark, that they could see him. He believed he felt the pressure of their gazes on his face. In slow motion, a rain of glass, the presences revealed. He paused it, rewound, watched it fall again.

The man with the black mustache kept asking him if he wanted something to drink and finally Darren said hot water. The man left to get the drink and the other man, who didn't have a mustache, asked Darren how he was holding up. Feel free to stretch your legs.

Darren was still. The man with the mustache returned with the steaming brown paper cup and a handful of red straws and little packages: Nescafé, Lipton, Sweet'n Low. Pick your poison, he said, but Darren knew that was a joke; they wouldn't poison him. There was a poster on the wall: KNOW YOUR RIGHTS, *then fine print he couldn't read. Otherwise there was nothing to stare at while the man without a mustache talked. The lights in the room were like the lights had been at school. Painfully bright on the rare occasions he was called on. ("Earth to Darren," Mrs. Greiner's voice. Then the familiar laughter of his peers.)*

He looked down and saw initials and stars and ciphers scratched into the wood veneer. He traced them with his fingers, keeping his wrists together, as though they were still cuffed. When one of the men asked Darren to look at him, he did. First at his eyes (blue), then at his lips. Which instructed Darren to repeat the story. So he told them again how he'd thrown the cue ball at the party, but the other man interrupted him, albeit gently: Darren, we need you to start at the beginning.

Although it burned his mouth a little, he sipped the water twice. People gathered behind the mirror in his mind: his mom, dad, Dr. Jonathan, Mandy. What Darren could not make them understand was that he would never have thrown it except he always had. Long before the freshman called him the customary names, before he'd taken it from the corner pocket, felt its weight, the cool and smoothness of the resin, before he'd hurled it into the crowded darkness—the cue ball was hanging in the air, rotating slowly. Like the moon, it had been there all his life.

THE SPREAD

(ADAM)

They were drifting on her stepfather's boat in the middle of an otherwise empty man-made lake encircled by large tract houses. It was early autumn and they were drinking Southern Comfort from the bottle. Adam was in the front of the boat watching a changeable blue light across the water that was probably a television seen through a window or glass door. He heard the scrape of her lighter, then saw smoke float over him, unravel. For a long time he had been speaking.

When he turned to see what effect his speech had had, she was gone, jeans and sweater in a little pile with the pipe and lighter.

He said her name, suddenly aware of the surrounding quiet, and put his hand in the water, which was cold. Unthinkingly, he lifted her white sweater and smelled the woodsmoke from earlier that evening at Clinton Lake, the synthetic lavender of what he knew to be her shower gel. He said her name again, louder now, then looked around. A few birds skimmed the undisturbed surface of the lake; no, those were bats. When did she dive or step off the boat and how could she have made no splash and what if she was drowned? He yelled now; a dog responded in the distance. From spinning around in search of her, he felt dizzy and sat down. Then he stood again and looked along the edges of the boat; maybe she was just beside it, stifling her laughter, but she wasn't.

He would have to pilot the boat back to the dock, where she must be waiting. (There was a dock for every two or three subdivisions.) He thought he saw a firefly signal slowly from the shore, but it was too late in the year for that. He felt a wave of anger rising and he welcomed it, wanted it to overwhelm his panic. He hoped Amber had dived into the water before his rambling confession of feeling. He'd said they'd stay together once he left Topeka for school, but now he knew they wouldn't; he was eager to demonstrate his indifference as soon as he found her safe on land.

See the outboard motor gleaming in the moonlight. For any of his friends, managing the boat would be easy; all of them, even the other Foundation kids, exhibited a basic Midwestern mechanical competence, could change their oil or clean a gun, whereas he couldn't even drive stick. He located what he assumed was a starter rope, pulled it, nothing happened; he pushed what must have been the throttle to another position and tried again; nothing. He was beginning to wonder if he might have to swim—he wasn't sure how well he swam—when he saw the key in the ignition; he turned it and the engine started up.

As slowly as possible he motored back to shore. When he approached the land, he turned the engine off, but failed to bring the boat in parallel with the dock; a loud crack when the fiberglass hit the wood, which silenced the nearby bullfrogs; nothing seemed damaged, not that he really looked. He rushed to throw the lines gathered in the boat around the cleats nailed to the dock, quickly improvised some knots, then pulled himself out of the boat; he prayed that no one was watching him from a window. Without taking the keys or her clothes or pipe or bottle, he sprinted up the incline through the wet grass toward her house; if the boat drifted back out on the water, that would be her fault.

The large glass doors facing the lake were always unlocked;

he slid one open quietly and went in. Only now did he feel the cold sweat. He could make out her brother's shape on the couch, pillow over his head, sleeping in the glow of the large television; the news was on mute. The room was otherwise dark. He thought of waking him, but instead removed his Timberland boots, which he assumed were muddy, and crept across the room to the white-carpeted stairs; he went up slowly.

He'd stayed over two or three times before when she'd told her parents he'd had too much to drink; they'd thought he'd slept in the guest room; they'd thought, correctly, that he'd called home. But the prospect of encountering anyone now—when he hadn't even confirmed that she was present—horrified him. Her mom took sleeping pills, he'd seen the oversized prescription bottle, knew she mixed them nightly with her wine; her stepdad had slept through a brawl at a recent party; they'll never wake up, he reassured himself, just don't knock anything over; he was glad to be in his socks.

He reached the first floor and surveyed the dark, expansive living room before he climbed the next flight of stairs to where the bedrooms were. He could almost make out the large generic hunting scene on the far wall: dogs flushing game from the woods beside a lake at sunset. He could see the red light blinking on the panel for the alarm system they thankfully never armed. And a little light collected around the silver edges of the framed family photographs on the mantel: teenagers in sweaters posing on a leaf-strewn lawn, her brother holding a football. Something ticked and settled in the giant kitchen. He went upstairs.

Hers was the first open door on the right, and without turning on the light he could see from the doorway that Amber was in her bed, under the covers, breathing steadily. His shoulders relaxed; the relief was profound, and the relief made more room for anger; it also let him realize how badly he had to piss. He turned and crossed the hall into the bathroom and carefully shut the door and without turning on the light lifted the lid. On second thought, he lowered the seat again and sat down. A car passed slowly outside, its headlights illuminating the bathroom through an open venetian blind.

It wasn't her bathroom. The electric toothbrush, the hair dryer, these particular soaps—these were not her toiletries. For an instant he thought, desperately hoped, that they might belong to her mother, but there were too many other discrepancies: the shower door was different, its glass frosted; now he smelled the lemon-scented gel beads in a jar atop the toilet; alien dried flowers hung from a purple sachet on the wall. In a single shudder of retrospection his impressions of the house were changed: Where was the piano (that nobody played)? Wouldn't he have seen the electric chandelier? The carpet on the stairs—wasn't the pile too thick, too dark in the dark to have been truly white?

Along with the sheer terror of finding himself in the wrong house, with his recognition of its difference, was a sense, because of the houses' sameness, that he was in all the houses around the lake at once; the sublime of identical layouts. In each house she or someone like her was in her bed, sleeping or pretending to sleep; legal guardians were farther down the hall, large men snoring; the faces and poses in the family photographs on the mantel might change, but would all belong to the same grammar of faces and poses; the elements of the painted scenes might vary, but not the level of familiarity and flatness; if you opened any of the giant stainless-steel refrigerators or surveyed the faux-marble islands, you would encounter matching, modular products in slightly different configurations.

He was in all the houses but, precisely because he was no longer bound to a discrete body, he could also float above them; it was like looking at the miniature train set Klaus, his dad's friend, had given him as a child; he didn't care about the trains, could barely make them run, but he loved the scenery, the green static flocking spread over the board, the tiny yet towering pines and hardwoods. When he looked at the impossibly detailed trees, he occupied two vantages at once: he pictured himself beneath their branches and also considered them from above; he was looking up at himself looking down. Then he could toggle rapidly between these perspectives, these scales, in a relay that unfixed him from his body. Now he was frozen in fear in this particular bathroom and in all the bathrooms simultaneously; he looked down from a hundred windows at the little boat on the placid man-made lake. (Touches of white paint atop the dried acrylic add a sense of motion and of moonlight to the surface.)

He swam back into himself. He felt like a timer had started somewhere, that he had minutes, maybe only seconds, to flee the house into which he'd unintentionally broken before someone emptied a shotgun into his face or the cops arrived to find him hovering outside the bedroom of a sleeping girl. Fear made it difficult to breathe, but he told himself that he would press rewind, quietly walk back out the way he'd come, disturbing no one. That's what he did, although now the little differences called out to him as he descended: there was a large L-shaped couch he hadn't seen before; he could tell the coffee table here was glass and not dark wood like hers. At the bottom of the stairs, he hesitated: the front door was right there, beckoning; he'd be free, but his Timberlands were downstairs where he'd left them. To recover them he'd have to pass the sleeping stranger.

Despite his fear that he might at any moment be discovered, he decided he must go after his boots, less because they were evidence, could be traced to him, than because he felt that he'd be risking ridicule, humiliation, if he returned to her barefoot. He could intuit the shape of the story, could sense that it would spread—how she'd left him first to mishandle the boat and then to lose his fucking footwear in the midst of whatever misadventure. Hey, Gordon, you got your shoes tied on? Got your slippers? A memory from middle school of Sean McCabe, coming home in socks, in tears, after he'd been jumped for his Air Jordans, flared up before him; Sean still got shit about it and Sean could now bench three hundred pounds.

The young man who had been her brother had turned his face toward the back of the couch; the pillow had fallen to the floor. The giant head of Bob Dole moved its lips on the screen as he crept past. He picked up his boots and slowly slid open the door; the rollers jammed a little; he had to apply some force, causing a loud squeak; the body on the couch stirred and started to sit up. (All over Lake Sherwood Housing Community the bodies stirred and started to sit up.) Without closing the door, he bolted, boots in hand, over the wet grass—indifferent to uneven ground, to sticks and stones—at a speed he might never match again, his body grateful for something to do with its adrenaline. No one yelled after him; there was only his footfall, blood thundering in his ears; he triggered a few motion lights and so moved closer to the water; he ran at full force for a minute before he realized he wasn't sure where he was going. He dropped to a knee, lungs burning, looked behind him to make sure he wasn't being followed. He pulled his boots on over his wet socks. Then he got up and sprinted between two houses until he reached the street.

His only goal now was to find his red '89 Camry parked in her driveway and go home, to bed. He was still scared—at any moment he might hear sirens—but away from the water and the scene of his ridiculous trespass he felt the worst was over. He patted his pocket to confirm the presence of his keys and walked quickly along the curb—there were no sidewalks—but he did not run, so as to minimize suspicion on the off chance he was seen. He walked and walked, ashamed to be on foot; he could not find his car, her house; he must have pointed the boat in exactly the wrong direction. After he'd searched for almost half an hour, had circled half the lake, he saw, was overjoyed to see, his car where he had parked it some hours before. The sound of the doors unlocking was deeply reassuring. He got in, found his pack of Marlboro Reds on the passenger seat, and shook one loose; he turned the key to the on position but did not start the engine. He lowered his window and lit his cigarette with a yellow Bic he took from the cup holder and inhaled what felt like his first full breath since he'd discovered her absence on the boat.

He started the engine and turned the headlights on to discover that she was standing, had been standing, in the threshold of her front door wearing an oversized sweater. Her almost waist-length dark blond hair was down. He cut the engine reflexively, turning off the lights. Barefoot, she walked to the car and opened the passenger door and got in. She helped herself to a cigarette, lit it, and said, as though he were a few minutes late for an appointment, Where have you been?

He was furious. He could not admit that he'd been scared, couldn't say he'd been unequal to managing the boat, or that he'd almost confronted the wrong young woman in another house. He demanded an explanation, What the fuck is wrong with you? I wanted to swim, she said, and shrugged and smoked when he pressed, tobacco mixing with the smell of her conditioner. Absently, she began playing with his hair.

My stepdad used to give these like endless speeches at dinner. Now he barely talks and anyway we don't eat together. I think he's depressed, like he should have a therapist, see your parents at the Foundation. It's weird now that he's quiet, because before he would make dinners into these long fucking discussions, except not really, because nobody discussed anything; he just talked in our direction. He'd ask my brother a question every once in a while, but it was always like, Pop quiz: What did I say made this a hard time for the aeronautics business? (You know he got rich off somebody else's invention. Some kind of screw that doesn't weigh anything.) And my brother would never have to answer because my stepdad answered his own fucking questions. The answer was always China, basically. Then there was this one night last summer when my mom was letting me sneak white wine and my brother was out and I had to be the one at the table getting talked at and it was getting on my nerves for real. Maybe it was because I was a little fucked up or because I'm just older now and so like more aware of my mom. What she's been through, starting with my dad. But anyway I did this stupid also kind of awesome thing. Really, really slowly I started lowering myself in my chair, like sliding down out of it, while he was eating his ravioli talking about whatever. My mom was already in the kitchen, loading the dishwasher; she never eats. It required a lot of core strength going down so slowly. All those crunches. All that crystal (joking). At dance they are always telling me to visualize a movement as I do it and I was visualizing myself as a liquid flowing down the chair. All the way down off my chair until I was literally under the table and my stepdad still hadn't noticed anything, and my mom was in there cleaning, and I was trying not to laugh.

Or maybe cry? Adam asked, and she looked at him.

At how fucking sad this dude is maybe. Or yeah like for my mom who is married to him. Like he doesn't realize the audience has gone home while he's just going on and on. And then I seal-crawl so slowly under the table across the carpet holding my breath into the kitchen. My mom has stopped cleaning and now she's on the other side of the island and doesn't see me and I stand up really quietly. She's holding her pink wine looking out the window at the lake or more at her reflection in the glass because it's night. I get the bottle from the fridge door and pour most of it into a plastic cup and come up to her with my like Big Gulp and she's coming back from Mars and about to say something to me but I shush her with a finger on my lips and whisper: Listen. We can hear my stepdad in the dining room telling nobody about Ross Perot. (He was obsessed with Ross Perot. Ross Perot and China.) And my mom maybe doesn't understand what's going on yet but we tiptoe over to the doorway and stand there looking into the dining room while he talks to the air like AM radio and wine is almost coming out of my nose. We stand there forever before he looks up, like we caught him beating off. He looks at my chair then back at us and now my mom and I start really cracking up. Then he gets this fucked-up smile that's pure rage. Like how dare you cunts laugh at me. But I give him the stepdaughter smile back and hold it, hold it. We basically have a staring contest and my mom's laughter gets all nervous until finally his face relaxes and it's all a big joke.

It would take Adam twenty years to grasp the analogy between her slipping from the chair and from the boat. He asked her some questions about her dad and she answered them. He considered telling her about entering the wrong house—maybe he could bring out the poetry of it—but he did not tell her, didn't want to risk it. To protect himself (from what, he wasn't sure), he imagined that he was looking back on the present from a vaguely imagined East Coast city where his experiences in Topeka could be recounted only with great irony.

But he was back in his body when they kissed goodbye and her damp hair was in his face and her tongue was in his mouth, running over his teeth, tobacco and mint, Crest toothpaste. The kiss deepened and as he moved his hands under her sweatshirt he saw against the black back of his eyelids little illuminated patterns flaring up. Phosphenes, tiny fading Rorschachs formed by the inherent electrical charges the retina produces while at rest, an experience of light in the absence of light. He knew these shapes from his concussion as a child and from his migraines and more recently from this kind of contact; he knew them from when he was little trying to fall asleep, watching gray circles migrate across the darkness; if he pressed his closed eyes near the temples, the forms would brighten. He'd wondered if these patterns were unique to him, evidence of some specialness or damage, or if they were universal, if everyone saw them. But they were so faint and difficult to describe that he was never able to figure out if his parents or friends shared this experience just above the threshold of perception; the patterns dissipated under the weight of language, remained irreducibly private. He'd hear people talk about "seeing stars" when they hit their head, but he saw no stars; he saw rings of red or yellow light or tessellated feather shapes that started to shake if he attended to them or dull gold spirals that spun across his field of vision—or whatever you call your field of vision when your eyes are shut. Instead of moving a hand toward the inside of her thigh as was expected, he moved both hands now toward her face; he held her head and ran his thumbs across her closed eyelids, carefully applying distinct but intermittent pressure; did she also see a few red sparks, a network of faint lines?

She pulled back a little, laughing, What are you doing? He told her the word for it he'd learned from Klaus, who said phosphenes might be triggers of psychotic hallucinations. That some people have tried to draw them and the drawings look strangely like those cave paintings, the oldest art. He hoped she liked the poetry he made out of it, how he wanted her to see what he saw, and to imagine seeing with or as her; the world's subtlest fireworks announcing the problem of other minds. Soon they were kissing again and he didn't know if they would fuck. But that night in Topeka's premier housing community conveniently located near West Ridge Mall, she separated from him gently, decisively; maybe she was on her period. Maybe she didn't really care about him. She climbed out of the passenger side with one of his cigarettes and the lighter; she walked around the front of the car and returned the lighter to him through the window. Where's the boat? He said he'd driven around the lake drinking for a while, wasn't sure where he'd parked it; he was tense again, worried he'd have to admit his various navigational failures, but she was unconcerned.

Win me a medal tomorrow, she said, smiling, when he started the engine again. Soon he was speeding away from the McMansions on Urish Road, cool air thundering through the sunroof that he'd opened. Where Urish hit Twenty-First he stopped at a flashing red light and saw to his right the Rolling Hills Nursing Home, a single-story prefabricated building where his now-nonverbal maternal grandfather had been a resident, a patient, a prisoner since moving, since being moved there, from Phoenix two years before; his grandmother, who was in fine shape, lived in Topeka's premier assisted-living community a few miles to the south. He flicked his cigarette butt out of the window, watched the embers scatter on black asphalt, and made himself look at the building. Bright streetlights in the almost empty parking lot; otherwise it was dark. Weird to think of the small old man sleeping in there now. Some brief but hideous analogy between the mechanical hospital bed and the reclinable driver's seat occurred to him, was gone. He pushed *All Eyez on Me* into the tape deck and turned it up very loud, wondered if anyone inside the home could hear it. Then he drove on.

♦♦♦

Four hours later his alarm clock woke him. Half-asleep, he showered and put on the black suit he'd bought with his mom at West Ridge. He tied one of his father's two ties. He drove the short distance to Topeka High, pulling up beside his coaches, Spears and Mulroney, who were looking over a AAA map, their breath visible in the streetlight. The former was drinking coffee from his large thermos; the latter sipped, as ever, her Diet Coke. Other formally dressed adolescents wheeled large plastic tubs from the school and loaded them into the backs of two nearby vans. He did not condescend to move his own tub; an underclassman would take care of it. He saw his partner, Joanna, and nodded in greeting; they weren't friends; their alliance was purely tactical. Once in the van, she wanted to talk strategy, but he leaned his head against the cool window, watched the rise and fall of telephone wires in the dark, and soon he was moving through tract housing in his dreams. He woke up when they pulled off the highway to stop for breakfast at McDonald's, familiar contours of the molded seating.

Dawn was breaking as they arrived at Russell High School. He would normally have skipped such a small tournament, but because Russell was Bob Dole's hometown, and because Bob Dole was running for president, the Russell Invitational would this year draw the best teams from across the state; the logic was unclear to him, but Mulroney had insisted they attend. From similar district-issued vans and buses, other awkwardly costumed adolescents were unloading their own tubs, hauling them across the cold parking lot to the school's main entrance. When he and Joanna walked through the doors, their would-be competitors made way.

He found the high schools strangely altered on the weekends, the spaces transformed when emptied of students and teachers and severed from the rhythms of a normal day. The classrooms, with their hortatory posters, BE THE CHANGE YOU WANT TO SEE, their rows of empty desks, equations or dates or stock phrases left on chalk- or dry-erase boards, made Adam think of abandoned theatrical sets or photographs of Chernobyl. He could occasionally pick up traces of Speed Stick or scented lip gloss or other floating signatures of a social order now suspended. As they walked down the main hall of Russell High he tried various combinations on the lockers. He touched a wrestling state-championship banner hanging in the foyer with the distance of an anthropologist or ghost.

They gathered for a brief welcome assembly in a fluorescently lit cafeteria that smelled of industrial-strength bleach. The host coach made announcements while they looked over their brackets. Then the teams dispersed, carts of evidence in tow, to the assigned classrooms, where a judge and timekeeper awaited.

He let Joanna lead him to their room. The daughter of two

Foundation neurologists, Joanna was a short, smart, Ivy-bound senior who scored, as she would let you know, a 1600 on the SAT. She compiled almost all of their research, having attended a "debate institute" at the University of Michigan over the summer to get a head start on the competition. (The topic this year was whether the federal government should establish new policies to reduce juvenile crime; their plan argued that strengthening child support enforcement would do so in various ways.) Adam's contribution to prep work consisted of skimming *The Economist* during debate class. His strength was thinking on his feet, exposing fallacies; his cross-examinations were widely feared.

These early rounds were a formality; they dispatched low-ranked teams in front of lay judges, often the reluctant parents of other debaters. That weekend at Russell a couple of sophomores tried to surprise them by running a version of their own plan against them, having reconstructed it from notes taken during elimination rounds, which were open to spectators.

Adam rose, smoothing his father's tie, to cross-examine the obviously nervous first affirmative speaker; his opponent resembled a waiter in his white shirt, black slacks. They stood facing a judge—competitors do not look at one another—who could barely fit into the combination chair and desk; he sat with his arms crossed, glasses resting atop his bald head, begrudgingly making notes on a legal pad.

"Could you please repeat this year's resolution?"

"Repeat it?"

"Yes, please."

"Resolved: That the government—"

"The *federal* government," Adam says, as if he's embarrassed to have to help him. "Take your time," he adds, knowing it will sound like politeness to the judge, and to his opponent, infuriating condescension.

"Resolved: The federal government should establish a program to substantially reduce juvenile crime in the United States." There's the slightest tremor in his voice.

"Why was child support established?"

"To support children, obviously"—the origin of the sarcasm is anxiety—"after their parents get divorced."

"Actually, unmarried parents accrue the same child support obligations in most states." Adam has no idea if what he's said is true. He makes a subtle show of ignoring, of transcending, his opponent's tone. "But let's set that aside. It sounds like you agree the program you propose to strengthen was not primarily intended to substantially reduce juvenile crime."

"No, I mean, that was among its intentions."

"Do you have evidence supporting that assertion?" His tone makes it clear that he hopes his opponent does, that he would welcome that debate; it also communicates to the judge that the round is over if he doesn't. (The ballot instructs the judge that "topicality" must be proved by the affirmative team. He and Joanna can crush these debaters in a variety of ways, but he'll start by seeing if his opponent trips himself up on this prima facie issue.)

"The evidence is that it cuts crime. That's why the advantages of our plan are—"

"So you're saying anything that has the effect of reducing crime is topical?"

"No. It has to be federal, a federal program."

"So if I advocate that the federal government build nuclear power plants and it constructs them shoddily and that causes horrible pollution and the pollution produces disastrous health effects and mass death ensues and crime is thereby reduced, that's a topical resolution?" The judge smiles—both at what Adam's said and at his delivery. And he has reminded the judge of his distrust of the Feds.

"Of course not," angry now.

"Why? Because it has to be an *intended* effect of the policy?"

"Okay, sure."

"Do you have any evidence that this was an intended effect?"

"It's common sense." He should argue that—regardless of *why* child support was established in general—they, the affirmative team, are now intending to expand the policy to reduce crime, arguably meeting the conditions of topicality. But he's too frazzled.

"I think what's common sense is that child support is designed to equalize financial burdens on parents following a separation. And that even if this equalization somehow *complicated* crime-reduction efforts, there would still be substantial arguments for its importance. And"—he realizes that, for the average citizen of Russell, Kansas, he might have just made a feminist argument; his pivot is without detectable hesitation—"I can think of strong arguments against that kind of federal intervention in private relationships. The point is that's not the topic of this year's debate."

"I— Look, you run this case all the time and topicality never—"

"Excuse me, I need to stop you there—you want the judge to award you this round because *we* have won other rounds with a similar case?" He's offended on behalf of debate itself.

"I'm not saying that. I'm—"

"That's an interesting idea, that what's argued in previous rounds should be relevant, can be used against us; should you lose this round arguing for the resolution since you presumably argued against it in a prior debate?" The judge is smiling again.

"No, of course not, but—"

"And, incapable of defending the topicality of your policy before the negative team"—he's deadly serious now, a prosecutor on *Law & Order* going in for the kill—"you're bringing up the fact that you copied your plan from our affirmative rounds." A pause. "Your defense against failing to meet the burden of topicality is plagiarism?"

Brief silence in which the judge, eyebrows raised, makes a note.

"I'm just saying it's a topical plan," he says meekly, the round already lost.

At Russell High it was not until the semifinals, when judging would be undertaken by a panel of three college debaters, that the competition really began. He and Joanna were on the affirmative side, facing a fairly formidable team from Shawnee Mission West. The room—a science classroom: microscopes on a big table in the corner, multiple sinks—was full: eliminated debaters and their coaches had become the audience. When the round was about to start, silence fell; for the first time Adam heard the aquarium filter running in a tank he hadn't noticed against the wall. He could just make out some slowly drifting yellow forms.

And now Joanna stands to deliver the first affirmative speech. For a few seconds it sounds more or less like oratory, but soon she accelerates to nearly unintelligible speed, pitch and volume rising; she gasps like a swimmer surfacing, or maybe drowning; she is attempting to "spread" their opponents, as her opponents will attempt to spread them in turn—that is, to make more arguments, marshal more evidence than the other team can respond to within the allotted time, the rule among serious debaters being that a "dropped argument," no matter its quality, its content, is conceded. (Competitive debaters spend hours doing speed drills—holding a pen in the teeth while reading, which forces the tongue to work harder, the mouth to over-enunciate; they practice reading evidence backward so as to uncouple the physical act of vocalization from the effort to comprehend, which slows one down.) The judges hunch over their legal pads, producing a flow sheet of the round along with the competitors, recording argument and counterargument in shorthand, making little or no eye contact with the speakers. During the brief intervals wherein their pens are idle, they twirl them around their thumbs, a signature habit of debaters.

To an anthropologist or ghost wandering the halls of Russell High School, interscholastic debate would appear less competitive speech than glossolalic ritual. See the cystic acned first negative speaker from Shawnee Mission—his dress more casual, typical of the rich kids from Kansas City—reading evidence at 340 words per minute to support his claim that the affirmative plan will overburden family courts, setting off a catastrophic chain of events. He lets each page fall to the floor when he's finished, along with drops of sweat. He inhales sharply, shouts out another tagline—"Overburdened courts lead to civil collapse"—then reads more evidence, getting briefly entangled in a stutter that, at such volume and such speed, makes it sound as though he's having a seizure or a stroke. As time runs out, he sums up his arguments, although few of the uninitiated could understand him: *Gregor evidence points to back-backlogged courts as result of increased child support enforcement judicial overload leads to civil collapse collapse leads to nuclear conflict China or North Korea nuclear strike in ensuing power vacuum out-out-outweighs whatever benefits affirmative plan offers and and and and Stevenson proves affirmative plan no solvency regardless because resistance from from internal agencies blocks imple-implementation must vote no on disadvantage impact alone but but even if you you consider plan as plan no solvency 1AC key source for Georgia courts not not applicable to fed program only state level so there is no way to vote but negative.*

The spread was controversial; if it happened in front of lay judges, there was shock, complaints. More than one highly ranked team had misjudged its judges and been eliminated in early rounds for speaking drivel. Old-timer coaches longed for the days when debate was debate. The most common criticism of the spread was that it detached policy debate from the real world, that nobody used language the way that these debaters did, save perhaps for auctioneers. But even the adolescents knew this wasn't true, that corporate persons deployed a version of the spread all the time: for they heard the spoken warnings at the end of the increasingly common television commercials for prescription drugs, when risk information was disclosed at a speed designed to make it difficult to comprehend; they heard the list of rules and caveats read rapid-fire at the end of promotions on the radio; they were at least vaguely familiar with the "fine print" one received from financial institutions and health-insurance companies; the last thing one was supposed to do with those thousands of words was comprehend them. These types of disclosure were designed to conceal; they exposed you to information that, should you challenge the institution in question, would be treated like a "dropped argument" in a fast round of debate—you have already conceded the validity of the point by failing to address it when it was presented. It's no excuse that you didn't have the time. Even before the twenty-four-hour news cycle, Twitter storms, algorithmic trading, spreadsheets, the DDoS attack, Americans were getting "spread" in their daily lives; meanwhile, their politicians went on speaking slowly, slowly about values utterly disconnected from their policies.

Joanna was too fast for the Shawnee Mission kids; Adam spent most of the semifinal round pointing out which of her arguments his opponents had dropped. In the finals, when they were back on the negative side, they hit rivals from Lawrence High. When they'd lost to Rohan and Vinay in the past, it had been Adam's fault; they were as well prepared as Joanna. But that day, for whatever reason, his mind was particularly swift.

And that day at Russell High as he enumerated in accelerating succession the various unpredictable ways implementation of his opponents' plan would lead to nuclear holocaust (almost every plan, no matter how minor, would lead to nuclear holocaust), he passed, as he often passed, a mysterious threshold. He began to feel less like he was delivering a speech and more like a speech was delivering him, that the rhythm and intonation of his presentation were beginning to dictate its content, that he no longer had to organize his arguments so much as let them flow through him. Suddenly the physical tension he carried was all focused energy, a transformation that made the event slightly erotic. If the language coursing through him was about the supposedly catastrophic effects of ending the government's Stingray surveillance program or the affirmative speaker's failure to prove solvency, he was nevertheless more in the realm of poetry than of prose, his speech stretched by speed and intensity until he felt its referential meaning dissolve into pure form. In a public school closed to the public, in a suit that felt like a costume, while pretending to argue about policy, he was seized, however briefly, by an experience of prosody.

Then he was back in the cafeteria for the award ceremony, eating Peanut M&M's a freshman had fetched him from the machine, half listening as Coach Spears tried to convince him that professional wrestling was real: I've seen the blood; I've been close to the cage. Adam nodded as he chewed. Everyone fell quiet when the host coaches arrived to announce the final results and hand out medals.

But there was a commotion around the cafeteria doors. They swung open and several reporters hurried in; a cameraman quickly set up a bright light on a tripod, shouldered his camera. Then, to the growing surprise of the assembled debaters, men who were unmistakably bodyguards entered the room, looked around, coiled tubes dangling from earpieces. He glanced at Coach Mulroney, who displayed a knowing smile. Finally, Senator Bob Dole appeared, the seventy-three-year-old Russell native who was less than a month away from being crushed by Bill Clinton, a landslide victory for the Democrat that would confirm that cultural conservatism was giving, had all but given, way to the reign of more liberal baby boomers. It would confirm that history had ended.

A few gasps of recognition, some applause. Dole, as ever, held a pen in his largely paralyzed right arm and waved his awkward wave with the left. He walked, flanked by aides, to the front of the cafeteria and shook the left hand of the host coach, who said, beaming, that the next president of the United States would be handing out the medals to the winners of this year's Russell High School Invitational. Before the medalists were recognized, Senator Dole wanted to say a few words.

"I'm not much of a debater myself," he said, maybe expecting laughter, which didn't come, "but I place great value on the skills that you are all developing here today." Even for a politician, Dole spoke haltingly. (From his chair in the audience, Adam involuntarily pictured Dole holding the pen between his teeth, reading backward; he pictured Dole trying and failing to do the debater's twirl with the cold, incapable hand. Then he pictured his grandfather's paralyzed left arm in Rolling Hills.) "You are the future leaders of America and I am very glad that you are all here improving your ability to communicate, to persuade. That's so important. In our democracy. Crucial. And learning so much about government and policy. Wonderful. I'm honored to get to be here and to let you know you're all winners in my book for the hard work you're doing. It will carry you far. Will be seeing some of you on Capitol Hill."

He was given an index card from which he read the names of the third-place team, the debaters rising to accept their medals, pausing for photographs with the senator. He butchered Rohan's and Vinay's surnames; they stood almost apologetically.

Now I am going to show you a picture and I'd like you to make up a story about it. We call this the Thematic Apperception Test, or TAT. A story with a beginning, a middle, and an end. It's a black-and-white photograph that appeared on the front page of *The Topeka Capital-Journal.* (Who is this unsmiling seventeen-year-old boy whose hair is drawn into a ponytail while the sides of his head are shaved, a disastrous tonsorial compromise between the lefty household of his parents and the red state in which he was raised? His left hand is almost touching Dole's right, which clutches the pen; around his neck the teenager wears a medal won by speaking a nearly private language at great speed. The senator, who often refers to himself in the third person, whose campaign is advised by Paul Manafort, will be the only former presidential candidate to attend the Republican convention in 2016.) What are these people in this picture thinking? Feeling? Start by telling me what led up to this scene.

♦♦♦

Adam had known Kenneth Erwood a little for as long as he could remember; Dr. Erwood—one of few openly gay men in Topeka, and so a frequent target of Reverend Fred Phelps and his followers—had been over for dinner, a guest at parties. He was a quiet, smiling, kind-looking man who appeared simultaneously older and younger than his age (prematurely stooped, then just stooped, but a boyish face that never seemed to change), and whose close-cut gray hair possessed no military quality (though he had in fact worked at the Naval Ordnance Test Station in Point Mugu, studying the optical assessment of self-guided missiles). Erwood listened carefully, but never held forth like other men. Although Adam couldn't remember it, his parents had taken him to Erwood, whose office was in the same building as his father's, for a consultation in the weeks after his concussion; they were given some meditation exercises to promote healing, reduce post-traumatic stress. He thought he could recall sitting on the off-white living room carpet with his parents, hands palm-upward in his lap.

Once, Adam had asked his mom if she knew anybody who was psychic, if she believed in that sort of thing; she'd said, without hesitation: Kenneth Erwood. Although he was careful to justify his research to administrators in the language of neuroscience, Erwood spoke openly with friends and colleagues about having been visited as a child in a waking dream and told, or given to understand, that he was under spiritual guidance. As a college student, Erwood had re-encountered his guide with the help of a well-known medium, and while simultaneously earning doctorates in physics and psychology, he'd had a vision in which he saw images of a clock tower. When he traveled to the Foundation in 1965, he recognized the building in the center of the campus; he knew it was where he was meant to undertake his work.

Erwood studied how mental processes influenced physiological responses. He was particularly interested in a person's capacity to alter the electromagnetic field surrounding the body. Soon after joining the Foundation, Erwood started a small department of psychophysics and psychophysiology. Its centerpiece was the Copper Wall Initiative. His research demonstrated that recognized healers and meditators from a variety of traditions could induce, from several feet away, significant voltage changes in a wall-sized electrode made of copper. The wall was established in the basement of the Foundation clock tower.

Now, as a senior in high school, Adam was going back to Erwood against his will. His parents had insisted, with rare resolve, that he either consult with Erwood or start conventional talk therapy. The intensity, they said, was out of control, how quick he was to rage, even if he was relatively quick to cool. He needed "strategies." His mom would ask him to get the dirty dishes out of the living room where he wasn't really supposed to be eating anyway. I'll do it later, he'd say; I'd like you to do it now, she'd respond; then out of him would issue an overwhelming barrage of ridiculous but somehow irrefutable arguments about her nagging, her hypocrisy, her failure to abide by the precepts she laid out in her books, her bizarre focus on conventional domestic order over the autonomy of others; again and again, she failed to prove topicality. The dishes remained where they were.

Or he would ask to borrow his dad's car because the check-engine light was on in the Camry and it was making ominous sounds and when his dad said, No, sorry, I have men's group tonight and I need it, but I can help you bring yours in tomorrow, he would suddenly lay into the whole notion of a men's group with vicious eloquence, although his arguments were contradictory. That's Robert Bly machismo bullshit, he'd claim, having heard mocking summaries of *Iron John* around the house, but when his dad said calmly, You've got that wrong, this is, as you know, a group of pro-feminist friends, he'd accuse them of being a bunch of emasculated yuppies who thought floating platitudes about fatherhood made them enlightened. You guys probably *should* go perform improvised masculine rituals in the woods. Play some drums, stew some squirrels. The calmer his dad remained, the more furious Adam grew: fights over nothing would lead him to slam doors; twice he punched holes in his bedroom wall.

His parents were, in addition to being exasperated, worried, but not *that* worried; as psychotherapists, they were much less afraid of open conflict than of the prospect of a kid withdrawing, disappearing into his room, into himself, a lost boy. As long as there was language, there was processing; and when he calmed down he would apologize for his intensity, deploying his Foundation vocabulary; he would often think along with them about its causes. When he wasn't being an asshole, he was funny, curious, kind; think about how wonderful he was around his grandmother, how many good questions he asked of their friends when they managed to get him to sit down for a dinner. Folk singers and community organizers and sexperts and writers and feminist scholars stayed in their big Victorian house when they passed through the Midwest; he was always interested, quickly picked up new ways of thinking and talking. They were proud of his politics. He got straight A's. (They didn't suspect he cheated in math.) He was a star at "public speaking." He was reading and writing poetry. He was probably Ivy-bound, although they'd be fine with KU. They rightly assumed part of his volatility arose from his fear of leaving home.

Then there were the migraines, their increasing frequency and severity. He would be looking at a page of text or a sign on a wall and suddenly find it impossible to read, letters like twigs floating away on water. Then large blind spots, as though he'd looked at a bright light. Then large tracts of peripheral vision fell away. Fast on the optical symptoms, on the sudden illiteracy, would be numbness in the hands, parts of the face, sometimes the tongue, which would cause him to slur his speech. Photosensitivity so severe that a little sun entering around the blackout blinds was a flashlight in his eyes, phosphenes loosed upon the world. He would have the sensation that his limbs were out of joint, that he could not control them; he would reach for a glass of water and miss it by a few inches or knock it over. When he pressed the Imitrex cartridge against his leg to give himself an injection, he could not tell leg, hard plastic, and hand apart; they were all dumb alien objects; the medicine did very little, maybe nothing. Within half an hour of the prodrome, there would be pain in his head so severe that he experienced it primarily as nausea. When the vomiting started, it wouldn't stop for hours; more than once he'd had to go to the hospital to be treated for dehydration. Here we are again, Nurse Eberheart. Say hi to Darren for us. Layered onto these symptoms was his fear of them, how the neurological distortions recalled his concussion; his disorientation was compounded by his panic at disorientation, and each migraine, which tended to last between eight and twelve hours, felt like a little repetition of that trauma.

Part of what made the migraines so terrible was his belief that he had caused them. You're going to give yourself a migraine, he often heard, often warned himself. If the cause of the headaches was stress, then every intense thought, wrong desire, real or imagined conflict, would return to him in the form of pain. The pressures of passing himself off as a real man, of staying true to type—the constant weight lifting, the verbal combat—would eventually reduce him to a child again, calling out for his mother from his bed. The migraines were his periodic full-bodied involuntary confessions that he was soft, a poser. And while he'd never had more than one in a six-week period, he thought he felt one coming on a hundred times a day: whenever he looked away from a light source to find his vision mottled, whenever part of his body fell asleep or felt slightly numb from an awkward posture, on the very rare occasions when he stuttered or grew briefly confused in his speech—terror arose within him. Each false alarm, because it caused anxiety, brought him closer to the real thing.

Erwood was a pioneer in biofeedback—especially in teaching people to warm their hands as a way of bringing automatic bodily processes under conscious control. The aim was to quiet fight-or-flight responses, increase blood flow to the extremities, and alleviate headaches caused by the buildup of vascular tension. Adam's parents had rightly assumed he would be more open to seeing Erwood for migraines than to seeing a psychotherapist to discuss his emotional life. Since Erwood worked unconventional hours, he could consult with him at the Foundation on Sunday afternoons.

The office resembled his father's except there was no desk; there were two chairs that faced one another for conversation and then meditation pillows and mats in a corner. A copper singing bowl and a little mallet. On the walls were a few framed pictures of what he assumed were famous Eastern healers—men, mainly, in white and red and saffron robes. The first session consisted of

Erwood soliciting a detailed description of the migraine symptoms, their onset, explaining how and why biofeedback worked, then hooking up a little temperature sensor to his hands, asking him to shut his eyes and visualize what the doctor slowly described. First he was to be aware of his breath, breathing deeply in, slowly out. Note the rise and fall of the abdomen and chest. Then he was to imagine a warmth spreading from the tips of his toes slowly up and throughout his body, before focusing on his hands. Although it felt like half an hour, they spent less than ten minutes on this initial session, Erwood showing him, after he'd told Adam to open his eyes, how he'd raised his temperature slightly. Erwood asked that he commit to ten minutes of practice a day for the first week, gave him the sensor, then wondered: Would you like to see the wall?

In the clock tower basement, Adam walked tentatively into the room Erwood had unlocked for him and sat cross-legged on the large glass cube, as he assumed he was supposed to; Erwood left, shutting the door. Adam looked up to consider the wall while his eyes attempted to adjust to what he at first experienced as total dark. He thought he smelled a faint coppery scent, but that must have been his imagination or his sweat. The color of the center of the wall soon became faintly visible to him. He could hear Erwood making noise behind the wall; why hadn't he switched on the lights? Some ambient light was present in the room, maybe filtering in below the door, and now he could more clearly differentiate a nebula of red and orange and brown from the surrounding blackness. Although his eyes were open in a dark room, he felt like they were shut while he was looking at a light source, as if light were penetrating his eyelids, taking on the color of the blood it passed through. Involuntarily, he attempted to open his already open eyes.

"How are you doing over there?" he heard Erwood ask from behind the wall, either through it or via a microphone, and he heard himself respond, "Fine"; his voice sounded bored, but he was not bored: he was looking into the secret power source of the Foundation dimly glowing in the clock tower basement, the thing behind or beyond all the talk, the unnameable energy that had drawn his parents and so many others from the coasts, helped gather Klaus and the old guard of analysts from their exile. He was looking at the gold ground of a medieval painting, then he was inside the painting looking out into a museum at night. He repositioned himself on the glass block, noticed how hot he felt, and almost demanded that Erwood turn on the light, if there was a light, but then he thought that it would sound like he was scared, which he was, if just a little. Because he'd picked that plant with special powers in the backyard of Bright Circle Montessori, because he'd hit his head, stopping time, because he brought the depersonalizing headaches upon himself. He was all ages at once as he sat in the dark before the wall, or he was flickering between them, moving through every house on the lake.

Now Erwood wasn't making any sound. It was too quiet; they had soundproofed the room so effectively that it approached the anechoic. He heard water moving through the clock tower pipes and the hum of electricity in the wires, but this was blood moving through his head, the hiss of idling auditory nerves. He imagined Erwood dead, slumped over some kind of control panel on the other side of the wall, which was a million miles away—he was adrift in outer space now, launched into orbit against his will; Erwood had been ground control. He shut his eyes to stifle panic and the wall was still there, phosphenes cycling across it; involuntarily, he tried to close them again. And now to fill the void came rage and language. Rage at whatever trick Erwood was playing on him, whatever test he was administering, leaving him here for minutes that were hours; he imagined kneeing the gentle doctor in the face, his nose shattering, the coppery smell of blood. *I warned you, motherfucker; I said step off. I said affirmative plan will trigger widespread particles of anger resulting in the declaration of martial law of migraine which does permanent damage to democratic institutions leads to collapse of NATO of the sound good rules that would enable thousands to live together in Rolling Hills Nursing Home with Darren and Dole.* Were his eyes open and/or shut? He wanted to deface the perfectly smooth copper surface, draw his keys across the metal like the car door of an enemy from Topeka West, make whatever minimal mark could inaugurate an alphabet.

Erwood opened the door; light flooded in, scattering his thoughts, if that's what they were. What do you think? Erwood asked. Cool, he said, indifference in his voice. Erwood approached him and, to Adam's surprise and discomfort, put a hand on the back of his neck, which was wet with perspiration, then moved both hands down his trapezius muscles to his shoulders, which were sore from his most recent workout at Popeye's Gym on Twenty-First. You're carrying a tremendous amount of tension, Erwood said. Here, and here. Why don't you try talking, since you're such a great talker, to those muscles? Ask them—with a lot of kindness, with a lot of humility—to relax.

There was an iron bench across from the clock tower, where he waited for his dad to pick him up. The clock said it was almost five. It was unusually warm for November, but the shortness of the days signaled the approach of winter. The red leaves of the nearby maples and the yellow leaves of the ash seemed to glow in the early dusk as if they were producing their own light. He wanted a cigarette. A siren passed in the distance; in its wake he heard the downward-sloping whistle of a cardinal somewhere in the trees. He tried to imagine what it would be like to be hospitalized here, to live on the campus, although hospitalizations were increasingly rare, since now insurance almost never paid. Then he imagined a huge debate tournament on the Foundation grounds, all of the competitors patients, most of them psychotic, some of them shaking and drooling from medication, involuntarily sticking out their tongues, smacking their lips. He imagined them withdrawing evidence from their plastic tubs, but instead of texts they produced random objects: an umbrella, a horseshoe, a pack of baseball cards, strange implements. The judges, the shrinks, Jonathan and Jane Gordon among them, would have to figure out what arguments had been made, which had been dropped. Resolved: A few red sparks, a network of faint lines.

The clock tower began to chime. A car drove slowly by, loud but unintelligible radio voices inside it. The driver, a bearded man he didn't recognize, recognized him, and waved. He noticed a small bronze plaque affixed to the bench, dedicating it, on behalf of the Topeka City Council, to the memory of Thomas Attison. His first, his most vivid memory of Dr. Tom was false; it was an image lifted from one of his dad's films; that's why the memory was black-and-white, set to piano music in his mind. He did remember visiting Dr. Tom's office with his dad when he was eight or nine to interview him for a school project. He could see the grandfatherly man extending a glass bowl of strawberry hard candies, the ones with the soft center. He'd read his questions off a yellow legal pad: Did you always know you wanted to be a psychiatrist? How does it feel to be world-famous? He'd visited again a year or two later for no particular reason. Again he was offered the glass bowl. Now, on the bench, he touched his tongue to the roof his mouth, remembering how the candies had scraped his palate. (After the session with Erwood, he was unusually aware of his body.) How many of his small gestures and postures in the present were embodied echoes of the past, repetitions just beneath the threshold of his consciousness? What would happen to the past if you brought those involuntary muscle memories under your control and edited them, edited them out? Now he felt the present absence of his babysitter's tongue, that first metallic contact years ago. Now more recent traces of tobacco, artificial mint. As his father pulled up to the curb, Adam bit down on a phantom pen.

May break my bones but words. Bounces off me sticks to you. The grown-ups had equipped him with weak spells to cast back against the insults. But the need for the sayings disproved them and as he grew they would if anything just feed the laughter. Nice comeback, Darren. If he still sometimes said those things or other private phrases to himself, it was only to interrupt the harmful thoughts before it was too late and he had set some trap for an enemy on a highway or country road. It's like there is a video game inside his head except what happens there will happen here. Recently it's been based on Spy Hunter, *which is among Darren's favorites at Aladdin's Arcade in West Ridge Mall. Same electronic music. From above he sees a strip of asphalt running vertically through a simplified landscape. The image is so vague it would be difficult for Darren to say if he's picturing graphics or real terrain. But he can make out the silver Fiero that is his avatar speeding down below and he knows that if he presses a button in his mind the car will release an oil slick or smoke screen in its wake. And while it is impossible to say when his enemies will encounter these fatal hazards, understand they will, they'll go through their windshields. Once, after they'd been talking about his dad, Dr. Jonathan asked Darren if he knew how he had acquired such powers. Darren said no.*

But he did know. It was at Bright Circle Montessori on Oakley Avenue when he was four, when he was still the same age as his body. It was warm for late September and the sky was cloudless when his mom dropped him off. Okay, sweetheart. At this point Darren no longer clung or cried. He would just walk to Mrs. Caldwell and hug her hello and then quietly build and knock over towers of wooden blocks and wait for Adam Gordon and Jason Davis to arrive. Then he would follow them around and they would let him. That day they were in the sandbox in the backyard during free play and Adam said that he had a plant with special powers that he had picked from along the chain-link fence. Like poison ivy or poison oak or the way spinach makes Popeye strong this was a plant Adam rubbed between his hands until it released some kind of force. You don't have to eat it. Adam gave the weeds to Jason who passed them on to Darren who got them to stain his hands a little and buried them as Adam instructed in the sand. Then Adam said you make a wish for something to happen and it does. Darren doesn't remember what Adam or Jason wished for, or if they told him, but Darren was obsessed with tornadoes and he said he'd use his power to make one happen and then they played some other game.

The chests of fifteen toddlers rising and falling on cots in the beige-carpeted room as poorly simulated wave noise issues from a portable stereo plugged into the corner. Mrs. Caldwell and her assistant Pam are preparing a snack in the adjacent kitchen, small paper cups of grapes halved lengthwise to mitigate the risk of choking. Darren wakes to rain falling on the school's metal roof. Quietly he rises and carries his stuffed rabbit to the window and parts the curtain to see unusually dark clouds he thinks are lowering. Acorns from the red oak in the school's front yard hit the window and he startles. Only gradually does he realize he is looking at his work. His hands are clean now, Mrs. Caldwell made him scrub them before lunch, but they feel at once raw and numb, like the time he touched the stove. Beneath the artificial lemon of the soap the smell of the magic plant is still detectable. He hurries back to his cot and pulls the Peanuts sheets up over his head and tries to call off the storm he's summoned. To his rabbit whose name is lost he says again and again that he is sorry. And then we hear the sirens starting up.

SPEECH SHADOWING

(JONATHAN)

I first read "A Man by the Name of Ziegler" on the 4 train, lights flickering in the shaking, almost-empty car; I was on my way back from seeing Jane, one of the first times we'd slept together; I'd leave Rachel for her within a year.

The story begins with Ziegler's visit to the city history museum—he's either in Basel or Berlin—which is free on Sundays. Alone in an exhibit of "objects of medieval superstition," he reaches unthinkingly beyond a rope to touch the forge and mortars and other implements from an alchemist's workshop; he is surprised to discover among the tools a "small dark-colored pellet, rather like a pill." Another visitor appears, startling Ziegler, who instinctively pockets the pill. Later, he rediscovers it over lunch, where, giving in to a "childlike impulse," he pops it in his mouth, washes it down with a beer. After the meal, Ziegler continues his day of leisure with a trip to the zoo. Wandering around the cages, he slowly realizes that, as a result of the mysterious pill, he can understand the language of the animals, who are, it turns out, viciously mocking the zoo-goers, whom they consider idiots and frauds and brutes. Ziegler is shocked less by the fact that he can comprehend the animals than by their contempt, the extremity of it; derided by monkeys and elk ("who speak only with their eyes") and ibexes and chamois (whatever those are) and llamas and gnus and boars and bears, he finally breaks down; tossing away his cane, hat, tie, and then his shoes, he collapses in sobs against the bars of one of the cages. At the story's end, Ziegler is hauled off to an asylum I pictured as Bellevue, where I'd interned.

Dr. Samuels, my analyst in graduate school, so rarely said anything—just "Go on," or "Say more about that," or repeated something I'd said to draw out its significance—that his recommendation alone would have imbued the Herman Hesse story with mystery. Was I supposed to be Ziegler? (Ziegler is unremarkable, "not stupid but not gifted," a man who respects money and science above all things, "one of those people we see every day on the street, whose faces we can never really remember, because they all have the same face: a collective face.") Was therapy like alchemy, or its opposite? Was Samuels, who knew about my affair with Jane, suggesting some parallel between my marital transgression and Ziegler's reaching across the museum ropes?

Rachel and I wouldn't have lasted regardless; we got married the year before I started grad school, after we both, within the space of a few days, lost a parent: my mom finally succumbing to breast cancer, her dad dropping from a coronary. It was a doomed attempt to shore up a sense of family in the wake of those deaths; we had history and grief in common, not much else.

Our wedding, our non-wedding, had been at City Hall, one distracted friend as witness, followed by a celebratory dinner at an uncomfortably upscale Italian restaurant. Soaked by a sudden shower, we arrived disheveled, hair dripping, a wrecked, ironic carnation in my lapel. The waiter poured out a little of the red wine for me to try; for an instant, I thought he was making a joke about my age, giving me a child's portion. Then I swirled it too aggressively, splashing a little on the tablecloth. I tried to make it into a Chaplinesque performance, but it all had a nightmarish quality—a couple of kids playing at adulthood with desperation. A year of nights spent staring at the ceiling, Rachel asleep beside me, the plaster yellow in the streetlight, the cracks seeming to spread before my eyes.

I felt fucked up about the deception—at least, when I wasn't exhilarated about Jane—and, probably because my attempt at substitute family was failing, it was like I'd lost my mom all over again, as if the news were fresh, not that the news was old, analysis no doubt also stirring things up. A movie poster with a leading man she liked at the New Yorker on West Eighty-Eighth, a turn of phrase she might have used overheard on the subway, "Remember me to your sister," Rachel blowing on her tea just so—suddenly I was bereft, but only briefly, like an episode of vertigo, like a crystal had come loose in my inner ear. (Ziegler, Hesse says, "especially admired cancer research, for his father had died of cancer and Ziegler firmly believed that science . . . would not let the same thing happen to him"; could Samuels have had this passage in mind?) Then there was the world: it was 1969, little improvised bombs detonating across Manhattan, perpetual campus protests; there was outrage, but also a sense of community, of carnival; we felt that history was alive. Jane and I were both increasingly active in the antiwar movement; my younger brother, who would prefer to be left out of a novel, was in the nascent Weather Underground; my father and I were barely speaking after our last fight over the war; all the orders, personal and political, were crumbling.

If I'd ever described my dissertation research to Samuels, I would have assumed that had prompted the Ziegler recommendation, but while I was open about desire and grief—a new erotic life with Jane, the recurring dream about my mom, the one where she's waving at the camera—I never mentioned my academic work in analysis, something Samuels didn't seem to notice. If my research became part of our sessions, if it was crossed with talk about my affair, my mom, etc., I thought I'd get blocked, paralyzed, especially if Samuels—dour, widely published, very

Swiss—even hinted at disapproval; I already felt like a fraud half the time. I assumed Samuels considered me—at best—"not stupid but not gifted."

For months I'd been conducting experiments related to the technique of "speech shadowing," in which a subject repeats speech immediately after hearing it. I'd have participants don cumbersome black over-the-ear headphones and listen to a recording of a text I'd selected more or less at random (a driver's ed manual I'd found discarded among other books on 109th and Columbus). As the subject parroted the recording, I gradually—almost imperceptibly—accelerated the tape; to my shock, I found that a significant number of the subjects would, past a certain threshold, begin to drivel, thinking all the while that they were repeating the recorded passage clearly. The first time this happened in my living room—two reel-to-reel recorders and a microphone atop the long rosewood coffee table my father had given us as a wedding present—I thought the subject (my downstairs neighbor, Aaron, who also sold us drugs) was having a stroke; Rachel rushed into the room to see what the hell was going on. But Aaron just sat there as he descended—or ascended?—into glossolalia, although without any apparent ecstasy; Aaron, in his one moth-eaten cardigan, looked as bored as ever.

My theory was that, under conditions of information overload, the speech mechanisms collapse—but, as Jane was quick to point out, this was more a basic description of the driveling than its explanation. I didn't really care; I needed a scientific-sounding topic, but I knew I wanted to be a therapist, and I doubted any of the graduate center faculty read the dissertations closely; the chair of my committee was totally checked out. (I'd focused on an auditory process in the first place because I'd already bought some rudimentary sound equipment for the short films I was making in my spare time.) Scientific significance aside, the shadowing was riveting to watch, at once disturbing and a little comic, an effect amplified by the grandiosity of the driver's education manual, which sounded like it was written by Hesse:

> **Shadowed passage, Task 1, 180 Words Per Minute, Presented in Left Ear (*Sportsmanlike Driving,* pp. 105–106)**
>
> When you have looked at a shiny, new automobile, have you ever stopped to think that, through all the countless thousands of generations that preceded this century, not even the most powerful kings on earth could have owned one like it? Nor could they have flown in an airplane, nor listened to a radio set, nor watched television.
>
> Of course you know why. It took those thousands of generations of technical progress, each building on the achievements of those who lived before, to make those common modern articles possible.
>
> Medicine has a similar history. Great plagues killed many thousands of people throughout the ages. Man's knowledge grew, with each new generation building on the past, until he developed ways of conquering those contagious diseases.
>
> Intelligent people would not want to destroy those hard-won accomplishments in technology or medicine, or to throw away the very valuable advantages we gain from them.
>
> Less understood, perhaps, is the long, long struggle man has had to devise good, sound rules which would enable hundreds, thousands, or even millions of people to live together.

It was as though Samuels had somehow intuited that, in my fourth-floor walk-up on 108th and Amsterdam, I'd become a kind of Ziegler. He'd come to understand the tongues of beasts at the cost of his reason, while I was destroying human language to reveal the river of nonsense coursing just beneath its "good, sound rules."

My research definitely played a role in what Jane and I still call my "Ziegler Episode." Instead of ingesting a mysterious pill found at a museum, we dropped some of Aaron's acid, sugar dissolving in our mouths on the crosstown bus, and went to the Met. It was late January, the city a mess of dirty snow, pedestrians walking with their heads down against the wind. We checked our heavy coats, ascended the grand staircase, and wandered into the galleries of medieval painting: tempera on wood, gold ground, elongated angels and Virgins, livid Christs. At first everything struck me as a little silly: the solemnity of the guards, the bombast of the wall texts; the babies who looked like little old men nursing at breasts that jut out of the Virgins' shoulders.

Then we arrived before Duccio's *Madonna and Child*, where we stood for several minutes, my jaw clenching and unclenching involuntarily as we looked. Old paintings usually bored me; this one stopped me cold. The foreknowledge in the woman's expression, as though she could anticipate a distant recurrence. The weird parapet beneath the figures, how it linked the sacred world with the world of the viewers. One instant I saw the gold background as flat and another I saw depths. But what really fascinated me, really moved me, wasn't in the painting: it was how the bottom edge of the original frame was marked by candle burns. Traces of an older medium of illumination, the shadow of devotion. The wall text claimed the painting helped inaugurate the Renaissance because Duccio reimagined the Madonna and Christ in terms taken from life. So in that sense it was a move against the sacred, a step toward paintings becoming objects of aesthetic contemplation, detached from religion, detached from altars, free or doomed to circulate in museums, in the marketplace. But the burns were like the fingerprints of an older time—before Ziegler and his brethren decided that traditional sources of value were merely superstition. "Those thousands of generations of technical progress" obliterated ritual, emptied out all meaning, glossolalia without divinity. I decided that's what the painted mother foresaw, that she was saying farewell to candlelight, that she knew she was trapped inside a painting addressed to the future, where it could only be, however great, an instance of technique. New cracks spread across the surface as I stared. Tears start in my memory.

We left the galleries of paintings and walked back down the staircase to find the ancient sculptures, which Jane loved. When we arrived in the skylit hall, I discovered that I'd somehow absorbed the colors from the paintings and could project them now onto the smooth marble of the statuary or let them play across the museum's high walls; I was a kind of magic lantern. I described this pleasant hallucination to Jane, who seemed to be tripping not at all, and she told me in what I called her "Barnard voice" that Roman marble sculptures *had* been vividly colored, that the image of pure classical form we inherited from the Renaissance was false; there was elaborate polychromatic painting, gilding, silvering, inlay. And these sculptures would have had eyes, Jane explained to me, not smooth vacant spaces, but lifelike organs of sight constructed separately out of quartz and obsidian and set into the sockets: blue or green irises; jet-black pupils. As Jane described them, the eyes materialized in a hundred marble heads, and soon the court was a vast network of crisscrossing gazes, encaged by them—like those laser motion sensors you see in heist movies; I could sense whenever I passed through one of the Romans' sight lines an almost imperceptible pressure on my face, like walking through mist or a succession of tiny webs.

I really started to lose it when I met them, the gazes, when I locked eyes with this or that sculpture and perceived the contempt, the "lofty and solemn contempt, a terrible contempt. In the language of these silent, majestic eyes, Ziegler read, he, with hat and cane, his gold watch and his Sunday suit, was no better than vermin, an absurd and repulsive bug." If, instead of a Sunday suit and carefully maintained whiskers, I wore a mustache on my collective face, had shoulder-length hair, a secondhand corduroy jacket over a plaid button-down shirt and faded jeans; if, instead of an uncritical faith in money and science, I believed, I claimed to believe, in the liberation of repressed drives and the reorganization of social forces, the contempt communicated by the statues was still overwhelming, their mockery specific to me, my hypocrisy. Your received jargon regarding the mind and its functions; the contradiction between the normalizing force of therapy and your supposed belief in revolution; your use of your mother's death to justify your behavior toward Rachel, behavior you'll just repeat with Jane. I read all this in their eyes and knew I didn't, still saw the unpainted marble underneath my vision; I understood that the drug had tapped and was now externalizing some vein of self-loathing. This isn't real, I repeated to myself, breathing deeply, and I started to calm down.

Until I heard the voices of the elderly couple near me; the man, black turtleneck beneath blue jacket, leaned over to read aloud from a placard beside the portrait bust of a powerful-looking curly-headed figure, some minor emperor. At first I thought the man was speaking a foreign language, maybe Hebrew, which I knew a little, but, as I listened, I grew convinced that I was hearing the garbled shadow of the wall text. Then I realized the collapse of sense was general: the girl in a plaid skirt who skipped past us, click of her saddle shoes on the mosaic floor, addressed to the grown-ups trailing her a stream of unintelligible if shaped noise. A red-haired woman in cat-eye glasses pointing out a detail on a Greek funerary relief said something to her friend that sounded like a recording played in reverse. I turned to Jane, but, instead of reassuring me, she opened her mouth and released, with the exception of one or two recognizable words, the rapid nonsense from my study. "Dejected and wrenched out of all habits of thought," Samuel's voice in my head, "Ziegler turned back to his fellow men in despair. He looked for eyes that would understand his terror and misery; he listened to conversations in the hope of hearing something comforting, something understandable and soothing." I tried to keep it together—I'd had a bad trip before—but there were guards moving in the periphery of my vision; they'd noticed my agitation; they'd haul me off to Bellevue. Chlorpromazine and electroshock.

I remember the next several hours of the Episode in both the first and third person, probably because I've depended heavily on Jane's account. At the time it was hell, but it would come to be an endearing part of our prehistory, a comedy—Buster Keaton, black-and-white, the action at once stuttering and sped up. Set it to piano music in your mind: I flee the museum, not allowing Jane time to claim our coats; she rushes down the steps after me, follows me freezing into the snowy park; I inadvertently lead us past the north gate of the Central Park Zoo (the animals laughing at my plight—although, since that afternoon in 1969, over half of the world's animals have disappeared); eventually we exit the park on Fifty-Ninth, the sudden smell of manure drawing Jane's attention to nearby carriage horses, whose blinders block the animals' majestic eyes; enticed by the heavy blanket she glimpses in the back of one of the white carriages, Jane more or less forces me to climb in; she instructs the carriage driver to take us wherever he wants, anywhere, just don't stop until I tell you, and we're off, huddling together under the coarse blanket, hooves echoing anachronistically on pavement, a sound Ziegler would often have heard on the Brauergasse in Basel or Berlin, while I'm babbling on about Samuels and alchemy and cancer and kings and cars and the lies of progress and civilization that horses and statues so easily see through, while Jane, stroking my hair, tries to shut the future father of her children up.

♦♦♦

The first successful hatching of a golden eagle in captivity took place at the Topeka Zoo in 1971; as a result, the American Association of Zoological Parks and Aquariums honored the zoo with the Edward H. Bean Award for the year's most significant animal birth; it also allowed the Topeka Zoo to officially change its name to the World Famous Topeka Zoo, a title only the association can confer (and which it would, twenty years or so later, following a string of animal deaths and failed sanitary inspections, revoke). When we arrived in Topeka for our postdocs at the Foundation, the ascendency of the zoo was front-page news, along with charmingly insignificant crime, crop reports, and cattle futures. (I remember visiting the zoo's "children's farm," Jane's laughter as the sheep's black tongue lifted the pellets from her palm.) In our first year in Topeka, my default joke was to describe everything as World Famous: this is the World Famous Topeka Howard Johnson's Motor Lodge and Restaurant; on your right, you'll see the World Famous Westboro Beauty Plaza; and so on. Like most of the staff at the Foundation—which was in fact a world-famous psychiatric institute and hospital—we initially thought of Topeka as the affordable and almost exotically boring backdrop to our professional lives. Most of our colleagues also came from the coasts or, in the case of several influential senior staff, from Europe, having fled, by whatever circuitous route, the war. We are now passing the World Famous Dillon's Grocery. The World Famous Kaw Valley Pawn and Gun. That's the World Famous Miniature Train carrying children through the World Famous Gage Park.

We planned to complete our two-year fellowships and return to New York, but we met Eric and Sima, Berkeley transplants, and we liked Topeka's lack of exclusivity, the unobstructed sky; we watched thunderstorms together on the wraparound porch of the ramshackle Victorian house we bought without having to ask my father for a dime. (Smell of ozone after lightning; green tinge to the clouds.) Jane found it easier to write in what she experienced as the quiet, easier to imagine starting a family where we were known only as a couple—no memory of Rachel, no complicated preexisting social networks, no potentially difficult relations nearby. I wanted children badly, maybe in part to mark how different my second marriage was from the first.

Jane was afraid Topekans would all be members of the John Birch Society or something, but we were treated with curiosity rather than suspicion by the locals, and even though I was a Jewish long-haired hippie from New York, I was good at drawing people out. I'd strike up a conversation with the neighbor about to pull the starter rope on his mower or the roofer who came to do some patchwork or an old-timer at a lunch counter and we'd end up talking about the antiwar movement or women's liberation; the key was to agree to disagree so respectfully that your interlocutor felt despite himself honored enough to reconsider whomever he had thought of as the enemy. (This was before the Reverend Fred Phelps of Westboro Church launched his ugly crusade, standing on street corners with his family and a few parishioners, holding picket signs that read GOD HATES FAGS, making Topeka world-famous for homophobia.) This kind of thing sickened my radical brother—"You're great at making fascists feel heard"—but it was what my practice as a therapist was based on, finding a way to get people, especially reticent Midwestern boys and men, to talk.

I was successful at the Foundation because I lacked ambition: I was a conscientious therapist, but had zero interest in ascending the ranks, wanted no power over my colleagues or fame in the field, and this meant, in an institution with its share of intrigue, that I made no enemies. My dissertation was long since filed—the findings fascinating, my analysis dialed in—and I had no real desire to publish, which meant that, unlike Jane, I never had to publicly offend partisans of this or that theoretical persuasion. As a result, I was one of the few people who got along equally well with everybody in the unspoken Foundation hierarchy:

psychiatrists ("real doctors") and analysts at the top, followed by us psychologists, who were above social workers; then came the nurses and activity therapists: art, music, exercise.

I was well liked and, for reasons I never entirely understood, Thomas Attison loved me, summoning me on one pretext or another to his large office lined with first editions and various antiquarian books. (There was rumored to be a copy of *The Anatomy of Melancholy* bound in human skin.) Really he wanted to talk about movies. I think Dr. Tom, as everyone called him, found in me a nonthreatening representative of a threatening counterculture that both drew on and attacked the canons of psychiatry. I was among the students who stormed the dean's office at Columbia in '68, but I wasn't, he told me, "one of these kids who had to act out an oedipal drama with every figure of authority." We'd talk about Sturges or Hitchcock (*Spellbound* was his favorite; "Did you know Gregory Peck and Ingrid Bergman had an affair on set?"), and our conversations would drift into Dr. Tom's reminiscences, his Kansan pronunciations flattened further by the mild facial paralysis that led him to speak largely out of the left side of his mouth.

I knew the institutional talking points—how in 1919 Dr. Tom had returned to Topeka after studying neuropsychology at Harvard to open a family clinic with his physician father, something like a little Mayo Clinic for the mind; how his younger brother, David, joined them in 1925, and would increasingly oversee daily operations as Tom gained fame through his publications; how waves of analyst émigrés arrived as a result of the catastrophe in Europe; how meeting Freud in '39—"despite his being an arrogant son of a bitch"—was pivotal for his and his institution's orientation; how the Foundation grew over the years from a small single sanitarium into a powerhouse of milieu therapy and training. But I was also treated to aspects of early personal history that Dr. Tom didn't widely volunteer: "You know my brother is 'Marie' on his birth certificate; Mother was desperate for a girl;

she put him in dresses for years." Did Dr. Tom really once tell me, apropos of nothing, how much he resented that his mother forced him to undergo frequent enemas as a child?

Everyone was aware of the ongoing struggle between the Attison brothers; Dr. Tom, while retaining some influence over the board and brand, was, by the time we got there, largely a figurehead. And there were the familiar transgressions—staff sleeping with each other (Dr. Tom himself divorced his first wife for a colleague), minor embezzlement, and so on; Dr. Tom told me little in this regard that I hadn't heard from others. More scandalous than the scandals were the norms, especially the practice of staff undergoing analysis with their senior colleagues, thereby assuring that boundaries were always blurred, that transference would be a fact or a suspicion, that a meeting could never only be about its ostensible subject (new state-mandated diagnostic insurance forms) but was also inevitably about repressed drives and aggression (what did Dr. Gibson's failure to bring enough copies of the form express about her feelings toward the group?). And who wouldn't think twice about challenging a superior to whom you'd described anxiety dreams (mine at the time was laughing uncontrollably at a suicidal patient), with whom you'd probed the origins of your sense of sexual inadequacy? The Foundation's setting on the northwest edge of Topeka in conditions, depending on your temperament, backward or bucolic, only made the institution more total; there was no big city into which you could flee by carriage or dissolve your workday, your contradictions.

Being Dr. Tom's confidant still had its advantages; while the Foundation was big—the campus consisted of more than twenty buildings, mainly red brick; there were over a thousand employees—it had echoes of a family business in which the affection of the patriarch carried weight. For me this meant that, after we joined the permanent staff, I was able to start, with Dr. Tom's support, a tiny "film and video department"—that is, me and a part-time secretary—with the stated purpose of investigating and eventually producing instructional films about therapeutic topics and techniques.

Initially this was a sliver of my work; my hours were devoted to patients, primarily teenage boys. I saw some adolescents (and occasionally their parents) from the Topeka community on an outpatient basis and had several hospitalized patients in my caseload. Still, I was grateful for any opportunity to link film with the Foundation; it gave me an excuse to purchase some equipment on their dime, to think of movies as part of my profession, not just as a hobby. (The joke at home was that, even if I was just getting stoned and watching *Bonanza* reruns on our new Zenith, I was conducting "research.")

But increasingly I saw real therapeutic value in my World Famous Film and Video Department. I started to curate screenings on the Foundation campus. Milieu therapy was based on the notion that patients and staff should mix, collaborate on treatment; we all ate in the cafeteria together, for example, though at different tables (small exhibitions of patients' paintings—sunsets, still lifes, winter scenes—were displayed on the walls); younger staff and patients might play basketball together at the gym, both groups almost comically careful not to foul; the senior staff might get their hair cut at the barbershop really intended for inpatients, in order to demonstrate how seriously they took this notion of integration; Dr. Tom was always joking in front of patients about how "Dr. Beatnik" could use a trim. (The Foundation—renowned, comparatively affordable, far away from the coasts—attracted an unusual resident population. As postdocs, we'd been tasked with administering the Rorschach and the Thematic Apperception Test to new patients; in my first week, I evaluated a star of daytime television, a peripheral member of the Qatari royal family, and a Vietnam vet who turned out to live a couple of blocks from us on Woodlawn.) My "festivals"—the first one showed movies set in Kansas; the obligatory *Wizard of Oz*, *Gunfight in Abilene*, the more recent *Paper Moon*—were mainly attended by patients, but some staff would trickle in and out; I can see Dr. Tom's white hair glowing softly in the front row for *The Rainmaker.*

More importantly, I could use my department as a way in with kids otherwise hard to reach. Some of my patients were severely traumatized or schizophrenic or coming from families in extreme conflict or duress; the nature of these patients' problems was, whatever their complexity, identifiable. (The psychiatrists—Eric was among the youngest—often put these kids on Haldol; more than one came to me exhibiting, as a result of the mysterious pill, "tardive dyskinesia"—involuntarily sticking out their tongues, clenching and unclenching their jaws, smacking their lips.) But I was also encountering more and more patients whose suffering wasn't clearly related to their circumstances, or whose circumstances were most notable for their normality—intelligent middle-class white kids from stable homes who were fine until they weren't: the lost boys of privilege.

Jacob, my first Film and Video Department "intern," was a lanky sixteen-year-old from a suburb of Chicago who went from years of excelling in school to failing in the space of weeks; he stopped doing homework, started skipping class, began to smell of weed, to smell in general; he shrugged when confronted with threats of punishment. At first his parents—two successful Realtors—blamed his peer group, the underwhelming teachers. But when they moved Jacob to a private school he became a kind of heavy-metal Bartleby (he preferred Black Sabbath), friendless and increasingly unreachable, scratching pentagrams into his desk. If they demanded that Jacob account for himself at dinner, he would stop eating at the table, maybe stop eating dinner altogether. If they suggested they go see *Star Wars* as a family, he would look at them as if they were speaking drivel. He would disappear into his room unless he was skateboarding, his injuries suggesting a growing taste for self-inflicted harm. He would come in through the kitchen door a patchwork of weeping abrasions and when they'd ask him how he was doing, need some hydrogen peroxide, are you hungry, I can heat up some pizza, there was the shrug again; he'd grab a Pepsi from the fridge and go upstairs and leave them blinking at each other across their kitchen island as the muffled fury of his music started up. (I imagined this scene taking place simultaneously in kitchens all across suburbia, a vast performance of which the actors are unaware, directed by a mysterious force that goes by the name or misnomer of "culture"; it was the opening sequence of one of my unmade films.) Everybody is in fine health; he's never been spanked, let alone abused; we make a good living; he wants for nothing; we don't think he's gay and we'd love him all the same. But soon Jacob isn't even hiding his Marlboros. Soon he can't be raised from bed in the morning and is raiding the liquor cabinet by night. They established a dry house, but Jacob had a plastic fifth of something in his closet, downed most of it one evening, stole their Cutlass, and crashed it into a parked car a few blocks away. For both parents and patients it all seems to happen so fast: one day you're going to Dairy Queen in the minivan after baseball practice, raucously singing along to "We Are the Champions," and the next day you're listening to a judge explain that Jacob has a choice between a length of juvenile detention and psychiatric care. A friend of a friend recommends the Foundation in Topeka; back then, decent insurance almost covered it.

What I knew as much by instinct as by training was that when a boy like Jacob shows up in your cramped but light-filled office, you should not under any circumstances ask him to account for his behavior (or the eraser burns all over his forearms, although para-suicidal rituals were much more common among girls); Jacob would be the last person capable of such an account; if he had the language he wouldn't express himself with symptoms. And by the time he finds himself looking over my shoulder at my diplomas (in the early years they required us to hang them), my mom's Chagall print in its silver frame, the picture of Orson

Welles at his *Touch of Evil* weight, Jacob will have encountered this impossible demand for explanation so often from parents and teachers and coaches and counselors and judges and mediocre shrinks that he can no longer imagine any other way of interacting with the supposedly expert and concerned. My goal—what Jane insisted was my gift—was to come in at an unexpected angle to those conversations that had only driven adolescent patients deeper into silence. I could initially get so little speech out of Jacob—couldn't even get him to complain about being at the Foundation ("It must be annoying that they won't let you smoke in the room"; nod)—that I started my own version of activity therapy.

When I bought a new Betamax camera in the second month of Jacob's hospitalization, I asked for his help testing it out; we spent a session taking footage of the white-tailed deer that were always bounding around the south edge of the grounds where a salt lick had been established some years before. A storm came up quickly from the west and we had to sprint back to my building, getting soaked by warm rain in the process; I was trying, awkwardly, to protect the camera under my coat; Jacob, catching his breath beneath the overhang, laughed at me a little; we laughed at me together. After a few more collaborative efforts, I asked Jacob to be my department's intern, a position, I went out of my way to note, that might be reported to parents and friends, listed on a future job application. Then we took an off-campus trip to Wolfe's Camera and Video downtown to see what new stock had come in; I was careful to consult Jacob as a colleague, to honor his competence. We saw a matinee at Gage Theater for the purposes of research: What did you think of that closing shot? Here is a book about the history of television I thought you might be interested in. Here is a flyer about the new film production major at the University of Kansas, something to keep an eye on in the future. However unconventional, a therapeutic alliance had been formed.

Then speech and signifying silence could do their work. Jacob, who is better, Led Zeppelin or Judas Priest? Because I hear the blues influence in Zeppelin, but Judas Priest just sounds like shit to me; maybe I'm already too old. (A little cursing could go a long way in forging a connection, gesturing toward a lexicon beyond the institution.) Jacob, were the kids at the private school less cool than the kids at the public one? Now Jacob would at least respond—he was the first kid to call me Dr. J—and if I could get the rhythm of quiet right, I could draw him out a little. I wasn't interested in extracting latent content, making manifest some deeper truth motivating Jacob's speech; my goal was to make the kid *feel heard*. I didn't mind the cliché; in fact, I admired the phrase, its rightness of fit, a mixture of the somatic and semantic; maybe it explained the desire for heavy metal that registered as touch as much as sound. How much easier it would be if when you played them slowly in reverse the lyrics really did, as some hysterical parents feared, reveal satanic messages; if there were a backmasked secret order, however dark, instead of rage at emptiness.

♦♦♦

I saw the young by day, the old by night. After dinner, Jane would ensconce herself in her study to write for a couple of hours. (By the sound of the Selectric through the closed door I could gauge how the book was coming; working now against the deadline of her pregnancy—red blood cells were forming in Adam's marrow; he was now capable of opening his eyes inside her—I could hear a steady rain of key strikes.) While she worked I'd circle Potwin's cobblestone streets with Klaus, who lived two blocks away, a six-foot-three incongruously elegant Berliner and senior analyst at the Foundation who'd moved in the late fifties to Topeka from Zurich, where he'd worked with Jung. As a young man Klaus had been an up-and-coming playwright, as well as a competitive amateur boxer, his nose broken twice by nineteen, the age at which he married Elke, who was known in artistic circles for her experiments with photomontage. They had a son, Fritz, in 1937; in 1940 Klaus attempted to smuggle them out of Berlin, paying to have them transported in a truck carrying dry goods to Holland, where he would join them. After the war he'd piece together the story of how they'd been betrayed; two gunshots forever echoing in the woods, in his inner ear. Klaus himself spent much of the war hiding in a chicken coop, dreaming of reunion with his family (although in his dreams, Klaus once told me, Fritz was a girl), composing dramas in his head to pass the time, his cramped conditions causing the large man constant physical pain. When you asked Klaus about those years—most people didn't ask—you got jokes, mainly about chickens, what you could expect from them in the way of conversation, input on your plays. His parents and three sisters died in Auschwitz. Only we chickens survived, Klaus told me, smile gone, when I pressed.

Picture us briefly illuminated by the headlights of a passing truck as it circles the roundabout on Greenwood Avenue: a thirty-three-year-old psychologist from New York who once smoked a cigarette with Bob Dylan on Clinton Street and a six-foot-three bespectacled Old World analyst in his seventies who'd been friendly with Einstein. We'd stroll through the punishing August humidity discussing my interns against a backdrop of cicadas. On the one hand, Klaus, surely the only man in Topeka outfitted in white linen, could not take these kids—with their refrigerators full of food, their air-conditioning and television, their freedom from stigma or state violence—seriously; what could be more obvious than the fact that they did not know what suffering was, that if they suffered from anything it was precisely this lack of suffering, a kind of neuropathy that came from too much ease, too much sugar, a kind of existential gout? And then, on the other hand, Klaus took them very seriously indeed; they are told constantly, the culture tells them, although "culture" is hardly the word, Klaus said, patting his forehead with a handkerchief cut from the same linen as his suit, that they are individuals, rugged even, but in fact they are emptied out, isolate, mass men without a mass, although they're not men, obviously, but boys, perpetual boys, Peter Pans, man-children, since America is adolescence without end, boys without religion on the one hand or a charismatic leader on the other; they don't even have a father—President Carter!—to kill or a father to tell them to kill the Jew; they have no Jew; they are libidinally driven to mass surrender without anything to surrender to; they don't even believe in money or in science, or those beliefs are insufficient; their country has fought and lost its last real war; in a word, they are overfed; in a word, they are starving. These kids, Klaus said, just need a good whipping and some physical labor; these kids, Klaus also said, are undergoing a profound archaic regression. Boys will be boys, Klaus dismissed them, and spoiled boys will be spoiled boys, but then, handkerchief held to the back of his neck: the abyss of non-belief, the vacuum, cannot be filled with *stuff* (Klaus loved the word *stuff*, which sounded German to me, but wasn't; from the Greek *stuphein*, "draw together"), and the violence will recur periodically—like cicadas. Then we're raked by somebody's rotating sprinkler, pleasant shock of cold water on my shins.

If I said, Klaus, you're claiming the problem is they have it too easy, but you're also saying having it too easy is too hard; you're saying that it's always been this way, but that it's also the sign of a specific imperial decline, this vacuum at the heart of privilege, then Klaus would respond by delivering his signature quotation from Niels Bohr, the quotation he always quoted when he seemed to contradict himself, a saying his conversation was inexorably working toward, one he loved so much he'd stop and stand still, smiling, to deliver it: "The opposite of a truth," Klaus quoted, "is a falsehood; but the opposite of a *profound* truth"—pause for emphasis, sound of sprinklers, insects, push mowers, felt absence of city noise, Kenny Rogers from a passing car—"may be another profound truth." It either is or is not August (Klaus removes his anachronistic glasses, round lenses, wipes his face, replaces them, resumes walking); if I assert it's August when it isn't—simply false; but if I say that life is pain, that is true, profoundly so; so, too, that life is joy; the more profound the statement, the more reversible; the deep truths are sedimented in syntax, the terms can be reversed, just as there is no principle of noncontradiction, no law of excluded middle, governing the unconscious. Then, briefly serious, Klaus would touch my shoulder: A quote like that can save your life.

I wasn't sure how much Klaus helped his patients—his analysands tended to be women, late middle-aged or older, although Sima, who was in training, was also being analyzed by Klaus—but I was sure he did no harm, letting his accent, which his patients associated with great psychoanalytic authority, do most of the work. What Klaus was known for at the Foundation were his "test reports," which all staff were required to submit at regular intervals—two- or three-page documents that were then disseminated and discussed at meetings. Klaus's were famous, or infamous, for their literariness; they brought something of the Weimar feuilleton to the Foundation bureaucracy. If he weren't an analyst, if Stanford hadn't bought his correspondence with Anna Freud, if he didn't speak four languages (although Klaus was surprisingly dismissive of his Yiddish), if he weren't old and elegant, weren't a survivor, he would have been reprimanded; instead, my colleagues and I could look forward to the single-spaced documents his secretary typed but that Klaus then often modified in his florid hand—not to correct typos or errors of fact, but to add an additional adjective or improve a sentence rhythm. "When the first snow falls in Topeka, transforming the out-of-doors into a vast interior, B—— turns her head to the flakes accumulating on the sill, and her memories turn to her white-carpeted living room in Ann Arbor, to her childhood's primal scene"; "When a trout rising to a fly gets hooked and finds himself unable to swim about freely, he begins a fight which results in struggles and splashes; in the same way, G—— is struggling on the hook of infantile personality disorder." Sometimes they reminded me of *Sportsmanlike Driving* crossed with Freud: "Human history, like the history of the individual, can be understood as a slow passage through conflicts of a sexual-aggressive nature. It is as part of this journey across millennia that we must understand K——'s disinhibited and egotistical traits"; etc. I could do a good imitation of Klaus's voice, would use it to crack up Jane and Eric and even his devoted analysand Sima ("One might say this marinara sauce came from a jar; but did not the jar, in a deep, perhaps deeper, sense, receive its identity from the sauce?"), but Klaus's charm, at least for me, was that his voice already sounded like an imitation of itself; Klaus was an actor bemused to be playing Klaus. And yet the effect of this doubling was generous, self-deprecating; it reminded me of how Charlie Chaplin—when the rich woman he loves enters the bistro—pretends, out of embarrassment, only to be playing a waiter for her amusement.

Klaus was always joking; Klaus was never joking—what underwrote the irony was a sense of the absurdity of having survived, or the absurd suggestion that anyone survives, even if they go on breathing, or the absurdity that language could be much more than noise after the coop, after the camps. Once, in the Foundation cafeteria, I watched him walk to the wall to adjust a slightly crooked painting of a sunflower, the work of a patient. Somehow—again I was reminded of a star of silent film—Klaus's gestures proclaimed that this was theater; without making a sound, he attracted the gazes of those eating at the tables. He overcorrected the painting—now it was too low on the left; he scratched his head; there was a little laughter; then he overcorrected it on the right, pretended not to notice, adjusted his bow tie, miming self-satisfaction, which produced more laughter; then, as if only the laughter drew his attention to his mistake, he held his chin in his hand, thinking. Suddenly an index finger shot up; instead of tinkering further with the sunflower, he walked to the other three paintings (bluebells, geraniums, coneflowers) on the wall and lowered their left edges until all the frames were equally askew; he sat back down to general applause.

♦♦♦

House lights fall in the Foundation theater, filled to capacity with staff and patients and various unaffiliated Topekans invited to the premiere. Strains of Friedrich Baumfelder's *Berceuse pour le Piano* play over half a minute of black leader, the recording a little slow, staticky, the pitch slightly distorted. Now a tall, if stooped, elderly man in a museum, his back to the camera, a homburg and cane in his hands, leans in to consider a pair of intricately engraved bronze doors. This is the City Museum in Berlin, circa 1909; this is the Nelson Atkins Museum in Kansas City, circa 1983. Cue title sequence. The tall man, who might have met Hesse in Basel, is and is not acting; his clothes are just his clothes; early twentieth-century Europe lives in his body in late twentieth-century Kansas; how often his mother pushed him in a pram down the Brauergasse. (The film is shot with a French sixteen-millimeter camera I found at a yard sale my third year in Topeka. Wolfe's Camera and Video donated the film—fast film they kept on hand for shooting high school basketball games in poor light; the effect is of a grainy period look, the motion at once sped up and stuttering, traces of an older medium of illumination.)

I, Ziegler, appear screen left; the camera, which is in the charge of an intern, follows me down the marble hall, a little (warm) laughter in the theater, my approximation of period dress less exact, my sideburns grown out for the role, my hair cut, for the first and last time in adulthood, to approximate a good bourgeois, "one of those people," Klaus says in voice-over, "we see every day on the street, whose faces we can never really remember, because they all have the same face: a collective face." In the next gallery, where I discover the pill atop a glass vitrine (we were granted permission to film, but not to touch anything), I'm surprised by a guard wearing a *schirmmütze* purchased at the military surplus on Huntoon; the guard's uniform is otherwise anachronistic, but nondescript enough not to compromise the scene. Fade to black.

Debussy, a passage from *La Mer*; fade in on a restaurant interior, which is in fact the Foundation cafeteria, long tables replaced with a few round ones my interns covered with white tablecloths, set with silver and china (mismatched; some purchased secondhand, some borrowed), although Hesse implies a more casual café. The paper Ziegler flips through, pretends to read, is *The Topeka Capital-Journal* (the Dow is up; the controversial Vietnam Memorial has opened), but it is also the *Berliner Lokal-Anzeiger.* At the table behind Ziegler's, Dr. Console and his wife, the parents of the future poet, are eating sausages; those two women in something like Edwardian dresses, having tea, are patients; one, whom Jane worked with closely, would jump to her death from the tallest building in Omaha three years after filming. Eating alone at a third table—his gestures unaffected, the gestures of the unobserved—a patient who almost won a Tony before the drinking got out of hand (it takes years of study to act, especially to eat, as though you're unobserved); I'd initially suggested he play Ziegler. Eric, awkwardly portraying a waiter, white towel over forearm, serves me the beer with which I wash down the pill I've rediscovered in the breast pocket of my vest; it's really a peppermint, a placebo. I scratch the pill with my fingernail, sniff it, try to crush it between my fingers, touch it to my tongue, then, surprising myself a little, pop it in my mouth. What's behind the raucous laughter in the theater at this moment? A testament to my aplomb as comic? Maybe, but there must also be something carnivalesque, cathartic, about watching a psychologist finger and ingest a mysterious pill with the aid of a Foundation psychiatrist; most of the patients are not yet on SSRIs, which will soon supplant the blunter medications. "Intelligent people would not want to destroy these hard-won accomplishments in technology or medicine, or to throw away the very valuable advantages we gain from them." Ziegler contentedly chews his kohlwurst, which is really an Oscar Mayer jumbo ballpark frank.

"At two o'clock"—Klaus's voice in the dark—"the young man jumped off the streetcar"—we'd tried and failed to get the Gage Park trolley for this transition—"and bought a Sunday ticket." Fade in on the front gates of the World Famous Topeka Zoo, located in the Tiergarten, a black rhino recently arrived from Ethiopia among 1909's chief attractions, cirrus clouds in the sky above Berlin drifting almost imperceptibly through the shot. Inside the gates, people on Sunday: couples are parading; everyone is in a holiday mood. Passing arm-in-arm in front of the impalas' cage there are the smiling Drs. Caplan, analysts both, soon to be divorced, since Allen Caplan has been sleeping with the psychologist Samantha Gibson, whom he supervised, to whom he now tips his cap as she passes in the Empire-style gown and feathered hat she borrowed from the Topeka Rep. (Strange for Allen and Samantha, a few rows from each other in the theater, to see themselves reproduce on-screen the false formality they maintain in daily public life.) There goes Dr. Atwal in dastaar and traditional dress. He is trailed by the bio-psychologist Dr. Erwood, who wears some kind of trilby. There goes our neighbor, Donald Peterson, in top hat and cape, his eight-year-old daughter, Anna, dressed for some reason as a boy, short pants and cap, holding his right hand. Donald is passed by the stately, obese J.M., who owns Mass Street Music in downtown Lawrence; he is arm-in-arm with his good wife, Laura, her face obscured by a large fan embroidered with a cabbage rose.

Chimpanzees leap from artificial branch to branch in an indoor cage. Now it's Ziegler's back we see, lacquered cane and straw boater in his hands, considering the monkeys. (Where did the boater come from? A failure of continuity.) In Nevada and New York, psycholinguists are trying to teach chimps to sign—believing them capable of language, although physically unable to produce a sufficient range of voiced sounds—but in Topeka, in Berlin, "a large chimpanzee blinked at him, gave him a good-natured nod, and said in a deep voice: 'How goes it, brother?'" It's going pretty well; ARPANET has adopted TCP/IP, enabling the Internet; Trump Tower just opened on Fifth Avenue, the first commercial cellular telephone call was made from the parking lot of Soldier Field in Chicago; Alexander Graham Bell's great-grandson took the call in Germany, the Germany of Wilhelm II, whose newspaper picture Elke is cutting up in her small flat for a collage, his mustache replaced with a wrestler's legs; for the only time, Freud is in America; in earnest, Proust has started *La recherche*, will, with the old technology of prose, describe his first phone call, first encounter with an airplane, what the motorcar does to the landscape. "Have you ever stopped to think that, through all the countless thousands of generations that preceded this century, not even the most powerful kings on earth could have owned one like it?"

Ziegler flees from cage to cage; now we hear the ominous *Scheherazade* by Rimsky-Korsakov. The footage of the stately elk is found, spliced; the Topeka Zoo didn't have one. The terrible dignity of animals on film. But Ziegler does look a lion in the eye through thick glass, learns of the "immensity of the wilderness, where there are no cages" or personality tests. At first there is laughter in the theater at Ziegler's antics, how, increasingly upset, he discards his cane in the bushes, loosens his collar (where is his hat?), but the gentle sadness of Klaus's voice as he describes Ziegler's depersonalization adds pathos to the frenetic comedy. Everyone knows how this story ends; that he will be transported from one World Famous institution to another; they know there is no outside, but one vast interior, even if the patient is behind the camera, the diagnostic eye, even if the animals mock the brutes beyond the bars, the coop. And now a crowd of Topekans has assembled around Ziegler, who has lost his faith in civilization, which is five years from mechanized warfare; he has lost faith in the image of antiquity he inherited from the Renaissance (a failure of continuity), in religion and science and the "Jewish science" of psychoanalysis; he has lost his reason. Two orderlies dressed in white (they are played by Foundation physical therapists) drag me from the frame, which is burnt in places.

One minute remains of the twelve-minute film. The crowd disperses, the camera pans left to show us two tall men engaged in animated conversation (no voices now, but the Baumfelder returns), presumably describing the spectacle they've just witnessed. One of the men is Klaus, whose back we saw in the opening shot; the other is Dr. Tom in tweeds. They look like dignitaries, presidents; they shake hands, maybe in parting, maybe to seal some mysterious pact between Old World psychiatry and new, then walk out of the shot in opposite directions. And here come two smiling women in hoop skirts, half a minute left, Sima and Jane, governesses probably, each leading two small children by the hand. Jason (Sima's son) and Adam, Darren Eberheart and a girl whose name is lost. (Their excitement when they were picked up from Bright Circle, where they were allowed to skip their nap.) They are walking toward us fast and slow, in the present and the past.

Things Darren dreamt began to show up in the bushes—the plastic figurine from a parachute firework, the small dull saw blade he thought of as a throwing star—and he pocketed those things. His pockets were large: all year he wore one of the three pairs of Army cargo pants he had purchased with his own money from the Surplus on Huntoon. Desert camouflage. Understand he had over four hundred dollars in mainly twenties. He had a dozen Buck folding knives. He had in the same drawer with cash and knives a Crosman pellet gun he had often claimed was an actual revolver and once pointed at the half-breed Jason Davis, prompting Davis to open a cut above Darren's eye. The coconut smell so strong he experienced it as a taste of the young nurse who stitched that up and the thin gold chain against her collarbone appeared now in his dreams, but that was okay, Dr. J said, the problem is when it goes the other way. It was like that paper TOPEKA HIGH SCHOOL *banner the cheerleaders held for the players to burst through when they took the field. More than to actually play that's what he'd wanted, imagined when he was a water boy in middle school. (See him in pure joy sprinting up the sideline when one of our running backs breaks away.) The banner between sleep and waking had torn and now people and things were passing through it.*

He'll be at the McDonald's on Gage Boulevard getting his hot water and he'll suddenly just know the man ordering in front of him is Dad, particles of windshield in his matted hair. So he walks right out head down and gets back on his Schwinn Predator and pedals full speed to the bushes of Westboro Park where he can breathe and pocket stray items from the dreams. What about the bushes makes you feel safe? Dr. J asks him every time he mentions sheltering there. Understand there is a network of tunnels through the big mass of honeysuckle and he has supplies, a plastic bag of small Snickers and PayDay for energy and some jerky lightly buried under brush in a place he will not reveal, not even under torture. Are there other places like the bushes? What about thinking of this place as kind of like the bushes, Darren?

Well, maybe he could do that if Dr. J didn't say at the end of every hour, Come on in, Ms. Eberheart, and then Darren has to listen to his mom complain. Most recently about how he ruined the perfect job at Dillon's that Dr. J had helped arrange for him, calling in a favor. Because Darren was dishonest, unreliable, and let's not even talk about the GED. What requires Darren to slow his breathing deliberately is how her voice goes very high-pitched, almost a squeal, animal in pain, right before she starts crying, then goes deep again: I don't know how much / More of this I / can take. His lies. My diabetes. Working night shifts at St. Francis. That's when Darren feels like he is about to cry himself or choke her out but instead just looks at the clown painting on Dr. J's wall hard enough that its colors start to change. Do you like it? That's by a painter named Marc Chagall.

It can't be like the bushes when that bitch is here. At first Dr. J would say we don't use words like bitch, faggot, pussy, but since he started catching glimpses of his dad there aren't really rules. Because understand Darren is not a faggot or a pussy no matter what Nowak or Davis or Dad said before he hit the median and went through the windshield underground. Darren had more than once confessed to killing him, at which point Dr. J said very slowly, like he was reading it off a billboard at some distance, No, Darren, you are not responsible—in any way—for your father's death. Having bad thoughts about someone doesn't cause their car to crash. But Darren had flipped the blue Honda over and over in his head before the wreck, pressed rewind, flipped it again. In his mind he'd sat bored and sweating through the service in the front pew of Potwin

Presbyterian before the highway patrol had even called them. Feel the starched collar against his recently shaved neck.

Ever since he was a boy he would drink hot water in the morning to pretend along with his mom and dad that he was having coffee, Here is your coffee, Darren, black no sugar, almost time for work. Rare shared laughter. The joke was that he was a man but now he is one, eighteen, and it's just what he does in the morning. At McDonald's they give you hot water for free although it can be hard to explain that you don't want to buy their Lipton tea. More than once he'd had to purchase the bag he would discard. (On Gage Boulevard they gave the steaming Styrofoam cup to him mostly without trouble, but the one time he'd tried at Twenty-First someone from among the cooks he might have known said tell the retard to fuck off.) When he'd started the job at Dillon's his dad had not yet come back through the tattered banner and Darren would sit in one of the red plastic swivel chairs near the front glass façade and watch through his own watery reflection the Phelpses holding their picket signs. He'd sip his steaming water, stir it with a plastic spoon, sip it. Then he would rise with a purposefulness he believed the other men could sense.

If you are going to your job, the scenery organizes itself differently around your bike as you cut through it, elms and silver maples lining up respectfully to let you pass. Stacy, the friend of Dr. J's, had showed him where he could lean his Predator just within the side entrance and where he could take a green apron from a hook. Tie it in the back like this. Then just ask me and I'll tell you which of the checkout lines you should help with first. Here come the heads of broccoli the box of frozen waffles Wonder Bread the two-liter Dr Pepper slowly over the black rubber conveyor to be rung up at which point he is to put them in doubled tall paper bags and, if asked, to carry them or push them in the cart to the trunks of cars, beds of trucks. Often he was transporting the food of people he knew, had known, and they would speak to him, and it was fine. Eggs and milk get their own plastic bag, don't ask me why. The satisfaction of jamming the empty shopping cart into another shopping cart in the corral. Four twenty-five an hour times thirty was more money than he could imagine once you timesed thirty by however many weeks there would be in the years he planned to work. One thing for sure: he would buy Ron Williams's silver Fiero and even let his mom use it if she followed certain rules.

Halfway through the first month a large can of something doesn't ring up and Mike the senior he is bagging for tells him to check the price which means first finding the aisle and then the shelf and then whatever number on whatever label corresponds to the can in question before carrying all that in his head and hands back to Mike who will have long since finished ringing up the other groceries, the customer pissed for sure. Stacy never said that pricing was his job. By the time he locates the right aisle he already sees himself returning to the register unable to account for how the label with the price was midway between two similar but distinct sets of cans, or how those distinctions blurred as he looked hard, the color of the labels transitioning until he could not define a border between what costs this, costs that. He would match the words if letters and numbers didn't go ants running across pavement twigs floating away on water as he stood there and if the other shoppers hadn't started to laugh at him until he turned to catch them. Only standing in a cold sweat before the shelves does he become aware of the Muzak that's been circulating through Dillon's all of 1996.

And then Mrs. Lewis demands he read aloud from How the Grinch Stole Christmas! *in fourth grade, sound it out, we can wait all day, the laughter, then Coach Stemple grabs him by the face mask during tryouts in seventh and throws him to the ground for being dumb as shit, ears ringing, cut-grass smell. He's also sitting in an office as Dr. Nelson says to his father think nine- or ten-year-old in a teenage body and then he's tripped up by Carter in a story about fingering Becky Miller some years later, do you even know what fingering means, same laughter around the fire, sparks crackling off the Osage orange. All these innumerable moments are present whenever one is, little mimic spasms around the corner of his mouth reflect that.*

You have to get away from where those moments pool in space so he walks head down to the storeroom, hangs the apron up, and bikes the four blocks to the Surplus where he can sit far in the back latching and unlatching a .50-caliber ammo can until Cut it out Stan finally says from behind the counter without looking up. Darren loved the smell of Cosmoline. Stan, even if he is fat and wheezy, and despite the missing thumb, could cup and clap his hands over your ears like all Marines in a way that kills you or shove your nose into your brain with his palm. These and other combat skills Darren sometimes believed he had absorbed, hoped he wouldn't have to use. Likewise Darren felt that he had had a little of whatever experience Stan recounted, the way a teacher once told Darren that to smell a thing means to get some particle of it in you. So if Stan said there were whores everywhere you barely had to pay them you'd just spit on your cock for lube Darren did not think that he was lying when he told a group of middle schoolers playing basketball on the Randolph court that he had fucked one, spit on, etc. He didn't have to pay her though he could, I have over four hundred dollars. If you say a thing that when it comes out holds together, that makes it true enough, so he didn't feel that he was lying, even though he often later felt he had. His whole life his mom demanded he confess he'd been dishonest before it was possible for anyone to know.

Yes and no the Surplus was like the bushes. Yes because no way a Gordon or a Nowak or a Davis could reach him here where Stan, who had known Darren's dad, was in command. You are free to hang around if you are quiet. Yes because this was like the bushes a dark place where Darren had tactical knowledge, even knew where locked behind the counter the antique but loaded Luger was. No because particles of Stan's anger would get in him. The girls all say they want nice guy sensitive types then bang the whole team is that not right Darren. I'm no racist Darren but do they not chase after them and beg for it. His name was always mixed up in these sentences when Stan was in a talking mood. The summer before freshman year they had dared him to kiss Mandy Owen, swore she wanted to be kissed by him, was just too shy to ask, and the way she screamed and reddened and held her hands shaking out in front of her was like when a bee landed on his mom who was allergic. The laughter. He was guilty even before his open hand connected with her face and while they were showering him with blows, dirt in the mouth, he wanted to say I'm sorry, Mandy; he'd known her since kindergarten, she only lived three blocks away. They have no idea how hard it is to taste your own blood, cut-grass smell, and not go home and get your knives or gun or flip their cars over in your mind. And when Stan's anger got in him Mandy just was a whore who held the banner the others jumped through. Understand it could be days in his mind before she wasn't.

Dr. J was not angry about the job, he had no particles of anger in him period. More than once Darren wondered if this made Dr. J a pussy. It was no trouble on my end, it's something we can try again down the line if that feels right. What concerned Dr. J was how Darren might be having at least some mild hallucinations, which isn't the same thing as telling stories. Darren, Dr. J said, Darren, until Darren looked from the painting to his eyes, what I mean is that it kind of sounds like you're seeing things that aren't there, like your dad. Dad didn't see things that weren't there, Darren thought, gaze back on the clown floating in its silver frame. Although in what Darren would come to understand as drunkenness, his dad would curse people who were not present, put his fist through the basement's Sheetrock wall. Or maybe you're just telling me you think about your dad, that it feels like he's right there, but that you know he isn't, really. If you think you are seeing or for that matter hearing things that just can't be, Darren, maybe it would help to repeat to yourself, or even to say out loud, this isn't real. This isn't real. You'd be surprised how much that's helped some other people that I know.

THE MEN

(JANE)

Do you remember how two winters ago it turned out that I hadn't bought our Florida tickets, how I only discovered the night before, when I tried to print our boarding passes, that I'd never actually purchased them? I had a clear memory of getting them through Orbitz, but since we go to Sanibel every January, I must have been remembering one of the previous years. When Dad asked me about them in the months leading up to the trip—were they direct or did we have to go through Chicago; how much did they cost—I wasn't lying when I answered: yes, they're nonstop, they cost around the same as last year. But I felt this low-level unease about them, or retrospectively I know I felt it, as if, just beneath the threshold of consciousness, or sometimes rising to consciousness and then sinking back down again, I suspected that I'd never bought the things, that I'd only meant to, then remembered falsely that I had. Whenever the trip came up, I experienced a mild dread, mild enough that I didn't really have to account for it to myself—maybe I was anxious about something else; maybe it's just that I hate flying; maybe thinking about the trip reminds me of how far away I am from you and the girls. Normally, like a good neurotic, I'd double-check the tickets on my computer several times in the weeks before the flights, just to reconfirm the times, that our seats were together, but this subtle dread, this knowledge that wasn't knowledge, prevented me from searching my email for the tickets, so that it wasn't until the night before the trip, when Dad suggested I check in, print the boarding passes, that I discovered—that I could no longer avoid discovering—that I'd never bought them. I can't believe this, I kept exclaiming, as I searched my Gmail, but in fact I had known it on some level all along. But that's not exactly it, or not only it: I think I'd felt that as long as I avoided looking for the tickets, they would be there; it was only if I searched the archive that they'd disappear, as if the past were up until that point indeterminate, that I might outrun it. Do you know what I mean? We had to pay a lot of money to get the tickets for the next day; luckily they still had seats, although I suppose there are usually seats to and from Kansas City.

It was kind of like that, recovering the memory of what my father had done. The knowledge was always there, I carried it in my body, but I didn't know what I knew, although I knew I knew something and that I dreaded knowing it fully, dreaded it as if only coming into the knowledge, into the memory, would make the event that I was repressing real. And I think Sima was the first person to intuit the contours of this unknown knowledge that I carried; she helped me see that what was missing had a shape, was a piece of the puzzle of my personality, and she made the edges visible—how what I wouldn't let myself know jutted out into other domains of my experience. And once its edges came into view, I could—in fact I could not *not*—confront the knowledge I'd both always and never had.

You can't really remember what Sima was like back then, when you were four or five, when she went from being my best friend to also being my therapist, although we said we were "consulting," a blurring of boundaries that was, needless to say, problematic; we should have known better—we did know. I don't offer this as an excuse, but there was so much slippage among Foundation people about professional and personal and psychotherapeutic relationships that I think to a certain extent it just felt normal to us. But we also felt like—we also *were*—two feminists forming a therapeutic alliance in a context where those slippages were typically used to reinforce patriarchal relations. At first I was in analysis with Allen Caplan, whom you remember from the neighborhood, because *not* to be in analysis was considered a strike against you at the Foundation, a sign that you were avoiding serious reflection on your own psychodynamics or something, and I had to put up with outrageously sexist shit. Once at a staff meeting I brought up the issue of salary differentials between men and women and later that day, when I was on Caplan's couch, he encouraged me to think about how my concerns about being paid less than men might relate to penis envy. He saw evidence of "phallic strivings." Once I asked another senior analyst why he referred to male postdocs as "Doctor" and female postdocs by their first names and there I was, on the couch again, getting the penis envy lecture. Objecting to the diagnosis of penis envy was a sure sign of penis envy. (I should find the leaked memo for you in which a senior analyst called me a "trumpeting virago" to Dr. Tom; you could reproduce a slightly redacted version in your book.) Now it sounds like parody, but that was the reality. Working with Sima felt like a form of resistance to that culture, a way that I could come to terms with aspects of my past without those terms being set by the Foundation's unexamined Freudian tradition, which pathologized women's experience when it didn't fit the great man's theory.

That said, it was one big overdetermined mess. Sima was in analysis with Klaus, who was like a second father to Dad, or maybe it was more that Dad was like a second son to Klaus; there was always some tension between Eric and us, even though we liked him, as we both thought he was overly aggressive with medication; he just had this tremendous uncritical faith in psychopharmacology as a cure-all. And then you and Jason were of course best friends, were around each other basically since birth, were like brothers; both couples had wills listing the other as the child's legal guardians in the event of a tragedy. (You and Natalia really need to make a will, by the way; quit putting it off.) And then there was what happened between Dad and Sima, which again was crossed with Klaus—you'll have to ask him about it if you want details; he told me about it years later, around the time of the Darren Eberheart situation—but I only had a dim inkling of all that at the time, another thing that I knew and also didn't. And if you want me to be completely honest, I'm not sure that my relationship with Sima—who was, by the way, the most gorgeous person, man or woman, in Topeka—was completely free of a sexual charge. It wasn't free of a sexual charge, in other words. Then there's the fact that Sima was, despite our methodological differences, the most insightful reader of my manuscript, which meant that I felt dependent on her, or indebted to her, in yet another way; it also meant that she felt, although she would deny it, some ownership over the book; certainly she would have a very complicated relation to its success.

Within a month or two of being in Topeka, Sima and I were having long, wine-soaked debriefings about the week at the Foundation, some debates about our respective theoretical orientations, but also these great talks about our pasts, our childhoods. The intimacy between us was quick and intense; there was something giddy about it; we were like kids at summer camp or freshmen at college who glom on to a new friend with an excitement tinged with desperation. We'd sit beside each other on the porch swing on Greenwood smoking cigarettes (I remember there was a little sugar on the tips of the Indonesian brand that Sima smoked) and drinking bad wine out of jam jars—Sima was very elegant, this was slumming for her—and we'd gossip and laugh and also talk openly about growing up in families with strong if accommodating mothers and fucked-up fathers. Her father, who never once visited Topeka, was a respected surgeon in Los Angeles, cardiac I think; he had emigrated from Iran, and was cut off from almost all of his family of origin. His focus was so exclusively on Sima's older brother, Amir, who was expected to be a surgeon in turn, that Sima felt entirely invisible. (You know how my dad favored Deborah, who'd probably rather be left out of your work; my dad didn't bother to conceal his preference.) Amir was a mess, had made a suicide attempt in his twenties—at least Sima considered it a suicide attempt; the family maintained it was just reckless partying, which drove Sima nuts. I remember Sima had this weird habit of smiling when she cried; I can see her perfect teeth glowing a little in the twilight as she told me about the family driving her brother back from the UCLA hospital, how her dad, from behind the wheel of their Mercedes, went on and on in a monotone about how a medical student should know better than to mix opioids and alcohol—talking about her heavily sedated brother's attempt to kill himself as if it were just another academic failure, a poor grasp of chemistry. I simply could not speak, Sima told me, smiling, sipping her wine, tears rolling down her high cheekbones, I simply could not make a noise. You will make fun of me if I say that when Sima did this crying-while-smiling thing—I can see her face illuminated by a cupped flame as she lit another cigarette—it was like that beautiful kind of weather when it's raining even though it's sunny, which is I guess the effect of the wind blowing rain from clouds some miles away.

It wasn't until Sima and I both had little kids—you and Jason are what, four months apart?—that our conversations about my father became more intense. Part of it no doubt was that having kids brought back our memories of our own childhoods, something you know about now, having the girls. But also what happened is that Grandma and my father started visiting from Phoenix to see you, and Sima picked up on some subtle but strange things I was doing—I mean beyond just being exasperated by the presence of my parents. For instance, one night when we invited Sima and Eric over for dinner, Dad making his one good chicken dish, she observed how I was simply incapable of being away from your side when my father was around. She said it was kind of like that Buñuel film *The Exterminating Angel*, when the guests at a dinner party are mysteriously unable to leave the parlor where they've retired after a meal. Except this time it was just me who couldn't leave: you and Jason were in your little bassinets in our living room, where we were having dessert. Sima observed that I'd get up and gather some plates and glasses to take to the kitchen, and then, as soon as I reached the edge of the room, I'd just suddenly turn around and sit back down, setting the dishes on the coffee table, "I'll deal with that later." Obviously, this was unconscious, irrational—even if I didn't trust my father I wouldn't have been worried in that context—but I just couldn't leave the two of you together out of my view. At some point I asked Sima, Do you want a cigarette? Yes, she said, and we got up, walked to the door, and then: Actually I don't feel like one, you go ahead; I just sat back down. If Dad observed any of this, saw that I was acting strangely, he would have assumed, reasonably, that I was feeling stressed about having my parents around, which is normal enough for anyone, and my father was pretty difficult company in conventional ways: he complained constantly, had little interest in other people. Sima later told me that when she went out to have that cigarette alone—a different era, nursing moms smoking with abandon—and she sat on the porch swing and looked in through the large window at all of us in the living room and watched me move a chair to position myself between my father and your bassinet—she suspected, and suspected that I didn't know what I knew. Maybe seeing it briefly from the outside, framed by the window, transformed into a painting or a silent film, threw it into relief for her.

—You keep calling him "my father" instead of "Grandpa" even though you say "Grandma" and not "my mother"—like you're still protecting me from having any relation to him.

That's interesting. You're probably right. Now I remember that night in the third person, like I'm looking into the living room from Sima's vantage on the porch swing—I misremember that moment as the moment I first started to recall more fully what had happened, but it wasn't. After that trip Sima mentioned what she'd observed and I kind of shrugged it off; I wasn't reactive, I checked in with myself about it, but it didn't seem to connect with any reality for me. I think I just couldn't let it surface when I was nursing a baby. I told Sima that I did feel a little crazy when he was around, that I was sure I acted symptomatically in all kinds of ways, but that I didn't believe anything had occurred when I was little and that, while my father was distant and totally disconnected from himself, I didn't think he would ever touch me inappropriately. It's to Sima's credit that she didn't press.

She and I went on talking about our fathers in particular and fathers in general, but it wasn't until a couple of years later that the deep past reasserted itself. My father had a stroke in Phoenix and we flew out there; I guess you were five or six—you were in Randolph, not Bright Circle. I remember you were really freaked out by how his face was a little paralyzed, the right side, by how he looked the same but different as a result of that, like he'd been replaced by his doppelgänger; you wouldn't go near him at first, not that he was the kind of grandparent a kid would ever run toward. The stroke turned out not to be that severe, but it was the beginning of the long process of trying to figure out how to deal with aging parents, so there was a lot of tension in the air. And then these two things happened with my mom. Nobody used the word "triggering" back then.

One night Dad and Grandma took you to rent a video. They didn't have cable and you were desperate for your cartoons. You guys came back with some Disney movie and this other video, *Fritz the Cat.* (An analyst might note that Fritz was the name of Klaus's murdered son, the one I think Dad was always related to in Klaus's mind.) Dad put on this video for you on the small TV Grandma had in the kitchen so she could watch the news in the morning and then he left. Eventually I came in to check on you and what I saw on the screen—it took me a minute to understand what I was seeing—was some kind of anthropomorphic animal gang rape; it was a fucking X-rated cartoon! I hadn't even known those existed. I'm standing there totally shocked, paralyzed—you're just munching away on your microwave popcorn; I don't think you had any sense of what was being depicted—and then my mother walks in and looks at the TV, at this cartoon gangbang, and says: "Oh my." Then she walked calmly out. I come to my senses, turn the thing off, tell you to go play with Grandma, which you do without protest (you knew something wasn't right); I yell for your dad, who comes running, and I put the tape back on for him. He was appropriately freaked out, although he also seemed to find it all pretty funny. He had no idea how it happened; he said he just glanced at the title when you handed him the box; he was very sorry.

That night I couldn't sleep. And it wasn't because I was worried the cartoon had done any kind of damage to you and it wasn't because I was mad at Dad for the mix-up. No, it was that "Oh my"—it was my mom coming into the room, seeing a child before a scene of sexual violence, and expressing her surprise in the exact same tone and with the exact same level of mildness that she used when she looked at a price tag on a pair of shoes. I was enraged and couldn't account for my rage; I spent the night in a cold sweat, listening to you mumble in your sleep on the inflatable mattress beside our bed. The next morning, I could barely look at her. I talked to Dad about what I felt—I knew it was crazy—and he was focused on taking responsibility for the rental; he thought I was just experiencing the intensity of the stroke, aging parents, and so on. But I decided to say something to her, or maybe I couldn't help myself. We were sitting in that little rock garden they had in the back, with all the succulents and cacti you loved, and I said: "Mom, why weren't you more surprised when you saw that horrible video? Why did you just leave the room?" And she said, not unreasonably, "Well, I thought it was your business, that you're the mother." "Well," I said, "what if I hadn't been there?" She could have said a million things in response to my question: she could have said, "If you and Jonathan weren't here, that video never would have been rented"; she could have said, "Of course I would have turned it off." Instead, she became very thoughtful, seemed to consider the matter carefully, and then said: "Adam would have been fine." I don't remember how or if I responded; the tape in my head just kind of ends.

The second thing happened a few days later, on the last day of the trip. I'd more or less gotten over the whole cartoon thing—at least, I didn't feel angry anymore—and Grandma and I were looking at some paintings and prints that she had, but had never had framed; she wanted to know if I wanted to take any back to Topeka. Grandma was already doing that thing you hate when I do; whenever I admired a painting or something, she'd say, "Take it, it's yours, I'd love you to have it"—as if she were saying goodbye to the world, divesting. So this wasn't a carefree exchange in the sense that, especially against the backdrop of my father's stroke, our talking about where the art might go was also a way of talking about mortality. (Where was my father during this trip? I guess he was just in his room or chatting with Dad, who I think was making some recordings; I can barely remember him being there at all even though his stroke was the reason we'd come.) But art was also something Grandma and I loved to discuss. You know how poor she was until relatively late in life, how impossibly frugal she was, how she'd never graduated from high school; I loved how she loved art, that she valued something beyond price, as you'd put it, and I really admired her taste—how a canvas at a yard sale in Midwood in like 1952 would catch her eye and over time we'd all realize that she'd found a really great little painting, something that deepened as you spent time with it. Some of my fondest early memories are of going with her to the Met; she particularly loved the ancient sculpture; "It soothes me," she used to say; the marble soothed her. As you know, she worked for various artists—helped get supplies, kept their books—and would get paid in paintings. Anyway, we were in the garage going through some prints she had pressed between big pieces of cardboard when my mom suddenly said to me: "I have a confession to make."

"I have a confession to make"—it was like she was quoting something she'd heard on TV; that just wasn't a turn of phrase she'd use. It was incredibly hot, of course, in that garage, but I went cold when she said those words. "Okay, go on," I managed to say. "Well, you know how I used to work for Lassiter." (Lassiter was the guy who made all the Chagall-like stuff that we have around the house; Dad likes them more than I do.) "Well, there was one painting of his—just a small watercolor—that I particularly admired. He actually drew my attention to it because it had a lot of rose colors; he said that since my name was Rose he thought that I might like it. And I did like it, I loved it, in fact—I guess because it seemed to accomplish so much with so little, which is what he was good at, making a whole world out of a few shapes and colors." "What," I said, trying to be patient, "is it you need to 'confess'?" "Well," she said, "he showed me this little rose painting and I loved it and I asked if I could have it as one of my paintings and, to my surprise, Lassiter said no, that he was saving it. I think maybe he was saving it for me, that he was going to give it to me as a gift so it wouldn't be payment, so it wouldn't have anything to do with debt. But I really don't know because this was quite late in his life and he never brought it up again." "Mom," I said, more exasperated than was reasonable, "get to the point." "Okay," she said, "so when Lassiter died, his son asked me to put together a list of his works. The son gave me keys so I could come and go and get everything in order; it was very strange being in the apartment, which was also his studio, without him. And I—I stole the rose painting. I didn't write it down in the catalogue I was making, I just put it in a brown paper bag and took it home; I ran down the stairs with it like a common thief, like the thief that I was. I'm sure his son would have just given it to me, he was so grateful for all I'd done, and maybe Lassiter wanted me to have it anyway. Certainly I could have bought it; his son would have sold it to me for very little, it's not like Lassiter was a big-shot artist. I had never stolen anything in my life and I've never stolen anything since. And I've never told anybody about this, including your sister, who has the painting now."

I remember leaning back against their big blue Volvo station wagon, that the metal was hot through my shirt, and I needed that sensation to stay anchored in my body as I tried to let the story sink in. I was confused, and confused about why I was confused; it was like I was hearing several stories at once, like I was hearing Grandma's story in one ear and then a different story in the other. And then I said—I remember my voice was very calm—"That's all you have to confess?" And she looked kind of puzzled and said: "Yes." And then I said, my voice flat now, like somebody else was speaking through me, "Is that the worst thing you've ever done?" She thought for a moment, no longer puzzled, as if this were the question she'd been expecting, and said: "Yes, I think it is, I think that's the worst thing that I've ever done."

When we got back to Topeka I went over to Sima's, rushed over really—Eric was at some conference—and I retold these stories, retold them as if their significance were self-evident. I was sprawled out on their big yellow leather couch and she was in an armchair across from me, her long perfect olive legs thrown over the armrest, and we were having our wine and smoking as ever. Sima just listened; I wish I could express to you how wonderfully Sima handled silence, how she calibrated it, how she somehow made you feel heard, met you wherever you were—maybe all these expressions seem clichéd to you, but you know, I think you sometimes have it, too, that ability, when you're not in debate mode. She just sat there smiling that very beautiful and also very sad and understanding smile and what she did, in part by doing nothing, was let me hear how my upset was *not* self-evident, how my rage at my mom's failure to "protect" you from the video or my rage that stealing the painting was to her mind the worst thing she'd ever done had not yet been integrated into a coherent narrative. Sima made a space for me to hear that there were depths beneath what I was saying that I hadn't sounded yet.

Then something happened in that space her silence made: my speech started breaking down, fragmenting under the emotional pressure, became a litany of non sequiturs, like how some of the poets you admire sound to me, or I guess what Palin or Trump sound like, delivering nonsense as if it made sense, were argument or information, although I was speaking much faster than politicians speak; my speech was accelerating as if I were chasing after meaning as it receded; it was like *I* was having a stroke. Sima would go on to point out to me that I kept saying the word "training"—like I would say, "Why would my mom give that painting to Deborah, well, my training tells me—" and then break off midsentence and start talking about something else entirely.

—Because it happened on a train.

When my father and I came back to Brooklyn from Seattle, where we'd been visiting family friends; I was six years old. When Grandma had to go to L.A. suddenly because her sister was sick. And she took Deborah and she left me alone with my father, which is the worst thing she ever did. And then at some point my speech just wasn't sustainable as speech at all; I dissolved into sobs, sobbing overtook me. I didn't see it coming, it was as involuntary and shocking as a muscle spasm. At first I was kind of laughing at the sobbing, sun and rain, laughing involuntarily at the force and unexpectedness of it, and then I gave in to it entirely. There was this incredible sense of relief when I let go: this language has ended in pure sound. This language has reached its limit, and a new one will be built, Sima and I will build it. I remember looking through my tears at Sima and seeing that she was *not* coming to me, that she was sitting there—now upright, very poised—full of sympathy, but that she was not going to approach and hug or hold me, and I thought—how strange that I could think anything at all—that she was right to sit up, to stay there, to wait; I remember thinking that we had started therapy.

◆◆◆

From a family systems perspective, a lot has been lost with landlines. Think about how often—before cell phones, before any kind of caller ID—you answered the landline as a child and had to have an exchange, however brief, with aunts or uncles or family friends. Even if it was that five-second check-in, How are you doing, how is school, is your mom around—it meant periodic real-time vocal contact with an extended community, which, through repetition, it reinforced. Now you never speak to anyone unless they call you directly. I love FaceTiming with the girls, I'm not just mourning the older technology, but I think it's actually a profound shift, even if among the subtler ones; maybe you should write about it somewhere.

It also meant that when the Men started to call the house you were often the one to pick up, and there was probably more than one time when you didn't hang up when I said, "Adam, I've got it." (How alien all of this would be to your twenty-first-century Brooklyn girls: two people picking up the receivers in different rooms in a big house in Topeka.) It was a point of pride for me to keep our number listed; getting it out of the phone book seemed paranoid or presumptuous, but I probably should have had it removed. I don't know how many different men there were because I suspect many of the calls were the same man, just disguising his voice, but there were definitely quite a few, especially after I went on *Oprah*; I feel like we averaged a call a week. They would often start off very politely, in a normal voice, "May I speak to Dr. Jane Gordon, please?" But then when I said, "This is she," or you fetched me and I said, "Hello," the voice would typically drop into a whisper or a hiss; then—almost without fail—I'd hear the word "cunt." Sometimes they just wanted to let me know that I was a cunt who ruined their marriage, or that cunts like me were the problem with women today, a bunch of feminazi cunts, or that I should shut my cunt mouth (stop writing); they'd deliver their message and hang up. But there were also threats of varying levels of specificity: that I was a cunt who should watch out, who was going to get what was coming to her, who might get shot while walking on the Foundation campus (that was just one caller, but he called several times), and so on. And there were variations on the theme of rape: I'm going to rape you; Somebody should rape you; You were probably raped; If you weren't so ugly, you'd get raped.

The calls upset Dad much more than me. I just felt that if somebody was going to attack you, they weren't going to call to tell you about it first, although why I thought this, especially given my experiences working with abused women, I can't say. Certainly it was unpleasant, but these guys were also so pitiful—I pictured them sitting in their La-Z-Boys, working up the courage to make their obscene call, maybe jacking off after from all the excitement, if not during—I couldn't really take them seriously, or only took them seriously as specimens of the ugly fragility of masculinity. (Of course, if we've learned anything, it's how dangerous that fragile masculinity can be.) Maybe I just wouldn't let myself register upset because under no circumstance was I going to give them the satisfaction of my sounding hurt or angry or scared. I never demanded, "Who is this?," I never said, "Don't you dare call my house again," I never said, "I'm calling the police," although Dad insisted that we call them; they said they'd "monitor the situation," whatever that meant. But then I invented this technique for fielding the calls that I'm still rather proud of.

When one of the Men called, and I said hello, and he dropped into his whisper to call me a cunt of whatever variety, I would pretend that I couldn't hear: "I'm sorry, can you speak up?" Typically what would happen is that the guy would repeat, confused, whatever he'd said a little more loudly, and while I could hear him fine, I would say, equally politely, betraying no knowledge of the nature of the call, "I'm sorry, it's not a great connection, can you be a little louder?" And I'd just keep doing this, keep politely asking the loser to speak up. He'd maybe repeat his message once or twice, but he would always eventually get too embarrassed by the sound of his own voice—or maybe he was worried about being overheard; I wonder how many of these men had wives or daughters in the next room—and finally their voices would waver or crack or, most often, they would just hang up in what seemed like a rush of shame. For a couple of these calls Dad was on the line and we would have to stifle our laughter as we sensed the threatening caller trying and failing to work up the courage to use his grown-up voice.

Then there were the Men at the store, at Dillon's. Do you have any memory of this? You and I went shopping at Dillon's most Sundays when you were in kindergarten—you loved grocery shopping, for some reason—and we were often approached while I was pushing our cart around, either by a man or a woman. If it was a woman, it was always gratitude, often very moving: "Your book saved my marriage"; "You changed my life"; etc. The woman and I would then "press hands." I remember reading in Russian novels about how so-and-so would "press the hand" of an acquaintance in a moment of emotion and I never knew what that meant. But that's what I did with these women; we weren't going to embrace each other, that wasn't going to happen in the American Midwest, but just shaking hands, which seemed very masculine, very businessy, felt insufficient. So we took each other's hand and applied a certain pressure, communicating solidarity through that touch—and then went back to our shopping. But the Men: they didn't call me a cunt in public, and sometimes they didn't say anything at all, but just let it be known by a look or snicker that they knew who I was. But one or two did approach me, very polite: "Are you Dr. Gordon?" When I said yes, I'd get something like: "I hope you're proud of yourself, home-wrecker," "I feel sorry for your husband"; that sort of thing. I'd say, "Have a good day," and that was it. (There were also the faxes the Phelpses starting sending out: one had my picture with horns drawn on it, called me a "Jezebelian switch-hitting whore," explained I used my "pulpit" to encourage sodomites who were worthy of death; I think we still have it somewhere. But then, the Phelpses attacked anybody from the Foundation who got attention since we refused, as an institution, to acknowledge the evil of homosexuality.)

This was unpleasant, but not much more than that; needless to say, plenty of women suffer a lot worse. Frankly, I think I was flattered by this measure of my book's reach, its effect; even the ugly aspects of recognition can give you a little rush and I was just generally amazed by the sensation the book had become. But fame of any sort, like a birth or a death, changes every relationship. I was naive about this at first, but I would learn. And I think I should have done more to shield you from the Men. You had a couple of episodes around then that I think were linked to them and to the changes more generally.

One took place at Dillon's. I used to ask you to go find stuff on the list we'd made together and to bring it back to the cart and we'd check it off—you loved the responsibility, felt very grown-up. "Okay, we need salt," I'd say, "where is the salt?" and then I'd kind of point you in the general direction and you'd either recognize the Morton shaker from home or, if necessary, ask somebody who worked there with your practiced, cute formality: "Would you be able to show me where to find the salt, sir?" You sounded almost British. Anyway, one day I asked you to get the milk—two percent, the one with the blue cap—and you went off to do it. But you didn't come back for a while and I grew concerned. When I found you—it was probably five minutes later, though it seemed like half an hour—you were wandering around in some other aisle crying, almost hyperventilating; I hadn't seen you so upset in a long time.

"There are men behind the walls," you finally managed to say, "there are men back there hiding in the walls laughing at me and trying to grab me." I was confused and also panicked, enraged: "What men, who tried to grab you, who touched you?" I really couldn't understand what you were saying, but eventually I said, "Show me where this happened," and you led me to the dairy section. "Where are the men who bothered you?" I demanded, and you just pointed at the milk case. I didn't know what was going on. "There are no men in there," I said, smiling to calm you, although I didn't feel calm, and I opened the glass door to show you, took a gallon of milk from the shelf. And that's when I heard the voices behind the case. After a moment of vertigo, an echo of your own terror, I realized that there were workers who supplied the cases from behind, that the back of the case was some kind of movable partition that opened onto the storeroom. I don't know if they laughed at you or even tugged on the gallon of milk you were trying to remove as a joke or if they were just working and talking and maybe laughing among themselves, but now I understood what you'd seen, why you'd freaked out. I calmed down, tried to explain the situation as slowly and clearly as possible. You stopped crying, but you were still upset. What I was describing—that there were men (and women, I insisted) working behind the walls—still sounded plenty ominous to you. And—is this the analyst in me?—I think it was worse for you that it was milk, that you were trying to procure, as you were playing at being grown-up, the nourishment I once gave you from the breast.

You had a few nightmares about it in the following months—that there might be men in the walls. Evil men. And then there were these men calling over the invisible wires. Klaus had an elegant and ridiculous Marxist reading of it as evidence of your precocious intuition of alienated labor, but it was clear that you were picking up on all the toxic masculinity swirling around. Dad also wondered if you felt he couldn't protect the family or something, if you were starting to contrast Dad's gentleness with the Marlboro Man culture around us, a contrast made worse by the fact that I was now the chief breadwinner, getting famous, and people were always asking what that was like for Dad, as if it were obviously emasculating, as if it were his loss. I also think you just knew that whatever was happening with my book, with the attention, was destabilizing, that it involved big changes. Anyway, the dreams didn't last. Then the chewing gum thing happened.

I bet you won't put this in your novel. One night Dad and I are watching a movie. It's many hours after your bedtime and as far as we know you've been sleeping soundly. And then you appear in the doorway, naked, totally calm, and I'm like, "What is it, Adam?" And you say, matter-of-factly, like we're just chatting, "Oh, I was going to the potty and chewing gum and the gum fell out." You'd recently been allowed to keep a pack of gum yourself with the understanding that you'd ask us before chewing any of it; you *loved* gum. Dad had kind of drifted off, wasn't really watching the movie, and said, without opening his eyes, "Well, did you clean it up?" And you didn't answer. And I sensed that something was wrong and I switched on the reading light beside the bed and said, "Come here."

When you were next to me I saw that you had carefully wrapped your penis and scrotum in chewing gum. I mean, you must have chewed it, flattened it out, worked deliberately to enclose yourself. Nothing was exposed. "Oh my God," I said, touching the gum, which had hardened. "What is it?" Dad said, totally awake now, concerned, rolling over. A pause. Then we both started cracking up, we couldn't help ourselves. And you laughed since we were laughing; you were relieved you weren't in trouble.

"How did this happen?" I asked, picking you up and depositing you on the bed between us. And you had your rehearsed line: "The gum fell out of my mouth and got stuck on my body." You were in this stage of using "body" to refer almost exclusively to your penis. If you said, "My body itches," you meant your penis. "Adam, this couldn't have just fallen out of your mouth," I said. "You did a really good job wrapping this," Dad said, trying to begin the process of disentanglement. "It must have taken a long time, a lot of pieces." But you maintained you'd been on the toilet, just chewing away, and that it fell out of your mouth, and voilà, you had this perfectly packaged little package.

It was funny until we realized that we couldn't remove it. And since you'd entirely covered your urethra you weren't going to be able to pee, which is serious. After a while—Dad was still chuckling, but I was starting to worry—we called and woke up Eric, since he was a "real doctor," and asked him what we should do. What followed was an hour or so of alternating comedy and panic where we were using Vaseline, peanut butter, olive oil—I can't remember which finally worked. But we got it off, gave you a gentle lecture, told you we were all taking a break from chewing gum, and then went to bed.

Dad felt this was just a kid exploring his body and that was it. I couldn't help but wonder if it was a kind of simulated castration thing, an attempt not to be a boy, a man, one of the Men. Now, understand, you were generally very happy, doing great in school, had great friends, etc., so we didn't think this was expressing anything specific. But I was personally very haunted by the gum thing; it got less and less funny and more and more upsetting to me, although I of course never let you see any of that. And that wasn't about you, that was about me—about my increasingly intense "consultations" with Sima, what they were dredging up. And while I knew—I mean, as much as a parent can ever know such a thing—that you had never been touched inappropriately or anything, I still worried you were communicating something, a fear if not a trauma. By the way, I think all of this is part of why I came down so incredibly hard on the Peterson girl, Anna, your babysitter, when I caught you guys kissing several years later. I mean, Anna needed a real talking-to, and for there to be consequences, but I basically scared the shit out of her and her parents, talking about her like she was a dangerous sexual predator, like she was lucky she wasn't going to the Foundation or jail.

Then when you were eight you did experience a trauma, which is a funny way to put it, since trauma is the collapse of experience as such. The concussion, I mean. Now that you're a parent you can probably imagine what it was like for us, or imagine how you can't imagine it. I know you remember the fall, a fall like a million others, but you banged your head just so. It was the alley behind Woodlawn. You managed to walk home. Retrospectively the scariest part for me is how close I was to missing it, to leaving you alone. Do you remember I was on the phone? It was an interview, I'm not sure with who—some paper. I was on the kitchen phone, twining the cord around my hand; you walked in, looking a little dazed. I covered the receiver and asked you if everything was okay, and you said, "I fell off my skateboard." I asked if you had any cuts or scrapes and you shook your head no. I looked you over quickly—you didn't have a mark on you, certainly nothing on your head; you weren't crying. I told you to grab a juice box from the fridge if you wanted one, that you could watch a little TV upstairs.

The interview was brief. Then I started going through some mail I'd brought to the kitchen table. I remember it, guiltily, as though I knew something was wrong, but that I didn't want to admit it, because that would make it true—like with the Sanibel tickets—but I'm probably making that up. What I know is that when I finally got to the top of the stairs and saw the unopened juice box lying there on the carpet I immediately knew in my whole body that something wasn't right; I can still see the red box, the untouched plastic straw in its plastic casing. It just didn't make any sense. It wasn't an instance of your making a mess; it couldn't have been something you'd forgotten (you'd just taken it); if you'd decided you didn't want it, you would have at least put it on a shelf or something. I could tell that it was the result of your having lost a relationship to the object—what is this thing in my hand?—or maybe to your hand itself. It's hard to explain how seeing a mundane thing cast out of the grammar of daily life can suddenly alert you to the irruption of violence. I ran.

You were in your room, in your bed, fully clothed, and there was vomit on your shirt. I had to shake you awake—Jesus, I'm sure shaking you was the last thing I was supposed to do. I must have been screaming your name. You did come to, thank God, and I carried you downstairs right to the car and buckled you in the backseat and drove as fast as I could to St. Francis. By this point you were crying out in pain, eyes shut. I was saying everything was going to be fine, trying to navigate through tears, biting my tongue when I wasn't talking, could taste the blood. I can't believe I drove you myself instead of calling an ambulance; I'm amazed I didn't crash and kill us both.

You've been told most of what happened next, must remember it in the third person. Dad got there from the Foundation as fast as he could. You needed a CAT scan and you were out of control with pain and fear—you thought everybody around you was trying to hurt you. You were tearing IVs out of your arms. And your speech was totally disorganized—the wrong words, slurred words, then just noise. Your vision was badly impaired, as was your balance, so your expressions and movements were strange, not your own. When it was clear there was no way to calm you down with speech they started injecting you with sedatives, my little eight-year-old boy, because there was no other way to administer them. Three adults holding you down, long needles. And then at a certain point you relaxed into unconsciousness and I thought: Okay, now he's going to rest, the drugs will wear off in an hour or two, everything will be fine. But then I heard a doctor say to Dad, "Now we just have to wait and see." The scan revealed a fair amount of swelling, and we didn't know when or in what state you'd wake up.

Soon I was doing something that approximated prayer. I was making promises to—bargaining with—a higher power, which I hadn't done since I was a child. If somebody in the family has to die, let it be me; If Adam is okay, I promise to do *X*, promise to do *Y*. The only promise I remember was: I will never write again. I felt—because I was doing an interview when you came into the kitchen? because I was guilty, despite my politics, about being a mom and having a career?—that it was my fault that you were in that condition, that I had failed you. "I feel sorry for your husband; I feel sorry for your son," the Men were saying in my head. "If you hadn't been driven by penis envy to write this book," said Caplan, said Dr. Tom, said a chorus of male colleagues, "none of this would have happened." Sitting beside you in the ICU in that horrible plastic-upholstered chair, I was defeated, desperate: "You're right, you're right, I'm a bad wife, a bad mother, a bad daughter, a home-wrecker (after all, I had helped wreck Dad's marriage; and I'd once—when I was very young—been with another married man; did that make it a pattern?); just let him be okay and I'll behave."

You were unconscious for fifteen hours. The awful beeping of those machines. There was a huge thunderstorm and at one point the hospital had to use backup power; I remember this involved the hall lights changing color, darkening from that unforgiving white to an ominous red. And then at about two in the morning, Dad whispered my name and I looked over at you to find your eyes were open. You looked very calm. Before we could bring ourselves to say anything, you said politely, "Hello." Dad said: "How do you feel?" "Fine," you said. "Do you know where you are, sweetheart?" I asked, trying to keep my voice from cracking. "The hospital," you said, chuckling a little at the silliness of the question. At that point the nurse came in—either because she heard us or because Dad summoned her with that beeper thing or because she was making her rounds—and said, "Well, look who is awake." And then she asked the same question, do you know where you are, and you repeated the answer, laughing this time as if this were a silly game, asking you where you were when it was obvious. And then she said, pointing to me and Dad, "And do you know who these nice people are?" And you looked at us, smiling warmly, and said: "Nope."

My vision swam. It was like the world had changed into a slightly different version of itself, one from which I'd been subtracted. My boy was going to be okay, but at the cost of no longer being mine. "You will," the nurse said, with reassuring confidence, "you'll remember soon that this is your mom and dad." And you said, "Oh," thought for a moment, and asked, "What are your names?" And this was an impossibly difficult question. I mean, you never called us by our first names; they weren't our names for you, although you of course knew them. "My name is Jonathan," Dad said awkwardly. "That's your mama, Jane." Somehow they didn't sound like our real names. And then the nurse said, addressing you, "And what's your name, sweetheart?" You opened your mouth to tell her, then stopped, a terrible pause. "Your name is Adam," I said. "Adam," you repeated, like you were trying it on, testing its rightness of fit. Then you said you were going to take a nap and you shut your eyes and went back to sleep. We looked at the nurse and she said, "Rest is good now, it will all come back, he's going to be fine; I'll page the doctor."

A few hours later you woke up again, sat way up in bed on your own, said you were hungry, all reassuring signs, but you asked our names again. This time Holly Eberheart was the nurse on call and she came in to ask you some questions. Holly

Eberheart, you'll remember, was a really large woman; still is, I assume. She had this sweater on and knitted onto the sweater was the alphabet—or maybe just A B C across the breast, I can't remember exactly. We were surprised she wasn't wearing scrubs, but it turned out the sweater had a purpose. She sat down beside you and she said, "Adam, hon, what is this—" and she indicated the giant A on her giant right breast. There was this long moment when you were looking at her breast, which she seemed to be proffering, then to us, as if for instruction. And Dad and I realized that you were trying to figure out if she was asking you to identify a body part, her breast, which she was basically holding in her hands, or the letter, and you didn't want to be rude. Dad had to cough his way out of laughter. We could tell that you knew the letter but weren't sure about the question and we thought you were going to say, "That's your booby," which is the word you would have used; but finally you said, very tentatively, "A?" "Right," she said, and then you looked relieved and answered all the other questions without hesitation. Now I was coughing, laughing; somehow it brought us a lot of relief.

At some point, maybe late morning, Eric and Jason came to visit. Jason had brought baseball cards for you, I remember, those packs with the sticks of gum inside. They also brought some food you couldn't eat; the doctors said you shouldn't ingest anything for a while. You were welcoming to Jason, but when we asked you who he was, you said you weren't sure, which Jason found amusing. We adults were amazed by how unbothered the two of you seemed about your no longer being able to recall the coordinates of your life. Eric reassured us about all of this, as by now several doctors had. Dad asked you again, "Do you remember our names, who we are?" And you said, "Jonathan and Jane, Dad and Mom," but it was clear that you were reciting newly acquired knowledge, although maybe it was also starting to sink in, linking back up with your memories as they returned. (Returned from where?) You were looking at the cards with Jason, also proudly showing him your IV, the electrodes. Dad and I suddenly realized we hadn't eaten anything in ages and began to devour the muffins or whatever it was that Eric had brought. And then Sima arrived—I don't know why she came separately; maybe she'd just been parking—and we hugged each other, a long and intense embrace. And while we were holding each other you looked up from the cards and, as casually as could be, greeted her by name.

♦♦♦

You have lunch with a friend you haven't seen in a while and she starts the conversation by saying, with a new trace of bitterness in her smile, "Wow, I can't believe you managed to find time for me." You ask her several times what she's been up to, but she keeps turning the conversation back to you and your book tour adventures, insisting that her life is ordinary, nothing of interest. You're five minutes late to a staff meeting because you spilled coffee on your blouse, ineffectually patted yourself down with paper towels in the bathroom, and there's murmuring: "I'm surprised she can be bothered to show up at all." A colleague mentions that he's received a big grant, and you offer your congratulations, but there's the slightly sour smile again: "Of course, I know this must sound like nothing to you." You protest, but that somehow makes it worse. At a case conference, the consultant discusses a patient's resistance to considering intensive therapy, and the chief psychologist quips, to general laughter: "She can just read Jane's book; it's sure to cure her and will save a lot of time and effort." A dentist's appointment has to be changed to accommodate a parent-teacher conference; the receptionist lets out an exasperated sigh: "Well, we're here to serve you, Dr. Gordon." At the conference you respectfully ask a question about the curriculum. "We might not be flashy or fancy, but we know how to teach our students language arts."

Even with Dad, who was generally so supportive and proud: if I forgot to do the dishes, now it was because I thought I was too good for chores—no matter that I'd been messy my whole life; if I was impatient about something, it was because I'd changed as a result of everybody telling me how great I was, even though I was also being told I was a man-hater or an intellectual sellout. He was tired of being asked what it was like to be "Mr. Jane Gordon" or being praised for "being a mom." People say of a person that "fame has changed her," or praise her by saying that it hasn't, but the trouble with that formulation is that fame or notoriety of whatever sort changes everything *around* the person, every relationship in which she is embedded, no matter what the person in question does. You can do a better or worse job of navigating your new reality, of course. And thank God my fame, such as it was, peaked before the Internet existed so I didn't sit around Googling myself or reading tweets and comment fields—which are infested with the Men.

But until the trip our families took to New York—you were in sixth or seventh grade—my relationship with Sima felt, at least to me, basically unchanged. The book was dedicated to her. She seemed genuinely happy for me, and at first she was my staunchest defender against the inevitable charge that I'd compromised theoretical rigor for the sake of popular success. Certainly Sima understood better than anyone why I was committed to accessible writing; first and foremost, I believed that I could help a lot of people by describing triangles or sibling dynamics as clearly as possible and that the translation of those concepts into practical advice was my strength as a therapist. I also had, as Sima knew, a deep—a bone-deep—allergy to anything that smacked of mystification, to the way professional jargon—especially, but not only, of the analytical sort—could be deployed to dismiss women as hysterics; this was related to what had happened with my father, all the secrecy and gaslighting abuse involves. Now, the hard-core academics and theoreticians found it easy to dismiss me; if your book is celebrated in *The New York Times*, then you're just peddling commercially repackaged ideology; you're not to be taken seriously. There are of course real arguments to be had regarding what's gained or lost with one mode of discourse or another, anti-intellectualism can be as bad as snobbery, but it was notable how, if one of the Foundation's old boys or his allies showed up in the *Times*, it was because his work was transcendent, but when a penis-envying virago like me received attention, it was because I'd reduced everything to a kind of psychological chick lit.

Sima and I had stopped "consulting"—that is, we no longer had any kind of scheduled sessions to talk about my father, sessions for which I had insisted on paying, to make it clear what was professional and what was personal; now what's painfully clear is the depth of our confusion. We'd stopped, but we were stuck in our respective roles: I was the patient, she was the doctor. We couldn't just switch back—I'd become the one who talked, she'd become the one who listened, gently pushed, advised. Here's Topeka in a nutshell: I was talking to Sima about my complicated experience of the book's reception, what it was doing to my relationships, including with Dad; Sima was talking about her relationship to my career (and her relationship to my relationship to it) on Klaus's couch; Klaus was probably communicating some of this to Dad—albeit in some encoded, maybe involuntary way—on their walks (or, since Klaus was starting to be less mobile, in his living room, where Klaus would smoke his pipe); I could go on. This is the backdrop against which Sima and Dad's own relationship got out of hand, but you'll have to ask him—

—If I want details.

If you want details. I'm interested to hear how you remember the trip to New York. Looking back, it was a horrible idea. I was doing an event at the Ninety-Second Street Y, a kind of public conversation about my work, and they asked me whom I'd like to have as an interlocutor. I thought that asking Sima, making a family vacation out of it—my publisher would pay for her ticket—would be a way to honor her, would be a lot of fun. She said yes right away when I suggested it, but my guess is that she started to feel, almost immediately, like my sidekick, second fiddle, choose your cliché. They made a flyer that didn't mention her name ("Jane Gordon in Conversation"; the Phelpses got hold of one of these and marked it up, faxed it around: "Jezebel Gordon Apologizing for Fags"), then misspelled her name when I insisted it be included; my publisher put our family up at a fancy hotel and Sima didn't want to pay to stay there, wanted a less expensive place, then got offended when I offered to pay the difference. Then I wanted us to all stay at the cheaper place so we'd be together, but she said that was ridiculous, insisted I leave it alone. All this before we took off from Kansas City.

The Y was packed, despite the weather—it was January; that night was alternating rain and sleet. I'm always nervous before public speaking (I probably took a lorazepam), but I was somehow surprised that Sima was; she was pacing around the green room, unwittingly ashing in one of the little bowls of salted almonds instead of the tray, asking me how she looked, which she never did, wanting to go over questions again and again, although we had more than enough topics. (Dad and Eric were with you boys; I can't remember where you went—somewhere touristy; maybe you ate at the Hard Rock Café.) After we'd been introduced, had taken our seats onstage—there were two chairs angled toward one another, a little table that held a glass pitcher of water, stationary mics—Sima turned to look at me, to ask the first question, and I saw in the instant before she spoke that her face had changed. There was a coldness now, a distance to her smile, trace amounts of bitterness. It was subtle, but more profound for being subtle—a face you know intimately is most disturbingly altered when it's altered only slightly; think about how you lost it when Dad shaved off his mustache for the first and last time—maybe you were too young to remember; he did it for a film.

And then her first question was about my parents, a topic we had never once mentioned as a possibility. It was about my parents, but I heard it as about my father: "We psychoanalysts are of course obsessed with parents," Sima said, had clearly always planned to say, "so I thought I would begin by asking you about yours," about my early experiences, how they informed my decision to become a therapist, my work. From the outside it was a totally reasonable question, but I felt blindsided. Was she daring me to divulge the abuse? To discuss how I'd recovered the memory with her? Or was I just being paranoid? It felt like Sima—or her doppelgänger—was threatening me, was reminding me that she, unlike my "fans," knew the real truth about me. "They won't believe you, I'm not sure I even believe you," I read in her face, however crazy that sounds—which is to say I briefly saw Sima as the abusive parent contesting the child's reality. I was both on that stage and back in Brooklyn in the fifties; I was very briefly on the train.

But then I heard myself answering her question, speaking quite naturally, talking about the dynamics in my household growing up, cracking a few jokes; the audience—made up almost exclusively of women—was laughing, warm. I swam back into my body. The feeling of panic and vertigo passed and the conversation went quite well; I remember feeling like I did great in the Q&A.

After I'd signed books at a long table in the main hall, Sima seated awkwardly beside me, although there was nothing for her to sign, we walked out into the cold and found somewhere to eat—a Greek place, dimly lit. As soon as we were seated, had ordered our wine, I thanked her for doing the event with me, for doing it so well. "I was surprised by your first question," I said after a minute or two, "since we'd never talked about starting that way." And that's when I realized that her face had not returned to normal—she had carried the new face off the stage, had brought that public face into our private exchange. "What do you mean?" she asked. "I just mean I wasn't expecting the question and it was disorienting for me given that you know a big part of the real answer, which I'm not ready to share publicly." She said nothing. "I'm just saying," I went on, "I was surprised and was curious how you understood it." "Well," she said, smiling her new smile—that signature mixture of warmth and sadness gone—"if you want to process how my performance tonight disappointed you, how my flying here along with my family to help celebrate you has made you feel aggrieved, then we can do that, but let's maybe wait until tomorrow, okay? I'm very tired."

My memory of the rest of the trip—we had two more non-travel days—has a nightmarish quality. Dad and I had decided well in advance to take you to see the house where I grew up in Flatbush, so close to where you teach; Sima and Eric had mentioned wanting to tag along; I tried to release them from the plan—I didn't want any other part of the trip to be about me—but I only managed to offend Sima further; I guess she thought I was trying to get rid of them. They came, but didn't want to be there—we just stood on the sidewalk of East Ninth near Avenue J, cold wind in our faces, looked at the façade, Dad took a picture, and we left—and it of course took forever to get there and back from the hotels on the Upper East Side. Then you and Jason started bickering—maybe you guys were picking up on the energy between the grown-ups—and you both basically became parodies of bratty tourists visiting the big city, whining on the trains, shoving each other. You wanted to go to some baseball-related store, Jason wanted to go to the top of the World Trade Center; you were both being exasperating. It wasn't a big deal, but I suddenly felt paralyzed: if I insisted we defer to Jason, Sima would feel patronized; if I suggested something that seemed to favor your desires, that would be evidence of my narcissism; if I thought we might separate for a while and meet up later, Sima could feel dropped; so I just became quiet and passive, which probably came across as sulking.

It was Dad's idea that we take Jason for the night and let Sima and Eric go out to dinner, and it was also Dad's idea that we would pay, a gesture of thanks; I told him I was fine with whatever plan, but that I wanted it to be clear that he was making it, not me. Eric and Sima reluctantly agreed and you boys were excited about staying in and eating room service and watching TV. I also felt relieved by the idea—I wanted a break from Sima. After their dinner—which wasn't far from our hotel—they'd swing by and get Jason.

The fighting resumed; maybe you wanted to watch *Terminator* and Jason wanted to watch *Terminator 2* or something, I don't know. I was leaving discipline to Dad, but Dad seemed only half there to me, was ignoring your aggressiveness. I found you both insufferable, was saying to myself, I can't believe I'm a mother of one of these acne-covered, baseball-cap-wearing, sports-obsessed Topekan proto-adolescents; God help me through the next six years. We ordered you billion-dollar hamburgers, which kept you quiet for a few minutes. Then you guys were starting to horse around, wrestle a little, although at least you were laughing now, seemed to be enjoying yourselves. I decided to take a very long shower—the bathroom was palatial, a spa—and leave you three to fend for yourselves.

At first I thought the shouting was part of the movie, but then I realized something was wrong. I turned the water off, managed to get into one of the hotel robes, and opened the door to find you two slugging it out, really going at it, Dad trying to get between you, but having trouble; in a flash I went from seeing you and Jason as kids to seeing you as young men, how there was real strength coiled in you guys, real rage, real violence. Now you two were grappling, each trying to throw the other on the ground, and either deliberately or incidentally you elbowed Jason hard in the upper lip. He screamed, you backed off a little;

Dad grabbed him and laid him across the bed and had to slowly peel his lip off his braces; there was a lot of blood; it was lucky the braces didn't go clean through. You'd retreated to a corner of the room and were ventriloquizing some kind of mash-up of masculine gibberish—"I warned you, motherfucker; dude, I said step off"—but you had tears in your eyes, a kid again.

An hour and a half later, Sima and Eric, both a little tipsy, arrived at the hotel lobby to find me waiting for them. "Everything is fine," I said, "but Jason and Adam were roughhousing and Jason hit his lip and might need a few stitches; they're at the hospital now. It's only a few blocks away." Eric had a rush of questions, which I tried to answer, but Sima, after an initial wave of concern, was perfectly cold. "I should never have trusted you to be in charge of my son," I projected or read on the mask her face had become. I kept apologizing as we walked to the hospital, I was feeling increasingly desperate for any human sign from Sima, but she repeated, as if she were talking to a stranger who'd bumped into her, "It's fine, don't mention it; boys will be boys."

You and Jason—whose lip was cartoonishly swollen—made up, got along for the rest of the trip, which was uneventful if also miserable for me. Although I wouldn't have believed it at the time, this was the beginning of the end of my friendship with Sima, despite several years in which I'd try to break through to her, imploring her to tell me what I'd done, weeping openly on the phone or in her doorway or over dinner at Steak and Ale when she'd condescend to see me, just tell me how to make things right, suggesting we see a therapist or ask a friend to mediate, anything I could think of, all to no avail; "Jane, you're making too much of this; we've just distanced a little since you've become so busy with your career," etc.; it's the only real adult friendship I've ever lost. I can't tell you what pain it involved, involves, in part because of how it was shadowed by the trauma she'd helped me to address. I'm not suggesting any equivalence between what my father did and Sima dropping me; I just mean I couldn't experience the latter without it being inflected by the former given the nature of our relationship, the blurred boundaries between therapist and friend. We hadn't spoken in a few years by the time we were forced briefly back into contact by the incident with Darren.

The only other part of the trip I remember clearly is the afternoon and evening that Sima insisted they would entertain you and Jason so that Dad and I could go out. "We look forward to seeing what kind of revenge Jason takes on Adam," Dad joked, "we can just meet you at the hospital," and everybody laughed, but awkwardly. And the entire time I was out with Dad, I *was* imagining you guys fighting again, you hitting your head on the corner of something, another concussion.

Dad on the other hand seemed almost manically excited to be out in the city for a few hours on our own. He decided that we should go to the Met, which I didn't particularly want to do, maybe because I'd so often been there as a kid, wasn't in the mood for any more childhood memories, but I didn't have any better ideas—it was too cold to just walk around. He wanted to revisit a couple of our favorite paintings—that Bastien-Lepage of Joan of Arc; that Duccio you love where the child is pushing away the mother's veil. Dad and I used to spend time at the Met when he was still with his first wife, and now, looking back, I think part of his weird energy that afternoon had to do with the fact that he and Sima were getting increasingly entangled—I mean we were returning both to an important scene in the history of our relationship and in the history of his—well, his struggles with fidelity. Anyway, the Met was a big part of our lore as a couple. There was one particularly memorable day when we ate mushrooms or acid and wandered around the museum and he kind of lost it, but that's another story. Now, twenty-two years later, as we moved arm-in-arm through the galleries, I was having my own experience of depersonalization, no drugs involved—an overwhelming sense of frames of reference giving way, of the past and present collapsing in on one another. I felt like a child who wanted her mom or Sima to protect her from her father and like a mother who was failing to protect her child, who was at risk of becoming one of the Men (I wasn't keeping the promises I made when you were unconscious; I wasn't learning to behave); I was simultaneously there with Grandma so the marble might soothe her ("Jane will be fine") and I was there with Dad in the more recent past as I helped wreck his home and in the present as a famous relationship guru who could no longer relate to any of her own. I kept seeing Lassiters out of the corner of my eye, kept catching glimpses of his rose painting, whispers out of time. We finally found the Duccio—I think all the galleries had been rearranged—and Dad was talking a mile a minute and suddenly I stopped understanding him, but that's not really right. He was describing a film he had made or wanted to make and an early photograph of his mother on horseback and these sculptures of horses his parents had had and blinded horses in Central Park and horses in Muybridge's *Horse in Motion* and the relation of still and moving images and administering the TAT to his lost boys ("I am going to show you some pictures and I'd like you to make up a story about each one. A story with a beginning, a middle, and an end") and the experiments about "blindsight" undertaken by a neurologist friend; all these topics were interfering and separating like waves.

A guard announced the galleries were closing. We had a dinner reservation downtown in the present, some uncomfortably upscale Italian place that Dad had chosen. At the coat check I remembered how—all those years ago, when Dad had had his bad trip—we'd rushed out of the museum so quickly that we'd left our winter coats; we almost froze to death. When I handed the woman the little numbered tile, I half imagined that she was going to bring us those coats from our student days. We'd put them on and twenty-two years would be erased.

Darren would help his neighbor Ron Williams move things from his garage to his truck or back, mainly tools and lumber. Darren can you help me with this filled him with pride. Cody Williams was Darren's age and while they had played together in the distant past, Cody, a quiet athlete, now looked right through him. Cody would not defend him from Carter or Nowak or Davis or Gordon types but he would do him no harm, never join the laughter. Whatever Cody's inclination he would not defy his father who had wordlessly made it clear you do not fuck with Darren. Sometimes Cody and Darren loaded or unloaded the truck together and Darren felt a brief commonality of purpose, lift on three. If Ron and Cody were shooting baskets in the driveway Darren could park and watch or maybe dismount and rebound for them. Take a shot, Darren.

On weekend evenings Darren had biked past Ron's and seen in the yellow light of the garage Cody drinking with his friends, Mandy usually among them. Sometimes Ron would be there smoking a Swisher Sweet, would wave to him, but never call him over. If it was summer and Darren stood in his own yard he could hear through the insect noise and the radio the laughter.

Until one Friday in November, after unloading heavy equipment until dusk, Ron said over Cody's mute objection, Stay and have a beer. In the garage Darren saw there was a silver keg in a rubber trash can filled with ice and he watched as Ron locked on the pump and tapped it. It's Cody's birthday and I'd just as soon they do their drinking here. He gave Darren a red plastic cup primarily of foam, then served himself and Cody. Ron indicated a stack of folding chairs and Darren unfolded one and sat beside the keg while Ron put away some tools on pegboard hooks and Cody took his cup inside, I'm showering.

To move only to drink or wipe the foam off on his sleeve and to pull down his Royals cap as far as possible over his eyes seemed to Darren his best strategy for remaining welcome. When Ron refilled his cup he refilled Darren's, but even without the alcohol Darren's anxious joy would have released into his bloodstream chemicals sufficient to prevent him from feeling through his sweatshirt the cool autumnal air. As if to mark the occasion Darren saw the closest streetlight flicker on and then around it first snow hovered moth-like more than fell. Hear the car doors slamming shut and the voices of Nowak Carter Gordon Davis types approaching. Ron was there so Darren did not move. No speech, but surprised, unreadable smiles were addressed to Darren as the types greeted Mr. Williams, one of the cooler dads, shook Cody's hand, the latter back now in baggy jeans and licensed sports apparel. Ron must have handed Darren the stack of red plastic cups because he found himself offering them to whoever approached the keg. A job, this one without prices. Working the keg, Darren, someone said, only mostly mocking him.

When did the girls appear, Mandy among them, and how did he know she wore black jeans, a red V-neck sweater, hair pulled up tight, since he absolutely would not look at her? But she said, Hi, Darren, matter-of-factly smiling lips freshly glossed and when he held the cups out to her she took one, thank you. He knew either from his two years at THS or his previous schools the names of almost everyone in the garage although he'd rarely had license to speak them. Let me fill that for you, Kyle Fulton said, and did. Cheers, dude, let's get fucked up. Like when he held a nine-volt battery to his tongue, the metal of the light beer in Darren's mouth.

Stan had given him a fund of anger about rap music and all those wiggers who love it now but what issued from the stereo had like the shopping carts or the ammo latch or one of his rare sentences that managed to hold sense over time that rightness of fit which made Darren feel his age, of his age, identical to his body, now his body with the night. Darren had not moved from his chair but the brim of the hat was raised a little and he saw that some of the girls while not dancing in the cold garage were nodding or bouncing a little to the beat. The intensity of the desire this inspired in him was closer to its fulfillment than anything he had previously known. Darren in that garage, in his chair, last century, his happiness. All eyes on me, the music said.

Then Davis was offering him cigarettes, hey man what's going on. No hard feelings about what went down last summer. Nod from Gordon. Darren knew to be on guard, but when the girl named Amber said let me see your hair, removed his hat, and ran her fingers tipped with ruby through or at least across the black matted mass not recently washed or cut he was too overwhelmed by pure sensation to care about the laughter here and there. Others began soliciting speech from him, where did you buy those awesome boots, is that a hickey or a bruise, do you still practice martial arts. You should hang out with us more, Darren. Yeah, we're tired of the same assholes in this senior class. He just laughed whenever others laughed, kept drinking from the cup they kept refilling.

From alcohol and sheer exhilaration a widening delay obtained between experience and its conscious registration, Darren realizing the party had broken up just as they were coaxing him into the back of a Jeep Cherokee, Nowak driving, Laura riding shotgun, see the cherry of her Marlboro Light, Davis beside him in the back, proffering a bottle of Mad Dog 20/20 Coco Loco wine, the bass of what Nowak called his system rattling Darren's chest, all eyes on me. It's as if by the time the cold air thundering through the sunroof Nowak left down to let out smoke makes Darren aware they're on I-70 they have already arrived at Clinton Lake some twenty miles away, mainly upperclassmen drinking around a bonfire, sparks flying off the crackling Osage orange, a few couples making out on blankets, same music from another system. Only when he rolls onto his back after puking painlessly in the grass somewhere beyond the bright circle of the firelight does he really hear them chanting Darren, Darren, Darren. And now he shuts his eyes he sees the stars.

THE CIPHER

(ADAM)

Hadn't they always been told to include him? The captain of the kickball team compelled to select him at recess on pain of punishment; a parent insisting on inviting him against her child's wishes to the birthday party, where he would play alone; Ron Williams telling Cody on the last Halloween of elementary school: Darren goes with you or nobody goes, his Spider-Man costume at least one developmental stage behind the increasingly sexualized genies flecked with glitter, the boys who fingered butterfly knives beneath their trench coats and wore on their faces only a trickle of fake blood. So now they were including him, the class of '97; there was irony, but not all of it was cruel. Was it, Adam wondered, really that different from how, the previous year, Coach Hawn let Aaron Nagel—an autistic boy who suited up for home games—play the last few minutes against Highland Park? Both teams trying to let him get a shot in, get on the boards before the final buzzer; his uncontested layup made the news. See the crowd go wild, run onto the court, classmates bearing him aloft. A heartwarming segment. As the seniors approached graduation, neared the end of their minority, the ritual reincorporation of Darren into their society closed the symbolic circuit of their childhood, Klaus's voice in the dark.

The opposite might also be true: that they were viciously punishing Darren for what he represented, the bad surplus. The man-child, descendant of the jester and village idiot and John Clare, the poet roaming the countryside after enclosure. The persistence of the mind of childhood—its plenitude and purposelessness—into the sexually mature body, which has succumbed to historical time, must log its hours. The man-child represented a farcical form of freedom, magical thinking against the increasingly administered life of the young adult. A teller of fantastic stories. Almost every object in the man-child's world reflected this suspension between realms: his alcohol that was also soda, his weapons that were toys, how he might trade you two paper dollars for one of silver, valuing not credit so much as shine. He had trouble managing his height or facial hair and when he injured actual children while demonstrating a wrestling move (clothesline, facehammer, DDT), it was a case of his "not knowing his own strength." He must, to fit the type, be not only male, but also white and able-bodied: the perverted form of the empire's privileged subject. If he were a woman or a racialized or otherwise othered body, he would be in immediate mortal danger from sexual predators and police. It was his similarity to the dominant that rendered him pathetic and a provocation: the man-child was *almost* fit for school or work or service, could almost get his license, finally discard the dirt bike; too close to the norms to prove them by his difference, the real men—who are themselves in fact perpetual boys, since America is adolescence without end—had to differentiate themselves with violence, Klaus's voice.

Milieu therapy, Jason said as he exhaled; they were in the backseat as they drove home from Clinton Lake, where they'd left Darren dreaming in the grass; the phrase would have been meaningless to the non-Foundation kids to whom Jason passed the roach in the front of the Jeep. The joke, insofar as it was a joke, was not only at Darren's expense, but also at the expense of the therapeutic culture that had failed him, that could not welcome him into the medicalized pastoral of in-treatment (who would pay?) or reconcile him with clinical hours to the larger world. In Jason's joke there was also bitterness at the folly of Foundation parents, how they thought Foundation kids would just "know better" than to binge-drink-and-drive or inhale crystal from a broken light bulb or throw forearms and elbows—a tactic capable of inflicting greater damage at close quarters that had spread among Kansans late in the millennium as mixed martial arts became a televised sport. Of course they knew better, but knowing is a weak state; you cannot assume your son will opt out of the dominant libidinal economy, develop the right desires from within the wrong life; the travesty of inclusion they were playing out with Darren—their intern—was also a citation and critique of the Foundation's methods; if they were at once caring for and castigating Darren, they were also modeling and mocking their own parents.

But that's not really right; no one decided, no one was in charge. He was in the garage because he helped Ron, because Ron had let him help (generosity toward the man-child often took the form of mock employment); he moved to the Jeep as much on a current of alcohol and shared energy as under his own power or the direction of his peers. Resentment and empathy and nostalgia and anxiety lived without their knowledge in their bodies, led them to stand just so, angled their shoulders thusly, opened or closed their faces, cut their hair, entered the prosody of their gestures, speech; no individual choreographed the sequence into which Darren was absorbed. How many of Darren's own small movements and postures in the present were embodied echoes of the past, repetitions just beneath the threshold of his consciousness? What's argued in previous rounds is always relevant. When Adam looked out the window of the Jeep, cold air thundering through the sunroof, the cue ball was already there.

It was cruel to leave him by the lake, but it was remorse about that cruelty more than its continuation that led Mandy to insist they stop by his house a few days later, leave visible traces of their company for his mom, a form of apology. And one could argue that sustaining the fiction of his inclusion and puncturing it were after that point at least equally unkind; easier to let him be a mascot through graduation, a kind of water boy, except instead of water he could carry keg beer, Everclear mixed with Sprite. Then there was their anthropological fascination: he was their Victor of Aveyron, their Kaspar Hauser. Could he learn their speech and customs? Only almost, and by failing, Darren performed a critical social function: he naturalized their own appropriated talk and ritual; Darren helped them keep it real.

No one was in charge, but Jason was central; he'd helped guide Darren to the Jeep at Cody's, then he'd insisted they leave him "sleeping" at the lake, a literal lost boy beneath the stars; looking back in twenty years, Adam would feel that Jason's eagerness to participate had had to do with Jason's own comparatively complex identity. While he physically resembled Eric much more than Sima, while he was thought of by most of his peers as white—which meant for most of them the question never arose—an element of ethnic difference was nevertheless present. For most of his life, the difference was barely visible; with his mom he'd more than once brought homemade lavash to World Food Week at Randolph Elementary (Jane was always pushing her to connect with her own history, to work against the cutoffs), but Sima did not speak in his presence a word of Farsi and her family had been intensely secular for generations, not that Jason knew them anyway; at home, Jason celebrated, albeit vaguely, both Hanukkah and Christmas, which meant he was if anything slightly less foreign than those Foundation Jews like Adam whose houses were not appropriately strung with holiday lights. Like a missing tooth on Greenwood, the Gordons' dark house in December. Phenotype and class and the insufficiency of available categories (at Topeka High, you were, in the minds of most white people, white, black, Mexican, or Asian; Pablo Figueroa, the one Chilean in the senior class, had long since given up on getting peers to make finer distinctions) meant that, for most of his childhood, Jason passed without knowing he was passing. But Desert Shield and Desert Storm and the truck bomb under the North Tower and his mom's pigmentation and foreign name meant that, by high school, shit-talking might involve the charge of "Arab." The summer before their freshman year, after Jason refuted a few of his lies, Darren had called him a "half-breed" and other names straight from the Surplus, then leveled his toy pistol; Jason hit him twice, the right cross opening a cut above Darren's eye. The violence was out of character for Jason; was he now including Darren to make it right? Yes, and the opposite: he was further punishing the perverted privileged subject of the empire.

Regardless, nobody would be allowed to strike Darren now; his tormentors were also his protectors. Two months after his long night at Clinton Lake, Darren was drinking a forty of Olde English on Amber's basement couch. He kept adjusting his posture when he felt he'd sunk too far into the cushions, soft brown leather. (Someone had tucked a cigarette behind his ear. He touched it periodically to confirm its presence—gently, the way a dazed person might touch a head wound, startled each time to find it there.) He'd been brought by a few underclassmen eager to be in on the ambiguous joke of his inclusion, but for many of the partygoers the novelty of his presence was starting to wear off; he was just another body getting fucked up. At this particular gathering were several seniors from Topeka West, Amber's former school.

In the twilit basement, Darren stood to find the bathroom. On the way he accidentally collided with Reynolds, a redheaded state champion wrestler from West, who responded, according to convention, by pushing Darren hard in the chest, telling the motherfucker to watch out. Darren spilled Olde English on himself, regained his balance, and prepared to resume his search without rejoinder or apology. But before he knew it, he was surrounded, briefly sure he had transgressed, ruined everything, would be jumped out of his new society. It took him a minute to realize the bodies closing ranks were threatening Reynolds, telling him to back the fuck off. (Darren had been defended before, but almost always from his peers, not by them.) Reynolds's two classmates came to the wrestler's aid and the glass doors slid open and they moved in a mass to the lawn that sloped downward to the man-made lake. Only Amber tried to stop it, attempting to force her way between the senior men, which allowed Adam the respectable out of moving her to safety. The threats both real and ventriloquized: step off motherfucker, what's up now. Reynolds peeling off his sweatshirt in the cold to reveal a six-pack, lats that made his torso appear hooded like a cobra.

In a minute Sean will head-butt Reynolds a beat or two before the latter expects first contact, breaking, almost exploding, the wrestler's nose. Reynolds's friends will come in swinging, only to be quickly separated and overwhelmed. When Reynolds, his face a mask of blood and dirt, is on the ground, they'll begin to kick and stomp him, Darren ushered forward so he can get a blow in with his awesome boots. At some difficult-to-determine point, among middle-class white boys in the Middle West, fights, instead of ending when a combatant hit the ground, took on new life there, the "boys will be boys" chivalry of boxing giving way to the archaic regression of overkill, a term that dates from 1946; every opponent must be spread; every offense, however minor, leads to holocaust.

Instead of focusing on the fight, zoom in on the fascinating and absurd spectacle of the gang signs that precede it: Reynolds, the son of Realtors, working his fingers into the word "blood," throwing up his set, miming the manual language of a Los Angeles street gang to which he could bear no coherent relation; see Nowak, who has a real if unloaded pistol tucked into the waist of his sagging jeans, respond with a rapid array of finger movements based on the signs of "Folks," which originated in the projects of Chicago, which may or may not have had a presence in Topeka, but certainly not among these white kids mainly bound for college who had no *volk* beyond their common privilege, Klaus's voice. "As Barack Obama eulogized the life and legacy of Nelson Mandela at a memorial service in Johannesburg yesterday, a man standing just a couple of feet away, who was supposed to be translating the speeches into sign language, was instead making a series of completely meaningless gestures with his hands." "As Hurricane Irma charged toward Florida, officials in a county on the state's west coast held a news conference to inform residents of mandatory evacuation orders. The interpreter wore a bright yellow shirt—a no-no for light-skinned signers, who typically wear dark clothing to help their hands stand out. Experts who reviewed the video said the interpreter gesticulated gibberish." "He heard voices and words, he saw movements, gestures and glances, but since he now saw everything through the eyes of an animal, he found nothing but a degenerate, dissembling mob" that had long since fought its last real war, history having ended at some point between 1989 and 1992.

They felt at once profoundly numb and profoundly ecstatic to be young and inflicting optional damage on each other; the heat was its own justification, but so was the cold—there was a second-order thrill in knowing you could kick someone in the chest without emotion. To have violent conflict without competing notions of the good, a kind of surplus. To have something to do on the weekends. Eventually they let the semiconscious Reynolds get dragged away by his friends, who were not badly beaten; they shouted something about retribution as they retreated.

Where were the parents? Most were sleeping. Some were watching *Friends* or *Frasier*, some were watching *SportsCenter*. Some were doing desk work or wiping down the kitchen islands. Some were reading Rice and some were reading Clancy, some were reading Adrienne Rich or "Non-Interpretive Mechanisms in Psychoanalytic Therapy." Or pretending to read. Some were coming back from date night in Kansas City or making perfunctory love or waiting for Internet pornography to load in an otherwise dark, carpeted basement office. Some were at a conference in Toledo. Some were on stationary bikes or the Bowflex or tinkering in the garage or cleaning guns. Some were trying email. Some were waiting for the beep of call waiting—for their kids to check in—while they spoke to others on the cordless. Some were worried and/or oblivious. Some were line-editing college applications or making rounds at St. Francis. Some were eating or opening a window or just walking dully along on a treadmill. Some were drinking gin and tonics in Taipei and some were writing this in Brooklyn while their daughters slept beside them and some were coming back on trains in dreams and some were at Rolling Hills in twilight states, mechanical beds.

♦♦♦

When he was a child he would call for his mom to recite the following poem at bedtime, a poem her own mother had taught her:

> I never saw a Purple Cow,
> I never hope to see one,
> But I can tell you, anyhow,
> I'd rather see than be one!

Then she would ask him to recite it in turn; he would always mess it up, at first because he actually had trouble committing the four small lines to memory, and then because she would mimic exasperation at his errors, which he found hilarious. Green plastic stars glowing on the ceiling. The smell of his freshly laundered Peanuts sheets. One more time, she'd say with mock gravity, and recite the poem with an air of formality; then he'd misquote it back to her, "I hope to never see one," so that the game could go on, postponing bedtime, a little Scheherazade.

It was nonsense, no such thing as purple cows, but it *made* sense: now in his mind he saw the cows to be avoided. (Try not to think of a purple cow.) Seeing was better than being the perverted thing but the poem implied they were related, that they had to be distinguished, could be confused. At a time when his personal canon of poetry consisted exclusively of taunts and weak spells to cast back at the taunters—sticks and stones, rubber and glue—"The Purple Cow" felt like another prophylactic speech act: this poem protects me from being what I see in my mind's eye. Among the phosphenes.

After his concussion the game continued for another year or so but now there was a dark energy underneath it or the ritual became about exorcising that energy; not being able to remember or commit something to memory was too evocative of cognitive damage or amnesia to be merely funny. His mother introduced the second poem:

Ah, yes, I wrote the "Purple Cow"—
I'm sorry, now, I wrote it!
But I can tell you anyhow,
I'll kill you if you quote it.

Now they were Batman sheets. George Brett was mid-swing in the Royals poster that adorned his wall. Why was this poem remarkable to him? First, there was the story, the prose around the poem, that his mother told, as her mother had told her: the author of both poems was a serious writer who had dashed off "The Purple Cow" while at work on ambitious poetic and scholarly projects. But the poem grew so famous that it overwhelmed all of his other work; the serious writer became identified totally with this nonsense poem, ruining his aspirations. (She never said the writer's name, as if even that had been swallowed by the black or purple hole of the verse.) At the age of eight, he located real sorrow and anger and violence in the second little poem; he was fascinated by the notion that a verbal object could circulate and become famous and destroy the man who made it, prompting a second poem, a spell against the paradoxical effects—as they say of medication—of the first. A poem is a mysterious pill. While the author hadn't become a purple cow, he'd become "The Purple Cow"; he'd achieved a bad exceptionality through language. Conjuring and seeing and being and the being seen (wrongly) of fame and killing and quoting and misquoting (to avoid sleep, to avoid being killed) and forgetting and misremembering at bedtime under plastic stars glowing softly.

"Once upon a time and a very good time it was there was a moocow coming down along the road and this moocow that was coming down along the road met a nicens little boy named baby tuckoo," he read for Mrs. Hackett's Senior Honors English. "His father told him that story: his father looked at him through a glass: he had a hairy face." In the opening of Joyce's *Portrait*, it was all there: the natal language of milk and men and naming and violence, in-groups and out ("—What is your name? Stephen had answered: Stephen Dedalus. Then Nasty Roche had said: —What kind of a name is that?"). Stephen's aunt Dante said he had to apologize or eagles would come pull out his eyes. Or were they crows, purple crows. Purple prose.

He wanted to be a poet because poems were spells, were shaped sound unmaking and remaking sense that inflicted and repelled violence and made you renowned, or renowned for being erased, and could have other effects on bodies: put them to sleep or wake them, cause tears or other forms of lubrication, swelling, the raising of small hairs. The fake-ass gangstas of Topeka were always threatening other fake-ass gangstas, accusing them of quoting, threatening to kill. Almost everybody—preschoolers, man-children, family therapists, analysts, biopsychologists, debate coaches—agreed language could have magical effects: just ask your muscles to relax. Even if he didn't want to be a poet, he always already was one, at least since he'd rubbed those weeds between his hands at Bright Circle. You're a poet and you don't even know it.

The problem for him in high school was that debate made you a nerd and poetry made you a pussy—even if both could help you get to the vaguely imagined East Coast city from which your experiences in Topeka would be recounted with great irony. The key was to narrate participation in debate as a form of linguistic combat; the key was to be a bully, quick and vicious and ready to spread an interlocutor with insults at the smallest provocation. Poetry could be excused if it upped your game, became cipher and flow, if it was part of why Amber was fucking you and not Reynolds et al. If linguistic prowess could do damage and get you laid, then it could be integrated into the adolescent social realm without entirely departing from the household values of intellect and expression. It was not a reconciliation, but a workable tension. His disastrous tonsorial compromise. The migraines.

Fortunately for Adam, this shifting of aggression to the domain of language was sanctioned by one of the practices the types had appropriated: after several hours of drinking, if no fight or noise complaint had broken up the party, you were likely to encounter freestyling. In many ways this was the most shameful of all the poses, the clearest manifestation of a crisis in white masculinity and its representational regimes, a small group of privileged crackers often arrhythmically recycling the genre's dominant and to them totally inapplicable clichés. But it was socially essential for him: the rap battle transmuted his prowess as a public speaker and aspiring poet into something cool. His luck was dizzying: that there was a rapid, ritualized poetic insult exchange bridging the gap between his Saturday afternoons in abandoned high schools and his Saturday nights in unsupervised houses, allowing him to transition from one contest to the other.

He was always practicing something like freestyling in his

head, although, when driving or showering or lying in bed at night, he might rehearse aloud. It was a typically silent and sometimes only semiconscious synthesis of the spread with poetry. An unheard melody. There were multiple tracks in his mind and he could conduct a conversation with, say, his grandmother using one track while on another he would be in an imaginary cipher, vocabulary from his actual conversation sometimes leaping into the virtual: *I'll be the poem you wish you never wrote / kill you with a quote / endless bills / from Rolling Hills* or whatever as they wait for the light to change on Twenty-First, Adam having picked up his grandmother, along with Jane, to take her shopping. I just need a few things. Yet to say he was "practicing" implies that he could choose to stop; in fact, while he was often barely aware of the rhyming, just as one might be unaware of a bodily tic, he did not feel that he could turn it off.

He and his mother and grandmother pulled into the vast parking lot of Hypermart, a big-box superstore, part of the Walton franchise, near West Ridge Mall; when it first opened, all of the stockers were on roller skates, which led to its association in Adam's mind with Starlite Skating Rink. It was the only place of business in Topeka open twenty-four hours a day. *Hypersmart / I make hyperart / while your mother mops at Hypermart* or whatever, while at the same time asking his grandmother, as they park in a handicap spot, how she came to marry his grandfather. When did you first meet? "In Brooklyn," she said in Topeka. "After I left high school to work as a typist to help bring in money for the family when my father fell ill, I would get home late to Avenue J; I always took the bus. And your grandfather would always be waiting there for me, asking if he could walk me home. This was in 1932," she said in 1997, "and we were worried about how we would survive." They'd entered the store and started to wander the vast and towering aisles of brightly lit, brightly packaged goods. "Finally he asked me to go to a dance. I was actually a very good dancer. But he wouldn't dance himself. And he wouldn't let anybody else dance with me." And then, as if this followed logically: "A few months later we were married." Adam and Jane laughed at this.

They had brought her here because it was located between her assisted-living home and their house and because it contained everything in the empire, but looking around he realized it was a ridiculous choice; his grandmother, a woman of Depression-era thrift who lived alone—although she kept careful track of what her increasingly vegetative husband needed—who made a discipline of consuming as little as possible, would find nothing small or sufficiently discrete to purchase here among the bulk. There were aisles of family-sized boxes of cereal: Cheerios, Cap'n Crunch; it might take her the rest of her life to finish one. She would, at least, note the lower unit prices as a result of the insane quantities, the overkill.

Jane asked his grandma what she needed and she said paper towels and the Comet cleanser she used to scrub the bathroom and a few other household supplies. They wandered at his grandmother's pace toward a pyramid composed of thirty-packs of toilet paper. They found a package of six rolls of paper towels, which Jane said they should buy: I'll keep four, Mom, you can take home two. Jane didn't need paper towels, but understood this was the only way her mother would assent to the purchase. But Rose was sure there was a generic, cheaper brand somewhere in the store, and they wandered on, Adam checking his pager when it vibrated—all the senior men had pagers—and saw Amber's code. To Jane, it must have made it seem like her son was playing doctor, pretending to be on call.

The paper towel issue was resolved but the bleach came only in four-packs and Jane couldn't pretend to need three containers of a cleaning product her mom knew she would never use. He recognized the strain of impatience entering his mother's voice as specific to her interactions with Rose, a kind of fast-acting exasperation that was not otherwise in keeping with his mom's personality. "You don't need this bleach in the first place; you pay—and we pay—for them to clean your apartment thoroughly. You shouldn't be breathing this stuff anyway. You shouldn't be hunched over the tub. We're not getting this. Come on, let's go."

"They never clean the tub properly. I've used bleach for fifty years and it's never done anybody any harm." Adam was silently reading the labels. *Dissolve you like soap scum / I'm the quicker picker upper when it comes to your mum / is the word*, and said: "We could stop by Dillon's on the way home where you can buy just one, Grandma," and shot his mom an empathic but gently chastising glance: "I know she's frustrating," it said, "but stay calm." He was at his most mature around his grandmother, and a help to his mother in her presence; generous, light, levelheaded. It was the context in which he most resembled his dad.

He left them for a moment so he could go in search of the creatine supplements he took to improve muscle recovery time. (Are there powders that hasten the recovery of memory? Klaus's voice.) He passed a worker using a small forklift to stack pallets of bottled water. Something was announced over the PA, and only after it resumed did he realize the Muzak had been playing all along. Since the beginning of time. He turned left and entered a vast aisle of protein mixes and tubs of vitamins and other products and experienced as he watched the packaging repeat into the distance a thrill not unlike what he'd felt in the wrong McMansion on Lake Sherwood—that banal but supernumerary sublime of exchangeability. To be a subject here was to be spread by objects. Later he'd recall certain aisles of Hypermart while looking at Donald Judd's boxes. Later he'd have a similar sensation looking at certain of Andreas Gursky's photographs.

He walked down the aisle until he found the most popular brand of the supplement and took down a ten-pound tub of the chocolate-flavored powder. Following no particular instructions, they would make a shake before lifting because it supposedly improved the intensity of their workouts and then they'd make a shake after lifting because it supposedly aided recovery and helped build muscle mass. Wikipedia says it was probably damaging their kidneys. He was retracing his steps now to rejoin his mom and grandma when on the edge of a forest of charcoal grills he encountered one of Reynolds's friends; perhaps the rival senior was also heading toward the supplements. Sagging jeans, Notre Dame football hoodie under letter jacket, baseball cap turned backward, a little bruising on the right cheek lingering from the fight. The adversary from West was accompanied by a woman who must have been his mother, white turtleneck under green Christmas sweater. They faced one another while the mother consulted a list, mumbling to herself.

Like any two men or man-children meeting in the playground or the marketplace they quickly, almost instantly, calculated who could take the other. They were approximately the same height and weight, but the letter jacket and association with Reynolds implied a wrestler's strength and training; you wouldn't want to end up on the ground, which means you'd need to risk the first punch, swing for the fences with a left hook, don't let grappling set in. They were as a matter of course imagining exploding each other's noses, breaking jaws or limbs in holds, choking each other out, running simulations that were mash-ups of *Street Fighter II: Championship Edition* and lived experience. Whenever he involuntarily made these calculations in his head, he also imagined one good punch or kick on the ground sending him back to St. Francis, collapsing his speech mechanisms, the beeping of the machines, the alphabet across Mrs. Eberheart's chest.

He knew, was relieved to know, the presence of the wrestler's mother would make a physical confrontation impossible; he also knew that the presence of the mother remained, even at this age, a structural embarrassment: Doing some shopping with your mommy? Adam decided to smile a smile that communicated this contempt, that also said: "You're lucky she's here or I'd fuck you up." Adam could quickly withdraw without a loss of face. I punked out one of those kids from West who I saw shopping with his mom.

"Adam"—his mother's voice—"tell your grandmother that prices have changed since 1945." To his horror his own family was upon him. Jews haggling over prices. A quick, preposterous desire to deny he knew them. The wrestler smiled a smile whose content was unclear, but it both frightened and enraged him. Was being in the presence of two generations of women worse than one? Was the wrestler aware of and mocking some form of difference?

Only seconds had passed since their initial shock of mutual recognition. Jane could tell that her son stood in some relation to the boy facing him from several feet away and so she said: "Hello, I'm Adam's mom, Jane." The wrestler's mother looked up from the list and smiled: "Oh, hello," although the speech had been addressed to her son. The senior men remained silent, smiles gone. "This is my mother, Rose." "Hello," the woman repeated. Adam's grandmother said hello. He imagined his mother launching into the story about how he wrapped his body in gum. This is my nicens little boy named baby tuckoo. He felt there was something effete about the way he was holding the creatine with both arms, cradling it, and he repositioned the tub.

Which of the seniors would speak and what would he say? "Mom, Grandma, I know this might come as a surprise, but this kid considers himself a member of an African American street gang from L.A. and my clique recently beat a friend of his unconscious because they threatened one of our inpatients; you know Darren." And then the wrestler's mother said to Jane: "Have we met before?" Jane said she wasn't sure, but Adam and Jane and Rose knew what was coming; they knew she wrote "The Purple Cow." "Oh, you're Dr. Gordon," the wrestler's mother said. "You were on *Oprah*!" Rose smiled, Jane nodded, Adam tried to calculate what this did to his status vis-à-vis the equally confused wrestler, who, to justify averting his gaze, consulted his pager; Adam wished he'd thought of that. Was it more, or less, emasculating to have a famous mom? "You must be very proud," the mother said, looking at Rose, who said she was.

For, since swallowing the magic pill, he understood the language of the products. (The film is in slow motion, but only to emphasize the speed, as if events would otherwise unfold at an incomprehensible rate.) From the Kingsford charcoal he fled to the Tostitos, from the Pop-Tarts he fled to the Slim Jims. They did not all insult him, but without exception they despised him. He listened to them and learned from the conversations what they thought of people in general. And what they thought was most distressing. Adam could sense that all of the materials inside the packaging—packaging as vividly colored as Roman statuary—had reverted to a kind of putty, a kind of gum, an abstract stuff out of which they'd have to make new languages, new bodies. And now the lights dim. The products withdraw into the walls, leaving only a giant expanse of rink. The only remaining source of illumination is a rotating mirrored ball throwing its ovals of light across the floor. Over the intercom Klaus's voice, unclear if it's live or a recording, instructs the mothers to line up on one side, the boys on the other. Human history, like the history of the individual, can be understood as a slow passage through conflicts of a sexual-aggressive nature. Now we hear the ominous *Scheherazade* by Rimsky-Korsakov. Now we see a procession of wheeled things: Darren on his Chicago skates, a grandfather in a wheelchair, a drink cart, a housekeeping cart, large plastic tubs of evidence that, if read quickly enough, reverts to stuff in the mouth: putty, poetry. And finally, an intern pushing the metal show box: see the cow, the purple of the hide barely perceptible, blood seeping from the small holes punched by a .22, ears tagged with plastic. Shitting itself, despite the tranquilizers, out of terror at being nearly real.

♦♦♦

He was good at debate, but he was great at extemporaneous speaking, the freestyle of nerds; indeed, he was arguably—and all over the country coaches and other competitors were arguing the point—the best extemporaneous speaker in the history of debate and forensics. ("Forensics" referred to competitive interscholastic speaking events other than debate, whereas "policy debate" denoted the evidence-heavy team debate in which the spread was dominant; all were governed by the National Forensics League. In Kansas, forensics started in the spring semester.) He'd placed second at the national championship his junior year in Fayetteville; he would have won the national tournament, which was held each June, but the panel of judges in the final round—two senators among them—penalized him for speaking too quickly. The general consensus: he was robbed. (So much adrenaline had coursed through his body during the final round that he could barely remember the speech in the first person; a video taken of the event had colonized his memory.) He was widely expected to win it all as a senior, an expectation under which he suffered; dreams of a sudden loss of fluency, of erupting into nervous laughter, of wetting his slacks before a live audience of thousands and whoever might be watching C-SPAN, which typically carried the finals live. He had no interest in becoming a nationally competitive policy debater; that would have required endless hours of research, filling those plastic tubs with evidence and briefs, summer "institutes." It would have meant, in his own mind, choosing the company of Joannas over Ambers, abandoning the fiction of his manliness.

As the name implied, extemp emphasized improvisation: a competitor draws three questions at random and chooses one, then has thirty minutes to prepare a five- to seven-minute speech delivered without notes. Topics might be frighteningly particular ("Will the Ukrainian parliament ratify the new constitution next month?") or frighteningly general ("What is the future of Mexico?"). Extempers had their own smaller plastic tubs of hanging folders specific to countries or issues that they'd stuffed with articles from magazines and newspapers, and they were supposed to cite sources in their speeches to substantiate their claims, but this was much lighter research than that required by policy debate: an extemper read several magazines a week, highlighted, photocopied. Extemp required less preparation, but it could be so nightmarish that even serious policy debaters respected it. They scoffed, meanwhile, at the other activities: original oratory, say, in which a student delivered a polished, memorized speech on any topic. See the sixteen-year-old in a "prep room" before a final round choosing among three questions of almost sadistic obscurity. (At local tournaments, the prep room was in the high school library, competitors wandering around mumbling to themselves like Foundation lunatics or Bluetooth users of the future as they tried to commit outlines to memory.) He goes with the question about water disputes in Djibouti because he at least knows what water is, but how will he project fluency and authority on a topic on which his tub is mute? Or imagine a speaker transitioning to her second major point in the third minute of a speech that's going well only to realize she's forgotten it; she has no notes, no way to call a time-out. Adam had seen novice extempers begin to stammer, fall silent, flee the room. He'd seen one vomit from sheer terror.

Extemp was officially about developing such a command of current affairs that one could speak confidently on a range of topics, but it was of course as much about the opposite: how a teenager in an ill-fitting suit could speak as if he had a handle on the crisis in Kashmir, how polish could compensate for substance as one determined the viability of a two-state solution. One learned to stud a speech with sources the way a politician reaches for statistics—to provide the affect of authority more than to illuminate an issue or settle a point of fact. Much of the coaching and practice focused on how to use one's body to lend a speech structure, when and where to step to mark transitions, when and how to gesture, opera without music. Unlike policy debate, in which the spread eclipsed all oratorical values, style and presentation remained primary in extemp, even if the goal was to project an image of erudition. One common defense of policy debaters' addiction to the spread was that students interested in the niceties of speech could go and do extemp.

Or they could do "L-D." In 1979 a representative of Phillips Petroleum, then the primary corporate sponsor of the National Forensics League, observed a round of policy debate at the national tournament and found it to be drivel. Phillips expressed its concerns about the direction policy debate was taking to the executive council of the National Forensics League. The result was the formation of a new, one-on-one debating activity, Lincoln-Douglas debate, which emphasized values, its format intended to prioritize oratorical persuasion. Speakers were expected to argue from a moral framework, not an empirical one. L-D—there were lots of jokes among policy debaters about the initials standing for "learning disabled"—featured resolutions that explicitly invoked justice and morality; e.g., "It is morally permissible to kill one innocent person to save the lives of more innocent people"; "In a democratic society, felons ought to retain the right to vote." The content of the resolutions was ultimately less important than the fact that the resolutions changed every couple of months, eliminating the tubs of evidence and encouraging competitors and judges to focus on delivery. Later Adam would perceive a fearful symmetry between the ideological compartmentalization of high school debate and what passed for the national political discourse: in the year of his birth—the year of the Iranian Revolution, the year before "the great communicator" thrashed Carter in a televised debate by dismissing points of fact ("There you go again") and focusing on framing—Phillips Petroleum helped formalize the sundering of values from policy in high school interscholastic debate. The parallel with the larger culture was imperfect, but undeniable: the supposedly disinterested policy wonks debate the intricacies of health care or financial regulation in a jargon designed to be inaccessible to the uninitiated while the more presidential speakers test out plainspoken value claims on civilians, a division underwritten by petrodollars.

By the time he was a sophomore, neither Spears nor Mulroney, Topeka High's two full-time coaches, had anything to teach Adam. For his senior year, they brought in Peter Evanson, a former national champion in extemp, the only national champion in the history of Topeka—who had graduated from Topeka High in 1990, attended Harvard. Evanson had recently left graduate school at Georgetown to return to Kansas and work on the campaign for the Senate seat Bob Dole had vacated during his presidential run. Many, including Adam, believed it was Evanson who was the greatest extemper of all time. A giant framed photograph of Evanson among his championship trophies hung on the classroom wall. He worked with no other student; he was Adam's private tutor, although Adam wasn't sure if he was paid; it was his job to make sure his protégé won the national championship in extemp that summer in Minneapolis. (The location of the tournament changed each year.) L-D was considered a less prestigious event, but maybe he'd take home a trophy in slow debate as well.

Like all Topeka High forensicators, he had seen the VHS of Evanson's championship speech. Freshmen watched it on the first day of class to see what greatness was possible; everybody watched it before the national qualifying tournament each spring. (Adam knew the speech by heart; his body could execute its gestures; he often misremembered giving it in the first person.) Evanson selected the most sweeping of the three questions he'd been dealt: "Does the fall of the Berlin Wall signal the global triumph of liberal democracy?" In the video, he walks deliberately toward the center of the stage after having his name and school and topic announced by an NFL official. Evanson has not yet put on weight, but his face has a boyish chubbiness. He stands stock-still in his black suit, red tie—his youth and pallor reminded Adam of Harold from *Harold and Maude*—until he receives from a timekeeper situated off-camera the signal to begin:

"You're most likely familiar with the character of one Wile E. Coyote and his nemesis, the Road Runner." His tone is crisp, slightly heightened; Evanson is a talented actor acting natural. He raises both arms, opens them out, a gesture that indicates confidence, welcome, that he has nothing to hide. "Again and again, Wile E. Coyote attempts to capture the swift if flightless bird"—such easily accessible but somewhat literary phrasing was a signature of Evanson's, would become one of Adam's—"often through absurdly complicated means. In a great many of these cartoons, after a mad pursuit of the Road Runner, Wile. E. ends up running off a cliff. Instead of immediately falling, however, Wile E. is suspended in midair, briefly oblivious to his predicament." What teenager spoke this way, let alone about a cartoon? "It is only when the coyote looks down and realizes his position"—Evanson slowly lifts a hand into the air—"that he plummets." The hand drops dramatically. "Ladies and gentlemen"—a pause in which tension gathers—"on November ninth of last year, state socialism looked down."

Throughout the audience of approximately two thousand competitors, coaches, alumnae, and spectators, applause begins, spreads, grows deafening. There is some cheering. Evanson devotes exactly five seconds of his speech to waiting it out, no doubt counting the seconds in his head, then resumes as if he's hardly noticed the interruption: "Now the question we must ask ourselves today is: Does the fall of the Berlin Wall signal the global triumph of liberal democracy?

"I contend"—swapping out the most obvious word (think, believe) for a slightly rarefied term will have an impressive cumulative effect—"the answer to this question is a resounding yes, for the following three reasons." Evanson has sped up a little; he's catching his flow. "First, because the fall of the Berlin Wall signals the collapse of the Warsaw Pact. Second, because the Soviet Union is in the process of dissolution. And third, because liberal democracy, combined with American-style capitalism, is the only viable political framework for an increasingly globalized world." Evanson will take a graceful few steps between each point, spatializing his areas of analysis. He will distribute his time among his points equally (two minutes each; he will never glance at the timekeeper; the pacing has long since grown intuitive). The coyote and roadrunner will return at intervals, stitching the speech together; how the elaborate but useless contraptions of the coyote resemble centralized economic planning, for instance. He will cite a startling number of periodicals from around the world. The array of proper names—not just Gorbachev but Honecker and Havel and Ceauşescu and Jaruzelski—is a kind of poetry. Evanson speaks familiarly of the Balcerowicz Plan, Lithuania's proclamation of sovereignty. It's not that the audience really learns anything about these people or events; it's about how naturally these foreign signifiers roll off the teenager's tongue. At no point in his six-minute-and-fifty-nine-second speech does he stutter or otherwise misspeak. You will find him, as he concludes, in the exact place on the stage where he began, a circuit that amplifies the sense of coherence and of closure. The audience is less following an argument than watching a tightrope walk, and when Evanson reaches the end of his flawless presentation there is an audible collective release of breath in the auditorium before the thunderous ovation.

Starting in January of his senior year, as Clinton was sworn in for a second term, as the man-made lakes froze over, Adam would meet with Evanson both during the academic period devoted to forensics and for one or two hours immediately following the conclusion of most school days. (Then he would drive to Popeye's Gym to lift weights before heading home for dinner with his parents.) After the building had largely emptied, Coach Mulroney would find and unlock a vacant classroom, radiator sputtering by the window, and leave them, as she put it, "to fight it out." Adam would give practice speeches that Evanson would interrupt with tactical advice about gesture ("Actually count the points on your fingers; hold your hand shoulder-high") or language ("You said 'in conclusion' at the end of your first point; this time say 'in fine'") or even appearance ("Push your glasses up so you don't seem to be looking over them and down at a judge"). Evanson taught him, trained him, to carry in his body the small ligatures of phrasing and transition and emphasis that separated a good speech from a great one. Adam found it much more difficult to give strong speeches in his normal attire—sagging jeans, hooded sweatshirts, a uniform more appropriate for freestyling or lifting—than in his suit; these sessions were as physically exhausting as his routine at Popeye's; the tension in his shoulders was extreme.

They'd focus on extemp, but they'd also undertake mock L-D debates, arguing over the moral permissibility of torture when it prevents a mass attack, for instance, or whether it is the purpose of government to redistribute wealth, directing their comments to a hypothetical judge in an empty desk chair, the bass of passing systems occasionally rattling the windows. They were less practicing here than battling, Evanson displaying his unsurpassed capacity to move between relative sophistication (a brisk refutation, say, of the political philosophy of John Rawls) and the plainspoken rhetoric of individual liberty, personal responsibility, etc.—Republican talking points. Adam simply had no experience of being tripped up in his own reasoning by someone capable of making finer and faster distinctions and quicker strategic swerves between language games. It was maddening and thrilling; he was the dumb but cooler type outwitted by the super-eloquent nerd.

But what was Evanson, exactly? He always wore khaki Dockers and a yellow, gray, or brown Polo; his face remained boyish, smooth, but the intermittent double chin foretokened middle age;

the standard haircut, too, could be read as either juvenile or professional, although his dark red hair had started to thin on top. Evanson sometimes appeared to him as an accomplished elder—the Harvard pedigree—and then suddenly he struck Adam as a species of man-child, a twenty-five-year-old coaching forensics at his former high school because he couldn't cut it "back East." As if he were always on camera, being judged, Evanson held very still unless he was executing a purposeful gesture; sometimes this seemed like discipline to Adam; at other times, it betrayed a kind of anxiety, as though all of Evanson's movements were part of a choreographed, memorized routine without which he'd be lost. One moment Evanson struck him as a precocious young man destined for the corridors of power—a conservative judge, a senator, the president of the NRA—and at other times Evanson seemed fated to drive sleeping debaters, sleeping drivelers, home from Junction City, plash of insects on the windshield of the district-issue van, glow of a single pair of ruby taillights in the distance.

Eventually they wouldn't be practicing L-D at all, following its format of speech and rebuttal, they'd just be arguing their own positions, feet on the desks, darkness falling—arguing about abortion, affirmative action, the Second Amendment, and other "hot-button issues." Adam was used to demolishing versions of the argument that abortion was murder—he'd been practicing since his mother, in the late eighties, had told an interviewer for *The Topeka Capital-Journal* that she'd had one in the sixties, prompting a dramatic spike in calls from the Men—but somehow when debating Evanson he found himself lost in a thicket of distinctions regarding fetal viability while also trying to defend the notion of "penumbra" in constitutional law. Evanson could spread him while speaking at conversational speed.

Evanson was also a master of what would come to be called "trolling." When Adam advocated the moral imperative of redistributing wealth to fund a welfare state, Evanson declared it, with a violent smile, a surprising argument for a Jew. When Adam grew furious, the wide-eyed Evanson clarified that he meant only that it surprised him that someone with such knowledge of the evils of tyrannical government would want the state to have the power to seize individual assets. ("Are you seriously suggesting I would make an anti-Semitic comment?" The sudden widening of the eyes, the animal mimicry of innocence, was one of Evanson's signature moves.) But what Evanson really "meant," Adam felt, was precisely to manipulate his emotions and show him to be a paranoid Jew. Evanson was gifted at committing the plausibly deniable outrage, then taking tactical umbrage, claiming the high ground. Adam was rarely if ever swayed by a position, certainly his mind changed little about key questions of value, but he was with every passing hour absorbing an interpersonal style it would take him decades fully to unlearn, the verbal equivalent of forearms and elbows.

What took the sting out of Evanson's superiority as a debater was Adam's misplaced certainty that Evanson, even if he always had the right words, was on the wrong side of the history that ended with Dole. Everybody hated the Phelpses, there'd been a lesbian wedding on *Friends*, Susan discussed her abortion, however ambivalently, on *Beverly Hills 90210*—maybe state socialism had looked down, but weren't American "conservatives" also doomed? The baby boomers were more liberal than their parents, and Adam's generation, however schizophrenic, was said to be more liberal still. He'd heard more than one person claim that all those "white kids wanting to be black" was evidence that the old racial fault lines were passing away. Eminem would soon be the bestselling rapper of all time ("In one 15-second segment alone, 'Slim Shady' spits 97 words, or 6.46 words per second"). The electorate, Adam had read in *The Economist*, would grow increasingly diverse and the Republicans would die off as a national party even if something remained the matter with Kansas;

Evanson might have a career writing reactionary speeches, or become another Rush Limbaugh talking into the air, addressing truckers on NoDoz, but meanwhile there would be a black and/or female president; Adam wanted to believe it was the end of the age of angry white men proclaiming the end of civilization. His mom was always saying Oprah could get elected, how she made such a diverse group of people feel heard, how she worked, like a good therapist, to overcome polarization without shaming.

Weird to look through the window of the classroom door with the detachment of an anthropologist or ghost or psychologist making hospital rounds and see these two men, if that's what they are, arguing in an otherwise empty room in a largely empty school eight years after history ended, snow flurries visible around the streetlights beyond the window. One, dark jeans sagging, is sipping a mysterious liquid; the other, khakis riding high, is explaining the slippery slope of so-called commonsense gun legislation a few years before Columbine. One of them will go on, when history resumes, to be a key architect of the most right-wing governorship Kansas has ever known, overseeing radical cuts to social services and education, ending all funding for the arts, privatizing Medicaid, implementing one of the most disastrous tax cuts in America's history, an important model for the Trump administration. And one will attempt this genealogy of his speech, its theaters and extremes.

♦♦♦

Adam had visited him once at St. Francis, where Klaus kept pretending to be at the Foundation, making jokes about being admitted against his will, addressing Adam as "Dr. Gordon"—"You've got to get me out of here, Doctor"—but within the space of a week Klaus was at home, in hospice, sleeping more or less continuously in a morphine haze. "What a pointless organ, the pancreas." And yet, when his parents left him to say goodbye at Klaus's bed, when he announced his presence a few times loudly, Klaus smiled faintly, raised his eyebrows, although he did not open his eyes. How amusing to be playing the part of a dying man in this amateur film, his eyebrows implied. Whether in Berlin or Topeka, Adam knew it was a triumph to die in your bed in a room that did not smell exclusively of urine and bleach, to die untethered to machines, although there was an IV on a wheeled stand, pale blue drip. He could hear the hospice nurse talking to his parents in the living room, although he couldn't make out the words.

He looked the room over so as not to stare at Klaus, whose consciousness had quickly retreated from his face. He looked for a clock so he could know when he'd been there long enough to leave without guilt, but there was no clock, although one of the three framed photo-collages hanging on the wall featured a watch face, the hands replaced with mustaches, maybe the Kaiser's. In the collage, it was 3:50, the perpetual end of a clinical hour. In the far corner of the large room there was a small writing desk; on the wall above it, a postcard of the Duccio *Madonna and Child* affixed with a single silver tack (on the other side of the card: a message from Jonathan written in a shaky hand). Atop a large dresser, among pill bottles: small photographs of family in oval frames—photographs so old that even from a distance Adam could see or sense that particular kind of innocence expressed by subjects in the early days of the medium; they wore a veil of ignorance; they couldn't quite imagine how their image would survive them, circulate, how they might end up in Topeka in 1997, snow falling beyond the window.

He imagined that instead of sitting on a wooden dining room chair brought into the bedroom for visitors he was on the glass cube in the clock tower basement and that he could, if he concentrated, alter the electromagnetic field around Klaus's body. Maybe if he really willed it, he could help Klaus die. He shut his eyes to try this the way a child might—a kind of serious game, you just rub the plant between your palms—but instead of influencing Klaus, Klaus began to speak through the channel Adam had opened with his mind. (Little webs of light floated across the black screen of his lids.) He had to tune out some noise—Tupac and Evanson and grainy piano recordings—to make out what Klaus was saying.

We know from Freud that the identification with the father is always of a precarious nature, and even in the "genuine" cases, where it seems to be well established, it may break down under the impact of a situation which substitutes the paternal superego by collectivized authority of the fascist brand. Adam heard a snowplow make contact with the asphalt on the street, pictured the salt it would scatter in its wake. Imagined the salt as rice, then cremains. *Chickens are capable of a large repertoire of different visual displays and at least twenty-four distinct vocalizations; their communication skills are on par with many primates.* He could hear the whistle of a Union Pacific train passing in the distance; the tracks were a mile or two away, along the Kansas River; Adam felt the sound was distinctly louder in the winter. *In fine, when the child had been lowered into the grave, and the earth was spread over him, all at once his little arm came out again and reached upward. And when they had pushed it back in the ground and spread fresh earth over it, it was all to no purpose, for the arm always came out again. This is the obstinacy of history.* Klaus said all of this in German, which Adam had been briefly given to understand.

Adam opened his eyes when Klaus surfaced to make an audible sound, smacked his lips. His mouth looked uncomfortably dry. Klaus tried to speak, maybe to ask for water. Adam looked at the bedside table and saw there a little plastic cup of water and a few blue foam swab sticks. He considered getting the nurse, using that as an excuse to leave, but then he found himself reaching for the cup. He dipped one of the sticks in the water, hesitated, then rubbed it across Klaus's faintly purple lips. His hand inadvertently touched the sandpaper of Klaus's sunken cheeks. Like a fish rising to a hook, Klaus tried to take the swab into his mouth and Adam let him; Klaus sucked out the water. Only now did Adam realize Klaus didn't have any teeth, that his dentures had been removed, maybe at this point thrown away. He repeated the action several times until Klaus seemed satisfied and relaxed into his pillow.

A series of outrageous images flashed before him: fucking Amber in the room while Klaus was there, unconscious; pulling the sheets and covers back to look frankly on Klaus's body; suffocating the sleeping man with a pillow; kissing him fully on the lips; Klaus's body riding shotgun in the Camry, propped up to appear alive. He imagined that Klaus was a recalcitrant analysand on the couch and that he must wait patiently for him to resume his symptomatic speech. Then he remembered Klaus visiting him in the hospital—Adam in the mechanical bed—after his concussion, a memory he hadn't called to mind in many years. It had a strange texture, the memory, because it was one of the first that he'd formed after his period of amnesia. A failure of continuity: he remembered climbing into his bed at home, then he remembered waking in a hospital bed, receiving guests, his parents in a kind of mania of relief. Everything he suffered in that interval was lost, at least to the first person; he possessed images formed from the stories he'd been told. The memory—Klaus was the last visitor that day—was burned in places, black at the left edge.

What he recalled clearly about the visit was what Klaus had brought him: a little box of blond wood, about the size of a box of kitchen matches. It had a floral pattern carved into it, silver hinges. Adam opened the box to see what the gift might be, then was embarrassed to realize, when he found it empty, that the box itself was the gift. Klaus had probably grabbed whatever knickknack was at hand on the way out of the house, Adam thought. (Now, sitting beside Klaus, he wondered why visitors were bringing gifts in the first place, offerings to his injury.) Klaus detected his mild disappointment and took the empty box from his hands. And then, impossibly, Klaus removed a silver dollar from it and handed the coin to Adam. For an instant, Adam felt dizzy—he wasn't, in his post-concussive state, capable of separating a sleight of hand from a breakdown in cognition. But then Klaus quickly revealed the secret, showed him how the apparent bottom of the box could be tilted to reveal another compartment; a box with an unconscious, his mom had joked as she looked on. Did he think of the movable partition behind the dairy case, the men in the walls? He loved the box, thought what he might hide there: candy, valuable baseball cards, one of his throwing stars might fit. (Adam tried to recall where the box was now; he thought it might be on his parents' dresser.) The box was very old, Klaus had told him at the time; only now did it occur to Adam to wonder what Klaus might have concealed there after 1933. One of those old photographs. Elke's jewelry. Baby teeth. A magic pill.

A branch of the Scottish pine near the bedroom window cracked under the weight of accumulated snow, returning him to the present in which Klaus was breathing shallowly. Adam shifted on the glass block and shut his eyes again and this time listened to Klaus in English: *Once upon a time, a small star full of water collided with a larger star, scattering ice across the vast expanse of space, creating the solar system. Satellites of ice still orbit the planets. Moons made of ice collided with the earth in prehistoric times, determining its geography. When a meteor filled with "divine sperma" struck our planet's surface, the human race was formed, the beginning of created things. Ice is the primordial element of the universe, more basic than fire, with which it is at war. All of this was revealed to Hanns Hörbiger—whom my uncle once met in Vienna—in a dream. When the Nazis came to power, they sought an authentically German worldview that could supplant physics, which was tainted by Jews and their notions of relativity. Hörbiger's theory, which already had a popular following, offered Himmler and Hitler a way to cleanse their Weltanschauung of Jewish science. The World Ice Theory was taught in schools, incorporated into textbooks. Germans believed or pretended to believe it en masse. It explained everything, whereas physics opened an abyss of non-belief. Events that occur at one time for one observer might occur at another time for another observer? That sounded like Freud's theory of trauma, not the basis of a strong cosmology. Today the question we must ask ourselves is: Should the United States support the reduction of greenhouse gases at the upcoming environmental summit in Kyoto?*

I contend the answer to this question is a resounding yes for the following three reasons. First, since the "global ether" is composed of very fine ice crystals, atmospheric warming could cause the moon to fall to the earth, destroying modern civilization, just as, according to Hörbiger, a previous moon destroyed Atlantis. Second, we must recognize that the concept of global warming was created by and for the Chinese in order to make U.S. manufacturing noncompetitive. You're contradicting yourself, Evanson said in Adam's head, even though Evanson would become a major ally of the Kansas-based Koch Industries, one of the world's great funders of climate change denial. *There is no principle of noncontradiction, no law of excluded middle, governing the unconscious,* Klaus responded. *And third, because the spruces rough in the distant glitter. Because of the "ice" in "voice." Echoing in the woods, weighing down the branch. According to a recent issue of* The Economist, *the brief sun flames on it. My love is like to it, and I to fire. Brief son. Experts agree that the Yukon is choked with ice. The Japurá is a pack of ice. The Loing is choked with fragments of ice. The Dnieper is still ice-bound. Indeed, grains of it are found in the molecular clouds where stars are forming, although global warming is a total, and very expensive, hoax! Like the moon landing or the Holocaust. Like Columbine and Sandy Hook and Parkland and Russian interference. When the first snow falls in Topeka, in Berlin, in Brooklyn, giving the out-of-doors the feel of a vast interior, you must have a mind of winter, must turn your head to the flakes accumulating on the sill*—Adam did as he was told, saw a sparrow hopping between small branches—*and return to your childhood's primal scene.*

Frost had hardened the grass and because his muscles had stiffened in the cold he imagined half-awake that he was caught in a web he had to sit up fast to break away from. It was early dawn. He was probably twenty yards from the no longer smoldering fire and he was alone. He smelled his own smell of woodsmoke, beer, and vomit. That part of him inclined to panic about how he would get home was checked by that part of him engaged in calculating if he'd been abandoned by his friends or if they'd first made an earnest search for him. He thought of the TV phrase: and left for dead. But he told himself they would have tried and when they couldn't find him assumed he'd found another ride. Maybe in their own drunkenness they forgot who had come with whom. He stood, joints cracking, and pissed onto the darker grass his body had protected from the frost. Best night of his life.

Where was his Royals hat? For years he had imagined surviving in the semi-wild, had places like the bushes to hide in, shortcuts through unfenced backyards mapped out in his mind; he'd memorized that dandelion, burdock, and fireweed were edible, but he could only identify the first of these. Although he slept on freshly laundered Star Wars *sheets and ate the meals his mom prepared for him and produced nothing himself that he consumed or used, Darren felt that he was trained or at least had been in training for a coming emergency that would establish the relevance of a skill set difficult to specify. If he had often claimed to be a black belt (ninth degree) in some composite martial art, could walk silently across rooftops, if he had been known to say that he was being recruited secretly for Special Forces, can't really talk about it, if he had "left" the Boy Scouts rather than reveal his own techniques for starting fires, purifying water, spearing and cleaning fish, etc., it was because imaginary disciplines were strategies, weak spells, for redescribing his exclusion as a manly way of living off the grid. Desert camo does not in Kansas disappear into the foliage but indicates a semiconscious wish to blend in with the soldiery of an empire whose enemies are so vague they're everywhere. Didn't Stan, a veteran of what he called the last real war, say that you could hardly ever see them?*

His parents, teachers, doctors, peers always demanded that he confess to lying, account for himself, but a spell is valued not by its truth but by its power, and what distinguished Darren from the types was not that his identity was a lie—so too was the dominant type he envied, white gangstas, many of them the sons of surgeons, lawyers, shrinks, cruising through Topeka bumping Tupac on their systems, their modes of dress and address, their ways of abusing substances and one another, modeled, however imperfectly, on rap videos—but that it had no purchase on his social world. If Darren, after patting his pocket to confirm the presence of the Buck 55 he always carried, did not think to start a fire, or break his fast on nontoxic autumnal berries, or derive the cardinal directions from the sun, it wasn't only because he was unable; it was also because the previous night's experience, however confused, made his survivalist mythology incidental as a strategy, however ineffectual, for surviving socially. Darren found himself in the closest thing to wilderness he had known, waking cold and hungry miles and miles from home, just as he perceived, for the first time since puberty, the glimmer of community.

He followed tire tracks in the grass to the dirt service road and walked along it until he reached a wider gravel one. A pickup passed him while he tried to figure out if or how to hail it. He could taste a little of the dust it kicked up, heightening his thirst. Trusting his instinct, which was wrong, he turned right and walked on the shoulder for half a mile before the road concluded in a trail. He retraced his steps past where he'd first met the gravel and headed south, trees on his left and open fields to his right, here and there a copse along a creek bed, a farmhouse in the distance, he wouldn't call there. It felt good to be walking, the fall of his awesome boots startling pheasants into flight, the pains diminishing, although that made more room for hunger; he'd last eaten three crustless peanut butter sandwiches at lunch the previous day. Soon he reached a three-way intersection and again had to guess where to turn and again guessed incorrectly; he realized his error fifteen minutes later when from atop an incline in the road the lake opened out before him, sparkling in what was now full daylight.

He reversed course, imagining Davis and Nowak laughing, we left the faggot there, but shook his head a little and the laughter became starlings calling in the roadside trees. Around the time he regained the intersection of his last wrong turn he thought of his mom. When she came home from her night shift at St. Francis Hospital and found his bed empty Darren was sure that she would think that he was dead. He involuntarily laughed aloud at this, but didn't find it funny, and wished he had some way to call her, and spoke into the air the number they'd drilled into him as a child: 601-2226. Again and again he repeated the number as he walked, a kind of marching song, until he reached East 250. Here stood several small grain elevators and an office and while the parking lot was empty Darren crossed the street and tried to peer in through the blinded window. A sign on the door said OTTAWA CO-OP*, a meaningless phrase, and Darren decided to keep walking on E 250, which he did for the next hour. He passed at one point a white cross hammered into the shoulder, bouquet of plastic flowers, and he thought, this is where my dad died, although he knew it wasn't, this is where Nowak flipped last night after they left me, asphalt slicked with oil.*

A few trucks passed him and one he thought had slowed as if to stop and inquire after him but did not, why would it. He met no fellow travelers although there were houses at long intervals between the fenced fields and Darren saw movement behind one window and thought how he could if he had to knock on someone's door, although he couldn't think what he would say. If he saw a street sign, he read it aloud, NO PASSING ZONE. *Chicken hawks eyed him from atop the telephone poles. When to the side of the road he perceived a dry creek bed he went down to it and hunted for fossils and arrowheads among the rocks, proving to himself that he was not afraid or lost, he was exploring. He pocketed what might have been a small crinoid stem and resumed his journey. He imagined that he'd entered* The Legend of Zelda *and tried to see himself from above as in its game play, moving across the overworld that links all levels, his life meter represented as a line of hearts. This was a landscape full of hidden keys, magic swords, boomerangs that could kill or paralyze Darren's enemies, except it wasn't.*

By the time E 250 met N 1600 he had been walking for a little more than two hours, thirst supplanting hunger, soreness more from the awkwardness of his sleeping posture than from the journey, but he felt blisters forming. Several cars passed on N 1600 and there was an abandoned brick building to his left, a newer stucco church to his right, and this was progress; he was closing distance between the country and the city. But when Darren read the black magnetic letters on the yard sign—STULL UNITED METHODIST CHURCH—little mimic spasms appeared around his mouth.

Every adolescent in northeast Kansas knew that Stull was one of the seven gates of hell, that somewhere in the town's cemetery were steps descending directly to the underworld, that in the old stone church, which had no ceiling, rain would never fall, even in a storm, that if you held glass bottles in the shape of a cross, then hurled them at the church's wall, they wouldn't shatter; Satanists still gathered here to perform their rituals, including human sacrifice. The legends drew tourists, kids who had been dared, annoyed local property owners and police, were the subject of campfire stories, death metal songs, and album cover art, and while Darren had spent much of middle school dressed in black, embossing pentagrams onto his Trapper Keeper, threatening his enemies with left-hand magic, he was not a devil worshipper. He didn't worship; what he feared since Bright Circle Montessori was that against his will he had been called, and now a sinister plot revealed itself, that the best night of his life had been a smoke screen, part of a plan to draw him here, if only to remind him that he both possessed and was possessed by powers he could not, if he were pushed, control.

He wanted to turn left, avoid passing the old church and cemetery he could see from where he stood, stone ruin and a row or two of headstones, but he intuited that Topeka was to his right, and so he ran in that direction on the shoulder of N 1600 until he was beyond the grounds, then stopped, hands on his knees, to catch his breath. Now he felt the creep of fatigue and doubt, could pick up derision in the remembered voices from last night, imagined the explanations they would demand of him—his mother, Dr. J, even Stan. Thus disheartened he resumed his walk, estimating that he must have at least two hours left before he reached Topeka, when in fact it would require six hours at his normal pace.

The almost imperceptible drift of cirrus clouds over Darren as he continues along the shoulder through the centuries, then the grass beside the road where it is level. In the wake of a passing car, the quiet intensifies, distant birdsong becoming audible. There are houses, the intervals between them diminishing, but also fields of brown wheat, green soy, vast prospects, until multiflora hedges obscure the view for a while. (He passes no inn or public house, no one throws him a penny from a hay cart that he might stop for bread or beer.) He makes eye contact with a lone cow near a barbed-wire fence, its ears tagged with blue plastic, the rest of the cattle clustered in the distance, some kneeling. Why, when he's gone another hour, is there a single tree exploding with purple flowers? In his mind he knocks on a door, asks for water, to use the phone, I'll call my mom collect, but he can taste the humiliation, although he can't quite visualize its form. Get off my property, Darren has often been told. But he is cramping now, mainly from thirst, and when he sees that a storage shed not far from the road has visible on its side a yellow spigot for a hose he is crouched down beside it before he can complete his assessment of the risks, drinking in the delicious water, gasping, drinking more. Refreshed, he runs back to the road, the wind stinging where his face is wet, Stull receding the way a dream does, maybe he'd always known that it was close to Clinton Lake, why the shock, her fingers through his hair.

It is a comfort to Darren that the scenery is looped, although the simulation plays at different speeds; he's passed that yellow house three times already, the huge American flag, knows that each time the road rises to a certain point a silver water tower will be visible on his left, its position constant, like the moon, that the clouds scroll steadily across the screen, their shapes recurring, as are the downward-sloping whistles of the birds, rudimentary electronic music, and here again is the exploding tree, Darren, Darren, Darren. It reminds him of when they'd drive to visit his uncle in Colorado, how he'd drift in and out of consciousness in the back seat, his parents playing Randy Travis cassettes, "Just waitin' on the light to change," Darren waking every sixty miles or so to see the same strip of restaurants, gas stations, and hotels, the sense that whenever they pulled off the highway they were in the town they had just left, although now everything is dictated by his gait, he can slow down or speed up what he thinks of as the tape.

This is how the hours pass or fail to, by being one hour, until long grasses give way to the lawns of tract housing, a different kind of repetition, and soon there are small groups of children regarding him from multicolored plastic jungle gyms or trampolines before the road widens out again into newer pavement, a four-lane avenue flanked by giant warehouse retailers and car dealerships with inflated balloon men seizing in the wind. What he longs for now is a McDonald's, hot water, the familiar contours of the molded seating, and while probability decrees that one is near him, he does not see the golden arches, and keeps walking, believing his surroundings, which are familiar as all prefabricated construction must be, will soon coalesce into an area of Topeka from which he knows his way.

He passes apartment complexes and office parks. A pair of joggers cross to avoid him. To travel by bike after early adolescence is ignominious enough in Kansas; to walk unless you are exercising purposefully in appropriate dress or moving to or from your car is to confess some kind of deviance; how many times have men rolled down a window to remind Darren he's a faggot? He almost stops at Arby's, but decides he will not rest until he's home, not at the Sonic or the Burger King or the Wendy's or the Walgreens or the Kwik Shop or the Dillon's, the sequence of which seems off to Darren, as if Topeka's syntax had been scrambled while the terms remained the same.

He begins to limp, his right ankle tingling, perhaps he turned it somewhere in the past, his fantasy now that Topeka has changed during his walk into a slightly different version of itself, one from which he's been subtracted. His house will still be here but on another street, his mom will be in his house but will not know him, the Phelpses will still be protesting but on a different corner with different signs. Something I can help you with, Stan would say, suspiciously, if he managed to find the Surplus, his bushes in the wrong park, his rations vanished, the conversations with Dr. J wiped from memory, the clown in the painting transformed into an angel. It is like the whole town has passed through the banner or he has, which also means his dad might be alive or living dead here, and the vertigo he thought he'd left in Stull is back, or he is back in Stull, the steps descending. Could you call collect from one Topeka to the other?

There should be a word for the relief he feels as the architecture around him grows particular enough to be unfamiliar and not uncanny in the way of chains, his relief at being lost, but in this world, not one like it, restored to time. A rightness of fit. He has arrived at a strip of interconnected masonry buildings, a main street. He reads the signs: FREE STATE BREWERY, LIBERTY HALL, SUNFLOWER OUTDOOR SHOP, THE PARADISE CAFE, businesses with but one location. Darren is at this point almost dragging his right foot and swelling ankle through what he has slowly come to recognize as downtown Lawrence, having been here often as a child, especially after the KU football games to which his dad would sometimes take him, the roar when one of our running backs breaks away, cheerleaders assembling into pyramids, followed by pizza and Ms. Pac-Man on Mass Street, the street he is limping down, searching for a pay phone, as many miles from home as when he rose from the ground six hours ago. Parents draw their kids near as he passes.

THE NEW YORK SCHOOL

(JONATHAN)

We were circling JFK, waiting for permission to land; the congestion was due to weather; we were at the tail end of a storm, suspended in turbulent air. We passed in and out of clouds. City lights visible below, then we were enveloped in dark gray. Then the lights again. Strange to spot other planes circling in the near distance; it felt like seeing our own plane from the outside, like I might catch a glimpse of myself in an illuminated oval window, first person and third. We sped up then slowed down, increased then decreased altitude, maybe in search of smoother air. Every five or ten minutes, the captain: Sorry, folks; we hope to be on the ground shortly. The announcements were so similar to one another they became a single announcement, which only made time pass more slowly, or kept it from passing. The flight attendants had long since come through the aisles for remaining garbage, told us to put up our tray tables, return our seat backs to their upright position, then taken their own seats in preparation for the landing that never arrived. I had the fantasy they'd somehow quit the plane, along with the pilot and copilot, that it was just us passengers being addressed by a recording. Eventually we'd run out of fuel, crash into Queens. The cabin was dim; some people were, miraculously, sleeping—including the slight woman beside me beneath the blue airline blanket, similar to a hospital blanket, Foundation-issue; she was snoring with her mouth open, the snore of a much larger woman, which made the sound seem dubbed. Others were reading newspapers or big hardcover thrillers—but how could they read?—under their overhead lights. Maybe they were only pretending to read. (I often suspected that people were only going through the motions of reading, or mimicking its stillness; did I pretend to read as a child, maybe as a way of escaping something—my father's anger? Walking through the library in graduate school, I'd think to myself: Not a single one of you people, if I shut your book, would be able to tell me what you've just read. Shadow-reading. And when I myself was reading, I was acutely aware of other people watching me, of how I performed absorption, which of course distracted me from the page.)

The plane bounced hard—bang of luggage in the overhead compartments; a few people gasped—then steadied. I was gripping both of the metal armrests. Normally I was indifferent to choppy air, was surprised at my discomfort, but I was almost never alone on a plane, was always with Jane and Adam, both of whom hated flying, were frightened of turbulence. Maybe I was only relaxed when I was with someone who wasn't, when I knew it would be useful for me to be calm, calming? Alone now, circling the city among the sleepers and fake readers, abandoned by the crew, unmoored by the absence of someone who needed me, I felt what I can only describe as homesick. We regress in the air. I wanted my mother, mom, mommy.

The first time I flew into New York, she sat between me and my brother to keep us from bothering one another; I was sixteen, the future revolutionary was fourteen. We were dressed up; everyone put on their best clothes to fly in those days. Like going to temple or church, touching the face of God; now you see whole families in sweat suits, pajamas, carrying those neck pillows; a form of regression. The deafening propellers. Cabin full of cigarette smoke, ashtrays in every armrest. I remember the in-flight meals were elaborate: the silverware real, a little fresh flower on the tray. Maybe we were flying business class, if they had that back then. We were returning to the States after two years in Taiwan, where my father was a low-level diplomat in the Foreign Service. I don't remember why he flew home separately, what excuse he gave.

In the fifties, even a low-level diplomat in Taipei lived like a king: cook, servants, driver. We lived in a big American-style bungalow in a neighborhood of nearly identical houses, all occupied by foreigners—Americans mainly, a few Brits. Freshly cut lawns sparkling with poison. One day I'm in Chevy Chase, shooting BBs at squirrels in our side yard, practicing kissing with Jackie Captain, who lived a few doors down, learning to drive in the Packard sedan (my dad would coach me slowly around department store parking lots, rare shared laughter), and the next day I'm being driven through the bustling streets of Taipei in a shiny black Imperial, scattering rickshaws and street vendors and goats and chickens—driven to the Taipei International School by Chang, who spared no one the horn, who referred to me, a lanky, pimply kid, as "Mr. Sir." ("When you have looked at a shiny, new automobile, have you ever stopped to think that, through all the countless thousands of generations that preceded this century, not even the most powerful kings on earth could have owned one like it? Nor could they have flown in an airplane.") No Chinese people at the American School, except for custodians, maybe a secretary or two; Chinese wasn't even offered as a language, only French and Latin; the students were mainly the kids of officers. My instant crush on Donna Selkie, the curve where her shoulder became her breast. My allowance, a rubber-banded wad of the weak, multicolored currency, a small fortune for the locals. How the servant Lin would silently appear in our vast, white-carpeted living room proffering a silver tray of gin and tonics for the adults, lemonades for the kids. Red jade sculptures of rearing horses flanked the fireplace; on the walls, a hanging scroll of a mountain scene, one of a bird on a branch, a red berry in its mouth, but also some incongruous Impressionist knockoffs we'd had shipped, and my mom's Chagall print. We had a pool in the back; there's Lin and his silver tray again, little wooden bowls of candied nuts beside the drinks. My mom in a one-piece dark blue bathing suit and cat-eye sunglasses turning the pages of a fashion magazine on the chaise longue. (On one occasion, a glimpse of pubic hair around the edge of her suit, a wave of rage that she'd "made" me see that.) Why did she never go in the water? You'd wake up in the morning and brush your teeth, and by the time you got back to your room your bed was made. At any point during the multi-course dinners of duck and red snapper and braised pork one of us brats could raise a hand and demand a hamburger. You could have an ice-cream sundae every night, a kind of lazy Susan of toppings would materialize: slivered almonds, whipped cream, sprinkles. Lin would put the cherry on personally.

We hope to have you on the ground soon, folks. I think my dad's job was largely arranging visits for more important versions of himself; it fell to him to make sure that Mr. X had everything he needed, the right room at the Grand Hotel, one with a balcony, the most reliable driver, the one with good English, that Mrs. X, when she had the inevitable stomach complaint, was taken to the right clinic, that the couple posed together for the right photos: here we are in front of Longshan Temple, here we are on Dalong Street, at the Confucius Temple (which looks ancient, but was rebuilt in 1939; Such a fine line, Klaus's voice, between memorialization and erasure). We thought the vagueness of his job was evidence of my dad's importance; maybe, my brother and I whispered, he was CIA? Certainly some of the other people around were CIA, must have been, including Jim Selkie, who spoke fluent Chinese—a dead giveaway. Jim was almost never around, always traveling for nebulous professional purposes. (Poor Paul Conway, some kind of business consultant, who impressed everybody with his determination to learn the language; he locked himself away to study Chinese from books;

when he emerged a couple of months later, he was talking up a storm—but in Cantonese instead of Mandarin; whoops. People just smiled at him politely. His pronunciation would have been unintelligible regardless.)

The silver trays, the beverage carts, like the one on the plane, only nicer: happy hour was at five o'clock, except on weekends, when it was earlier. People were always dropping over, or we were dropping in, sitting beside a pool identical to ours, turquoise water in tiki light. Somebody's "man" coming out with fresh ice, limes, another bottle of tonic or seltzer. Emptying and replacing ashtrays. Would music be playing? "Unchained Melody"? There were cigarettes and highball or martini glasses in every adult hand. I'm not sure we kids thought of the grown-ups as smashed, but we were aware of their distance, its hysterical edge. Like those Peanuts cartoons where the adult voices are just some kind of "wah-wah" noise, probably a trumpet or trombone; speech was addressed to us every once in a while, but we experienced it as meaningless shaped sound. My brother, maybe on my dare, cannonballing into a neighbor's pool fully clothed, making a splash that soaked the hosts; it produced only uproarious laughter among the tipsy adults, including my dad, who would have whipped him with a belt in Maryland for that kind of spectacle. Donna Selkie, dark blond hair in a tight chignon, sitting one evening beside my mom; Donna had been given a half-real drink, a thimbleful of gin mixed with soda; what are her plans for college, some diplomat asks, making an effort not to slur, leaning in to hear her better, a hand landing on her thigh. My dad coming around the corner of the house one night arm-in-arm with somebody's wife, "I think you'll want to see the wisteria," then stopping to admire her necklace, lifting the little pendant from her collarbone—to discover me in the bushes smoking one of Lin's cigarettes, which he'd only reluctantly surrendered. My dad just took it from my mouth, said he'd finish it, ordered me back to the house; I would have been grounded for a month in the States.

We were representatives of the most powerful country on earth, the power was in our every cell, look at how the "natives" bowed, their gratitude for our supposedly civilizing force, the future was ours. But we were also Jewish, one of two Jewish families in our neighborhood, our complex, our compound, and the ovens had been active only fifteen years before. Later I'd map the distant losses in a genogram. And we were less than a thousand miles from Hiroshima, even closer to Nagasaki. (Circling JFK I imagined our plane had a bomb bay, that we were waiting for the right moment to let our payload fall.) I never heard mention of the camps or of the bombs—not in the American houses, not in Taipei International School. The collective effort of repression was tremendous, made the alcohol indispensable. An intense but contentless optimism about the future was the only protection against the recent past, in which all the regimes of value had collapsed, irradiated or gassed. Public repression, private repression: What I knew and also didn't know was that my mom was sick; the official story was that she had been ill in the States, but was better now, that the years abroad would be a welcome rest; but we kids knew she wasn't cured, although nobody ever—not even near the very end—said the word "cancer" in our presence. Those two years my mother usually looked fine, but her weight fluctuated, her smile was too unchanging—too much of a mask, like a parent hiding how frightened she was of turbulence.

This is your captain speaking. James Toomey, son of a rear admiral, captain of the Taipei International Tigers basketball team, which only played other international schools on the island, was always followed around by this kid Robert Russell. Russell was a dim, crew-cut giant, a Lenny to Toomey's George. Except Toomey was always egging Russell on, daring him to eat a leech or grab a girl's breasts or put a laxative in a teacher's mug of coffee. One day, on a hill near the school, Toomey handed Russell his .22-caliber rifle and instructed the man-child to shoot almost every scrawny cow in a local farmer's herd. I saw some of it before I fled, tears in my eyes, wimp that I was; a pop, more the report of a cap gun than a weapon, and then a cow would take a knee, lie down, eerily calm, while Toomey kept barking instructions at Russell like a commanding officer. (Each dying cow spoke with his eyes, "two big brown eyes. His silent gaze expressed dignity, resignation, sadness, and with regard to the visitor"—the American—"a lofty and solemn contempt.")

The farmer, whose life, or at least livelihood, was destroyed, showed up, to everyone's amazement, at the International School the next day, screaming, crying; I was told that what he demanded was not compensation, or that Russell be punished, but that someone apologize, face him and apologize. I don't remember what happened beyond the fact that kids made fun of the farmer in mock-Chinese, Jerry Lewis gibberish, mimicked how he crossed his arms and refused to budge until the police dragged him away. (Half of what came out of American adolescent mouths was that racist travesty of speech.) Maybe somebody peeled a few multicolored bills off a wad and told him to get lost; maybe they gave him nothing; maybe they gave him a beating. Boys will be boys, my father said. Boys will be boys, Confucius says. (There were endless Confucius jokes: Brush your teeth, Confucius says, etc.) On the other hand: an archaic regression. I remember a standoff between a couple of local teenagers and a few Tigers, maybe Toomey's friends; somebody stole somebody's bike, or was anyway accused; the details are lost. When Russell and another Tiger started whaling on one of the Taiwanese guys, the latter just took it, ducking here and there, but never hitting back. And his friends stood there, smoking those local Banana cigarettes; not just passive, but impassive. Nobody was going to hit a white kid. Was there really a school play in yellow-face?

We could go wherever we wanted, but we could never penetrate the image our power projected, so in a sense we went nowhere; so much of what I saw was through the glass of the

Imperial window, which Chang of course kept spotless. Even when we roamed those streets we'd been told to avoid, people made way for us, didn't want trouble. We didn't even exist in an economy; we'd either be charged five hundred percent over market for dumplings or they'd be given to us for free. America was one vast institution; it had no outside. With every passing week, the adults got further away from us. I became best friends—friendships had that summer-camp feel, a quick and desperate intimacy—with Frank Selkie, who was much more adventurous than me, who even spoke a little of the language, who did help me get around a bit. That I was obsessed with his sister was a bonus: sneaking into the bathroom at night when I slept over to bury my face in her towel, inhale the smell of her Prell, the dampness transferred from her body; I'd masturbate as quietly as possible, coming into the sink; I'd always be careful to flush the toilet in case someone was listening.

Soon the Selkies were the family closest to us in Taipei; they'd drop by without calling ahead, without it meaning we were "entertaining"; nobody had to change for dinner. Soon I wasn't even hiding my cigarettes. Was it Eleanor Selkie my dad was with when he caught me smoking Lin's? Eleanor was my mom's closest friend. Three afternoons a week, they offered free typing classes to young Taiwanese women. They'd shop together and do whatever else diplomats' wives did—I remember they took a class on bamboo weaving, our living room filling up with baskets. Lin always made sure they held fresh fruit. I can see the persimmons on the long rosewood coffee table, the table my father later gave me and Rachel.

Frank was full of energy; he'd convince a Taiwanese lorry driver to let us hitch to Hsinchu or another nearby city and we'd have cuttlefish soup and beer in a night market, then hitch back; unless I'm misremembering, you could flag almost anybody down. Once we skipped school and went out with some shrimpers off Qianshui Bay; the seas were a little rough—"moderate chop," not much worse than the air over JFK—and I spent an hour puking over the side of the boat while the professionals smoked and watched me with that mixture of boredom and fascination I associate with zoo-goers.

Then there was Beitou—Frank and I thought about, we talked about, Beitou incessantly. The dancing girls of Beitou. Or Peitou. It was either another city or just another district of Taipei. The hot springs were famous, you could say they were your destination, but everybody knew that some of the bathhouses were brothels where you could pay for a "water frolic." Frank claimed he'd already lost his virginity to one of the "fallen women," a lie so obvious I didn't bother to dispute it. With more dread than excitement, I felt that I would ultimately have to visit, that there was no way I could avoid it, that I owed it to myself to return to the States a man, that this was the only conceivable way. Frank and I went at least twice to the district for what we decided, after we'd chickened out, was reconnaissance. We were both somber about the whole thing, almost grim, like we were gearing up to fight a battle or submitting ourselves to surgery.

The actual event, which took place at the end of my first school year, was hazy even at the time, thanks to a bottle of Kinmen—grain alcohol, like solvent on the tongue. The room was wood-paneled, the bed very low to the floor. A smell of incense. The thin girl, around my age, had long hair in a style intended to be Western, long bangs, and she lay down on her back, wearing a bra and panties, both very white. Or was she wrapped in a towel? I stood there, frozen. Eventually she got up and came to me, gave me head for a few seconds, dizzying, and then embarked on a hand job, very matter-of-factly. I remember looking down at her; I stared at the part in her hair, the whiteness of her scalp. I worried I was too drunk. Then all of a sudden I realized that was *me* calling out as something like pleasure tore through my body; I shut my eyes to better picture Donna. There was a sink where she went to wash her hands and face.

Then she went back to the bed and lit a cigarette and smoked it while I said who knows what nonsense in a wave of relief and guilt. I talked and talked. Then Frank and I were running through the streets—it was raining or had been; we kept slipping on wet stone—ecstatic at our triumph. I described in detail how "mine" had screamed out in pleasure while we fucked.

The guilt was a surprise, the intensity of it, the impulse to confess—to confess to my mother specifically, who I thought could absolve me. All these memories of approaching her, almost saying where I'd been, if not exactly what I'd done. Walking up to the large green lounge chair where she sat reading or pretending to read. Standing in the threshold of her bedroom door while she hunched over her writing desk, addressing postcards to Bethesda. There was the dream where the girl from Beitou or Peitou rang the bell in the middle of a dinner party, small gift-wrapped box in her extended hand. Lin admitted her, silence fell. What was in it? A wedding ring? Semen? Somehow the guilt was caught up for me in what I knew, at least semiconsciously, was happening with my dad and Eleanor. I had committed a kind of sexual wrong, was becoming a man, while the man of the house, in the way of men, was betraying my mom, who was sick, who we were making sick. There was the dream wherein Frank and I returned to the bathhouse only to find, when we were admitted, that it was my parents' house in Chevy Chase, my mom there to greet us, asking if we'd like a root beer while we waited. Meanwhile, I *wanted* Donna to know, thought it would make me experienced, mature, mysterious in her eyes. I was increasingly obsessed with her, but darkly, because she was Eleanor's daughter; adolescent desire was getting caught up in a network of crisscrossing relations whose overdetermination charged almost every exchange. And my mom and dad were fighting now, we'd overhear it from upstairs, raised voices, a tumbler shattering in the unused fireplace. I wonder where my dad and Eleanor met up for their trysts. A hotel? The embassy? Whatever Donna knew—about bathhouses, about our parents—she did become interested in me, or suffered me, whether she pined for Toomey types or no. Making out on the observation platform at Bamboo Lake. Struggling with her bra in the movie theater's artificial dark during some dubbed matinee. Maybe *Creature from the Black Lagoon.* I slipped a finger into her in the backseat of the Imperial one night when it was parked in the garage. Donna Selkie, who, two years after my mom died, would become my stepsister when Eleanor finally left Jim for my dad. They were married at City Hall, Frank the only witness. The next year I met Jane.

♦♦♦

One of the planes circling JFK was waiting to land in 1961, the first time I'd approached the city from the air, my crew-cut head against the oval window, the pane vibrating from the propeller; the Soviets had just detonated Tsar Bomba, largest man-made explosion ever; all the clouds looked like mushroom clouds to me. And one of the circling planes was waiting its turn in the winter of 1991, the last time I'd flown into the city, in-flight smoking only recently banned, Jane and Adam on either side of me, Sima and her family two rows behind, aerial bombing of Iraq in its twentieth day. A note of Sima's perfume, if it was perfume, somehow detectable even in the foul, canned air of the plane: sandalwood, rain. A little floating signature of another world. Watching her walk past our seats to the lavatory through a patch of rough air, how the turbulence didn't affect the smoothness of her gait. Her arms, instead of being occupied by the effort to balance, reach behind her neck, confirm the presence of the pendant, adjust it a little. It was an ancient coin, Greek maybe, a drachma set in gold, but she typically hid the pendant in the back, just below the nape, so it looked like she was wearing only a thin chain. When she was talking she might reach back for it, bring it around; if she was talking about something intense, intimate, she might, unthinkingly, obeying a childlike impulse, bring it to her mouth, bite it gently, as if assaying the metals. Maybe that only happened once or twice; maybe I'd looped the image in my head.

The change took place soon after Jane's book was published, on the Foundation campus. I walked by Sima—I'd just finished a meeting with Dr. Tom—without noticing her there, smoking on a bench across from the clock tower, and she said my name. She said it quietly, as though giving me permission to pretend not to hear. And I knew, instantly, that I shouldn't turn around; a feeling low in the stomach, half anxiety, half arousal; a soft voice in my head saying: "Don't." Don't what? She was my wife's best friend; our families were together most weekends; we'd chatted a million times before. She was incontrovertibly gorgeous but there was no particular charge; we weren't compatible; she was an elegant analyst writing about Wilfred Bion; I was a specialist in lost boys.

There wasn't a charge until there was; I sat down and we made small talk, but now the few inches between us were all static; my imagination, no, my awareness of her thigh beneath the white silk of her slacks; I could barely look at her; I stared at the clock, the trees, every leaf more sharply delineated than it had been a few minutes before. The content of that conversation—it probably lasted twenty minutes—is lost, but it was the first time I noticed her reach back for the pendant, move it forward. It marked a difference, signaled a shift. And that was the start of it, our meetings, our walks around the grounds. Private, but in plain sight.

Early on, Eric was a topic, probably because that was safe and unsafe at once; an acknowledgment of our delimited relation and a challenge to it. "Did I ever tell you about the first time we met, how his girlfriend, who knew me a little from a class we'd taken together and in which we'd often disagreed, a class on psychoanalysis and literature, drunk at a grad student party, her teeth stained with red wine, kept insisting that I was making eyes at him (a beautiful phrase, already anachronistic at the time); in fact I'd barely noticed him, certainly I had no sexual interest. But his girlfriend was so drunk and so insistent that he came up to me, after she'd left in a huff with friends, to apologize; that's how everything started." What was the moral of that story, the point of that prehistory? That her connection to Eric was tenuous, founded on misrecognition? That all desire in some Lacanian sense involves misidentification? That people project their own fears and desires onto Sima? It was not like me to ruminate, to get caught up in analytic spirals, but an hour with Sima would fund seventy-two hours of obsessive thinking. One night, late, when Jane called Eric with a medical question about Adam, I realized how my consciousness was on the wrong end of the line: I was with my wife and child, but my mind was picturing Sima half-awake beside Eric: fall of her hair across her pillow, slight part of her lips, curve where her shoulder met her breast.

My role was to listen. She listened to everyone else, but she talked to me; that was supposedly my gift, to make people feel heard, but this was more complicated, involved transference, transgression: she was talking to Klaus through me, maybe desiring him through me, a body her age. I could feel it. And she was telling me what she felt she couldn't tell Jane, and, by inviting me into intimacy, punishing Jane for that feeling. Once their "consulting" positioned Sima as the therapist, Jane as the patient, it became impossible for Sima to share, as she had in the past, her own emotional experience with Jane. Sima resented that, no matter if it was in part her doing. Those conversations about Jane's dad stirred up Sima's own troubled relationship with her father; Jane was the person who, in the past, Sima would have confided in about those very feelings. It might have been okay, they might have eventually reset, if Jane hadn't become famous. But when the book took off, Sima felt like she'd been sacrificed: she'd disappeared into the role of therapist to help Jane heal, and meanwhile Jane was getting the kind of fame her own father might have finally cared about. She was jealous, Sima said, of how Jane had me—someone who listened, who knew how to hold feeling, whereas for Eric, everything was dopamine or serotonin. You just needed to get the chemical balance right, find the magic pill. That's why Sima's dad had approved of Eric ("Eric is the only decision I made that my father supported, one of the few he seemed to notice"); that's part of why their marriage was increasingly distant.

I saw these dynamics, thought seeing them protected me somehow, which is the stupid mistake psychologists make, a very Foundation mistake; we thought that if we had a language for our feelings we might transcend them. More often we fed them. I could explain our mutual cathexis in relation to Jane's success. I could explain my sudden and severe investment in Sima as a repetition of my father's behavior. And I had to acknowledge and admonish myself regarding how, if I betrayed Jane, my betrayal of Rachel would form part of a pattern more than indicate a single course correction. Maybe I was a man who sought substitute mothers, then left them like my father. (We would visit them, my dad and Eleanor in Maine, and I would never mention my own mom, couldn't bring myself to say her name, as if her name were cancer.) Soon Sima and I were processing the overdetermination of our relation over lunch, then meeting later the same afternoon to process the lunch on a walk. Hiding it all by not hiding it. Jane was often traveling for the book. I would drop hints—both voluntarily and involuntarily—to Jane about the new intimacy with Sima and then be furious when she didn't seem concerned (a fury I hid). Then I was furious when she did seem concerned: Are you seriously suggesting that I, etc. Soon Sima was stopping by my office when she knew I was free. Our first shut door. For all the world, we were consulting. Then one day she's standing looking out the window, talking about a film she'd seen, that she wanted to see with me, lifts the pendant to her lips. And maybe that's the day I'll stand and start to walk to her. I'll close the venetian blinds. I'll press against her from behind. I'll take the pendant from her hand, her mouth, and rotate it around and then pull on it a little, thin chain applying pressure. To avoid the risk of it breaking, she'll bend her head back, at which point I'll kiss her, run my tongue over her teeth.

But the phone rings, the phone rang, and it was gone, instantly, everything between Sima and me. I spent most of the time he was unconscious praying for forgiveness in a plastic-upholstered hospital chair: If somebody in the family has to die, let it be me; If Adam is okay, I promise I will never be distracted from my wife and child again; I will never, not for an instant, begrudge Jane her success. I will not become one of the Men, won't let him become one; just let him be okay and I'll behave. Asking forgiveness not from God, but from my mom. And when Sima visited the hospital the next day after the long nightmare and she and Jane embraced, I was amazed by how thoroughly eradicated it was, the energy between us. She and Jane had been knocked back into the right position, were best friends again. Eric was reassuring us; we were grateful for his cool, competence, confidence. We were a mutually supportive quartet, focused on our kids. Adam—who was just starting to remember who everyone was—gave me a stick of chewing gum from the pack of baseball cards that Jason had brought him as a gift. I accepted the gum like a Communion wafer, some sign of absolution, new resolve.

After that we were never alone together, stopped all our talks. Desire and guilt about desire would come back to me, but only in flashes, not as obsession. And then the charge was there again. An involuntary alteration in the electromagnetic field surrounding the body. Maybe it had to do with another fall: Klaus, our substitute father, who made Sima a version of Donna, tumbling down the stairs. A broken hip, a very slight concussion. Maybe it had to do with how I was reaching out to relatives on my mom's side of the family, many of them in Russia, trying to reconnect with that part of my history, which stirred stuff up. Maybe it had to do with a million things, including just a brute and basic appetite that interpretation obscures as much as it clarifies. The *x*-year itch. A midlife crisis. But in 1991, when she returned to her seat in rough air and smiled her perfect smile as she passed us, I felt a wave of terror and desire. A distant note of jasmine in her wake.

Well, folks, from the flight deck, because nothing could happen on a family trip, something did. It was the day after Adam had sent Jason to the emergency room. It was the day of the evening Jane and I were going out to dinner, as Eric and Sima had gone out to dinner the night before. I brought—probably Jane's idea—some things from the pharmacy to their hotel: a soothing rinse the nurses had recommended, an ice pack. Jane must have called to tell them I was coming, confirmed they were around. Sima answered the phone when I had the front desk call, and told me to come up. When the door opened, I found she was alone. With Sima it was impossible to tell when she was dressed to go out; she was always "put together," a phrase my mom used of women she admired; she was wearing earrings, gold crescents, that quietly quoted the pattern on her skirt. That's not the kind of thing I'd notice, but she heightened my sensitivity. She was put together, always poised, but beneath it, a river of reckless energy. Or maybe I—like everybody else who became fixated on her—was just projecting my own destabilizing desire. The poise and elegance made her seem more grown-up than the rest of us, like we were only playing at being adults, but the sexual undercurrent threatened all our staid routine; she seemed older and younger than me at once.

She didn't say anything about where her family was. She neither invited me in nor suggested I leave. We didn't shut the door. It was a way of denying it was happening as it happened. There was an abandoned housekeeping cart, like an airline drink cart, like Lin's, near us in the carpeted hall. Someone would appear at any moment and we'd need to disentangle instantly; so that limited it. And limitation enabled it. Hedging coexisted with a feeling of total abandon. Like we were in our bodies and floating over them. I was aware of the plastic bag from the pharmacy where I'd dropped it on the floor, a dim awareness tethering me to reality as my tongue was across her teeth, in her ear, lifting salt off her neck. Did she know Eric and Jason were far away? Or did she want to be discovered, bringing the whole overdetermined structure down on top of us? In 1961, in 1991, I had my fingers inside her, no pubic hair along the edge of the silk. The heat shocked me. It was its own justification. The desire was so intense, it was referred, as they speak of pain being referred: she was grabbing me through my jeans, but the pleasure, although "pleasure" is the wrong word, was distributed over my body, a receptivity I've always associated, rightly or wrongly, with women. Maybe I felt like a woman, like Jane, like she and Jane were making contact through me. Like the sound that indicates the captain has illuminated the seat belt sign, the ding of the elevator arriving down the hall. We separated and she walked into the room, into the bathroom. I followed her immediately in my head; we'd fuck in the shower, on the black-and-white tiles. But I didn't move. Then I picked up the plastic bag, put it on the bed, and left.

Jane and Adam were in our hotel room; Adam was watching a football game, Jane was pretending to read. I greeted them and told Jane I was going to shower, get ready for our date. I got into the shower and jacked off. Then I sat down in the tub, like I did when I was hungover or sick, waiting to cry. Instead, uncontrollable laughter came up out of me, as in an anxiety dream: I was masturbating like a teenager while my soon-to-be teenager was in the other room. I'd made it to third base. I couldn't wait to tell Frank Selkie, who'd died in 1988. I couldn't wait to tell the men's group. But it was going to be tough to tell my mom or Eleanor or Rachel, although I *wanted* Donna to know.

Jane and I went to the Met. The odor and taste of Sima was in my sinuses, would not be dislodged. I was aware my speech was manic; I kept telling myself to slow down or shut up. I found myself describing to Jane the only existing film of my mom. Kodachrome, 1960. She was on horseback, or maybe it was a pony. It was at some kind of festival or carnival outside of Taipei. I remembered shooting this film very clearly, I explained to Jane. It was the first time I ever held a camera. I remembered it as the origin of my interest in the medium. But just a few months before, I told her, I'd found the reels in the attic and brought them to the Foundation to watch. It was just as I recalled, except in washed-out color, not in black-and-white; silent, of course. She was smiling, a little off balance, wind blowing her hair into her face, the bored pony or small horse being led around by a long purple ribbon. I remembered the weight of the camera in my hand, trying to hold it steady; I remembered calling out to her as I filmed, to get her to look my way. She did, she waved. But suddenly a teenager appears in the shot, seems to say something to my mom. And as I watched him walk out of the frame I realized he was me.

♦♦♦

We were cleared to land in 1999, the woman beside me still snoring in her sleep, her seat still reclining despite the injunction to return it to its upright position, Adam, twenty years old, collapsing or on the verge of collapse below us in New York, which is a logarithm of other cities, other times. At first I was reluctant to pick him up, to bring him home; I worried we'd be sending the wrong message, failing to honor his competence, making him feel like he couldn't make it through the semester, or that Jane and I doubted that he could, but finally we were just too concerned—terrified is more like it—about how severely he was crashing to care what signal we were sending; we wanted him in our sight.

He'd never gotten his footing in New York; even before his breakup, his breakdown, there was something a little manic in his voice. Natalia had gone to Barcelona for the semester and he'd decided that, in lieu of also going abroad for part of his junior year, he'd spend the fall at Columbia—he had friends there and wanted to study with the poets, maybe find a way to meet some of his literary heroes; he was probably also scared to leave his language. He and Natalia would remain a couple, and as soon as the semester was finished, he'd meet her in Spain, travel around a little, mark the new millennium in the Old World, fireworks on the Nova Icària or something, then they'd both return to Providence.

He underestimated how much going to New York for a semester would be—without Natalia as a stabilizing force—like leaving home all over again. They'd gotten involved so early in his freshman year at Brown; she was his substitute family. He'd had no real experience of the city, which is overwhelming, especially if you grew up in Topeka. The bipolarity of the place: glittering plenitude one instant, an abyss the next. Its lofty and solemn contempt. And their relationship had been messy in familiar undergraduate ways; he was coming home during breaks (the more expensive the school, the longer the breaks), getting entangled with old girlfriends; Natalia was waiting for him to grow up. Then she went to Spain and didn't want to wait any longer; she fell in love with a Spaniard, a musician of some sort, an underground rap star or an aspiring one, moved from her host family into his apartment. I imagined spliffs on a little iron balcony overlooking a narrow street. The stiffness of sheets dried on clotheslines strung across internal courtyards. That drink they drink: Coca-Cola mixed with red wine.

She kept not telling him about the guy, maybe hoping he'd get interested in somebody in New York, break up with *her*, maybe thinking, at least at first, that she'd just drop the Spaniard as the semester drew to a close and real life reasserted itself. But a few weeks before the end of the term, before the end of the millennium, before he was supposed to fly to Barcelona, she sent him an email: Don't come to Spain; I've been dishonest; I'm in love with a man I'm living with; I will always care about you, but it's best if we don't speak again; I'm not coming home.

When he first called us from a pay phone on Broadway—minutes after he'd received her email, which he'd read in the lobby of the Columbia gym, where they had a couple of computers—he was in shock. Can you believe this shit? he kept asking; he clearly couldn't. (That it was the most familiar story in the world, an undergrad relationship foundering on a romance abroad, was neither here nor there; nothing is a cliché when you're living it.) Jane and I were both on the phone—she was in her office and I was in the kitchen—and we were repeating how sorry we were. I asked him what he was going to do for the rest of the day and he said: I have to track her down, reason with her. (That he didn't have a way to reach her, that he only had the host family's number, didn't seem to occur to him.) And later that night, he explained, he was supposed to attend a big poetry reading at the 92nd Street Y; his professor, a poet named Stoke, or maybe Coke, was going to read, and so was John Ashbery, Adam's hero. There was some chance he might get invited to the dinner after; this was the kind of thing he'd dreamed about when he'd opted for New York. We told him to call us later, to hang in there, that we were in his corner, and we hung up, at which point I went upstairs to Jane's office to process the news he was taking surprisingly well.

By the time I got to her office—less than half a minute later—the phone was ringing again. Jane picked up, said hello, and then, audible even from where I was standing in the doorway: sobbing. What am I going to do, I love her, I need her, I hate her, fuck her, etc. I stood there as Jane did all the right things: listened, didn't minimize, but made reassuring statements about his strength, his support network. Then I walked back downstairs to the phone in the kitchen and rejoined the call. Had I ever heard him so upset? I pictured him losing his shit on Broadway in his gym clothes, oblivious to the cold, although my image of the street was from my past New Yorks. Snow flurries from 1969. A copy of *Sportsmanlike Driving* in a nearby pile of discarded books.

Eventually he quieted down, which is not to say he grew calm. I asked him if he was still going to attend the reading at the Y and he said he doubted it, doubted that he could compose himself; I said I thought that it might be a good idea, even if he was just going through the motions, that sticking to his schedule, trying to let himself be distracted, might be helpful. We knew one of his Columbia friends, Dan, who had stayed with us for a night when he'd driven across the country the previous summer—and we asked Adam to please get in touch with him, have Dan accompany him to the reading. We also asked that he stay away from any substances, drugs or alcohol, when he'd experienced such a shock; he said he would. Eventually he said he had to go—no doubt he was going to start calling Barcelona, however futile the calls—and we told him we'd be home all night, that he could call at any point, but we certainly wanted to hear from him before he went to bed.

We were worried, but not *that* worried; we knew that healing might be a long process, but we—or at least I—thought he would bounce back pretty quickly; after all, he'd only really decided to commit to Natalia right when she was leaving; he'd clearly been ambivalent about being in a long-term relationship at the age of twenty. Around the age I lost my mom, married Rachel. But when he called a few hours later we didn't like how confused and fragmented his speech had become.

From the fragments, a montage formed in my mind. He leaves Morningside Heights for the reading, forgetting his winter coat in his room, walks across the park at dusk with Dan. There are seats near the front reserved for the students in his poetry class, so he and Dan sit quite close to the stage. The place is packed. His professor, Coke, is slated to read first; Ashbery will introduce him; then Coke will introduce Ashbery. Before the reading, Adam had changed his clothes, washed his face, stanched his tears; while he feels sick to his stomach, as he has since getting the email, he can, however briefly, and from a distance, access a little of the excitement of his circumstance—the chance to hear and maybe meet the great man.

The house lights, the cabin lights, dim, signaling the beginning of the event, the initial descent. And in the dark, the anticipatory quiet, Adam starts to lose it again: panic symptoms indistinguishable from migraine symptoms; his right hand goes numb, his tongue feels like it belongs to someone else, he thinks he might throw up. He must reach Natalia. He tries a little biofeedback, to warm his hands, to no avail. Ashbery is at the podium now, saying good evening, introducing the program. Adam has to get out of there, fight or flight. He rises, loud creak of his chair, has to move through a thicket of legs, more noise when people shift to let him pass. He has to walk right by the stage. And that's when Ashbery pauses, makes a harmless joke ("That bad, eh? Wait till you hear our poems"), and everybody in the auditorium laughs. At my son. Laughter at his failure to set out; laughter at how his soul mate is on the back of a moped in Barcelona at that moment, clinging to her man, the real man she is fucking, a magic pill flooding her brain with serotonin as they weave through El Barrio Gótico; laughter at the idea that he could ever make it in New York, whatever that means for a poet, be a cool or sophisticated writer, leave the protection of his mother, mom, mommy.

The cold air feels good in his lungs, wind stinging where his face is wet with tears. Without waiting for Dan, he walks back toward Columbia—stopping en route to call Spain from a pay phone on Madison, even though these calls succeed only in waking the increasingly angry host mother; the first couple of times he called, he asked for Natalia in broken Spanish; now he's just hanging up. It's six hours ahead in Barcelona; it might as well be sixty years; it's a world from which he's been subtracted. (See him cursing, crying, beating the metal bank with the black plastic receiver.) Whatever conversation he overhears on the streets, even music from passing cars, seems a joke at his expense. On any other night, he would be, although he wouldn't admit it, scared to walk through Central Park in the dark, even though it was probably much safer than driving around Topeka with its armed lost boys, but now he's indifferent to whatever might befall him; if somebody were to stab or shoot him, it would be a relief; not only would it stop this agony, but it would also punish Natalia, who would never forgive herself, who would realize the horrible mistake that she had made. The very trees conspire against him, wind in the leaves the prolongation of the laughter from the Y, but he meets no fellow traveler. He passes no inn or public house, no one throws him a penny from a hay cart that he might stop for bread or beer. It starts to rain, then it's alternating rain and sleet.

He called us when he got back to the dorm, to his room on the ninth floor. Bare walls, books and clothes strewn on the floor. After he told us about the reading, he was alternating rage and sorrow. "I'm going to go to Spain as planned, bringing her home, I'm not afraid of this guy," etc. Then: "Mom, I love her so much. I can't handle this. I need it to stop." Adam, are you thinking of hurting yourself? I asked, I was trained to ask. No, he said, without hesitation, but without any "of course not," any reassuring emphasis. This time Jane and I were in our bedroom and Adam was on speakerphone. I was imagining the child version of him sitting on the bed between us, but would have settled for 1997, the world still all before him. We could tell by the nature of the pauses, when he did pause, that he was smoking a cigarette, cigarettes, one after another. Those Banana cigarettes from Taipei. Soon the swerves between anger and anguish and disbelief were happening in single sentences punctuated only by sobs: "Spain I'm going to go there it's like a sinking feeling that won't stop sinking she'll come to her senses won't she isn't happening." Cascades of such speech. And he was responding to our questions less and less ("Where is Dan?"; "Have you had dinner?"; "Do you think it might help to try some breathing exercises?"; "Would you like us to arrange a call with Dr. Erwood for tomorrow?"; it was like we were adults in those Peanuts cartoons.) And then he said that he thought he was being punished. Punished for what? I asked. For Darren Eberheart. For Mandy. Natalia is only part of this, he sobbed. Sweetheart, Jane said, you're a wonderful person and you're not being punished for anything. You're going through a breakup, a serious betrayal. What's important right now is that you focus on breathing and let us help you calm down.

But he went on, less about Natalia now than about the pointlessness of everything, phrases from his college reading entering his voice. He kept saying "instrumental reason," which seemed apt to me because I thought the music of his language was overwhelming its meaning. At one point it was like he was speaking nonsense rhyme. All his vocabularies were colliding and recombining, his Topekan tough guy stuff, fast debate, language he'd lifted from depressing Germans, his experimental poets, the familiar terminology of heartbreak. And something approaching baby talk, regression. He wasn't driveling, but, from our bedroom in Topeka, I pictured him wearing over-the-ear headphones in New York, receiving 180 words per minute in his left ear, speech mechanisms on the border of collapse. Jane was taking the lead, trying to interrupt him, redirect him, while we kept looking at each other with alarm, a sense of helplessness. And then Jane said his name forcefully and he stopped, returned to himself (returned from where?): "What?" he asked. "I'm having trouble hearing you," she said. (I gave her a puzzled look; we could hear him loud and clear.) "I'm sorry," she said, "it's just not a great connection. Is there another phone you can call us from?" "What do you mean?" Adam said, confused. "It's all staticky, you're too quiet." "Maybe it's the storm," Adam said, the rain apparently heavy now in New York. "Is there a pay phone in or near the dorm?" Jane asked, and now I understood what she was doing, and understanding knocked the wind out of me. "I guess there's a pay phone in the basement, near the washing machines," Adam said. Near the copper wall. "But I'll just speak louder," he said, and did. "I'm sorry, we just can't hear you," Jane said, like she used to do with the Men. "You'll have to call us back from downstairs." "Okay," Adam said, finally, and tried to gather himself. "Okay. I'll call you back in a few minutes."

He hung up the phone, collected his keys and cigarettes, and left his room on the ninth floor, its window open to the storm. Without noticing, he passed the doorway in which Sima and I were going at it, and got in the elevator. I was traveling furiously toward him in the dark. I was in the plane, finally cleared to land, flash of distant lightning. The metal doors shut, the landing gear unfolded, and we made our descent, first person and third, together through the clouds. Jane had talked us down.

From the ceiling there was suspended a rotating ball whose surface was a thousand mirrored facets throwing ovals of colored light across the walls and concrete floor and bodies of the skaters as they circled the rink to the deafening popular songs. Around their necks some of the girls wore plastic tubes of green glowing chemicals. Roller skaters at rest or those afraid to skate ingested sugar from straw-shaped packages or ate spun sugar from white paper cones. Chaperones from the school must have been there in the dark overseeing the Randolph Elementary Intermediate Winter Skating Party but the children could not sense their presence and their parents or guardians had merely dropped them off at Starlite on the northwest edge of town. Outside in the vast lot snow fell on the few parked cars.

While you might expect to find the younger Darren alone in the concession area envying the swifter skaters as they pass, he is in fact one of them, balance maintained without visible effort, strides strong and fluid. He can do a two-foot spin, a spread-eagle. Having been taught by a neighbor at a young age who gave him a pair of black Chicago skates, Darren by this point possesses an ease and rhythm unavailable when his shoes are unequipped with wheels. A dim inkling that this is the last year roller skating might be cool provides him now with extra grace and courage.

There is fructose coursing through their bloodstreams and music loud enough to register as touch and the hardness of the floor they slide across in a dark shot through with light effects. When a novice skater falters, she might take your hand. Risk and mystery and violence, the collective memory of Nick Dewey's attempt at some sort of rotating jump the previous year, how mundane lights came on to reveal him facedown and motionless, gasps when the grown-up turned him over. Then there is the tension between the flowing continuity of skating and the discreteness of the 4/4 time of popular music, an incommensurability that intensifies the feral sexual hysteria, because what would reconcile repetitive rhythm and pure lubricity except for fucking, an act that shapes the young imagination it's beyond?

What Darren remembers from this night because of its intensity in the first and third person simultaneously is the Snowball, an event signaled by the scattered lights going only white. Over the intercom comes the DJ voice, unclear if it's live or a recording, instructing the girls to line up on one side of the rink, boys on the other. In preceding years, Darren, like many of the unpopular, would at this point quit the rink and purchase sugars or a plastic tray of tortilla chips with a well of liquid yellow cheese and wait for free skate to resume. But this time, perhaps sensing admiration for his skating, Darren lines up along the wall. When the DJ voice shouts "Snowball," he skates directly to Jessica Baker and takes her hand, which she does not withdraw. Slowly they circle together to "Lady in Red" until the DJ voice shouts it again, "Snowball," cuing a change in music, "I want to know what love is," and before he can decide who he might pursue, Darren himself has been selected by Morgan Jensen. How she depends on him utterly for their motion, sweat of their palms commingling. Show me love is real, yeah / I want to know what love is.

So when he finds himself seven years later in a twilit basement redolent of marijuana, beer, and kitty litter, the bass rattling his chest, and the half-breed Davis pushes a drunk freshman toward him, saying, Darren, this hottie has a crush on you, Darren, make your move, and the hottie, who is approaching incapacitation, throws an arm around him, slurring, What's up handsome, it is Starlite Darren remembers, the last time he was cool or chosen. If now the sugars are fermented and the violence is willfully inflicted and the parents are out of town and oblivious is he wrong to feel the continuity, that even standing still they are moving rapidly over a hard surface? Kiss her, dog, kiss her, Davis says, but Darren just smiles and drinks from his red plastic cup and adjusts the brand-new Raiders cap he bought at West Ridge Mall.

Darren's uniform is changed. At West Ridge, at JCPenney's, where his mom had dropped him off and picked him up, he'd also purchased two pairs of black and baggy wide-leg jeans and several solid-color hooded sweatshirts, little Nike swoosh above his heart. In the Foot Locker he had pondered both Air Jordan IXs and brown Timberlands but it would, despite the Christmas money from his mom, erase his savings and his boots still represented for him a kind of combat readiness from which he could not bring himself to part.

When she'd clipped his hair at his request to the length of half an inch, a sheet thrown around him at the blond wood kitchen table, Mrs. Eberheart had almost convinced herself that Darren's increased interest in his appearance indicated only a new maturity. Even she could see his style was a little off, non-native: the thin beige braided belt he wore to secure his sagging pants for instance somehow constituted less a single bad decision than a deep incomprehension of the language game in which he was attempting to feign fluency. But he did look better, older and younger at once, looked more his age. And when you pick up your intermittently hallucinating son encrusted in sweat and dirt and vomit twenty miles from his bed you are relieved when the most immediate subsequent change in his behavior is to dress and perform his toilet with more care. Since the day that Darren had called collect from downtown Lawrence, he'd showered and shaved with regularity; instead of his returning late in the afternoon from park or parking lot stained with grass or oil, Mrs. Eberheart would find him watching music videos in the La-Z-Boy, or resting between sets of push-ups, clothes immaculate.

She was at St. Francis when they came for him, pre-partied, but she knew it by the beer cans and glass bottles of alcoholic soda: Seagram's, Zima. The different species of surprise offset one another: that anyone was seeking out Darren's company, that they were brazen enough to leave evidence of their drinking, but also that the bottles and cans had been emptied and rinsed and arranged politely in the sink and that the house was spotless otherwise. And whatever they had done and wherever they had gone in her absence, Darren was always after that first night in his bed when she returned exhausted from the hospital near dawn. First thing she would climb the carpeted stairs to crack his door.

After she'd picked him up, she had carried the cordless phone beyond Darren's earshot to call both Ron Williams and Laura Simms's mother, with whom she'd gone to high school. Ron confirmed he'd invited Darren to have a beer, just as soon they do their drinking here, and named the kids he'd left with; Laura, her mom had called back quickly to report, had felt just awful when she'd learned that Darren hadn't caught another ride. We wanted to include him, it's our senior year. Understand that Mrs. Eberheart had known these young people, at least known of them, all their lives. Adam Gordon, Martin Nowak, Jason Davis—all Foundation kids. She simply would not believe that Jonathan Gordon's son—a boy she'd cared for at St. Francis—would torment hers. The Owens were neighbors and, despite what had happened, almost friends. These seniors, all college-bound, maybe even out of state, would be aware of how easily Mrs. Eberheart could reach their parents and raise whatever necessary hell. Would that not be a check on their behavior?

Beyond that she was powerless. An adult in law if not in spirit, Darren could not be restrained. To imagine a yelling match with Darren over, say, a curfew was only seconds later to imagine the bang of the back screen door, then homelessness, jail, or death. In her head she could hear the phone ringing, some officer asking, May I speak to Mr. or Mrs. Eberheart? Ma'am, are you sitting down? She was so far from being able to afford the few special programs Dr. J had attempted to describe over the years that she did not retain any of their details: something on a farm, something on a lake; insurance covered none of it. Would you blame her if a particle of hope got in her that the cool kids just wanted to end their time at Topeka High with a lasting act of kindness, to let Darren, who'd dropped out at sixteen, feel like he had friends and classmates before they left for college? The Gordon and Davis boys had known her son since Bright Circle Montessori.

Kiss her, dog, kiss her. The freshman disengaged from Darren and said relieved and laughing He must be a faggot and stumbled back toward the center of the basement where there was a pool table, drinks and bongs on the green expanse of baize. Davis laughed. Rage followed Darren's absorption of the slur, but he did not move or quickly lose his smile despite the little mimic spasms as the laughter pooled. Act and time were separating now, the distance between them rapidly expanding, so that only after he'd inhaled the acrid vapor from the light bulb beneath which Davis held the flame did he resolve to just say no. You gonna let her say that, Darren? I'd tell that bitch to watch her fucking mouth. The meth, a purer, measured version of which was circulating as prescribed through many of the bodies in the basement, dissolved the present, the future was the instant past; he already had the cup that he would reach for, less foreknew what track was coming next than heard it as it played in memory, Gotta grind, gotta get mine. The music was fast and slow and complex in its harmonies but Darren could separate out each layer as he approached the pool table to tell the girl to watch her fucking mouth. A circle formed around them.

PARADOXICAL EFFECTS

(JANE)

The Reverend Fred Phelps was a Primitive Baptist minister and disbarred attorney who'd made it his spiritual mission and full-time job to eradicate homosexuality from the planet. Every day, Fred and his followers—which included the few remaining members of his congregation, most of his thirteen children, and many of his grandchildren, some of whom were under ten—gathered on a Topeka street to display huge picket signs that read GOD HATES FAGS, DEATH TO FAGS, FAGS = DEATH, etc. Some signs featured stick figures engaged in a kind of anatomically abstracted sodomy. You'd see the Phelpses in parkas or puffy down jackets on Gage Boulevard midwinter, their breath visible, stomping their feet to keep warm. (Fred, who was in his seventies, was tall and lean, had been an amateur boxer in his youth.) Or you'd see them in sweat-soaked T-shirts—some customized, indicating verses in Leviticus—fishing around in a cooler for a Tab, holding the can to the back of a neck. (Fred, beneath his signature cowboy hat, wore those large, fit-over plastic sunglasses, same as my mom, the kind they give you at the optometrist after they dilate your pupils, the ocular equivalent of orthopedic shoes.) As they protested, the Phelpses were often jovial. You might hear them singing, "I hate fags, I hate fags," to the tune of "Jingle Bells." The Phelpses picketed parades, the performing arts center, most events at Washburn University, and funerals—especially if they suspected an AIDS-related death. ANOTHER FAG IN HELL, a sign might say. In 1994, after *20/20* aired a segment about Fred entitled "A Gospel of Hate," the Phelpses became World Famous.

Fred hated "fags" and "fag-lovers" and Topekans hated Fred. There were periodic counterdemonstrations, broad support for the victims of Fred's harassment. Ordinances were passed restricting his picketing at funerals and private homes. But I always felt uneasy about the nature of the condemnation. A patient once told me how much she despised Fred. Her daughter danced with a local ballet company and Fred and his followers had protested *The Nutcracker.* "I could hardly keep from swerving my car into the whole group of them. Why should my daughter have to know about those people?" At first I thought she meant the Phelpses, but it quickly became clear that the irate mother was referring to "the gays." Besides Ken Erwood and a courageous professor at Washburn Law, I knew exactly no one in Topeka who was out. (I always wondered about Klaus.) Billboards on I-70 showed smiling, crew-cut men who had been "cured" by Bible study. "There is hope."

Given that I was famous in Topeka (Jonathan said "Famous in Topeka" would be a great name for a band), that I was outspoken about gay and lesbian rights, given that I was Jewish, that I worked at the Foundation, I should have been one of the Phelpses' primary targets. For mysterious reasons, however, they went easy on me. There had been the faxes, documents I found more funny than upsetting—we kept one on the refrigerator ("Remember Lot's Wife!")—but I'd given talks or workshops without the Phelpses even bothering to show up. Whereas the Renaissance Faire held just outside of town was picketed from morning till night because it somehow encouraged cross-dressing. Whereas families had to pass the Phelpses to attend a Raffi concert. The Phelpses picketed openly homophobic politicians at the statehouse for not being homophobic enough. And yet when they recognized me—if they saw me at an event or spotted me in the car at a corner where they'd gathered—their way of mocking me was strangely gentle, almost flattering. "Oh, here is the Brain," they would say sarcastically. (They had preprogrammed chants and taunts for particular "fag-loving" Topekans.) "Here is the brilliant Dr. Gordon." This, coming from people who laughed and screamed at grieving parents: "Hope you're happy your son is burning in hell."

Over the years, Jonathan and I had spent a lot of time trying to account for the Phelpses' relative neglect, or was it mercy? Maybe it had something to do with the fact that Jonathan had briefly seen a member of their congregation, a teenager, in court-mandated therapy. But that didn't make much sense; Jonathan and the boy never really connected and, regardless, how would he have had the power to influence the others—to get them to show restraint with me? Could it be that the Phelpses agreed with, were even grateful for, my article in *Mother Jones*—republished in the *Capital-Journal* (surely the only time that's happened)—in which I discussed the hypocritical nature of Topeka's universal condemnation of the Phelpses, how they were denounced for extreme representations of beliefs so many Topekans held? That seemed a little subtle.

Regardless, they showed up in force for my keynote at the Kansas Association of Women Conference. I was both accepting an award and celebrating a new book on the topic of forgiveness. I gave relatively few talks in Topeka, and White Hall, the largest auditorium on the Washburn campus, quickly sold out. (Proceeds went to the Battered Women's Justice Project.) I was surprised that Adam not only seemed eager to go—the association had made a point of requesting that my family attend—but had asked if he could bring Amber, who wore what looked like a prom dress for the occasion: low V-neck, open back. I was happy that Adam considered my talk something to show off; maybe he was getting more mature as college approached, more integrated.

The five of us—my mom joined us—went to dinner before the event at the new sushi restaurant on Southwest Ashworth, which used to be the Rib Crib. Over California rolls full of mayonnaise, I tried to get Amber to talk, asking open-ended questions about her family, school, her plans after graduation. But it was difficult to get much out of Amber—both because she was quiet, if poised in her way, and because Adam kept talking over her or for her, sucking up all the space. After Jonathan lightly vetoed Adam's attempt to order a glass of wine, telling the waiter, "My baby boy is only eighteen," Adam's voice took on an angry edge, disappearing only when he addressed my mom.

(Brief moment of wonder when Amber discovered a ladybug on a leaf of iceberg lettuce in her salad, holding up the scarlet beetle on her chopstick. It had avoided the thick ginger dressing and so, when she blew on it, proved capable of flight.)

Part of my consciousness was devoted to rehearsing lines of my talk (I'd have it in front of me at the podium, but I wanted to consult the text as little as possible, make it seem extemporaneous); part of me was trying to tune out the drunk man at the sushi bar explaining to the young, most likely Korean chef that he forgave him for Pearl Harbor; part of me was trying not to react to my mom's palpable concern about how much the meal would cost. The remainder of my consciousness was devoted to trying to think of my bully of a son as a vulnerable young man passing through a complicated social and hormonal stage.

I did this by remembering—by willing myself to remember—some episode from the past that emphasized his sensitivity; I'd been doing that a lot lately, a variation on *metta* meditation; Erwood hadn't suggested it, but it was the kind of thing he might have. That night, as they served our punishingly large portions of green tea ice cream, I recalled the saga of *SpaceCamp*. (Maybe it was all the talk on the news about the comet, which was visible to the naked eye.)

In the mid-eighties, we'd taken Adam and several of his

friends to see the movie by that name in which the young attendees of a NASA training camp find themselves accidentally launched into orbit. (Adam had been obsessed with all things related to space for more than a year, seemingly undeterred by the *Challenger* disaster; the producers had pushed the premiere of *SpaceCamp* back by several months after the shuttle broke apart on live TV.) Eric and Sima had even suggested, building on the kids' shared interest, that we consider sending Adam and Jason to the weeklong sleepaway camp in Huntsville, Alabama—"where children work as a team and confront mission scenarios that require dynamic problem solving and critical thinking skills." Adam had been thrilled by the idea, and we were pleasantly surprised that he'd even consider spending time away from home without us, especially so soon after his concussion.

Adam was unusually quiet after the movie, said his stomach hurt. That night he burst into our room crying about how he didn't want to go to Space Camp, please don't make me, Mommy, how he didn't want to be launched into outer space. We'd assured him that he didn't have to go; we also wanted to be clear that, if he *did* go, there was no way he'd accidentally end up in orbit. But Adam wasn't entirely convinced; our eight-year-old boy spent weeks afraid that we would change our minds, send him to Alabama, that he'd be impressed into NASA, watching earthrise from a lonely shuttle. (What could be lonelier than a child in space?) As part of the effort to calm him, Jonathan had repeatedly explained how incredibly difficult it was to become an astronaut—how thousands of people devoted decades to training, but few were ever selected. It was like being afraid you'd be forced to be a professional baseball player. Afraid you'd be forced to be president. It wasn't something that could happen against your will. But Adam was not completely reassured: there was the evidence of the movie, there was the dead teacher in space, there was Laika, a stray dog from the streets of Moscow who was the subject of one of Adam's children's books. (The book said nothing about the dog dying several hours into the flight from stress and heat.) Klaus had suggested we think about all the resonances of the word "camp."

I looked at the young man holding forth at the table and remembered the weeks, maybe months, we spent promising him (especially at bedtime) that we would keep him on this planet. Not under it, not floating hundreds of miles above it. He didn't have to be a hero, he didn't have to take a giant leap for mankind, which was always calling on the phone, watching from the walls.

Even though I'd handed the waiter my credit card, he returned the check to Jonathan; I reached across the table for it. Then, even though I signed the receipt, retrieved the card from the little tray, even though I was the one who made more money, Amber thanked Dr. Gordon—meaning Jonathan—for the meal. I was deciding if I should ask, as lightly as possible, why people always thanked the man, if that would be good modeling for Amber or just embarrass her, but Adam, in a brief flash of maturity: "And thank you, Mom." Suddenly I felt good about my boy as we all walked to the car, the glass of chardonnay and fresh air lifting my mood, settling my nerves. (The talk was two blocks away; it was a beautiful late spring evening, but few people in Topeka would have ever thought to walk.)

What happened next happened fast. We parked in a reserved spot at White Hall. We passed the knot of Phelps protesters, some of whom started yelling at the Brain. Jonathan and I responded not at all, but Adam, maybe showing off for Amber, snapped back at them, told them to shut the fuck up, told them they were pitiful mouth-breathing morons, pieces of shit. Jonathan sternly said Adam's name, surprised that our son would give the Phelpses the attention they craved, and tried to keep him moving toward the auditorium entrance, but Adam resisted. One of the Phelpses' followers told Adam he was a faggot and, in response, Adam called her a bitch; I couldn't believe it. The woman was laughing now, cackling, and shouted at me: That's the kind of son you've raised? You must be very proud. And I said, although I knew it would have been better not to speak: No, I am not proud. I am ashamed that he is talking that way. Adam turned from another protester, with whom, as Adam would say, he was "squaring up," turned to me in fury, and said: You're ashamed of me? I'm defending you from these assholes and you're ashamed of me? And I said to him, commanded him: I don't need defending; go in the building right now. Amber tried to pull him in that direction, toward Jonathan, who was leading my mom through the glass auditorium door. The Phelpses laughed, delighted, and the man Adam had been facing shouted: Listen to your mommy, fag. Listen to the brilliant Dr. Gordon. Go into the building and sit by your fag dad and listen to the Brain talk about her trash book.

Then I was talking, blinded by stage lights, acknowledging how honored I was, how grateful I was to be there with my family, my loving husband and precocious son, my rock of a mother. But was Adam in the audience? Yes and no. He was a flickering presence, rapidly changing ages in his reserved seat: a baby in a bassinet, protected from my father, who unfortunately could not join us tonight, much as he would have liked to. A student at Bright Circle, developing special powers. Unconscious, concussed at St. Francis. Unable to recite "The Purple Cow." Rhyming instead about bitches and blunts.

♦♦♦

First they find the animals with the most potential, my sister explained. Monkeys mainly, because monkeys are the smartest, even if they only speak with their eyes. But also certain kinds of genius parrots. African gray parrots are as smart as anything. They can sing opera. They can sing Bach, which is classical music. But it is hard to hold the brush in your beak and the hands of monkeys are like our hands. Parrots probably only paint the leaves. The roses are for the monkeys who also know how to mix the colors. Pink roses are the hardest. Animals are selected from zoos all over the world and moved to a tropical island where they train them in the basics. Before they can teach them to paint they have to help them understand the human language, which requires a lot of patience. You have to reward the animals with treats and when they misbehave you have to be firm with them, but careful not to hurt their feelings. So you have the world-famous scientists and trainers and artists from France working with the animals. Paris, the capital of France. I learned about the school on the tropical island when I was in Mrs. Michener's class and a man from Prospect Park Zoo visited. He told us how proud he was that one of their monkeys had been selected. There was an assembly, this was when you were still just Baby Jane. A marmoset, which is tiny. But he was also nervous because what if the monkey wasn't good enough and was sent back to the zoo? Animals can die of shame. They can die of sadness, too. But when they are on the island the animals are happy because they eat only the finest things and are treated like little movie stars and when they aren't painting they are allowed to roam free. Every one of the leaves and petals on this box is the work of an amazing creature. That's why I was speechless when I opened mine. I know you wanted a bicycle but this is worth a lot more than a bicycle. Than an automobile, probably. You can't just go into Macy's and ask a saleswoman for one of these. No matter how much money you have or how famous your name is. The man from the zoo said the Metropolitan Museum of Art wanted to purchase one of the boxes but couldn't. Forget about the Brooklyn Museum. The people on the island decide who gets them but nobody knows how. That's why when I opened mine, I cried, too. Not because I was sad, but because I couldn't believe that Mom and Dad got not one but two of the tissue boxes for us. Dad must know somebody who knows somebody on the island and must have convinced them that we would love them and take good care of them forever and that it wouldn't be fair for only one of us to get one since we're sisters. Like I said, they aren't only for the rich. You should go back downstairs and get yours where you left it and thank Mom and Dad and tell them that you're sorry and this is better than the bicycle anyway. I bet our flowers are identical because that's how smart the animals are. They never make a mistake or smudge anything. I'm not even telling people about mine. I'm going to put it on the shelf with my other treasures and be quiet about it because of jealousy and the fact that everyone will want to touch it and people have oils on their hands that damage things. Identical means the same.

What's remarkable is how I went on believing my sister's story about the tissue box for decades, long after I'd discarded the box itself. Or maybe "believing" isn't the right word; while the power of the box faded over time, I never subjected the story to reason, never exposed it to the elements, the damaging oils. It was a small but vital story surviving on the edge of consciousness, where it formed a hinge. Then in November 1969 there was a downpour and Jonathan and I ducked into the Woolworth's on Seventy-Ninth to wait it out. On a discount table we were perusing with half attention, a tin tissue box identical to the one I'd received as a child. Identical pattern of pink and white roses. What's wrong? Jonathan asked me, as we stood there dripping in the bright aisle. I had one of these when I was a kid. Except the one I had—

The feeling of a fiction collapsing inside you. A fiction you'd forgotten was there. Frame, crossbeams, slats, braces, joins. Revealing the softer sapwood, which is marked by candle burns. Half an hour later we were at the Greek diner on Ninety-Eighth with the gaudy dime-store box between us; I was weeping openly if quietly, Jonathan holding both of my hands under the table, one of the first times we'd really touched. You must think I'm a lunatic. No, I think it's a beautiful story. About family and art and memory and meaning, how it's made and unmade. (You can't actually hear what we're saying; it's a silent film.) All the edging, shaping, drying. Have you read any Herman Hesse?

It was the second tissue box that I kept in my office at the Foundation, this one holding actual tissues for my patients. Tissues made by specially trained spiders who spin the fibers. Its ugliness had faded over the years as it began to appear antique. The original box, the one painted by animals, was never recovered, even though I asked my mom about it—my mom who threw nothing away. That's when I'd learned more about why, instead of the Schwinns we'd been all but promised, Deborah and I had received identical tissue boxes that Christmas morning. (Why we were celebrating Christmas in Flatbush, I can't really say; my mom hated all kinds of religious orthodoxy—maybe it was her way of making sure we didn't become "too Jewish.") Because my father had, without consulting my mom, spent half of the money she had been saving for our gifts on "business expenses" he could not explain. (A clerk at the unemployment office had no "expenses.") When my mom made the inevitable discovery, he'd assured her that he'd get wonderful replacement gifts. Leave it to me. He must have picked up the boxes as an afterthought on Christmas Eve. That morning when I'd hurled the box across the living room was one of the few times I'd seen tears in my mother's eyes.

A meditation: remembering when I told the tissue box story to Adam. He must have been ten. I'd intended it to be a sweet story about the power of the imagination and the bond between children, but he was distraught at the thought of me as a poor kid in Brooklyn—not at the thought, but at the vivid image. He'd wept imagining the young me weeping, Space Camp all over again. (Some monkeys are sent into orbit, others learn to paint.) And, while I skipped the part about my dad taking the money for the gifts, Adam had been furious at my father for failing to provide the promised bike. Why didn't he save? Why didn't he work a little more? Why had he let you expect the bike if he couldn't figure out how to buy it? Adam had felt vulnerable and he'd felt protective. (Was he expressing an unconscious intuition that my father had done far worse?) That's what he was feeling when he yelled at the Phelpses. It didn't excuse his behavior, but it gave me a fund of empathy.

I needed that fund. As his departure for college drew nearer, even the most casual conversations with Adam would devolve into policy debates and screaming matches. I'm not sure if it was in spite of Adam's intensity or because of it that Jonathan and I decided to attend—over Adam's protestations—the National Forensics League championship tournament in Minneapolis, which was held in June, just a few weeks after graduation. We were also overdue to visit Jonathan's Russian cousins on his mother's side—whom he'd helped track down and helped bring over as part of his effort to connect more with that part of his history. But most importantly, we'd come to feel a little guilty about how we'd never paid that much attention to "competitive speech"—save for lamenting Adam's argumentativeness; how we'd more or less accepted his own cynical account of it as a silly activity that would help him get into college. We asked about it every once in a while, we congratulated him on all the victories, but we never pressed; we were alarmed to think we'd never expressed an interest in seeing him compete. Maybe some of Adam's anger was anger at neglect.

Regardless, it was clear to me that Adam was terrified about the tournament, that it bound together his diverse anxieties. He was expected—even *The Topeka Capital-Journal* said so—to win a national championship in extemp, the culmination of his high school "career." (As a bonus he might place highly in value debate.) He was equally afraid of making it to the final round and failing to. He was scared he would get a migraine, scared being scared would cause one. All this crossed with imminently leaving home, with moving back East. Even if he didn't want it, we were determined to be there, to offer our support.

Thus I found myself seated between my husband and the young Coach Evanson in uncomfortable desk chairs in an over-air-conditioned Minneapolis high school classroom, running my finger over the stars and initials scratched into the hard plastic surface. This was an early, low-stakes round and few people besides us were watching: a handful of kids and coaches. There were six competitors in a round and Adam was scheduled to go last. I was strangely nervous, as if on everyone's behalf.

A tall and long-limbed young woman strode into the classroom. I thought she was, despite an excess of foundation, quite pretty in her long blue slacks. An anachronistic beauty, probably lost on her peers; very 1920s. She confidently took her position in the front of the room and, smiling, asked the judges in a chipper meteorologist voice: Please tell me when you're ready. The speech that followed about the prospect of Korean unification was repetitive and bland; what stood out were her gestures—or how she only gestured with her right hand, as if she had no control over the rest of her body. She made the Clinton thumb, she opened a palm, she indicated different levels of analysis—but only with one arm. She never took a step in either direction. I stopped listening, paralyzed by her paralysis; I imagined her internally willing her other arm to move, but finding herself incapable. Was she having a stroke? Was it an old war injury? The second competitor, who entered half a minute after the first departed—to my relief, the first speaker's body came back to life as she exited the room—was an underdressed heavy kid (dark blue sweater over light blue button-down, khakis with no belt) who gave a rapid-fire speech full of statistics about Chinese economic power; he seemed indifferent to the quality of his delivery. He made eye contact with only one judge. He left two minutes of his allotted time unused. I could smell, even from that distance, a mix of sweat and Old Spice. (Evanson whispered to me that the speaker was a top-ranked policy debater from California, clearly just going through the motions with extemp.) Then there was a strong speech about funding the UN—delivered by a young woman with a southern accent, the only person of color in the round—that went awry in the final minute. Blanking on her first main point as she tried to sum up her speech, she was suddenly tongue-tied, nervous, repetitive, making jokes at her own expense as her time wound down. It was excruciating to watch. (Why did I feel Evanson relished it?) The girl rushed out of the room with an embarrassed smile, maybe to cry. I listened to the scratching of the judges' ballpoints on their ballots, imagined cruel comments, diagnoses—borderline personality, penis envy. Then there followed the disorienting experience—at once eerie and comic—of two speeches on the same topic given by two similar-looking boys in black suits and red ties, both boringly and competently arguing that, yes, NAFTA was good for Mexico. (This repetition of topics within the same round was an administrative error, Evanson told me, a violation of the rules.) They made similar gestures to indicate the smooth flow of goods and services across the border. They both concluded with the same vaguely offensive quote about Mexican politics from P. J. O'Rourke. They both had red bumps on the skin above their collars. I had to keep from looking at Jonathan or we'd crack up.

After the second of the identical speakers left the room, I heard one of the judges say to another: It's Gordon next. And then, as Adam entered, Evanson leaned toward me and whispered, grinning his lupine grin: Now watch this.

♦♦♦

Yes, you're winning these rounds easily, Evanson said to Adam, with an intensity I thought might have been for our benefit, but you're winning them in the wrong way. (This was two days later; we were in another empty classroom after the afternoon's competition had concluded. It was Wednesday, halfway through the tournament. Spears and Mulroney and a few student observers were also in the room. I got the sense only Evanson had the authority to address Adam in this way.) You're giving fast and fluent speeches from left on the spectrum and you're going to easily carry judges who share that orientation. Liberal cosmopolitans. Judges from San Francisco and New York. Of which there are plenty. (My eyes met Jonathan's; maybe I was being paranoid, but I half expected Evanson to come right out and say "the Jews.") But imagine you're running for president and now you're in a swing state. You're an hour or two outside of Pittsburgh, and while you need to be intelligent, you need to be winning hearts as much as minds. What you have in your favor is Kansas. You have Midland American English. I want quick swerves into the folksy. "You can put lipstick on a pig, but it's still a pig." That kind of thing. I want you saying, right after some hyper-eloquent riff about Yeltsin breaking a promise, "Now, in Kansas, we call that *a lie*." After you go off about a treaty regulating drilling in the Arctic: "Now, in Kansas, we wouldn't shake on that." I don't care if they're not real sayings, just deliver them like they're tried-and-true. Say "tried-and-true." Say "ain't" if you want. You can go agrammatical so long as they know it's a choice, that it's in quotes. Interrupt your highbrow fluency with bland sound bites of regional decency. Why do you think they elect Texans who went to Yale, Arkansan Rhodes Scholars? Anyway, deliver little tautologies like they're proverbs. Things your Grandma Rosie used to say. Back on the farm. Back when America was America and not the plaything of coastal elites. And I want arms thrown out, palms up, while you do it. Let me see it. No, watch me; my shoulders are relaxing, relaxed, almost a shrug. Like you're briefly breaking character, the fourth wall, if you know what that means. (A fictional wooden parapet.) And then, *bam*: I want you all business again, back to wunderkind analysis and the movements we practiced. But you're a hometown boy wonder, you're playing for the Hoosiers, okay? You're not the son of Jane Gordon (grin flashed toward me) who always expected to be here. And you need to slow everything down two clicks. Oh, and I want you citing the Cleveland *Plain Dealer.* I didn't ask if you had it in your files, I said I want you citing it. For every *Le Monde*, I want the Cleveland *Plain Dealer.* Just use "as reported in the Cleveland *Plain Dealer*" for something that probably was. The Mexican economy has enjoyed strong growth, as reported in the Cleveland *Plain Dealer.* Roman Herzog is less influential than Helmut Kohl, as reported in, etc. You can be too general to be disprovable. Finally, the bouncing your head thing has to stop. We talked about this. I know you don't think you're doing it, but believe me, you move your head to the rhythm of your own speech when you get going, when you enter your zone. Ask your parents; they'll tell you. Am I right, Dr. Gordon? (He meant Jonathan, who just smiled noncommittally.) This isn't a bunch of kids sitting around rapping. You aren't Tupac Shakur. May he rest in peace. You don't get to groove to your own beat. (The other coaches and students—everyone in the room was white—laughed at this.)

The nodding. I was suddenly back in New York, 1969, debriefing with Dr. Porter, my supervisor and, for a time, my analyst. Book-lined walls, smell of pipe tobacco, although I never saw him smoke. After observing me in session through a two-way mirror, Porter fastened on my "nervous habit" of moving my head and insisted that I put a stop to it. It was true that during my sessions I nodded a little to the rhythm of a patient's speech. The gesture wasn't meant to affirm anything, except that I was listening. The nodding was subtle, I was barely aware I was doing it; certainly, no patient had ever seemed to care. But Porter had been adamant, summoned a strange intensity—as if he wanted to come down hard on me and couldn't think of anything else to criticize. (Anything besides my entire theoretical orientation; if I were an analyst, jotting down notes behind a prostrate patient, my nodding wouldn't be an issue in the first place.)

But when I stopped nodding, tried to suppress the impulse, something was thrown off in my thinking. To my surprise, the physical movement wasn't stifled, but displaced: I began to bounce my left leg a little, which would make a patient think I was fidgeting, restless, not concentrating. But when I stopped the movement of my leg without allowing myself to nod, I began to twirl a pen in my writing hand—like a high school debater. When I got rid of the pen—which meant I no longer jotted down observations—I became distractingly aware of my hands as such, kept shifting them from my lap to the arms of the chair and back again. I felt like I was trying to pose for a photograph, like I was still being supervised, operating under a pressure to perform my role in a way that kept me from fulfilling it.

Then I made the mistake of bringing up these almost comic struggles with Porter in analysis, when I was on the couch. At which point the focus became my transference, my father, how allowing myself simply to resume nodding would constitute a cowardly retreat from my own psychodynamics. (What was Porter doing with his hands as I spoke?) Yes, I was resistant to having my body disciplined by a famous analyst (famous, too, for sleeping with his students). Was that pathological? Why not analyze why he had made this small tic into a significant issue?

And suddenly it was significant. While suppressing the nod, I forgot important aspects of my patients' history and had to be reminded; I spoke too little or too much, mismanaging silence; I became clumsier at keeping track of time, and was often surprised to find the session was nearly over. And so on. Finally, I just stopped trying to monitor myself and everything was back to normal. I even developed something like pride in the subtle nodding, the way an athlete might—a little ritual that helps you keep your rhythm at the free throw line, for instance, an analogy I would never use. In that way, I had refused to be trained. I refused to be a trained monkey. Or genius parrot.

I was back in Minneapolis now, listening to Evanson train

my boy. I felt suddenly protective of Adam's bouncing, nodding, whatever it was, his semiconscious acknowledgment that a channel had been established, that language was coursing through him. Because even though it happened while he was speaking, it was also a form of listening, of making himself a medium. It was the poet part of him. Watching Adam compete, Jonathan and I had been both fascinated and unnerved by his fluency, his dominance; the young Evanson embodied what disturbed us—the choreographed spontaneity, all in the service of manipulation, of winning. But the little gesture Evanson was trying to edit out stood for something else. It was like Glenn Gould's humming in *The Goldberg Variations*. It was a sign that the artist was alongside an art that exceeded him. Except, instead of engaging Bach, these kids were arguing about the viability of a European currency.

Look at my boy, divide him into zones. Erwood was working on the tension in his neck and his temples and his general vasoconstriction, asking him to ask his muscles to loosen, but Evanson was working at cross-purposes, making even relaxing the shoulders a momentary gesture in a linguistic martial art. Maybe we should have raised him among the liberal cosmopolitans of San Francisco and New York. Maybe I'd offered my boy up to the wrong tutelage, the Brain had offered him to the Men, thinking he would somehow know better. And now he was a graduate of the Topeka School. As reported in the Cleveland *Plain Dealer.*

Even though Adam and Evanson didn't care much about them, I preferred watching the Lincoln-Douglas debates. Adam's gestures and posture were less routinized, his eloquence seemed to have more substance, and, in those moments when he was actually arguing for something he believed in—like the redistribution of wealth—I could entertain fantasies of his fluency eventually being harnessed for important social work. He was polite—more polite when we were present?—in cross-examination and, in addition to being impressive in his ability to shape arguments, make fine distinctions, he was often very charming. While his focus was on extemp, he kept winning easily in L-D, and on the Thursday morning of the tournament, we observed him in the quarterfinal debate. (All "elimination rounds" were held at the event center at the Mall of America.)

A hundred people were packed into a conference room. There were miked podiums. Five judges sat in the front row. Resolved: The United States ought to provide a universal basic income. Adam was the affirmative speaker; I loved the poetic passages of his speech, his insistence that we must privilege collective flourishing over concentrated wealth; instead of just defending a welfare state, he was going all-out in heavily iambic prose (see him nod) against the maximization of profit as the organizing principle of a society. It was ludicrous and I loved it, my man-child quoting Rosa Luxemburg to a bunch of future corporate lawyers or their lobbyists in the shadow of the world's largest mall. The second half of the speech was more moderate, Scandinavian, describing the concrete advantages of democratic socialism, but the overall effect was to make Adam refreshingly weird—who was this red-diaper kid from a red state, his tie removed, his shirt collar yellowed, a tough-guy poet (with a silly haircut) waxing eloquent in front of nerds and his parents about the theft that is property and the freedom of the species-being? He was eclectic, after all, despite his training; I beamed as I listened. Evanson hadn't bothered to attend.

Adam seemed surprised by how little his opponent, a kid from Austin in a powder-blue suit, asked during the cross-examination: a few points of clarification about who was cited when, a confirmation of Adam's position that wealth was arbitrary from a moral point of view—that a person didn't deserve to have ten billion dollars while another starved. A brief discussion of the concept of "moral luck." (His opponent's recently cut black hair covered his forehead, which seemed both stylish and, I noticed when he wiped sweat from his brow, served to conceal bad skin.) Then

Adam sat down, ready to take notes, and the young Texan, before beginning his speech, gave a kind of overview that I found strange. "Just a brief road map," he said. "I'm going to go first to the Rawlsian framework, then to the Marxist analysis; then I'll offer a Utilitarian counter-framework I think is superior for this debate, and from there I'm going to enumerate the consequences—moral and empirical." Jonathan and I glanced at each other, confused; there was a murmuring in the room. We could tell Adam was surprised; his posture over his notepad changed. For what this "road map" signaled—unbeknownst to us, but clear to everyone else—was that Adam's opponent was going to attempt to spread him. Apparently there had been rumors about the spread spreading to value debate in certain states, if not in Kansas.

I knew about the high-speed rounds in policy debate, I'd listened to Adam demonstrate the crazy rate at which he could speak and read, but I was nevertheless unprepared for what I witnessed. The negative speaker, after his "road map," proceeded to read piece after piece of "evidence" indicting theories of "justice as fairness" and "distributive justice" and "Marxist-Hegelian Romantic theories of community," letting the sheets of paper fall to the floor one after another. I could understand very little of the language, but I knew it was the shadow of speech, of reason. The breathing, the gasping for air—I'd heard hyperventilating patients make similar sounds; it sounded a little like the barking of a seal. While the young man seemed to have a sort of swagger, my primary experience was of a body in duress. Or possessed. I watched Adam, who was taking rapid notes, but also looking up at intervals to try to read the judges: Were they participating in this madness, noting each argument? Or were they going to protect the integrity of L-D debate, which was, Adam had explained, developed precisely to avoid this kind of babble? I couldn't tell. When the negative speaker concluded, again wiping sweat from his brow, there was a murmuring among the observers I thought implied approbation.

After a moment of hesitation only a mother was likely to perceive, Adam rose for the Q&A. Smiling, he asked: "Are we having a quantitative or qualitative debate?"

"Both," the speaker said.

"I suppose my question is: If this is a debate about logic, ethos, pathos—why the rush to make more arguments than we could possibly consider carefully?"

"I think we can consider a lot of arguments carefully. Maybe we should get to the arguments right now instead of wasting time" (laughter).

"Okay, but do you agree that dropped arguments are not conceded arguments, as in policy debate?"

"Well, I think that it's problematic to separate value from policy, as your question implies. Do you think policy should be made without thinking about—"

"I'm asking a question about our mutual understanding of the activity that we—"

"I think we should let the judges decide who has made the better arguments in the better way."

"It's clear you've been a policy debater, so you know that arguments about what constitutes a voting issue—topicality, etc.—are often contested, form part of the debate. Shouldn't we be able to do something similar here?"

"Okay, sure."

"So my parents are here today. They came all the way from Kansas to watch their boy compete. It's very touching" (laughter). "Now, they're intelligent people, but they're unfamiliar with the spread. They looked pretty confused to me while you were speaking" (laughter). "Can you explain to my parents why debating at such rates is conducive to the careful adjudication of questions of value?"

"Well, I would say"—he seemed unprepared for this question—"to your parents that—that to people who are familiar with debate, I was sufficiently clear."

"With policy debate, you mean. At the high school or college level. Not to anyone else. Since this is a value debate, I'm asking you to account for the *value* of the spread. Not just right now, in this Q&A, but in your next speech; I'm suggesting that's a burden you've assumed."

Adam used all the time they give you for preparation, making furious notes, before returning to the podium. The atmosphere was tense; there was palpable excitement. Would he demonstrate that he could match his opponent's speed, try to respond to all of his points, unleash a barrage of arguments in turn?

No: Adam spent most of his speech elaborating an analogy between the spread and a blind commitment to economic growth—he argued that his opponent's fascination with speed and his claims about competition being stifled by a societal emphasis on equality were in fact related. A crisis of content and of form. For they both depended on the belief that more is always better, accumulation at all costs. Adam toggled—elegantly, I thought—between arguments about the need for societies to free up human capacities from profit-seeking and the need for new regimes of language starting right here, in this debate. Now let us turn to the most significant of my opponent's arguments, which can easily be grouped into three main areas . . .

When the boy from Austin rose—this time he left his jacket on the chair, rolled up his sleeves—he did, as Adam requested, defend the spread, but he did so at several hundred words per minute, providing a dizzying array of arguments ranging from the positive cognitive effects of rapid information processing (he had evidence from psychologists) to the importance of including as many diverse points of view as possible in value debates so as to avoid hegemony. (The perversity of this last point bothered me particularly—that speaking at the far edge of intelligibility was actually about inclusivity.) Not that the content of his speech mattered. Then he went on to "pull across" the various arguments Adam had "dropped" from his earlier speech, claiming

Adam's attempt to group them was just a strategy for dodging what he could not refute.

I was moved by seeing my son defend a more human scale of exchange, by his rejection of linguistic overkill—his own version of which his dad and I so often had to suffer. I liked to think he was channeling us, maybe paying a kind of homage; would he have made the same arguments if we hadn't been in the room, or would he have descended—or accelerated—to his opponent's level? Regardless, we congratulated him with real warmth on his performance as we all waited in the carpeted hall outside the room for the results to be announced. I felt that my own example had, at least for the moment, edged out Evanson's.

In the final debate of his career, Adam lost 4–1.

♦♦♦

Sonia Semenov's nursing home was close to our hotel; we would meet Nina, Sonia's daughter, and her husband, Leon, there, visit for a while, then cross town to Nina and Leon's house, where we'd all have dinner. I was pleased that Adam would join us; surely he needed a night off from meals with forensicators at the Applebee's and Olive Gardens, at the Mall of America's Hard Rock Café. And maybe his rising anxiety about the championship round of extemp made him eager to be in our company, where he could speak frankly about his fears and we could reassure him.

It was storming when we picked Adam up at his hotel in our rental car—we had booked a separate place from the competitors—and together we moved slowly, wipers at high speed, lights on although it was still day, toward the Summerset Nursing Home. Adam asked to be reminded who everyone was, who was related to whom, as he'd only met the Russians once before. Jonathan explained that Sonia—who had been a physician, who was in her nineties now—was his mother's second cousin. Jonathan's mom never met her, but Jonathan had made contact in the late 1980s, and had ultimately helped Sonia and family move from Moscow to Minneapolis, where friends of theirs had immigrated before them; the Semenovs arrived in 1991. Sonia hadn't been in the nursing home for long; her dementia, probably Alzheimer's, had rapidly worsened over the last year. Although she was in great shape physically, she'd started wandering out of the house, including one January night in a bathrobe, and Nina and Leon didn't feel they had a choice. (As Jonathan explained all this to Adam, I pictured the ancient woman—who'd been a medic in Afghanistan, who'd survived famine, repression, buried two husbands—babbling in Russian in subzero temperatures as she circled the man-made lake.)

We stopped at a red light. The rain had slackened and Jonathan turned the wipers down a click. Through my window I could see a break in the clouds to the west, a sliver of bright blue sky.

"Mom," Adam said from the back seat, "you told me once how you had to give a big speech somewhere, maybe in New York after your first book came out, and you were really nervous, almost panicking. And you said you took one of those pills you had for turbulent flights. And that it took the edge off the fear but didn't knock you out or anything, right? Did you bring those—don't you always have them with you when you travel?"

For an instant I considered lying. "I have an ancient prescription for Valium. Or lorazepam. I almost never take one."

"If I break to finals, can I have one? I'm walking around imagining pissing myself in terror. And I realized last night that if I could have one of these pills I could stop worrying. At least worry less. About giving myself a migraine or otherwise melting down."

"But you're doing great without it," Jonathan said. "And you can't take those things all the time—which means you have to develop other strategies. Biofeedback. Breathing techniques."

I braced myself for the spread. For fifty reasons why Erwood was bullshit, why Jonathan's logic was profoundly flawed. Why our faith in such practices revealed our own charlatanism. But Adam responded calmly: "I'm not saying this could take the place of the other things. That it's some kind of magic solution. But this is a uniquely terrifying situation, don't you think? This is speaking without notes, without a net, in front of a huge crowd. Broadcast. Being recorded for classrooms everywhere."

"But you don't want to try a medication for the first time around a big event," I said. "Pills can have paradoxical effects—some people are made more anxious by a tranquilizer. More wired." What if he wanted one on the nights before he left home for school? Then to help him with the inevitable stresses of school? Started mixing them with alcohol? Not that it would be hard for him to find the drugs on his own.

"Also, it's not really appropriate," Jonathan said, "for us to be doling out prescription medication."

"We're not real doctors," I joked, or half joked.

"And they might dull you. Not good for extemp," Jonathan said. "Evanson would kill us." Again we braced ourselves, and again he was calm:

"If you're worried about a bad reaction, give me half of one tonight and I'll see how it feels. I hear what you're saying, but I'm not a junkie, I'm not going to start sneaking them from Mom's purse. This once. My last speech. We could call Erwood or something if you're worried. To ask about side effects. Maybe I won't even take it, but knowing I *could*— Just think about it, please."

"You'll win this thing without it," Jonathan said.

"If you say no, I'll respect that. But just think about it, okay?"

"Okay," I said. I'd want a Valium before drawing three topics out of a hat and addressing an auditorium of Evansons. I might take one just to listen.

The rain had stopped by the time we parked in the Summerset lot. The humidity was gone, the air washed cool. There was lightning in the direction where the storm had passed. I took a deep breath, as I always did before plunging into the distinct medium of nursing homes.

Muzak was circulating through the lobby, linking Summerset in my mind with the Mall of America, where Jonathan and I had wandered around that afternoon. From a brown couch rose Nina and Leon, who greeted us with Old World enthusiasm, Adam awkwardly receiving Leon's kisses. The Russians were particularly moved—as they always were, always would be—to see Jonathan, whom they considered a hero. (He'd helped with visas; he'd loaned Leon money—or rather, we'd loaned him money—for his car dealership, which had flourished, largely because of his loyal Russian clientele.) Next they heaped heavily accented praise on Adam, "our Mr. Champion Talker"; they couldn't wait to attend the big speech. I saw Adam blanch a little as he explained that he might not make the finals, that it would be boring regardless, they really shouldn't bother, all of which the Russians waved away. As we approached the desk where visitors signed in before entering the true "facility," I asked Nina how she felt Sonia was doing, and Nina replied, "My mom is happiest here I have known her," which I thought must be sarcasm, a grim expression of Nina's unwillingness to entertain such questions, or a failure of her English.

Doors slid open to admit us to the actual home. I noted the little black box on the wall, the alarm that would be triggered by a bracelet if a patient tried to escape. It was like every other nursing home I'd visited, if on the nicer side. Wheelchairs were grouped around a large television where white heads nodded in and out of consciousness before a muted episode of *Seinfeld*. There was a cafeteria where a few residents were eating or being fed from trays. From the individual rooms, I heard more televisions, some sounds of routine distress as a resident objected to being moved or changed; down a corridor, from deep in his neurodegenerative disease, a man was calling out in a private language.

I preferred it to Rolling Hills: the inevitable unfortunate smells were subtle; the staff interacting with patients seemed warm enough; the schedules on the walls—July Fourth decorations were still up, sparklers and flags—said that a children's choir would be visiting that week, along with puppies from a local shelter. (I tried not to think of the analogy between institutions.) I didn't relax entirely, but my shoulders lowered as I stopped expecting to see my father, who'd been declining rapidly, wherever his wheelchair had last been abandoned.

Instead of leading us to a room, Nina indicated that we should sit in a cluster of beige chairs while she went to find her mother. There were old issues of *Time* and *Newsweek* on a little table. Cover stories about the Roswell Files, Generation X. A painting of sunflowers on the wall; where did nursing homes purchase art? Soon Nina returned with a short, smiling old woman in what looked like a white doctor's coat. The woman quickly handed each of us something in turn, talking rapidly in Russian; it was a red and white mint; I'd seen the large bowl of them on the counter of the nurses' station. Having distributed the gifts, the woman appeared to excuse herself—but Nina took her arm and said something to detain her. While the two women argued politely, Leon explained to us that Sonia didn't know who Nina was; she thought we were all just visiting the "hospital." Sonia was saying that she didn't have time to chat because there was too much work to do. (There was a stethoscope around Sonia's neck; was it a toy?) We are your family, Nina responded. These are your cousins who have traveled to see you, she explained, gesturing toward the three of us; we all smiled awkwardly as Leon translated. Sonia condescended to wait while Nina stood behind each of our chairs, reintroducing us in turn—first Jonathan, then me, then Adam. (Somehow they didn't sound like our real names when Nina said them.) Sonia looked down at her wrist, where there was no watch, while she listened. But something Nina said about Adam—she'd rested her arms on his shoulders—interested

Sonia, and she came over to him, pinched his cheek, pulled on one of his ears, and felt one of his biceps, making a face to indicate how impressed she was with his muscles. (The nimble expressiveness of the pantomime reminded me of Klaus.) Nina said: My mom thinks Adam is Jonathan, the cousin who helped us move to America. She thinks she moved to America to practice medicine here. Sonia kissed my son again, the young Jonathan. (The child is father to the man.) Then I looked at the real Jonathan, saw how moved he was to see a maternal relative connecting to his child. Adam was saying *spasibo* over and over again in his American Midland accent.

Sonia was the happiest she had ever been. Late in her career, for political reasons, she'd been prohibited from practicing medicine in the Soviet Union, but here she was, working; when she'd moved to Minneapolis, she was, despite Nina's best efforts, entirely isolated. Now she had concerns—Nina said she complained about the thin blankets, a lack of certain medicines, some incompetents on the staff—but she spent most of her days performing both real and simulated tasks, the embodied memories of her training. The nurses—one of them was Russian—embraced her delusion so long as she didn't attempt anything beyond fluffing pillows, feeding people applesauce, auscultating someone occasionally with her fake stethoscope. (Through a fake stethoscope, you can still hear a real pulse; through her fake doctoring, Sonia provided some real comforts.) Sometimes she remembered who Nina and Leon were, usually she didn't; either way, she was always a little put out by their visits, how they wanted to talk and talk when there were patients in need of care.

Since Nina couldn't convince Sonia to stay in one place, she asked her to give us a tour. We followed Dr. Semenov around the home, nodding as if we grasped what she was saying, as she gestured to this or that patient. (Sonia seemed to have lost all concept of linguistic difference, convinced that everyone could understand her, as if, in her senescence, she were speaking Esperanto.)

At various points Sonia winked at Adam, indicating her particular affection, but I also imagined the wink was saying: Of course, I'm only pretending to have this fantasy about being a doctor; I know I'm just a demented old woman in a nursing home; I'm doing this for my daughter, so she thinks I'm happy here. I'm aware that the flowers on this hideous wallpaper weren't painted by monkeys.

When they reached the sliding automatic doors, Sonia took her leave, kissing each of us in turn, pressing my hand, doing the bicep thing again with Adam. We watched her walk to the nurses' station and pick up a clipboard and start babbling to one of the nurses, who smiled and nodded in response without looking up. Then we left the Summerset Home and got back into our cars. After a moment of stunned silence, we erupted in shared laughter, shared wonder, at Sonia's triumphant decline.

As we followed Leon's taillights across town, Jonathan started and stopped several sentences about his mom. I put a hand on his thigh to indicate I was aware how many emotions were stirred up by the visit. After we'd driven in silence for a while, Adam calmly brought up the pill again, and I found myself saying: Fine, I'll give you a half now and you can see what that feels like. It wasn't like me to make such a decision suddenly or unilaterally; I felt the muscles of Jonathan's leg tense beneath my palm. Is that okay? I asked him, and he shrugged as if to say: Too late now.

In the driveway of the Semenov house, which Adam said resembled Amber's, I located the bottle of yellow pills in my purse, broke one of them in half; regretting my impulsive response, I gave the fragment to Adam. What I regretted wasn't the half pill—more of a magic feather than a therapeutic dose—but how I'd assented casually to sharing the medicine after both Jonathan and I had expressed our reservations.

The house looked like a hotel, displayed mass-produced prints that could have been in Summerset—I half expected Muzak—but it smelled particular, like fish and cabbage and whatever else

Nina had left simmering while we'd visited her mom. Leon offered all three of us small glasses of vodka from a silver tray, but, before Jonathan or I had to intervene, Adam said he'd just have water. I watched him take the pill. When Leon compelled Adam to come with him to the garage to see his customized car, and Nina withdrew into the kitchen, I said:

"That was totally inappropriate of me, giving Adam the medicine without our talking more. I'm really sorry."

Uncharacteristically, Jonathan said nothing.

"I think it's fine for him to take something around all this insanity, but I know that's not the point and I apologize. If you're concerned about it, we could call Eric—"

"We are not calling Eric," Jonathan snapped. "To say we've drugged our child. We are not calling Eric and Sima to announce that we—"

"Lower your voice."

Jonathan stood up, stormed off in the direction Adam and Leon had gone. Clearly this wasn't about .25 milligrams of lorazepam. I took a deep breath. In my head, my mom asked how much the black leather couch I was sitting on cost. Then I tried to picture a fairy-tale form of dementia for her if she ended up at Rolling Hills. But that thought was immediately overwhelmed by my realization—no less profound for being obvious—that, when my mom lost her memory, she would lose the memory of what my father had done to me, what he'd finally acknowledged doing before they'd moved to Topeka from Phoenix. Leaving only Jonathan and Sima in the know. "In the know"—I sounded the phrase in my head. The trauma was perpetual when you were left in it alone. A child on a train, in outer space, out of time. Would I ever tell my son?

Adam was involved and charming at dinner; it was hard to say if that was an effect of the pill or evidence of its ineffectuality. Jonathan was restrained, if smiling, and I was suddenly exhausted, almost groggy, as if I'd been medicated. (That plaques and tangles form in your brain and all that's left, if you're lucky, are the traces of your training. That I might be left alone with the knowledge, then lose it myself.) I tried to listen, then just tried to appear to be listening, to Leon, who was going on and on about Audis, how much better they are than Volvos. I had to take my plate into the kitchen so Nina would stop serving me impossible quantities of sturgeon and potatoes.

Leon had persuaded Jonathan to have some vodka. Jonathan didn't seem tipsy, but, when the meal was finished, when Leon had tearfully hugged Jonathan goodbye several times, even though they'd see each other the following day, Adam suggested that he drive, at least to his own hotel; Jonathan said sure, handed him the keys. Weird to see my husband and son from the back seat, especially with Adam driving, as if Sonia's misrecognition had scrambled everybody's role. (Adam wasn't an authorized driver on the rental; letting him drive was a little like letting him take someone else's medication; I could use that against Jonathan in an argument. The debaters were rubbing off on me.)

When Adam pulled into the parking lot of his hotel, he turned and told me that the pill had had a mild calming effect and he would appreciate my giving him one the next day. I nodded and he opened the back door to hug me where I sat, where I remained, as if kept there by a mysterious force, while Jonathan switched to the driver's side. I didn't know what was coming, but I knew that something was, and, after an interval of silence while Jonathan navigated out of the parking lot and back onto the street, he began to speak, in a kind of muffled fury, about my sharing the medication, not consulting him, I'm equally a parent here, etc. I was in a hurry to agree, but I also noted his uncharacteristic intensity, which made him angrier. It was like he wasn't addressing me, but some shadowy presence in the front seat. "And then you want me to call Eric—"

"What was so crazy about that?"

Because you have no respect for boundaries. Because Eric isn't

Adam's doctor or our doctor or even a close colleague. He's the husband of a friend you made your therapist and look what that got us. Because (he didn't say) you can't reach across the museum ropes for a magic pill to make Darren or Adam fluent or to touch Donna's leg at a dinner in Taipei in Sima's basement.

"It might well have been the wrong decision," I responded. "And independent of that I totally mishandled it, I get it. I am sorry, full stop. But I don't know if it's the nursing home or the alcohol, but—"

But Jonathan was Adam—the aggressiveness, the speed, the tension at his temples—proving how my sharing the pill was irrefutable evidence of my inability to maintain borders. How I made everything a network of crisscrossing relations. I was the Brain who wrote the purple cow that Darren shot from a nearby hill and now Jonathan's mom had to ride it forever in the first film he never made. I hope you're proud of yourself, home-wrecker. Penis-envying virago. Cunt. Jezebelian switch-hitting whore from Beitou or Peitou, he didn't say. Is it any wonder your friendship with Sima had—

"I don't want to talk about Sima, okay? It doesn't have anything to—"

We pulled into a space at our hotel. He turned off the engine, but remained facing straight ahead. As if the windshield were a teleprompter from which he was reading his lines at increasing speed. Why couldn't we just go one fucking night without blurring the distinctions, crossing the wires. Between the personal and the professional. Between doctor and patient. Real doctors and fake, with their toy stethoscopes. (Ziegler particularly admired cancer research.) Policy and value debate. I was looking at the headrest. Then I shut my eyes. I could barely understand him; it was like I was having to translate from a foreign tongue in which I'd once been fluent. It required more and more of an effort, however positive the cognitive effects. And yet, paradoxically, I already knew what he was going to say. That he had a confession to make. (Jonathan's tone had started to change.) That he had stolen the painting. He'd stolen the *Madonna and Child* in its burnt frame. It was the worst thing he had ever done. And then the joins broke open to reveal the softer sapwood of his voice, the anger gone. He was so sorry. (He'd started crying.) And I was still trying to stop him—"I don't want to talk about Sima"—but it was too late. I am so sorry, he sobbed, tossing away his cane, hat, tie.

♦♦♦

House lights fall in the Mall of America's event center auditorium filled to capacity with competitors and coaches and family and reporters covering the championship rounds of the 1997 National Speech & Debate Tournament. To my right is Jonathan; to my left is Nina; in the row in front of us: Evanson and the other coaches and students from Kansas. A giant blue banner (THE FUTURE OF SPEECH) forms a backdrop to the stage. Beneath the banner on tables covered with blue cloth stand the rows of tall pewter trophies for which the teenagers will compete. There are TV cameras set up in the aisles; men with headsets have trained them on the stage. The excitement in the auditorium is unmistakable, mounting, ominous—as if many in the audience are there primarily in the hope of watching someone crack under the pressure. Americans consistently report that their greatest fear is public speaking—greater than nuclear war or flying or drowning or snakes or spiders, greater, according to the surveys, than death itself. But why, exactly? Is it obvious that it should be scarier than driving at high speeds or tearing through the atmosphere? (Not even the most powerful kings on earth could have driven a shiny new automobile, nor could they have flown . . .)

Because it's a linguistic primal scene, Klaus's voice in the dark. The assembled, the community, demand that the speaker be at once individual (your speech must be original to be prized) and utterly social (your speech must be intelligible to the tribe). Through the individual mouth we must hear *the public speaking*. Or: you are not just speaking but ritually performing the human capacity for speech as such; to be victorious is to be a poet who refreshes the medium of sociality, who is beside himself as language courses through him—like Glenn Gould humming along, nodding like me or my son; to fail in this endeavor is to lose your status as a social person—to regress to infancy (from the Latin *infans*, without speech) or, worse: to the status of a beast. That the speaking here is supposedly extemporaneous—no notes, no net—only heightens the stakes of the archaic contest. The speaker has in fact prepared, has been trained to ape naturalness, but that puts you at risk of being revealed to be an ape. (An animal can die of shame.)

A short, bald man, stage lights reflecting off his polished scalp, walks onto the stage. This is Arthur Naylor, president of the National Forensics League. In the lapel of his dark gray jacket, a little diamond pin catches the light; each coach whose student has won a national championship receives one. He removes a note card from his breast pocket and reads the first finalist's code, name, high school, and question. He repeats the question slowly: What can the Colombian government do to end the conflict with the FARC? I can hear hundreds of people jotting down the question in the dark, a scratching I associate less with language than with the frantic activity of mice. If an animal can be trained to paint, why not to write? Naylor departs stage left. I try to remember who the FARC are. A guerrilla group. A group of ibexes and chamois and llamas and gnus and boars.

See the first speaker, the child dressed as a man, take the stage. He makes eye contact with the judges, who are on a dais at the front of the auditorium—a senator and a minor ambassador among them—and, when the timekeeper nods that she is ready, he steps onto the tightrope. Despite my allergy to Klaus's grandiosity, a grandiosity that has only increased since his death, I do sense something primal behind the veneer of current events: a boy mimicking the language of politics and policy, the language of men. Soon this one is explaining the peril of paying ransom to a paramilitary force, how it only leads to more kidnappings and hostage situations, but perhaps the young speaker is, with his theatrically raised eyebrows, trying subtly to signal his own captivity—a cry for help directed to the grown-ups in the audience? But there are no grown-ups, that's what you must grow up to know fully; your parents were just two more bodies experiencing landscape and weather, trying to make sense by vibrating columns of air, redescribing contingency as necessity with religion or World Ice Theory or the Jewish science, cutting profound truths with their opposites as the regimes of meaning collapse into the spread.

In the artificial dark, as the first speaker concludes with a joke, the audience roaring with laughter, the presences around me begin to flicker: now I'm flanked by Porter—traces of pipe tobacco—and Caplan and all the other men who have observed me, trained me; they are here to evaluate my son (not a man, obviously, but a boy, a perpetual boy, Peter Pan, a man-child, since America is adolescence without end). He is only weeks from leaving my supervision, leaving Jonathan and me an empty nest. What is the future of his speech? I shift on my padded seat, blink the presences away, only to discover that I'm looking at the back of Jonathan's and Sima's heads, a few strands of silver just perceptible in the jet, the pendant turned to the back of her neck, a note of sandalwood where tobacco was. They are whispering; they think I cannot hear. Jonathan is saying: The tournament is his to lose, no, Evanson is saying that, has turned around to flash the lupine grin, grilled onion on his breath.

Jonathan takes my hand in the dark. His hand is warm, eloquent: I will make this right; I will do whatever it takes, for as long as it takes. Naylor returns to the stage. Speaker 433NN from

Apple Valley High School, Minnesota—a few cheers for the hometown favorite erupt from one side of the auditorium, but are immediately stopped by a stern look from Naylor. The question is: Has the embargo been good or bad for Castro? The question is: Did you always know you wanted to be a psychologist? How does it feel to be world-famous (your speech at once original and intelligible to the tribe)? Like one of those fragmented friendship necklaces, the other half of Adam's pill is in my pocket. (I gave him a full one this morning.) As the young woman from Apple Valley introduces her speech by enumerating some of the failed CIA attempts on Castro's life (exploding cigars, poisoned pens), I—obeying a childlike impulse—put it in my mouth.

The pill has a paradoxical effect. The speaker is still moving her lips, counting things on her fingers, but I can't hear her speech. At first, all I hear is the blood moving through my head, the hiss of idle auditory nerves. Then, its origin obscure, I perceive a kind of quiet piping, like a barely perceptible Muzak. It is spreading out from the stage into the Mall of America and the Summerset Home and Rolling Hills and the Hypermart and the Foundation and the Dillon's on Huntoon. The white noise at the end of history. Unintelligible, if shaped. The young woman is walking a few steps to her right, transitioning between points, but her mouth is shut. She's speaking only with her eyes.

I close mine. After a few minutes, audible applause indicates the silent speech has reached its end. Then I imagine the auditorium has emptied around me, except for Jonathan on my right, who still has my hand. The next speaker is XN722, Adam Gordon, Topeka High. The question is: Can you read the alphabet from Holly Eberheart's chest, the natal language of milk and men? The question is: Can you use it to write a poem? About family and art and memory and meaning, how it's made and unmade? I open my eyes.

I can see that Adam's gait is not his own, that he's performing uprightness, aping naturalness, projecting calm while flexing, no matter the benzodiazepine. The silence in the auditorium is total now; I hear the click of his dress shoes, the hard rubber soles, on the marley floor. Once he's in position, when he turns to face the audience, when he squares up with the judges, I can tell that he's a little blinded by the stage lights; Evanson has taught him, however, to feign eye contact, to pretend he can make out faces (beyond the parapet). Suddenly, although I know it is impossible, Adam seems to look directly at me, smiling slightly, politely, but without recognition. (Do you know who these nice people are?) He stands there motionless, as if he's holding my gaze, waiting for me to start his time.

Darren thinks of it, will always think of it, as already there, the cue ball, a heavy polished sphere composed of skating rink, a moon or dead star infinitely dense suspended in the basement firmament, a rotating disco ball that throws no light, only absorbs it. Darren feels that he has turned and hurled it back toward the table before he's picked it up from the corner pocket, felt its weight, the cool and smoothness of the resin. Before the freshman hottie shouts faggot, screams retard, before Darren reaches for her hair, but—her friends stepping between them—settles for the ball, before he is pushed back by a couple of seniors toward his original position along the wall, it is already there, spinning in the air, in place, the cue ball, the snowball, the baseball Brett Nelson "pegged" him with one summer, breaking a tooth, the tooth ball, composed of his teeth and poor Nick Dewey's, calcified, enamel, rotating slowly around its axis, viewable from every angle, leaving plenty of time for people to get out of its way, for the party to disband, to clean things up, spray the lemon-scented Glade, for the parents to come back from date night in Kansas City, too tired to notice it hanging at eye level when they come down to say good night, time for the seniors to graduate and go to college, for Darren to get another shot at Dillon's, to price the instant coffee, cash accumulating in his drawer until he's driving the silver Fiero home from the party at Clinton Lake, all eyes on me, passing a version of himself along the highway, rolling the window down to call him faggot, call him retard, Mandy riding shotgun, the cue ball visible through the window to his left, its position constant. Understand he would not have thrown it except he always had. If I make the sign of the cross it bounces off me. Sticks to you.

OLDE ENGLISH

(ADAM)

In the dream the trophy was so heavy he had to drag it down the carpeted corridor by the raised arms of the pewter Greek orator while he searched alone for his grandfather's room, but in reality his mom just brought a copy of *The Topeka Capital-Journal* to Rolling Hills, a photo of Adam cradling his prize above the fold.

He and his mom and grandma waited on the cement patio in the late July heat. There was no one else outside. They sat at a metal table protected from the sun by a large red umbrella that rattled in the intermittent gusts of wind. Poorly positioned sprinklers darkened the cement. He watched a jet draw contrails against an otherwise cloudless sky. Eventually his dad wheeled the small man out through the automatic doors and parked him between Adam and his grandmother. As ever, his grandfather was dressed, had been dressed, in a kind of thin sweat suit, this one beige with white piping. His knees were close together and angled up and to the right. Like a skier or skateboarder holding a position in midair, Adam thought; doesn't that require a lot of core strength? All those crunches, all that crystal. His grandfather's feet looked impossibly small in the brown slippers. Like the bound feet he'd seen in a black-and-white photograph, probably in a textbook.

Rose made a series of rapid adjustments to her husband's body:

pressed his thin white hair down where it stuck up in front (it sprang back up), pushed his knees toward the center of the chair and helped extend his legs a little, wiped the flecks of white from the corner of his mouth with a wad of tissues that, to Adam's alarm, she then returned to her purse. She executed these gestures without affection or contempt, as if she were tidying a desk.

Daddy, look at this article about Adam, who is a national champion in—in a kind of debate. Oratory. His grandfather did seem to look at it, reached a tremulous, half-opened hand toward his mom as if to take the paper, but just brushed the newsprint instead. He turned his head to Adam and less opened his mouth than let fall his jaw, which trembled slightly. Everyone waited to see if he might speak. Adam felt involuntary laughter rising inside him, coughed it away. Finally his grandfather's mouth shut and Adam watched the attention dissolve in the old man's eyes, which were pale blue, rimmed with red, and rheumy.

"Your grandson is a nerd," Adam said slowly, loudly, smiling, willing himself to place a hand on his grandfather's slight, rounded shoulder; he felt obliged to address some number of lighthearted statements to the body in the chair, and to demonstrate that he did not fear contact with the body. Adam was sweating now, could smell his own deodorant. It was difficult to determine what to say to someone who may or may not hear you, could not respond (the profound opposite of talking to an analyst). "Unfortunately, I wasn't a talented enough pitcher." His grandfather had been a baseball fan—in the halfhearted way that his grandfather had been anything; some norm of baseball fandom had been placed within him earlier in the century. Adam withdrew his hand from the shoulder, inadvertently grazing the skin of the old man's neck, which was somehow cool and dry; maybe the old no longer sweat.

Do you remember seeing Adam play baseball, Daddy—when you visited from Phoenix? His grandfather looked at his mother and something like recognition passed across his face, a ripple effect, the muscles tightening slightly, which also tightened the silence: Was he on the verge of speech or at least internally forming phrases? Again they waited awkwardly to see if he might speak, although increasingly this felt like a formality; his grandfather hadn't spoken a word in almost a year. Adam listened for highway traffic beyond the sprinklers, tuned in to the whistling of grackles on the home's low roof. He tried to remember his grandfather's voice, to hear it in his head, but could not. In fact, Adam wasn't sure he could "hear" anyone's voice, sound something internally. But didn't people always talk as though they could actually hear things in their heads—not only know and recall what they knew about voices, music, sounds, but actually re-experience properties of pitch and timbre? His head was always full of language, but there was never any noise. The voices were unvoiced. Adam wondered if this meant there was something wrong with him.

His dad was talking now, for the sake of talking, about Little League—about the brutality of other dads routinely reducing their kids to tears, getting into fistfights in the stands—but Adam was trying to listen inside his head; he'd talked to Amber only hours before, and now he willed himself to hear her voice, which felt like attempting to flex a muscle he didn't have, exercising a phantom sense. He shut his eyes for a second, wiped the sweat from his forehead with his forearm; maybe he could catch a distant echo of her intonation; it helped to picture her speaking, to read her lips. (Imagining the movement of her lips, her tongue, the slight gaps between her front teeth, was going to give him an erection; what kind of a pervert, Adam wondered, gets a hard-on visiting family in a nursing home?)

Evanson's voice, he was disturbed to realize, felt closer to him than Amber's—maybe because his body knew how to approximate it, mimic it, to let it issue from his larynx and palate; was a voice only truly present if you could imitate it, become its medium? Maybe Evanson's voice felt near because of how often

Adam had encountered it as recording, as if his brain had already learned to separate it from its embodied origin. That would explain why the contours of Tupac's voice were easier for him to imagine than Jason's, why he could retrieve the voices of relatives he spoke to on the phone, however rarely, more readily than many people he spoke with often and in person. (It wasn't obvious what voices got in you, were implanted; it didn't follow a hierarchy of intimacy; it wasn't under your control.) But even the voices that felt most firmly lodged within him made no sound. Klaus, for instance, his grandfather of affinity, was often in his head, but Klaus's voice—its literary syntax, his constant quotation—"sounded" like writing. It was like how, when he read a poem to himself, the rhymes were neither sound nor silence. Unheard melodies in the mind's ear. The muted music of consciousness. Maybe it was this way for everyone—that to speak of hearing voices was metaphorical; if you really heard voices, you belonged in the Foundation.

Suddenly his grandfather made a noise. It was a groan or croak—deep, hoarse—and it lasted two or three seconds. At the beginning and end of it Adam detected slight modulations that might have been attempts at phonemes, at sense, at language. Little linguistic phosphenes. Was it a word or phrase or expression of pain or an asemantic involuntary expulsion of air, meaningless vibrations passing through him? His grandfather's face was expressionless, gave no clue, although he'd turned his head toward Rose. He didn't know if it was an instance of the old man's voice or its negation, signifying nothing. Whatever it was, it was horrible, indecent: maybe he'd soiled himself. Against his will, he imagined it as a sound accompanying orgasm. He was surprised at his disgust, at his anger, shame. Are you speaking to us, Daddy? Is there something you want to say?

This length of sound that was almost speech—not pre- but post-verbal—got in his head. It was still resonating within him as they said goodbye, each of them, except for his grandmother, hugging his unresponsive grandfather in turn. Accompanied by his dad, he wheeled the body back inside, parked it in the common area where the body would await lunch. He approached the desk where a few of the staff were sitting and thanked them, as he'd often seen his parents do, for taking such great care of his grandfather. We really appreciate all your work, the care you provide for our family, he said, he heard himself say, but his speech was shadowed in his own mind by his grandfather's obscene complaint. Look at my famous baby boy, his dad said, handing the folded newspaper to the woman in green scrubs; he won a national championship in speech! The woman took the paper and, looking from the photo to Adam, smiled politely. Adam said something self-deprecating and again he perceived his grandfather's groan beneath it.

By the time they'd dropped Rose off and returned home, the noise had receded into memory; it no longer felt as though it originated in his body. Instead of immediately heading for his room, or the living room TV to watch *Rap City* on BET, or the phone, or back out in his Camry, he sat with his mom at the kitchen table, his dad preparing coffee in the silver stovetop espresso maker.

"What is it like for you," he asked his mother, in a voice he was preparing for college, "seeing him like that? Mute. It must be hard."

"Well, it would be better if he could let go. For everyone. I think he's too strong for his own good. He was never sick. I mean not even a cold."

"Do you think he knows who we are, where he is?"

"I think he does. Most of the time."

"So you think he can listen but not respond."

"Yeah."

"That sounds like the worst to me. A nightmare. Not being able to talk back."

"Yes."

His dad set a chipped blue mug down before his mom and joined them at the table. Adam didn't drink anything with caffeine, because of the migraines.

"When was the last time you had a real conversation with him?" he asked.

"He was still talking a fair amount last year," his mom said.

"But a substantial conversation, not just him managing a few words here and there."

"Years," his dad said.

"We had some real talks when you were in middle school, and when you were a freshman," his mom said.

"About what?"

"We processed a lot of things." She sipped her coffee. Sipped it again. "The family dynamics growing up. How he favored my sister, for instance."

"Do you think he ever read your books?"

"I think he skimmed them. He said he read them. He always said they were 'very interesting.' He would say, 'Jane writes books for troubled women.'"

"He was probably threatened," Adam said.

"In what sense?"

"By your success."

"Maybe. I'm not sure. He seemed indifferent."

"Did you ever confront him about the tissue box?"

His mom laughed. "Not really."

"I can't remember what it sounded like, his voice."

"Your dad has recordings."

"Of him saying what?" Adam asked.

"Reminiscing," his dad said. "Nothing in particular. I just got him talking. I used to do that with a lot of people—I have reels of Dr. Tom. Klaus reading his plays in German. I know I have tapes from Phoenix. After his first stroke. Can you remember that trip?"

"Kind of. Can we listen to them?" Adam noted how his dad looked at his mom, awaited her answer.

"Sure," Jane said.

"Why don't we listen now?" Adam asked. Maybe the tapes of the voice would obliterate the traces of the croak.

"Jonathan, do you know where they are?"

His dad went to get the cassette tapes from the messy basement room they called his studio. Maybe it would be too discomfiting for his mom to listen to her father's voice issuing at once from before and beyond the grave. Certainly Adam felt an ambient intensity. "We don't have to listen to the tapes if it's weird."

"No, I'm curious. He was actually very eloquent. He would have been a good extemper."

"I would have destroyed him," Adam joked.

"But not a good debater." She didn't hear him. "He spoke very slowly. It could be exasperating."

"I would have totally destroyed him."

"I can only find one," his dad said, returning to the table with a gray portable cassette player and recorder. "I also have the reel-to-reels from my dissertation down there," he said to Jane. "I should transfer those to cassette for Adam. Talk about 'the spread.'" His dad put the cassette into the player but did not press any buttons. His mom finally reached over to press play.

For the first few seconds, they heard nothing but the hiss of the tape. Then it was Jonathan's voice, tinnier, younger (it was hard to sort the youth of the voice from the age of the medium): *Okay. Okay, here we go, so we were speaking, you were talking about the Brooklyn house, Avenue J. And how you made almost—*

Most of the furniture and many of the girls' toys. Despite how this hand, how my right hand, has never opened completely, or closed properly. Now it would be described as a disability and I could probably draw welfare for my entire life, never work a day. But this was back when one made do. And in fact it never—

It was a little more high-pitched than he'd expected, maybe due to the tape. (Or did voices deepen in memory?) The *r* sound disappearing after vowels—like a Brooklynite aspiring to be British. Adam heard it as pretension. This was reinforced by the slowness, a patriarch holding forth, convinced that whatever he said, it was of interest. The pronunciation—despite the recent blockage of blood flow to the brain, the mild facial paralysis—was crisp.

—*interfered with my carpentry. We saved a considerable, a not inconsiderable amount of money. Because what I didn't make I could fix up and Rose would bring home chairs or other discarded furniture and I would restore those pieces. In fact, I could have probably turned that into a lucrative business. Rose is fond of talking about how little income we had in those days but if you were to calculate what I made and salvaged we were in fact in a very strong position. We spent little on the house but had a fine home. Certainly the girls wanted for nothing. I remember in fact how Deborah was always begging me to make toys for her friend Alice, who lived on Carroll Street, a wealthy family, and I did make her a very pretty rocking horse but refused to take*—

"That's a lie," his mom said over the tape, "he had promised several people these rocking horses; he never made them."

—*money from, what was her mother's name? Her husband had died in the war. A career officer. The Asian theater. I wouldn't have accepted payment under any condition whatsoever. Something with an* S. *And I did all of our repairs. And I made many of the frames for Rose's pictures. I had some good Disston saws. I could measure the pilot holes without using a tape. Those are to prevent the wood from splitting. Some of those artworks you have hanging in your house in Topeka are as you know my frames. I think her name was Sarah. I'd give them a classical look, age them. A coat of red paint, a layer, and when that dried I'd coat it with two layers of a light gray or gold. Then I'd sand it with a very fine paper and let some of the red come through, especially at the corners and edges. A dishonest person could have sold them as antiques. I intended to make some frames for the prints Rose has in the garage but now I can't even work the miter. I wonder if Deborah has kept up with Alice. She was like one of the family in many ways. A darling. I felt terribly sorry for her, that she didn't have a father. I don't know what the money was from, but they had a Chevy Bel Air, which was a gorgeous automobile. The four-door hardtop. It had those chrome—*

His mom stopped the tape abruptly. The three of them looked at the player on the table as if it were an urn. The voice continued in Adam, then faded, but he knew that it was somewhere in him, had been and would be. How do you rid yourself of a voice, keep it from becoming part of yours? He wanted to break the silence in which his grandfather was still involved. He imagined stomping on the player, unspooling the magnetic tape from the mangled cassette. (He knew he could not account for the violence of his response, which only increased it.) He wanted to say something to and for his mom. Come on, Mr. Champion Talker. But what if he opened his mouth and his grandfather's voice came out? Or worse: the disgusting noise from their visit? Or Evanson, citing the Cleveland *Plain Dealer*? Or rhymes about bitches? You kiss your mother with that mouth? a Little League coach asked silently in his head. He hated that expression.

"I hope to never see one," Adam said. And without missing a beat, his mother responded, corrected him, smiling now: "I never hope to see one." In his mind, he was rewinding the tape, pressing the red button on the player, so that they were recording over his grandfather. He misquoted the line again, as if he were trying to get it right. "Jonathan," Jane said, eyes beginning to shine, "I can't believe our boy, a poet, a national champion in competitive speech, can't memorize a single simple line." She corrected him again, his split infinitive, that little broken future, and now his grandfather wasn't in the room; it was just the three of them, an immediate family. If he ever needed to summon her voice, Adam knew, all he had to do was quote his misquotation, their ritual refusal of repetition across the generations, their shadowed passage, weak spell, and then his mother would answer in his head, overwhelm the Men, however briefly. ("I'm sorry, it's not a great connection.")

♦♦♦

At first the dream absorbed the voice—a woman a few seats behind him on the small plane began to yell—but soon it overwhelmed the fiction and he woke, sat up suddenly. Maybe it was shouting in a movie. No, it was too loud, and they wouldn't be watching so late; according to the red display of the alarm clock, it was 2:17. A weeknight. Now he recognized his mother's voice, although he also found it unrecognizable; he had of course heard her yell before, but this was primal. For a moment he wondered if the sounds had to do with sex, although he had never to his knowledge heard his parents "making love." (The phrase, even when he thought it, was in scare quotes.) This was some kind of argument, or had been an argument before it became something worse: he could hear, when his mom wasn't yelling, his dad speaking; his voice was also raised, but in an effort to calm her. (How much affective information travels through the walls, even when the words are unintelligible.) Then the screaming again, maybe sobbing; Adam wasn't sure.

He looked around his room. Now that he was days from leaving home, his possessions seemed to belong to the past, to pertain to a childhood from which he'd graduated. On the desk beside the wooden incense burner and stacks of CD cases, there was a large plasma globe someone had given him years ago, maybe for his Bar Mitzvah. When you switched it on, shifting beams of blue and pink light ("Lichtenberg figures," Klaus had called them) moved between the inner electrode and the outer glass. A terrarium for phosphenes. If you touched the globe, the current curved to your hand, the electricity buzzing beneath your palm; he'd often worried touching it would somehow lead to migraines.

It seemed childish to him now, this novelty item from the eighties; he hadn't turned it on in a year, maybe two; he should get rid of it. As his mom's yelling started up again, he wondered—he forced himself to wonder—how would one dispose of such a thing? Can you just put it in the trash? What kinds of noble gases are trapped within the glass? If it cracked, what would be released? Maybe Erwood would want it.

The globe, he remembered, also had an audio setting; the electricity would pulse in response to sound. He imagined that if he turned it on, it would register his parents' voices from that distance, the electrical patterns somehow communicating the content of the fight to him, flickering hieroglyphics. But he didn't want the content to be manifest; he just wanted the yelling to stop. (An instant ago he'd been older than himself, his room; now he was a little kid, afraid of the noise.) He coughed as loudly as he could, kicked the wall his bed was next to.

But his mom went on, animal in pain. He rose and stood in the middle of his room beside the wedge of moonlight on the off-white carpet. He was in his boxers and the undershirt they called a "wifebeater." Calm down, he said to himself: parents argue; mom is stressed out about her (hopefully) dying dad; they're worried about an "empty nest"; transitions in multiple generations. Maybe he could wrap his body in chewing gum and walk into their room, "It just fell out of my mouth," distract them. Maybe put on his debate suit and reason with them, adjudicate questions of policy and value. He decided he'd go to the bathroom, make a lot of noise in the hall.

He moved with exaggerated clumsiness, Buster Keaton, and moved quickly, so as not to comprehend much language; he couldn't have explained his desire not to understand the nature of their fight. From the hall he heard his mom use the word "Flatbush," the word "museum," but soon he was flushing the toilet, then flushing it again. But they didn't hear him or she didn't care, was too far gone. He returned to the bathroom door and slammed it, They'll hear that, then walked to the sink, opened the taps, and stared at himself in the mirror.

How his dad would help lather Adam's face and then apply the remaining foam to his own cheeks. Back then Adam had his own safety razor without a blade that stood beside his father's in the little stand. He would position the stepstool next to his dad and they would "shave" together before breakfast, Adam very serious about removing the lather in even strokes, rinsing his razor between each row; he loved the smell of Barbasol. Even on the stepstool Adam wasn't tall enough to reflect in the mirror but he could look up and see his father's image in the fogged glass. He'd synchronize his motions with his dad's until the child became the man; Adam believed he could feel the blade scraping his rough cheek, had to be careful to avoid the mustache he now wore. A collective face. Until they splashed the cold water and he became himself again. How his dad wiped the remaining lather with a towel, making him laugh by pulling a little on his earlobes. Then they'd drive to Bright Circle, often picking Jason up en route.

Back in the present he heard not only yelling, but things being knocked over, maybe thrown. He couldn't picture what was happening; he'd never seen his mom or dad wreck anything in anger.

It was less than ten feet from the bathroom to his parents' door. He walked slowly, his footfall purposefully heavy in the hall, making the floor creak. His dad was talking now: about the painful process of clearing the air, about not living up to expectations, about patterns, someone named Rachel, but Adam was trying not to hear. (Trying not to hear felt like flexing a muscle he didn't have.) He wanted to call out—Hey, what's going on, everybody relax—so that they could prepare themselves for his presence, but he felt incapable of speech. He doubted that the sounds he was making traveled through the air; he was in a different dimension than his parents, a ghost, inside the walls. He could hear his mom responding now, but she wasn't saying much—cursing, something derisive about the men's group, then noises that weren't words. His dad had fallen silent.

Adam knocked loudly on the half-open door, then pushed it fully open and walked in. He tried to make his voice sound a little sarcastic, a joke about his being the mature one, the parental figure: Let's all take a deep breath here. The only light was from a reading lamp on the bedside table. His dad was standing in his underwear, what Adam and his peers would have called "tighty whities," his arms crossed; he always looked slightly blind and vulnerable without his glasses. His mom had put on jeans and a dark sweater (which made no sense; even at night, the temperature was in the eighties), her hair wild and only half held back by a clip; sitting on the floor, she was pulling on a pair of boots. That wasn't something she would normally do—sit on the floor of her room, unless she was stretching. The shoes she typically wore were downstairs near the door; she must have taken the boots from the closet. With a deliberateness that betrayed his upset, his dad said finally: "Everything is fine, Adam; go back to bed. We're just having a disagreement." But his mom stared at Adam as if shocked not only by his presence, but by his existence. Concussed, she failed to recognize him. Then she yelled: "Some fucking privacy, okay?" Stunned, he heard himself say—heard a much younger kid say—"Mom, where are you going?" In the ensuing silence, the pulsing of the off-hook tone from the phone beside the bed.

"Ask your father." She scrambled to her feet; there was something childish about her motions, which disconcerted him further. Then she made herself smile and said to Adam in a strained approximation of her normal voice: "I'm sorry, sweetheart, I need to get some fresh to think—air, I mean." Distress had scrambled her predicates. She walked past him and down the stairs; he heard her grab her keys from the hook near the front door, which she then shut hard behind her, rattling the front windows. Footsteps on the porch, car door slamming, the engine starting up. He walked to the nearby window and parted the venetian blinds and watched her pull out of the driveway, head toward Sixth.

Adam turned and watched his dad take his glasses from the dresser, put them on, then start to pick up some of the things his mom must have thrown. He retrieved the brass table clock, set it back on the bedside table, then the small but heavy stone Inuit sculpture that Rose had acquired somewhere. It went on the dresser. Adam had the strange sensation that the various objects strewn across the floor had less been scattered by his mom than drawn into their position by a magnetic force, some principle of attraction his dad now had to fight against as he restored them to their place. He imagined that the water glass his dad lifted from the carpet—by the darkness of the stain he could tell it had held wine—weighed thirty pounds, like one of the barbells Adam curled at Popeye's. In the corner, along with a few books that had been swept from the surface of the dresser—including one of his mom's, a new translation into some Eastern European language—Adam saw the blond wood box that Klaus had given him. We've been processing a lot and tonight it got out of hand and I'm really sorry that we woke you. It's all fine, really; your mom will be back soon; let's just get some sleep. The desire to know more and the desire to know less fought each other to a standstill within Adam, making it hard to move. He sensed his dad was bracing himself to field the difficult questions.

But Adam said good night, turned around. He softly shut his parents' door behind him. His legs carried him past his bedroom to his mom's study at the end of the hall, where the carpet gave way to hardwood. He didn't turn on the lights. Large unblinded windows opened onto the backyard. The branches of the walnut tree around which the back deck was constructed were moving in the wind, throwing shadows on the floor. He stood as quietly as possible, listening for the sound of a car returning. Atop the backyard fence an animal crawled slowly; was it a large cat or a raccoon? It was a cat. He turned from the window and walked to the desk and sat down on the rolling chair. To the right of her computer monitor, a few green and purple Alebrije turtles from Oaxaca, heads trembling slightly. A triptych of hinged frames with him and his mom at different ages. By the low hum from the tower underneath the desk he could tell that she'd left the computer on. Only the beige box monitor was off; he found the square button on the back of the screen and pressed it.

Word for Windows, 1995. She didn't have Office 97 yet. The open document consisted of notes his mom was making, maybe for an article: "Cut offs in first families—see Bowen, process view of change"; "pursuit cycle and anxiety"; etc. He had the fantasy that anything he typed in the document would end up in one of her books, that she would later mistake it for her own language and incorporate it into her writing, which would then circulate around the world, maybe influence her readers' relationships. He knew the notion was absurd, but it frightened him.

He opened a new document. He typed out fragments of what his dad had said, but now he organized and broke them roughly according to their syllables and stresses, something he'd been experimenting with in his poems:

It's painful when you clear the air
I haven't always lived up to
Especially when there is so much

He let the cursor blink four times. Then he went on:

A process view of change becomes
Two layers of light gray or gold
Electricity beneath your palm

And so on. There was some kind of special power involved in repurposing language, redistributing the voices, changing the principle of patterning, faint sparks of alternative meaning in the shadow of the original sense, the narrative. The power was both real and very weak, a distant signal. He wrote a few more tercets, none of them particularly good, but the process of composing them, or letting some other force compose them through him, relaxed him a little, a kind of meditation. He closed the document, clicking on "Don't Save."

He hesitated, then double-clicked on the Netscape icon and listened to the dial tone. Then the automated dialing, the beeps and hisses, the sound of the modem communicating with another modem across the landline, the language of machines. When he was connected, Adam typed "ALS Scan" into the search bar and waited for the results to load, at which point he clicked on the appropriate link. It took a while for the thumbnails to appear. It wasn't his favorite site, but he felt confident that if the name ALS Scan was somehow discovered by who knows what surveilling power it would sound innocuous. Wasn't ALS a disease? He could claim he'd been doing some kind of research.

He clicked more or less at random on the small image of a young woman probably around his age giving head to a purple dildo she held in one hand while she spread her labia with the other. The image began to load; the muffled sounds that issued from the computer tower were reminiscent of construction noises heard from a distance. Sawing and hammering, as if little men lived in the computer and had to manufacture the image by hand. It began to appear from the top of the screen down, a curtain of color falling millimeters at a time. It would take a full minute to appear in full, the striptease of slow bit speed.

That part of the screen the image hadn't reached was dark, and he could see his own reflection in the glass. Then, without warning, there was another face reflected there, someone looking over his shoulder; horrified, Adam dove awkwardly at the computer under the desk and hit the power button; by the time he sat back up, he already knew it was a false alarm, that the room was empty. He would have heard someone approach. He inhaled deeply through his nose, exhaled audibly through his mouth. Exhausted now, he got up to go to bed.

But he stopped at the threshold of the study: when his mom turned on the computer in the morning, would the image still be loading? He knew that couldn't be, but the mental picture was disturbing, and there might be some other trace of it, his browsing history. (The image would appear on screens everywhere, and somehow people would know it was his doing, his responsibility; Amber would see it on her own PC, Rose would see it the next time she passed the electronics department at Hypermart, it would show up on the Phelpses' picket signs, are you proud of your son, it would somehow load in the frames beside her desk, take over the dust jackets of her books, but it would also load on the screens and surfaces of the past, *Fritz the Cat*, the George Brett poster and his *Star Wars* sheets; it would replace the Chagall in his dad's office, ruining his practice. And the evidence would appear on the screens of the future: your iPhone, the cover of this book. Foreknowledge of the humiliation had caused his mom to flee. The obstinacy of history.)

He returned to the desk and turned the computer back on. He heard the six-second Windows start-up sound composed by Brian Eno. He needed to find and clear the cache. Only now did he wonder if his mom's changes had been saved.

♦♦♦

He parked the car a few houses away from the party and cut the engine just as the streetlight nearest them came on. Do you think they're on timers, he asked Amber, or do you think they're photosensitive? I think there's a little bird inside each light, like on *The Flintstones*, she responded. They lit cigarettes and smoked and watched some of their classmates arrive, most carrying bottles or boxes. They played a game of trying to identify the brand of beverage from this distance: Zima, Mad Dog 20/20

Coco Loco, Mickey's Fine Malt Liquor. Amber covered one eye, like when they have you read the letters off the chart.

When their cigarettes were finished they got out of the car and walked to the trunk, which he'd popped, to retrieve their own drinks, both taken from Amber's parents: a lightly used fifth of Absolut and a bottle of white wine. When he slammed the trunk shut the streetlight went out as if with the noise. Amber slid in front of him so she was between him and the car and pulled him near her: Quick, before the lights come back on. He tasted the sugary gloss and tobacco, the hints of mint and metal that made him when he kissed her think of blood. It was good to be inflicting optional damage on your bright pink lungs; it was good to be two young people tasting of Lancôme and Philip Morris, synthetic pheromones and carcinogens, to be at the point of their most intimate contact, their most interchangeable, corporate persons; clichés, types.

I have a cousin in Joplin, she said, pulling away (she was always suddenly pulling away), who says they go out when she walks under them. She thinks it's like a superpower she has, or whatever you call a bad superpower. A curse—that there is something wrong with her.

Maybe it has to do, Adam said, with the electromagnetic field around her body.

But the fucked-up thing (she ignored him) is that we—my brother was there—were all stoned and she was telling us this and we were teasing her, talking about Stull, *The Exorcist*, and then she was like: Come on. And we all walked to the downtown, which was like half a mile from my aunt's house, totally deserted. This was one in the morning on a Sunday. There were all these old-school streetlights. And she told us to wait and watch and she walked slowly under them on one side of the street and nothing happened. We were cracking up. Then she came back toward us on the other side of the street and one of them *did* go out. We were like, holy shit, but also said it was luck. And so she did the walk again and another one went out, I swear. It was totally fucked. Like she did it with her mind. She's pretty nuts and on Prozac now and they're homeschooling her. I think she might be a witch or something.

This is your dad's side—his older sister's daughter, he confirmed.

Yeah, she said, laughing.

You sound like a bunch of crazy fucking stoners, he said, in case his desire to map her family, to hold the system in his mind, made him appear weird or soft.

They walked holding hands toward Jason's house but let go of each other as they approached; nobody held hands, it wasn't the 1950s. More people were arriving and Adam was surprised by all the cars—neither Adam nor Jason had ever hosted a full-blown house party; Sima and Eric, like Jane and Jonathan, wouldn't mind a little drinking, wouldn't be scandalized by a little pot, but they wouldn't tolerate harder drugs or incapacitated underclassmen or a brawl; any one of those would lead to a year, maybe years, of "processing." Jason's parents were in Kansas City for the night, but it could be difficult to control a gathering once it started, ensure everyone disbanded in time. Jason was bound for Stanford in a month and a half; maybe he didn't care if he got into trouble.

From the voices and music (the Fugees, *The Score*) they could tell that people were in the back. A wooden gate on the side of the house led to a stone path flanked with small lights to the yard where other recent graduates were distributed among the patio furniture, smoking and drinking. Here and there a case of Natural Light; Nowak imbibing Evan Williams from the bottle; a jug of Carlo Rossi; etc. Adam, after the customary greetings, now mixed with mock congratulations on his triumph—"Hey, let's all toast the champion of dorks"—went inside to find a mixer.

Why on that night was it strange to enter Jason's house, a house he'd known for as long as he could remember? Why did he rifle through the refrigerator and kitchen drawers like an anthropologist or ghost? Why did he set the orange juice down beside the bottle on the counter and, instead of preparing the drinks, walk into the living room and regard the yellow leather couch and paintings on the walls—a small Lassiter in an antique frame, a gift from Jane, among them? He sought out the tooth marks he knew he'd left on the coffee table a decade or so before, a fall when they were playing; he ran his fingers over the impression and recalled watching his dad peel Jason's lip off his braces in the hotel some years later. (What happened to their baby teeth? he suddenly wondered. Did their parents just throw them out? He imagined rejoining the party and finding the senior men and women flashing smiles of little deciduous teeth, gaps here and there where they'd been lost, the missing teeth left under pillows for the tooth fairy, who'd exchange them for silver dollars.) With no destination in mind, he climbed the stairs, hardwood creaking under his feet. Jason's bedroom and the TV room were to his right, but he went to his left, opened the door to the master bedroom, which he'd never entered before. He could smell a scent he associated with Sima. On top of their dresser was a large open jewelry box inlaid with silver and pearl and he picked up some of the bangles, looked at the rings. There was a locket unattached to a chain that he tried to open, but could not; maybe it wasn't a locket, was just a pendant, but he sensed that it concealed something, an old photograph, a sliver of World Ice. The large windows opened onto the backyard and he walked to them and carefully parted the venetian blinds and looked down onto his milieu. See Darren arrive in the company of Cody and Laura. The exaggerated enthusiasm with which Darren is greeted, its hysterical edge. What's up, my brother? Yo, now this is a fucking party. Adam imagined he could see himself on one of the wicker armchairs, Amber in his lap, pulling her blond hair into a ponytail over her right shoulder in a way that displayed the toned muscles of her tan arms.

But it was Amber who touched his back, causing him to recoil from the blinds in shock. Jesus, he said; how had she made no noise on the stairs? What are you doing up here? she asked. Not knowing what to say, he smiled conspiratorially and walked to the door and locked it by depressing the button in the silver handle and then returned to her and led her to the large and carefully made bed. Here? she asked. Unexpected firmness of the mattress, the memory foam. More voices outside the window, the party growing larger fast. They made out for a while with her on top of him and then he flipped her over, kissed his way slowly down to the top button of her jeans, which he undid.

Understand his sexual knowledge, such as it was, represented a synthesis, or a workable tension, between porn and *Our Bodies, Ourselves*, the closest thing to porn he'd ever located in his parents' possession; he'd heard his own mother talk about the erasure of the clitoris from psychoanalytic theory and he'd of course heard boys and men speak endlessly of the female body as a plaything to be wrecked for male pleasure. How to interact with Amber in a way that at once asserted his good difference as poet, proto-feminist, Ivy-bound alternative to the types without neutering himself in the process? Cunnilingus, cunning linguist, as the joke went, a joke that might have been made for him, he who tried to cover the body in speech. (The gum, Klaus's voice, indicating a transfer of orality to the genital.) He could hardly have been the only boy who "ate pussy" in Topeka, but he might have been the only kid in the class of '97 who read up on techniques, consulted the famous sexpert when she passed through town, who solicited frank feedback from his partner in the act. (This talk itself, after her initial shyness, seemed to affect Amber almost as much as physical contact.) To flatten the tongue instead of pointing it. The dialectic of circular and vertical motions. The choreography of his fingers. Not to instinctually speed up in response to rising pleasure, not to succumb to the instinct to spread. In college he would have to unlearn the beautiful adolescent myth that "writing" the alphabet with his tongue was a universal code for the female orgasm, but it at least expanded his range of motion. You could practice by trying to read with a pen in your mouth. The bar was absurdly low for this form of articulacy. To use the edge of the tongue, essential for alveolar plosives, such as */t, d/*. If all he knew was to listen and respond and hold steady through the shaking, that was more than enough—combined with straight fucking—to make Amber declare him by far the greatest of her many lovers. But while he hoped she publicized this ranking, he didn't want her divulging the centrality of oral stimulation, which would put his reputation at risk among the types. Again his tongue was both his strength and weakness.

She pulled one of the large pillows over her face to muffle the noise she made when she came, or seemed to come. When she was no longer trembling, he repositioned himself carefully and removed the pillow and they made out slowly for a while. Then they were both on their backs staring at the motionless white ceiling fan just visible above them in the darkness. Instead of immediately going down on Adam to reciprocate, Amber began to speak.

Even though my mom doesn't want me going too far out of state I bet she could be convinced that I have to move east to find the right mix of dance and academics. She has a niece who went to Swarthmore which is basically Philadelphia and that's a long drive to Providence or a short one to New York. I don't know if I could get in because my transcripts from West have a bunch of C's because I was fucking around but I'm 4.0 since then, 790 math SAT, and while I'm not a dorky debate champion I can write a good essay or you will for me or there are other schools. (Did you know there's a medical school in the Bahamas where you can go and then come back here and be a doctor? How great would that be. After college I'll be there learning how to operate and then be chilling on the beach, stoned as fuck. That's what I'll do if dance doesn't work out. Maybe pediatric, like how they fixed my brother's arteries because he was born with them reversed. That's why he couldn't play football even though he's awesome.) I'm not saying we're going to be some kind of couple always but I want to be in New York some weekend with you, I want to go to the museum and ride in one of those horse-and-buggy things through the park like your dad did after his bad trip and make some other memories there. I can't believe they just tell you what it was like for them getting together and doing drugs and losing their grip. My mom will be shitfaced and full of pills but swear she's had half a glass of wine. Like we could see art or hear music or poetry or something or the clubs or just walk around the streets from movies. My brother says the last time he was there they bought forties of Olde E and got on a ferry and spent the night getting fucked up going back and forth and looking at all the city lights from the water, which sounds cool to me, we could do that together one night, okay? You don't know how much when you're not being an asshole I love being with you, how it feels to know the sameness and the difference even though you can't represent my voice, the problem of other minds, phosphenes, phonemes. Like now the wide and vacant blurrings of my early life thicken in my mind. We just need fake IDs. Scarce know I at any time whether I tell you real things, or the unrealest dreams. If you rub this plant between your hands, the streetlights will go out, the sirens on. Hale-Bopp is about to pass perihelion, a trail of blue gas pointing away from the sun. Blue ice. You'll see it if you shut your eyes and press. Always in me, the solidest things melt into dreams, and dreams into solidities. There is a spaceship behind it and while we lie here the members of Heaven's Gate are mixing phenobarbital and applesauce and vodka and climbing into their bunk beds and covering their heads with purple cloth so that they may be transported from their bodies and this planet where history has ended, class of '97.

In the kitchen they poured the vodka and orange juice over ice into the tallest glasses and returned to the backyard, which was loud now with the assembled crowd. A wave of underclassmen had arrived. Within minutes Adam was back to refill their glasses, less orange juice this time, and then without transition he was being handed a third, maybe fourth by Amber. He could not have told you how the cipher formed, who the first actors were, but he found himself with his arms around a couple of seniors' shoulders while they tried to rhyme about bitches and gunplay and so on. If you take this mysterious pill you can abstract from the absurdity and offensiveness of their vocabulary to regain a sense of wonder before the mere fact that any kind of formally pressurized language game held social weight, that the masculine types would in this appropriated manner create a theater where speech might be recycled, recombined, however clumsily or outrageously. On this night Adam managed to rise above the stupid violence of the battles and misogynist clichés and enter a zone in which sentences unfolded at a speed he could not consciously control. At that point it didn't matter what words he was plugging into the machinery of syntax (a sublime of exchangeability), it didn't matter if he was rhyming about bitches or blow or the Stingray surveillance program; it didn't matter that he looked like an idiot; what mattered was that language, the fundamental medium of sociality, was being displayed in its abstract capacity, and that he would catch a glimpse, however fleeting, of grammar as pure possibility.

Whose idea was it to incorporate Darren? Darren moved, was moved, on a current of alcohol and shared energy, into the circle without surplus; the types placed their arms fraternally around his shoulders as in a football huddle and passed him the invisible mic or conch or talking stick and while he was purely mute the first time, incapable of any vocalization whatsoever, see the terrified smile, they returned to him eventually, and now he spoke, if haltingly. And while his contribution was but a clumsy attempt to repeat word for word what Adam chanted about fists in faces and catching cases, his brothers all shouted their encouragement and amazement and bobbed their heads to the nonexistent beat as though Darren were disclosing new territories of thought and feeling, new worlds, as though he were their Caedmon. For they had always been told to include him and this constituted the zenith of inclusion, the assimilation of Darren to corporate speech, their busted prosodies, and if there was irony, not all of it was cruel.

But it was too loud out back; the neighbors would complain. Eventually Jason broke the cipher up and said they had to go inside, downstairs to the basement with the large TV and the beanbag chairs and the copper wall and the billiard table Eric had with Jonathan's help and Ron Williams's pickup hauled from Klaus's a couple of years before. It was time to take their positions around the imperceptibly rotating cue ball, satellite of ice. There was, there is, no rush; the interns have to set up the cameras, the actors need to adjust their period dress, angle their hats just so, fasten their pagers, apply their secrets of wash and finish. This is 1909; this is 1983; this is early spring of 1997 seen from 2019, from my daughters' floor, dim glow of the laptop, "Clair de lune" playing in a separate window, as Bone Thugs-N-Harmony plays in the basement. From outside, because tonight is recycling, I hear the sound of people picking through glass; from inside the novel, laughter and slurred speech, the mechanisms near collapse. The cases of beer have been placed along the wall; the bongs have been placed atop the green expanse of baize; McCabe shows Jason the plastic bag of crystals, how you heat the bottom of the bulb from which the filaments have been carefully removed. It took thousands of generations of technical progress, each building on the achievements of those who lived before, to make those common modern articles possible. Tempera on wood. Kodachrome marble. Rubber and glue.

When everyone is in position in the crowded basement, the

lights go off. Here and there the glow of a lighter held to a bowl, the blue electrical display on the portable stereo. Click on the cue ball and drag it to the edge of the table and place it alongside Mandy Owen's face, which is in profile; when the mouse is released, it strikes her three inches below the temple, shattering the jaw in several places, dislodging multiple teeth, knocking her unconscious, forever altering her speech. When the lights come back on, she is facedown on the floor; there is screaming at the speed and spread of blood; the music is finally cut. Some rush to Mandy, slowly turn her over (more screaming); others rush to Darren, restrain him as if he were trying to escape, little mimic spasms around the corners of his mouth; many flee the basement altogether, stampeding up the stairs. Locate the cue ball where it's rolled beneath the table and click again, drag it left. The blood and teeth reenter Mandy's head as she regains her footing, her jaw re-knits; the lights go out, clouds of smoke reenter mouths, the music plays backward as the little moon spins through the basement firmament, all in a span perhaps no longer than / an arrow takes to strike, to fly, to leave // the bow. How much easier it would be if when you played them slowly in reverse the lyrics really did, as some hysterical parents feared, reveal satanic messages; if there were a backmasked secret order, however dark, instead of rage at emptiness. Now it fills his hand.

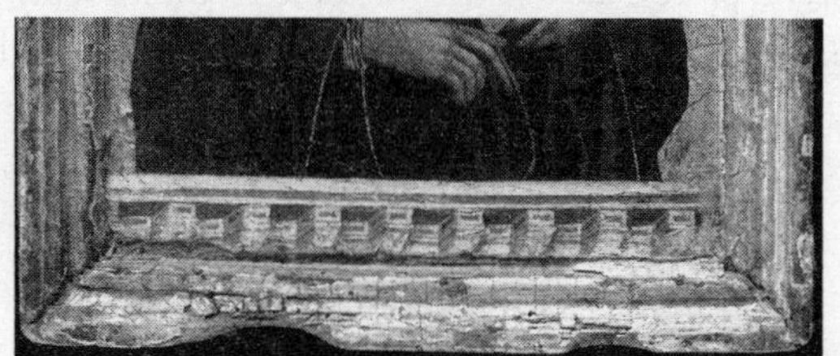

THEMATIC APPERCEPTION

(ADAM)

From Doña Alana's one-bedroom apartment on 108th and Amsterdam, an apartment that had not materially changed since 1942, when she'd arrived from Vieques, the apartment in which she'd raised two daughters on her own, the carefully made twin bed her girls slept in still there beside the carefully made queen, which was next to a little table that held a rotary phone, the last rotary phone in my life (that my own daughters will never know landlines, a profound change from a family systems perspective), an apartment that felt like the one still point around which the neighborhood constantly rearranged itself, we walked, Natalia and I, pushing the double stroller through unseasonable November warmth toward Riverside Drive. From our own girls we were trying to hide our sadness at the latest signs of their great-grandmother's advancing dementia: how she called Natalia by her mother's name for most of the visit; how she thought Luna, our eldest, was a boy, Natalia brushing Luna's brown hair back to reveal the little gold studs; how Bisi, as the kids called her, grabbed a coquí refrigerator magnet from the young Amaya's hand with sudden desperation, *Es mío*, the way another child might, then looked at the magnet in her palm, confused by what she'd done, as Amaya's wailing started up. We stopped on the Broadway traffic island, waiting for the walk sign, Natalia greeting the old-timers on the bench to our left, the Spanish unintelligible to me because of the swallowed vowels, birdsong audible in the wake of a passing bus, as I pretended not to watch a homeless man picking through the green metal trash can to our right, confirming that he was not a threat to the girls, unable not to think in those terms, Amaya napping now, pacifier in mouth, Luna singing a song about hippos to herself, clouds moving rapidly through the space between the buildings when I looked up, Cardi B issuing from a double-parked car. When we didn't want the girls to understand our conversation, Natalia and I spoke to one another in polysyllabic jargon, ten-cent words, something I could only do in English, which also allowed us to make serious topics a kind of game—we felt like children mocking grown-up speech—and so I said, "Neurodegeneration is onerous to behold but her fundamental personality is intact," or whatever; Natalia said, "My hope is that she can reach her terminus without relocation to an institution," or the like. The light changed, we crossed the street, Luna indicating the Mister Softee truck: Dada, you promised ice cream; No, I said you could have cookies at Bisi's or wait and have the ice cream, guilt at projected levels of sugar in her blood. Luna began to whine, Natalia, who only spoke Spanish with the girls, told what consequences whining might bring; Luna let it go, resumed her hippo freestyle, incorporating the word "onerous" now, which she pronounced "ownrust," the language putty in her mouth, clapping to scatter some pigeons as we coasted downhill toward Riverside, Luna delighted by a man doing pull-ups on the scaffolding, Dada can you do that. What a life your grandmother has had, I said to Natalia, as I always did, and what a particularly insane century to have spanned, to be born in the early days of automobiles and airplanes and now to be FaceTiming (on Natalia's phone) with a cousin on the island, the power just tentatively restored, as her great-grandchildren run around her. Natalia nodded at the platitudes, *Sportsmanlike Driving*, smiling the particular smile designed to hold back tears, to exert an upward pressure on the ducts, Trump throwing paper towels into the crowd after Maria, FEMA handing out Skittles and other corporate sugars, as I pushed the stroller over the curb and onto the main path of the thoroughfare; we turned left and headed south toward the Hippo Playground on Ninety-First.

When we arrived at the playground, Luna hopped off the stroller so Natalia and I could carry it down the stone steps and then I unstrapped and lifted Amaya out (why does it feel dangerous to fictionalize my daughters' names?) and started to wake her (why is she heavier when asleep?), singing my own song about hippos, who are classified as "vulnerable" but not "endangered," Dada wants to push you on the swings, my little hippo, eventually plucking the pacifier, which she calls her bobo, from her mouth, which caused her to open her long-lashed eyes and speak, if only to demand her bobo back, "Dada bobo few more minutes." I gave it to her, set her down, pulled on the waistband of her rainbow-striped pants to check her diaper, then released her, watched her waddle toward her sister, who had climbed one of the small stone hippo sculptures in her tentative way, smiling and waving at me. I half-consciously scanned the playground, could not not, for potential bullies or broken glass on the asphalt and made mental notes about the relative height of the playground equipment, what kind of injuries this or that fall might entail. Then I checked my phone for messages coming from beyond the frame, checked in with the pacifying spread of headlines, scandals, archaic regressions, the latest in World Ice, before powering it down as part of my renewed effort to be present with my girls. I was also making a renewed effort not to intervene at every instant, not to be too present in that sense, and so I let Luna and Amaya, without my spotting them, climb the little yellow metal ladder (a fall would probably not involve concussion) onto the jungle gym, kids of different ages running from feature to feature, swinging from monkey bars; there was a wide metal slide. Natalia was some distance away retrieving the water bottles from the book bag stored in the basket beneath the stroller.

Luna lined up behind a couple of taller girls for the slide; Amaya lined up in eager imitation behind her sister. That's when I became aware of the boy—maybe seven or eight, a few years older than Luna; he wasn't sliding, but was sitting atop it banging his feet on the sheet metal. When one of the older girls asked the boy to move so that she could have a turn, he said: This slide is only for boys, no girls on this slide, go away. The girl called for her own father, who was nearby, to help her with the boy who wasn't taking turns, Luna and Amaya watching intently to see how this would all unfold, preparing, it seemed to me, to internalize whatever life lesson. (That particular look in a child's eyes, a mixture of presence and absence, when she is about to be impressed, to receive an impression like wax, the pressure it places on the speech and gestures of those of us pretending to be adults.) The father, whose accent was probably French African, asked the boy gently and with a smile to give the other kids a turn, and the boy shot back: No, no girls on this slide, no, go away. At which point the father, still smiling, said: And where is your daddy or mommy today? The boy, after a moment of hesitation, in which he scratched at the scabs on his knees, reluctantly nodded toward a man on a bench about ten yards away who seemed to be watching from that distance the scene on the slide. I tried to distract Luna and Amaya, have you girls seen these monkey bars, but they were riveted, following with their eyes the father as he walked, holding his smile, to the father on the bench, while the boy went on making the thunderous noises and the older girls waited patiently if unhappily in line for adult intervention. I pretended not to track the exchange between the two fathers, but soon the father of the girl returned, perplexed, a little shaken even; he told his daughter that it was time to go to the swings, that they had to leave soon anyway. The father and I made eye contact and he raised his eyebrows to indicate that the father on the bench was bad news. I looked frankly over at the bench to communicate to the bad father who had not come to rein in his son that I stood with the good father, while also taking the opportunity to size the bad father up, couldn't not: he was taller and thinner than I; he was dressed more formally than any of the other adults on the playground, as though he'd come from work, although it was Sunday; he had on khakis and a jacket and a pink button-down shirt, no tie; I imagined he worked in finance, securitized something. He was clearly not a tough guy; he wore black-rimmed glasses like mine, like a million other fathers in the city. He was white, so there was no question of that complicated political dynamic between us, however it had inflected his interaction with the other father. I looked back to my girls, who were still waiting, perturbed, all of us watching the boy who would not yield the slide, who kept making that metallic thundering sound, now in my mind an approaching storm, a large cyclonic system with a warm core. I told Luna there were swings open for us, and let's get some water from Mama, who was talking to a woman she seemed to know near the strollers, but Luna and Amaya, along with one older girl in front of them in line, would not budge: I want to go down the slide, Dada, the boy isn't being nice.

How about we let the girls have a turn now? I said to the boy, smiling as the father before me had smiled, but the boy, after kicking the slide some more, shouted: No, these girls are stupid, these girls are ugly, no stupid ugly girls allowed. This was to my knowledge the first time my four- and two-year-old daughters had ever been called such things. I involuntarily imagined lifting the boy off the slide by his neck; instead I said, smile gone, but my tone even, Those aren't nice things to say. The taller girl started crying, followed by Luna, and then Amaya, who removed her bobo to wail. Do you see how you've hurt their feelings? I said, looking toward the bad father on his bench, the bad father who no doubt saw what was happening. Please get off the slide right now, I said, but the boy just kicked the metal again and, before I knew it, I was walking toward the bad father, my own father's voice in my head: Don't do it, get your girls and go to the swings, leave the slide to the boy (boys will be boys), that's what you should be modeling for your girls, there is nothing to be gained by confrontation. As I closed the distance with the bad father, I made sure to smile again and, as I drew near, saying, Hey, how is it going? I tried to channel my own father's voice, a voice that somehow disarmed other men, gave them permission to act other than according to their macho scripts; the bad father barely nodded in acknowledgment. Can you help me out a little, I said, as calmly as possible; your son is playing on the slide and some other kids, including my girls, would like a turn, and he's having some trouble sharing the space. The bad father responded angrily: No, I'm not coming over there; absolutely not; let the kids work it out.

My father said: Adam, this guy clearly has a lot going on, look at how he's shaking; maybe he feels incapable of managing his son and doesn't know what to do, maybe his marriage is falling apart, maybe he has a horrible diagnosis—who knows; what we know is further conversation won't help. And while I disagree with him, my father said, while he's handling it poorly, the kids *will* work it out, that is, Luna and Amaya will just find some other place to play. I nodded, maybe imperceptibly, to my father, to Dr. J, to his sanity, as my own voice—which sounded calm, although my breath was coming faster now—responded: I cannot allow your son to bully my daughters. Please come and get your son. And the bad father said: No; I don't take orders from you; this conversation is over. The bad father took his right hand by the wrist and held it awkwardly against his chest as if to still a tremor, tardive dyskinesia, or to keep the hand from striking me of its own volition; I couldn't tell if this was posturing meant to intimidate me or if it indicated imminent nervous collapse. We were a couple of privileged crackers with divergent parenting strategies; we were two sovereignless men in a Hobbesian state of nature on the verge of primal confrontation. I said, sounding measured, but feeling the tenuousness of my own self-control: What I'm asking is for you to come and help the kids play together; I know another parent has already approached you; I know you probably feel incapable of managing your son and don't know what to do or maybe your marriage is falling apart (why weaponize my father's empathy?), but I'm not going to let your son call my daughters names. Get away from me, the bad father said, removing his glasses, putting them away in his jacket's inside pocket, Get away from me now. Was he taking them off in preparation for a fight? Because it somehow helped him to calm down? I forced myself to inhale deeply through my nose, held it, exhaled audibly.

I left the bad father on the bench, returning to the slide, where all the children, the boy included, had been watching us in silence. Come on, I said to my girls, and when Luna said no, I snapped at her: Now, I hissed; come right now or we're going straight home; I'm the father, I'm the archaic medium of male violence that literature is supposed to overcome by replacing physicality with language. At this point Natalia arrived, asking what was going on, and I explained, with forced nonchalance, that the boy—the young man—was having trouble playing, that I'd spoken with his father, that fathers had spoken through me, that it was time for the girls to find another activity. Natalia could tell that I was upset and managed in her graceful way to redirect the girls to the swings; the boy started up another round of thunder; I felt the gaze of the bad father, sensed his sense of victory. I told myself not to turn around and see his smile.

I turned around, saw his smile. Then, as if I'd closed the distance with one step, I was inches away from him, the bad father, looking down on him, very white scalp where his black hair was thinning, my hands cold, a familiar sign of migraine and/or rage, a symbolic system breaking down inside the body. He was tall, had the advantage of reach, would score high on the so-called ape index, whereas my own habitus was monitored closely by doctors for signs of a genetic syndrome I prayed nightly I had not bequeathed to my girls, tracking the dilation where the aorta meets the heart; still, I felt that I could take him, not that I'd been in a real physical fight since I lived in Topeka. Unlike in Topeka, it was improbable he was armed; I saw no handgun printing through his clothes. Instinctually, I went for an element of discursive surprise: I've been trying to enlist your help, I said, leading with a Foundation vocabulary, but delivering it as though I were talking shit; I've been asking for your help in making the playground a safe space for my daughters; I recognize that my reaction to your son is not just about your son; it's about pussy grabbing; it's about my fears regarding the world into which I've brought them. The bad father, clearly startled by the mixture of passion and dispassion, the tangle of vocabularies, responded: Let the kids figure it out. My boy's playing on a slide; he's not harassing anyone. He's seven years old, okay? No, I said, it's not okay; the child is father to the man, what the kids will "figure out" is repetition. (I helped create her, Ivanka, my daughter, Ivanka, she's six feet tall, she's got the best body, she made a lot of money. Because when you're a star, they let you do it. You can do anything. You have the authority. A moon or dead star infinitely dense suspended in the basement firmament.)

The father said nothing; he took out his phone and started texting, making a show of not finding my presence threatening. Are you ignoring me? I asked stupidly. The father looked up at me, both of us bad fathers now, and said: I am not talking to you anymore; I asked you to leave me alone, now I'm telling you to fuck off. Only when I heard it clatter on the asphalt was I fully aware I'd knocked the phone out of his hands.

♦♦♦

Our flight had been delayed several times due to a mechanical problem—we'd taken the girls back and forth on the motorized walkway, plied them with exorbitantly priced processed foods from the airport markets, let them watch videos of themselves dancing over and over again on our phones. By the time we landed in Kansas City (significant turbulence during the descent; I hid my terror from the girls by reading to them through it, before Amaya, indifferent to the choppy air, took the book out of my hands) and fetched the gate-checked stroller, met my parents, retrieved the baggage from the carousel, drove the hour back to Topeka (chicken hawks atop the telephone poles, fields of brown wheat and green soy, Grandpa and Grandma leading the kids in song, "Billy Broke Bolts," "The Golden Vanity," Luna puking outside of Lawrence, a change of clothes at the rest stop), and finally pulled up in the driveway where I'd so often drunkenly parked my Camry, I only had a couple of hours left before my reading at Washburn University. Standing in the shower, I felt as though twenty years had been erased, washed off me, as if I emerged eighteen again, an unsettling feeling compounded by the fact that Natalia had taken the girls for a walk around the neighborhood of Victorian houses and cobblestone streets, no sound of the family I'd made, it was all a dream, my mom typing something in her study, letting the machine pick up the landline when it rang, my dad gone to Dillon's for a quick shopping, whole milk and macaroni, organic if they have it, etc. I dressed up slightly, although not in a suit from West Ridge Mall—I was reading poetry, not preparing for a debate, although my coaches might well be in attendance—and told my mom I was going to drive around a little before the event, would see Dad and her there; she told me where to find the keys to the white Prius; Leon Semenov had cut them a deal. I texted Natalia to let her know that I would see her and the girls later that night, decades in the future, then turned off my phone, which hadn't been invented yet.

The quiet of the electric car added to my sense of being a ghost, at least not coeval with myself, let alone the landscape, history not over but paused. I passed Klaus's house, the white repainted a light blue, a stranger mowing the lawn; I waved and he nodded suspiciously. I drove past the alley where I hit my head just so, then St. Francis on Seventh, where I was briefly comatose, a child in space, my mind a false-bottom box. Soon I was at Bright Circle on Oakley Avenue, where Darren and I first developed our powers. I rolled down the windows and crept past the single-story preschool; I imagined I could hear children playing in the backyard, even though the kids would have all been home by now. I could smell, although it was only memory, a bass note of mud and decaying leaves, a tinge of ozone indicating an approaching storm.

From Oakley, Cardi B playing on the radio, I headed to the former Foundation campus on Sixth. The campus had been abandoned since the Foundation, or what was left of it, moved to Texas in 2003. In 2005, many of the buildings were to be leased as office space, the clock tower had been extensively renovated to that end, but then vandals struck; the damage was so severe—or perhaps so disconcerting—that the leasing had been indefinitely postponed. As with the Topeka Zoo, I imagined the honorific "World Famous" had been officially revoked from the Foundation, stricken from the record. "In my 29 years as a law enforcement officer, I don't know that I've ever seen a building attacked this savagely," Randall Listrom told *The Topeka Capital-Journal*. "This is the result of someone being very, very angry. Someone spent a great deal of time in here. This was not one hour of kids having a good time." According to the *Berliner Lokal-Anzeiger*, the perpetrators, who were never apprehended, "turned over a bookcase in the building's library, set a fire in a restroom, destroyed bathroom fixtures, left piles of human waste in one room, destroyed an elevator control panel and spray-painted obscenities throughout the building." Did they deface the copper wall?

I turned off the radio, the way I might when driving through a cemetery, and parked the Prius in the empty parking lot nearest the tower. I found the iron bench dedicated to Dr. Tom, looked at the stopped clock—it was 3:50, the perpetual end of a clinical hour—which always reminded me of *Back to the Future*, touched my tongue to the roof of my mouth, jackhammer in the distance, a downward-sloping whistle in the trees, which had started glowing in the early dusk. I tried to warm my hands, anxiety about the reading encroaching now. I imagined that all the speech that had ever been uttered at the Foundation was somehow still in the air, if only I could tune in, the way old radio broadcasts have started returning from space, where they've bounced off heavenly bodies made of ice, a ham radio operator picking up Herbert Morrison's *Hindenburg* disaster broadcast from 1937, the year of Fritz's birth, in 2014, Oh, the humanity, electromagnetic radiation falling back to earth. I shut my eyes and listened, but there was too much interference, noise from the Big Bang, the crackle of sparks, lightning, stars, a charged body beneath white silk, wires crossed.

My hands were still cold on the steering wheel when I left the campus and its ghosts, taking Southwest Wanamaker past Starlite and Hypermart to Lake Sherwood. Facebook told me Amber—M.D. from American University of the Caribbean, a residency completed at KU Med—now lived in Omaha, had two sons, a husband who sold insurance, was a big Huskers fan, ate strictly Paleo, but she was also in her house, all the houses, moving behind the curtains as I navigated through the planned community, green static flocking spread over the board, an echo of juvenile desire surprising me, tongue across the teeth, first intensity, wind off the man-made lake, a voice I couldn't represent. When I left Sherwood and stopped at the light on Twenty-First, I looked at Rolling Hills, the prefab Stull, but it had lost its power: my grandfather, ashes now, was back in Potwin in a little cardboard box. (As I waited for the light to change, I remembered the scene at the Penwell-Gabel Funeral Home on my first trip back from college, one of my fondest memories of my grandmother, who is also ashes now, but scattered surreptitiously, lovingly, at the Brooklyn Botanic Garden one spring as the cherries blossomed. The funeral director kept showing Rose what he called "vessels for the remains of the dearly departed" in a heavy binder, but Rose found each option too expensive; after nearly an hour of negotiation in which she repeatedly asked the director to put the cremains in a plastic bag, "I can carry him in my purse," which he insisted was illegal, he agreed to sell her—for forty dollars cash—the pine box in which one of his marble urns had shipped. At first my mom had been exasperated by her mom's stubbornness; by the end, we were all laughing uproariously, cathartically, at her refusal to give an inch. If only they'd offered an urn of painted tin.)

Back in town, I passed through Westboro, but avoided Jason's house for fear that Sima or Eric would be coming or going or working in the yard, would see me, requiring me to stop, catch up awkwardly, and maybe because I didn't want to be near their basement, where a version of myself was, is, permanently waiting to take up his position. Instead I bought a pack of Marlboro Reds at the Kwik Shop on Seventeenth, and after parking in the Washburn lot as far from White Hall as possible, I sat on the hood and smoked two, one lit from the other, while I flipped through my books, dog-eared pages I might read as darkness fell around me. Like house lights in the Foundation theater. Who would attend such a reading? A handful of local poets. Several Washburn English classes had made it compulsory. Many former stars of the Ziegler film and others in my parents' extended community. Assorted teachers from Bright Circle and Randolph and Robinson Middle School and Topeka High. A few friends, too, Mandy among them, who'd messaged me that she couldn't wait to catch up a little after. Erwood, if he could put weight on the new knees, cobalt-chromium and titanium. The Phelpses would be there, were there, I saw, as I finally approached White Hall, as

I flickered between ages, the tranquilizer starting to take effect, not because I was a "well-known poet," but because I was the Brain's son.

Now I am going to show you a picture of one of the protesters. Darren is heavier than the last time you saw him, bearded, almost certainly armed, although no printing is visible in the photograph; he is wearing the red baseball cap, holding his sign in silence. If your eyes were to meet, only the little mimic spasms would indicate recognition. What is happening in this moment? What are the characters thinking and feeling? Tell me what led up to this scene.

♦♦♦

It was overcast when we entered the subway but we emerged from the City Hall stop into full sun. We walked the few blocks north to Foley Square, which had been the fallback site after Zuccotti was dismantled. The classical architecture of the government buildings loomed around us. Luna asked me to read the mottoes inscribed on the courthouses' stone façades and I did so, but my attempts at paraphrase and explication were weak and halting. "Who gave them permission to write on the buildings?" Luna asked.

Luna wanted to throw a coin in the fountain surrounding the large black granite sculpture, a memorial to the slave trade; I didn't have any pennies so I gave her a dime. She spent a long time figuring out what to wish for before she threw the coin, which caught the sun just before it struck the water. "Don't even think about asking me about my wish, Dada." ("Don't even think about" was a new locution, no doubt copied from some idle parental threat; she usually misapplied it, at least a little: "Don't even think about how hungry I am right now," when she wanted a snack, etc.) Above us an anachronistic-looking airplane trailed a white-and-red banner advertising car insurance, a kind of signage

Luna had never seen. "What happens when they come back down, the airplanes?" I had no idea; did they detach the banners in the air before landing? Couldn't a banner get caught in the landing gear? "Great question, sweetheart." We walked on, Luna stopping here and there to collect winged samaras from the pavement, one of the seedpods I'd called "helicopters" as a child in Topeka. Soon we approached the Jacob Javits Building, 26 Federal Plaza, an imposing glass slab where the ICE offices were located, Natalia texting with other protesters who were now converging. What had Luna wished for?

As we entered the security line, we pretended, as agreed, not to know any of the other families involved, but Luna greeted a few kids she remembered from previous actions; we hadn't asked her to dissemble. Although she'd been told that we were going to a protest, she kept wondering—because of the metal detectors and plastic bins for our belongings—if we were going to get on a plane. "A plane with one of those things that people down here can read?" The guards asked us very little, despite the sudden influx of visitors; we said we had Social Security paperwork to fill out at one of the administrative centers the forty-story structure housed; Luna, as if this answered the guard's query, announced that she was almost five, extended her fingers in case he wanted to count the years; "My sister isn't here, she's two." We'd thought it best to leave Amaya with friends in Brooklyn.

At the big bank of elevators in the main lobby, the families gathered quietly, choreography of the peacefully enraged. We waited until two elevators could be occupied simultaneously so that we would all arrive at ICE at once. Luna pressed the button for the ninth floor and began playing happily with the stockinged foot of a baby dangling from her mother's carrier as the doors closed. It was uncomfortably hot. I smelled sweat and powdery deodorant and drying breast milk and the watermelon gum of the visibly nervous dad beside me. As we ascended, one of the organizers thanked everyone for coming, "Congratulations on making it in," and rapidly explained to the group that we would need to "push past" the first guard; this made Luna nervous: "Isn't pushing wrong?" Great question. Natalia explained quietly that everything was fine, safe, that we were just going to get to the place where we could make our voices heard. I raised my eyebrows at Natalia; we hadn't understood that we would have to force our way past anyone; I'd thought we would just occupy whatever space the elevators opened onto, sing our songs, chant our chants, deliver our messages, a little upbeat teach-in for the children, then leave when asked to leave, careful to avoid any kind of conflict a kid might find disturbing.

A metallic ding signaled our arrival; the doors of the two cars opened simultaneously, and our combined group of some fifteen families walked toward the hall where a single guard was sitting at a desk. Confused by our determined approach, the guard stood, then extended his arms to stop us, Hey, no, everybody check in, register, show ID, restricted area, but the parents pushed through him and broke both to the right and left. There was a brief crush of bodies and Luna said to me, frightened, "Up, up, up," so I picked her up and she buried her face in my neck as we ducked under the guard's arms; I could smell last night's Mr. Bubble in her hair, the sunscreen I'd over-applied to the back of her neck. We regrouped in the narrow hall off which the ICE enforcement offices were located. Through one of the few windows I saw a woman with a white hijab at a desk flanked by men in blue suits. The room must have been thoroughly soundproofed; they didn't seem to register a disturbance. The reconstituted group began to sing ("This little light of mine"; as ever, I had to overcome my embarrassment at the sound of my own voice), while some parents and their children withdrew signs from backpacks and tote bags. Several cell phones were recording now; there was one person with a camera from act.tv, a live stream. A few adults unattached to children tried to enter the rooms where ICE proceedings were taking place, but they were violently pushed back by guards and the doors were slammed; the scuffles further upset Luna, who was repeating in my left ear: "I want to go outside." "We're just going to sing our songs here in the hall and send love to the children and go," I said, but I was conflicted about exposing her to such intensity, although many of the other kids were laughing and singing along as if on a school trip, a visit to the Museum of Natural History. A mother with a baby sleeping through all the commotion gave a brief speech about tearing children from their mothers, about kids in cages, about not being fooled by that day's executive order; the voices and cheering echoed through the narrow hall. Luna pressed her face harder into my neck; I reassured her, although she could probably less make out my words than feel the vibrations of my voice.

I began to experience a sensation I hadn't felt in at least a year. As a toddler Luna had been underweight—"failure to thrive," a battery of inconclusive tests—although now she was growing just fine. During periods of particular anxiety, often when I was rocking her to sleep, I would imagine that she was growing lighter and lighter in my arms, until I started to lose my sense of the material fact of her altogether, as though she were evaporating. It was like a nightmarish version of the "floating arm trick" I first encountered at Bright Circle: you pressed your arms against a doorway, counted slowly to ten; when you stepped away, they involuntarily rose above you (The Kohnstamm phenomenon, Klaus's voice; a first experience of automatism). I was grateful for the pressure of her face against my neck.

Natalia initiated a chant in Spanish. There was no more shoving, but police had started to arrive from other floors, many of them sporting bulletproof vests, tactical gear. (What did it feel like to be outfitted like that only to face a singing collective of families?) The hall was as hot as the elevator now; they'd probably cut the air-conditioning, a common first response to occupations. The police walked through our crowd deliberately, menacingly, one bumping me and another father as he passed.

Soon police were positioned at both ends of the corridor; they seemed to be awaiting orders about whether to clear or just contain us. There was little chance of arrests, we'd assumed, given the babies and young children, given that nobody was trying to further penetrate the offices, but I sensed that even as seasoned a protester as Natalia wasn't sure what the rules were, what the agents of the state were capable of, now that America was great again. Luna didn't like the look of the police and asked her mom, who had finished chanting, which of the men was ICE. "Is he the ICE?" Natalia explained again that we were totally safe, that we were there because other families were being treated badly by the government and police. That ICE wasn't a person but a group of people following orders from the president and being unfair. (Ice is the primordial element of the universe, sweetheart, more basic than fire.) *¿Somos activistas, verdad, Luna?* Natalia tried to take Luna from me, to sit with her on the floor and make another sign—if she wanted she could give it to a policeman—but Luna would not let herself be taken from my arms; I found it almost physically impossible to release her, even to her mom.

Were we wrong to bring her? Luna was by no means panicked or hysterical, but she was upset, and I was worried that one of the more aggressive protesters would try to push into a room again, causing the police to rush us, frightening Luna further. Another chant: "Families and children deserve to be safe"; in between the yelling, I said to Natalia, exaggerating my enunciation since we were largely reading lips: I'm going to take her out, okay? I think she's fine here, Natalia responded, I think she'll calm down. FAMILES AND CHILDREN, we yelled, then the others: DESERVE TO BE SAFE, and in the brief intervals between chants we tried to determine whether Luna and I should leave or stay, Luna quiet now but refusing to pull her face away from my neck, which was wet with tears and sweat. Finally Luna did pull back, but it was only to say—to say decisively, in a voice we almost always honored—that she wanted to go. Okay, I said, and Natalia nodded her assent, maybe a little reluctantly, and I made my way through the protesters toward the police, who made a show of barely letting us pass. By the time the elevator doors closed, Luna was calm, smiling. She demanded fruit leather.

Outside the building we located the group of protesters who had gathered in solidarity—either families who didn't feel comfortable occupying the building or non-parents who came to show their support. This was where the protesters inside would convene when they left the ICE offices. A camera crew had set up to await them and tried to interview Luna, but, smiling shyly (see the chip in her left front incisor), she ran off to where a few other children were playing in the plaza, jumping from one large paving stone to another without touching a crack. Someone had brought sidewalk chalk and a young boy was drawing and soon Luna was, too, making what she called a "heart fountain"; she said it would stop ICE, then asked me again what ICE was, where the kids in cages were, aren't cages for zoos, for animals ("Who speak only with their eyes"); I responded as best I could. I received a text from Natalia that they were coming soon, no arrests, that it was calmer and some of the kids were giving speeches, "Wish Luna was here."

I was still looking at my phone when a cop in tactical gear, military-grade weapon slung across his torso, approached me and asked with clear contempt if I was one of the organizers of the protest, "Is this your show?" I smiled noncommittally, the smile of someone who doesn't speak the language. The cop, heavy, broad-shouldered, white, said to me: "We've let you all have your little protest here—but this can't happen, this is a no." "What can't happen?" I said. And he pointed at Luna and the boy, who were drawing hearts and spirals on the ground with yellow and red chalk. "These kids are defacing government property."

"I don't understand," I said innocently.

"What don't you understand?" the guard said impatiently.

"I guess I don't understand what government property is," I trolled. "Is 'government property' like 'public property'? Because I know we're allowed to use this chalk—it washes away in the rain—on sidewalks."

"Are you going to tell these kids to stop or am I?" Luna and the younger boy looked up at us, not hearing the words, but registering the intensity.

"I think they're almost done with their drawings," I said. "Go ahead and finish, guys." They resumed, Luna now writing her name.

"You stop them or I'll have to stop them," almost a hiss. "Understand me?"

"No," I said, lowering my voice. "I'm afraid I don't. Understand you. What would stopping them look like, exactly? Are you going to put them in cuffs? Cages?"

"You're going to instruct your—"

"Anyway," I interrupted, my tone now as light as I could make it, although I felt both rage and fear, "my daughter barely listens to me." Luna was drawing stars around her fountain. "Like this morning, before we got on the train, I told her that I wanted her to wear the high-tops with Velcro and not ones with laces, but—"

"This is the last time I'm going to ask you."

"—you see what shoes she's wearing. Do you have kids? Because I have no authority, is what I'm trying to say. I just have no authority over these kids. Do you have authority? Where does your authority come from again?"

The protesters nearby started cheering as the group that had occupied the building emerged. Luna stopped drawing and pulled on my shirt: Let's go clap for Mom. The younger boy also stopped and joined us. Then they held their chalk out to the cop as though he'd been asking for a turn.

We found Natalia, and Luna hugged her and asked her to lift her up onto her shoulders, which Natalia did. One of the organizers stood on a stone bench and yelled, "Mic check," and we all yelled it back. The "human microphone," the "people's mic," wherein those gathered around a speaker repeat what the speaker says in order to amplify a voice without permit-requiring equipment. It embarrassed me, it always had, but I forced myself to participate, to be part of a tiny public speaking, a public learning slowly how to speak again, in the middle of the spread.

ACKNOWLEDGMENTS

Duccio's *Madonna and Child* is a real painting with a fictional parapet, enclosed by a burnt frame, although the Met didn't acquire it until 2004. Its anachronistic appearance throughout *The Topeka School* can stand for the unstable mixture of fact and fiction.

Some of the scenes and sentences in this book first appeared in the essay "Contest of Words," published in *Harper's Magazine*. Excerpts from the novel appeared in *Granta* and *The New Yorker*. The opening pages of the section "Paradoxical Effects" repurpose passages from Harriet Lerner's article "Hating Fred," which appeared in *Psychotherapy Networker* in 1994.

Thank you, Ari. Thanks to my editor, Mitzi Angel, and to my agent, Anna Stein.

For encouragement and criticism I am indebted to: Harriet Lerner, Stephen Lerner, Matt Lerner, Annie Baker, Michael Clune, Joshua Cohen, Cyrus Console, Stephen Davis, Jeff Dolven, David Grubbs, Michael Helm, Violaine Huisman, Aaron Kunin, Rachel Kushner, Maggie Nelson, Jenny Offill, and Ed Skoog. Thanks to Susan Goldhor for the tissue box story. Geoffrey G. O'Brien read this book so often and so closely that our conversations approached collaboration.

Lucía and Marcela, I love you.

A NOTE ABOUT THE AUTHOR

Ben Lerner was born in Topeka, Kansas, in 1979. He is the author of the internationally acclaimed novels *Leaving the Atocha Station* and *10:04*, three books of poetry (*The Lichtenberg Figures*, *Angle of Yaw*, and *Mean Free Path*), and the monograph *The Hatred of Poetry*, as well as several collaborations with artists. Lerner has been a finalist for the National Book Award in Poetry and has received fellowships from the Fulbright, Guggenheim, and MacArthur Foundations, among many other honors. He is a Distinguished Professor of English at Brooklyn College.

Keep in touch with
Granta Books:

Visit granta.com to discover more.

GRANTA

Also by Ben Lerner and available from Granta Books
www.granta.com

NO ART

'I did not walk here all the way from prose
To make corrections in red pencil
I came here tonight to open you up
To interference heard as music'

This book brings together for the first time Ben Lerner's three acclaimed volumes of poetry, along with a handful of newer poems, to present a decade-long exploration of the relationship between form and meaning, between private experience and public expression. *No Art* is an exhilarating argument both with America and with poetry itself, in which online slang is juxtaposed with academic idiom, philosophy collides with advertising, and the language of medicine and the military is overlaid with echoes of Whitman and Keats. Here, clichés are cracked open and made new, made strange, and formal experiments disclose new possibilities of thought and feeling. *No Art* confirms Ben Lerner as one of the most searching and ambitious poets working today.

PRAISE FOR BEN LERNER'S POETRY:

'Lerner's curiosity and thinking are far-ranging and iconoclastic, and his writing is similarly aphoristic and electrified. This is poetry bred of poetry, boldly set down by an "unfettered" mind'
C. D. Wright

'The poems are charged with the full force of Lerner's monumental talent, which begins with the finely chiselled line and extends to the architecture of the book entire' **Poetry Foundation**

Also by Ben Lerner and available from Granta Books
www.granta.com

LEAVING THE ATOCHA STATION

Winner of the Believer Book Award

A *Guardian* Book of the Year
A *New Statesman* Book of the Year

'Luminously original . . . like a comet from the future . . . intensely and unusually brilliant' ***Observer***

Adam Gordon is a brilliant young American poet on a prestigious fellowship in Madrid, and things are not going well. Fuelled by strong coffee and self-prescribed tranquilizers, Adam's 'research' soon becomes a meditation on the possibility of authenticity, as he finds himself increasingly troubled by the uncrossable distance between himself and the world around him.

'Utterly charming. Lerner's self-hating, lying, overmedicated, brilliant fool of a hero is a memorable character, and his voice speaks with a music distinctly and hilariously all his own'
Paul Auster

'Seductively intelligent and stylish' ***Independent***

'The best new novel I've read for a long time' **James Meek**

'Funny, uplifting and moving . . . [You'll] finish this book feeling a little cleverer, and a little happier' ***Financial Times***

'The sharpest and funniest novel I read this year' ***Mail on Sunday* 'Books of the Year'**

Also by Ben Lerner and available from Granta Books
www.granta.com

10:04

Shortlisted for the Folio Prize

A Book of the Year in the *Observer*, the *New Yorker*, the *New York Times Book Review*, the *Wall Street Journal*, the *Village Voice*, the *Boston Globe*, NPR, *Vanity Fair*, the *TLS*, the *Globe and Mail*, the *Huffington Post*, *Gawker*, *Flavorwire*, *Electric Literature* and the *San Francisco Chronicle*.

'Extremely funny . . . a dazzling, absorbing novel' ***Guardian***

The narrator of *10:04* faces a future of uncertain fortunes. Living in a New York beset by frequent super-storms and social unrest, he has recently been diagnosed with a potentially fatal medical condition and received the unexpected windfall of a large book advance, and now his best friend Alex has asked him to help her conceive a child. As he contemplates the anxieties of fatherhood, the imminence of the city's extinction and the challenge of making art in unsettled times, a brave new kind of novel emerges: a shimmering portrait of the multiple futures we might inhabit and the connections we have yet to form.

'Wry, witty, always surprising' ***Evening Standard***

'Even if he writes nothing else for the rest of his life, this is a book that belongs to the future' ***New York Review of Books***

'[In] *10:04*, Lerner is saying that life is too fragmented, too multifarious to be narrowed down to one single narrative, but that doesn't mean it can't be captured, in all its heartbreaking variety, in the pages of this novel' ***Observer***

'Contemplative and tender . . . I doubt I'll read a finer novel this year' ***Telegraph***

'Generous, provocative, ambitious . . . a near-perfect piece of literature' ***Los Angeles Review of Books***